On a Strange Ship from Atlantis . . .

Gwalchmai, the godson of Merlin, laid his hand upon the girl's shoulder, then recoiled. Here was nothing human to be a companion for him in the wastes. It was an image only, formed from the same odd metal as the ship.

As he inspected this cunning creation of some long-dead artist, he remembered how Merlin had amused him when he was very small by causing a mandrake root to leap and prance before him.

He knew the spell. Should he try it now?

Smiling at his own ridiculous folly, he looked at the beautiful statue and muttered: "Come here and talk to me . . . if you can!"

With a tread that was feather light, the metal girl quitted her pedestal, advanced toward him and sank upon her knees with bowed head, murmuring in soft tones like a muted golden bell: "I am here. What does my lord require of his servant?"

THUS BEGAN THE MYSTERIOUS QUEST OF GWALCHMAI AND CORENICE, PRIESTESS OF ANCIENT, LOST ATLANTIS!

Also by H. Warner Munn
available now from Ballantine Books:

MERLIN'S RING

Merlin's Godson

H. Warner Munn

A Del Rey Book

BALLANTINE BOOKS • NEW YORK

A Del Rey Book
Published by Ballantine Books

ISBN 0-345-30499-3

Manufactured in the United States of America

First Ballantine Books Edition: September 1976
Fifth Printing: October 1981

Cover art by Darrell Sweet

To my Wife
My own Gold Flower of Day

Contents

BOOK ONE

King of the World's Edge

Prolog

After the hurricane which swept Key West almost bare, a cylinder of bronze, green with verdigris and thinned by the years, was dug out from coral and debris by a veteran engaged in the work of reconstruction. He, perceiving it to be a most ancient relic, though he mistakenly believed it to date from the Spanish occupation of that island, realized that it might be of more value if unopened. So he took it to the museum in his home town, at which I happen to be curator.

I opened it in his presence, being promised ten percent of any valuables it might contain, should they chance to be of only ordinary interest.

We were both surprised to find in it a tightly rolled bundle of parchment, upon which was painted in rugged soldier's Latin the following letter.

As I translated it, the eyes of my caller sparkled, for he recognized a bold kindred spirit across the years.

I, too, thrilled, but with the zest of the antiquarian; for I knew that at the time of writing, Rome had perished, the barbarians had dismembered the Western Empire, and only in Constantinople survived anything of Roman pomp and power. Yet here, at a date forty years after the fall of Rome, was a man writing to a Roman emperor!

Had the letter been in time to have been of use, the history of the world would have been far different; but it miscarried, and with it all the hopes of its valiant writer. Let him speak now for himself.

1

The Lost Legion

To whatever Emperor rules in Rome—Greetings:

I, Ventidius Varro, centurion under Arthur the Imperator of Britain, and now King of the Western Edge of the World, known here by such titles as Nuitzition, Huitzilopochtli and Atoharo, send these relations by my only son, who seeks your confirmation of my kingship, that he may rule in my stead when I am done.

It is now, I estimate, full five generations since the legions finally withdrew from Britain, and though I may be, in the early part of these writings, but retelling what by now is common knowledge in Rome, I cannot be sure of that and it should be told. Bear therefore, I pray, with the garrulous reminiscences of an old soldier, scarred in the services of a country he has never seen.

It is hard for me to believe that since I left Britain forty years ago it may not have been recovered from the Saxon pirates; yet I must assume it, for I remember well that for a hundred years previously we received little or no help.

Nay, when in my great-grandfather's time we Romano-Britons sent to Aetius for aid, pleading that the recall of the legion he had sent left us defenseless, did we get even one cohort in return?

Not though we warned that Britain would be lost— as it has been, unless indeed it is true, as Myrdhinn the seer has told me, that Britain was discarded willfully as of little value to Rome.

How can I credit this, knowing well the fertile soil, the rich mines, the teeming fisheries of Britain? There must be another reason, and Myrdhinn has said it.

An age is dying, the whole world tottering to ruin, overrun by barbarians as we in Britain were; yet for a hundred years no news crossed the seas to us, other than garbled rumors brought by Saxons who were no friends to Rome.

They met our galleys and warships, twenty to one, and sank them. They harried our coast, burning, marauding, pillaging, till hardly a roundship dared venture the crossing of the channel, and trade died. Communication with the continent was shut off. Even the fishing-vessels dared not leave the sight of land, and everywhere the Saxon dragon-ships held the seas.

So, understand then that at the risk of boring you with an old tale, I must review the events following the recall of the legions, when in all Britain the only Roman soldiers were those of the sadly decimated Sixth Legion, Victrix, stationed at Eboracum and on the Wall.

If this be known to you, pass on. There are things to follow that will be new, for I am the only Roman left alive in all the world who has knowledge of the marvels I shall describe.

First, after the Emperor Honorius' letter of recall, the Twentieth Legion embarked—leaving Deva and the west country exposed to the fierce mountain tribes of the Silures. Then from Ratae the Ninth marched away and all the low country was helpless.

Two years later, the Second Legion left Isca Silurum and nothing hindered the pirates from sailing up the broad Sabrina.

Lastly went the greater part of the Sixth, and, too weak to hold the Wall, the Consul moved his forces farther south, deserting Eboracum to the Picts and Saxons, who promptly occupied it, settling there to stay.

If the various cities could have agreed among themselves, and together have assembled an army, Britain might yet be free. There were plenty of men with stout hearts and Roman training, and some of these the Sixth recruited to bring up the full strength of the legion, but this was like diluting wine with water.

The cities from which the levies came bickered among themselves, each trying to keep its fighting-men at home, and so, singly too weak to fight off invasion, they fell as they fought, singly. Meanwhile the various British princelings gathered a following and set up petty kingdoms, quite separately from the city-states, and most of these were later destroyed or absorbed by the invaders.

Eventually what remained of the Sixth after three generations of fighting, recruiting and dilution, still calling itself Roman and Victrix as well, clinging to its eagles, retreated into the mountains of Damnonia, the last stronghold of Britain.

And here I must in more detail begin the story of my own particular family and tell how it was affected by these events.

Stranger! Know me first. I am Ventidius Varro, then —Roman to the core of me, though I never have seen that lovely city by the Tiber, nor did my father before me. He was British born, of a British mother, and on *his* father's side was possessed of only one quarter of pure Roman blood. Yet am I Roman, my allegiance is to Rome, and to her goes my love and my heart's yearning—to that delectable city which I shall now never see in life!

The story of my family is the tragedy of Britain. When my great-grandfather was called into the troops, my grandfather was a babe in arms. The island was bled white of fighting-men, only skeletons of garrisons remaining, but by the time of my grandfather's entrance into the Legion firm sturdy substance had formed upon these bare bones of organization. One might say that the brains were still Roman, but all the flesh was British.

The Sixth fought the Picts, the Scoti and the Saxons, and although the barbarians had gained a foothold, they were all but dislodged again and were held with their backs to the sea. Then, just as another year might have decided the struggle, Rome called.

Men were needed—Rome itself was in peril—my grandfather followed in his father's footsteps, into mystery, and never returned. None of the levies returned, and his wife, left lorn with young children, my father among them, moved west toward the mountains of Cambria and brought up her brood in Viriconium.

Rome sent us no more governors, no more high officials or low. Our fortresses in the west continued to be held by the decimated Sixth, but the very best men were gone, and I do not know where even their graves may lie.

Then the Jutes, Saxons and Angli, who had occasionally fought beside us as allies against the Picts, turned against us, and my mother fled across the Cambrian border, looking over her shoulder at flaming Viriconium, where my father with other brave men fought and died that Rome might be perpetuated in Britain.

My early childhood was spent in wandering about among the wild Cymry, whose bravery had challenged and broken all the power that Rome could hurl against them, and which now remained the only corner of Britain which was free from the Saxon peril and which, strangely enough, now protected the culture of Rome. And at last I come to my own time and the story you must know.

Among these Cymry dwelt the strange man known to them as Myrdhinn, but to us across the border as Ambrosius; a man of noble aspect and terrifying eye, of flowing white beard and majestic carriage; a man whose very origin is shrouded in mystery.

If the tale is true, Myrdhinn was sired by a demon in the reign of King Vortigern, baptized instantly by Blayse, the mother's confessor, thus becoming a Christian, but retaining the demoniac powers of magic, insight and prophecy. Others have considered him so wise that he could not be even slightly mortal, and maintain that he was born at the age of eighty at a time co-exis-

tent with the construction of Earth and has since been
growing wiser!

It is more probable, however, that he was a found-
ling brought up in childhood by Druids who still keep
up their ancient practices in Cambria, and taught by
them their mystical lore, though he in later life em-
braced Christianity. Druidism warred in his heart with
Christian tenets.

It is well known that the sages of antiquity possessed knowledge lost to us in these times of decadence,
and locked fast in Myrdhinn's brain were many secrets,
including that of prolonged life.

I am beaten down by years, grizzled, gaunt and
almost toothless, yet Myrdhinn in all the time of my
acquaintance remained the same as that of my mother's
description, when as a young woman she first saw him
among the hills of Cambria, striding along a lonely glen,
hale, rugged and strong, the child Arthur holding his
hand and half trotting to keep up with the old man's
vigorous pace.

They must then have been going to find his friend
Antor, to whom Myrdhinn delivered Arthur for tui-
tion, and whose diligent care developed the stripling
into Arthur, the hoped-for, the undying—Arthur, Imperator, the great Pendragon, dictator—Arthur, save
only for treachery's intervention the savior of Britain.

At that time he was about fifteen years older than I
who, still a suckling, knew nothing of the stirring events
around me. By the time I was growing calluses prac-
ticing with sword and spear, Arthur already was leading forays into Saxon land.

Old crippled soldiers of the scattered legion remnants
trained the savage youth of Cambria to a fantastic
semblance of the iron ranks of Rome. Again the smiths
pounded red iron into white blades, again sow and
pig* talked on carroballista and catapult, and at last
a ghost of the old Legion marched over the border,

* Ratchet and pawl.

with tattered standards, battle-scarred armor, dented shields.

But we marched in full strength! Our metal was bright and polished, our bows strong and arrows sharp (every man an archer, whether a member of the cavalry, engineers or simple legionary), and leading us all the glittering eagles gave us courage.

Sixth Legion, Victrix! Hail and farewell! Thy bones make the fields of Britain greener now.

Something of the old imperial spirit came back. Viriconium was captured, lost and held again, and the Cymri streamed over the border, rebuilding all possible of the past glory. On the plain outside the walls scampered the shaggy Cambrian ponies in laughable contrast to the thundering charge of the Roman horse. But the Saxon footmen scattered before the charge, and as time went by we penetrated deeper into hostile country, winning back foot by foot the soil of Britain to be once again free land for us exiles and lovers of Rome.

Here and there we came upon noble steeds and mares in the fertile lowlands, and by the time Arthur's forces were strong enough to meet in pitched battle a superior force of Saxons, three hundred horsemen smashed the shield walls.

The Saxons, streaming away, left us masters of the field in the first great battle to break the invaders' power, and harrying the retreat the cataphracts pursued, hacking them down and wreaking such havoc that from the survivors of the troop Arthur formed his noble band of knights.

Their leather armor, knobbed with bronze, was replaced with plate; stronger horses were bred to carry the extra weight; and as Arthur came victor from field upon field, armies, chieftains, kings thronging to him, naming him amheradawr (or imperator)—the Round Table came into being and held high court in Isca Silurum.

Thus from battle to battle we passed—our glory increasing, our confidence growing, recruits coming in—sneaking by night along hostile shores in coracles of hide and wicker, creeping by the moored Saxon longships—until flaming hilltop beacons farther than the eye could see marked the boundaries of recovered Britain.

Grumbling, growling to ourselves, watching the Legion grow to double strength, we waited for the word to sweep over the Saxon remnant. Then came unexpected help from Armorica—our compatriots across the sea sailing in roundships and galleys to our aid.

Myrdhinn had asked for their help, and nobly they answered.

At that time we had but one warship, the *Prydwen,* a great dromon built as an experiment from a design found in an old book, modeled to be a cruiser which could meet and plow under the enemy galleys. Its like had not been seen in British waters for hundreds of years. Armed with ballistas and arrow engines, driven by oars and sails and with overhanging galleries the better to repel boarders, it towered over the hulking roundships and low galleys, like a proud cock who struts among his family, protector of all.

Already the barbarians were marching upon us, out of Wessex, while at sea a fleet sailed to land forces in our rear.

We met them at Mons Badonicus and spent the day and most of a long moonlight night in killing, while upon the water the allied fleet covered itself with glory.

Armorican, Hibernian and Saxon galleys crashed and flamed to heaven, while among them, ramming, casting firepots, roamed the *Prydwen* in the arrow-sleet, trampling the foe under her forefoot.

Then to us at last came peace, time to live and love and rest—and for some, time to plot treachery.

Myrdhinn had planned for Arthur a marriage with Gwenhyvar, daughter of a noble chieftain, Laodegan of Carmelide; and journeying thither in disguise to see the maid before wooing, Arthur arrived at an opportune time. The walled city of Carmelide was besieged by a wandering foray of savage mountain raiders, but

Arthur's armored knights scattered them and drove them far.

Entering the city, Myrdhinn spoke for Arthur, beseeching the hand of Gwenhyvar as a reward to the city's savior.

It was open talk afterward that Myrdhinn had engineered this attack and rescue to bring about his own plans, but I know nothing of the matter, having been far away. I believe him capable of it, for his mind worked in devious ways and he was not a man to do a thing in a simple way if something spectacular could complicate it.

This time, however, if he was at bottom of the matter, his love for a brave show ruined himself, Arthur, Gwenhyvar—and Britain. You see, Gwenhyvar was already in love with a young man named Lanceloc.

Arthur was approaching middle age, Gwenhyvar and Lanceloc much younger. Theirs was the proper union, but how could an ambitious father refuse the great Pendragon, savior of the city? Laodegan commanded, Gwenhyvar obeyed like a dutiful child, and evil began.

"Forbidden fruit the sweetest of all"—so runs the ancient saw. Others knew what went on in all its seamy detail, but noble Arthur, the soul of bravery and honor, remained in ignorance for years.

Then Agrivain and Medrawd, kinsmen who aspired to be mighty themselves and who thought that could be best done by bringing low those already mighty, came sneaking, telling tales, spewing venom upon all that Arthur held dear, and down crashed our hopes for Britain.

Lanceloc, Agrivain and Medrawd fled into Wessex, fleeing their outraged ruler, taking their kinsmen, their vassals, and their friends.

Here they allied themselves with what remained of Saxon power, sending word overseas that it was safe again for pirates to come and murder, rape and pillage, for Arthur was stricken to the heart and Rome had forgotten her lost colony.

So the Sixth marched and the Saxons marched, and both great armies came toward the fatal field of Camlan—and the end of all glory!

2

Arthur, Myrdhinn—and Vivienne

It is not for me to describe that tragic calamity to my Emperor, feeling certain that during the passage of these many years the sad events of that cursed day have been so fully described to you that by now you must have a clearer picture of the battle than any I could give. After all, I was but a centurion, nor had I any knowledge of the whole plan of battle. Still, all plans were frustrated by a thick cold fog that shrouded us from the beginning, so that soon we broke up into troops hunting for similar small enemy bands, killing and being killed in many bitter encounters.

Then as the daylight grew more dim, the clash of arms became feebler, and wandering alone, separated from my century, I dismounted from a charger I had previously found running masterless through the slaughter, and now led him along a beach where the waves of an ebbing tide came slowly in, whispering a mournful requiem to all my hopes. The clammy, darkening fog seemed pressing down upon my very soul.

The narrow strand separated the ocean-sea from a small brackish lake at which I meant to water my steed. So I turned to my left, hearing the plash of little waves among the sedges of the salty marsh surrounding the fresher water. There was no other sound, save the occasional croak of a sea bird flying blindly through the mist.

My horse was raising his head from his drink, with a long sigh, when the fog abruptly lifted and gave me a clear view of perhaps a hundred yards. We were standing at the edge of a narrow inlet, and upon its other shore I saw the wreckage of a furious encounter.

Dead men lay in the water and carpeted the sand beyond as far as I could see into the farther haze. But not all there were corpses.

One lay bleeding, partly raised upon an elbow, while bending over him was a ghastly knight. Much of their armor was hacked away and that remaining was dabbled with blood. I recognized the pair.

The dying man was Arthur; the other, with whom he weakly argued, was Sir Bedwyr, one of the most trusted of his knights. I hailed them, but Arthur was too far gone or too absorbed to hear me, though Sir Bedwyr looked across the water and lifted his hand for silence.

Again Arthur commanded and this time Sir Bedwyr agreed, picked up Arthur's great sword, Caliburn, and walked away into the mist. Then the cold gray curtain fell again, and through it I rode around the inlet until the sound of voices halted me.

"This time you did not fail me?" queried Arthur.

"Regretfully I obeyed, my King."

"And what did you see and hear?"

"I threw the sword into the mere, as you commanded, and as it circled flashing, something cried out most dolefully, while up from the mere there raised a long arm in a flowing sleeve of white samite. Caliburn was caught, brandished thrice and drawn under, while from all the mere rose up a various keening of sorrowful voices."

"So Caliburn returns to the hand that gave it, to be held in trust for another who shall succor Britain. Strange that I heard no sound."

"Sadly I say it, my King, but your ears are becoming attuned to other rhythms than those of earth."

"So soon? With my work barely begun?"

With that exclamation his eyes closed. As I approached, I could not tell if Death had touched him or if it was but a swoon.

Sir Bedwyr met me before I reached Arthur, and explained, whispering, the scene I had just witnessed.

"He seems out of his head with despair. His wounds are grievous, but I think not fatal could I only stop the bleeding. I think it is his soul that is dying. He is firmly convinced that the end is come, for himself, for all of us, and for Britain. That is why he bade me cast his great sword into the mere.

"God forgive me! I am a forsworn knight! I have lied to a dying man. You can understand, Centurion? How could I cast it away? The brand has become a symbol to men. With Arthur gone, the scraps of our army will rally only to something they cherish. You know how the rabble need something to follow, a hero, an eagle, a sacred relic. With something to protect or follow they are giants; without it they are only men, afraid of death, afraid of pain. They would fight like demons to keep Arthur's sword out of the hands of the Saxons."

I had dropped upon my knees, examining the deep wounds in side and thigh, but my efforts at stanching were no better than the other's had been, and we worked together while he continued:

"So I cast the jeweled scabbard into the mere and lied! There was no arm in white samite, no wailing, only ripples on the mere and a sea bird's croak!"

"Nor would there have been more had you hurled the sword after the scabbard," I grunted. "Hand me more of that linen shirt."

He smiled sadly.

"Now if he dies, he will die happy in that respect, thinking I obeyed him, and if he lives he will understand I meant it for the best and will forgive me, I hope. Do you think I was right?"

"Unquestionably," I agreed. "With Arthur's sword in our hands we can flee to the hills, gather strength and strike again. If I could only stop this cursed blood!"

His lips had become the color of clay, and I marveled that he still breathed, for it seemed that each faint gasp would be his last.

Hearing the approach of a company, I looking up and clutched my own sword, then relaxed. Robed men, sagely bearded, were about me. Myrdhinn and his Nine Bards had come, and never had I been so glad to see that mysterious person as now.

He wasted no words, but brushing us both away, deftly probed the wounds, pressed at the base of the skull and at two places upon Arthur's back, then motioned for us to stand guard.

"The great Pendragon is departing."

The bards began a sorrowful keening, cut short by the sage.

"Peace! That will not help us. I cannot cure him. Time only can do that, but I can prevent a further sinking while we seek safety."

The groping tendrils of fog swirled thicker about us all as we watched those nimble fingers. Deftly he bound up those dreadful wounds from which the blood no longer pumped, his lips moving in a swift patter of mumbled words. Here was a scrap of Latin or a Cymric phrase, but mostly it was merely a sibilant hissing which belonged to no language of our ken.

And it seemed to us that in the pause between the longer incantations the mist became thicker and thicker yet, while just beyond the circle of our vision there sounded muttered rejoinders, as though Myrdhinn prayed for the life of Arthur and the cold lips of that great host of British dead on Camlan field must supply the responses.

And ever through the mist came the lapping of water on the distant shore. But *was* it distant? The sound seemed closer than it had been.

Once Myrdhinn paused to listen, but went on to complete his charm.

A cold touch lapped my ankles. I was in a puddle of lake water without having realized the fact. I moved closer to the mound upon which the others stood.

"Is he dead?" gasped Sir Bedwyr, and Myrdhinn shook his head.

"He would have been by now, but his breathing has stopped and he will live."

"Stopped his breathing? Then he must die!"

"Not entirely stopped, perhaps," smiled Myrdhinn. "He will breathe possibly once a day, until he has recovered during a long sleep the energy and the blood he has lost. He has been almost drained dry. We will take him to a safe and secret place where I can hide him away until he is recovered and ready to fight again for Britain."

I moved out of the water again. Was I sinking in a marsh? The ground seemed solid.

"How long must he sleep?" Again Sir Bedwyr questioned.

"Longer than you would believe. *Your* bones will be mold and your very tomb forgotten, before Arthur has well begun to sleep! I cannot explain now—hear that clank of arms? Enemies are prowling in the mist! Quick, Varro, help my men to lift him across your saddle. We must flee!"

As I moved to obey, I saw again that I stepped from water to reach higher ground. I looked about me. Unperceived by us, the water of the mere was stealthily rising to surround and cut us off.

Quietly I showed Myrdhinn. His eyes widened. Then he laughed.

"Ah, Bedwyr. It would have been better had you returned Caliburn to the lady who loaned it. My wife, Vivienne, a somewhat grasping person. She may bear us a grudge for cheating her. She held me ensorceled in the wood of Broceliande for some time, I remember very vividly. Come quickly, before the water rises!"

A huge wave came up from the mere and hurled itself along the inlet, swirled about our knees and fell back as though loath to release us.

"Hurry! Hurry!" urged Myrdhinn.

Again we heard the clinking of accouterments, this

time much closer, and soon the gruff words of Saxons could be distinguished.

They were hard upon us. Sir Bedwyr looked at me, and I at him. We were the only armed men in the party. With common consent we turned back, but for only a few steps when we again heard the rumble of a monstrous wave breaking upon the lowland we were leaving.

This time other sounds followed—cries of horror, of pain; the screams of tortured men; then groans, and bitter sobbing, awfully intermingled with mumbling, munching sounds, as though in the fog mercifully hidden from us some monstrous thing was feeding.

We stood aghast as Myrdhinn urged us to join the party.

"Come quickly! Tarry not! The mistake will soon be discovered. Let us get far from this evil place."

"What is back there?" I gasped.

"Vivienne's pet, the Avanc. The Worm of the Mere. We have cheated it and her as well. She is probably jealous that I have aided Arthur and she is surely enraged at the loss of Caliburn, which was due her by the terms of the loan.

"Listen, my good wife, and heed!" He called into the fog. "I hold Arthur's sword, and shall now keep it. This to repay for my years of imprisonment in the Ring of Smoky Air.

"Run, for your lives, men, run!"

We ran, beside the trotting horse. For the first few minutes all was still; then the ground surged in waves beneath us like an angry sea. Once, twice, thrice it rolled and threw us from our feet. We picked ourselves up and ran blindly in the fog.

Then somewhere a crash, as though the ocean-sea was hurling itself violently upon the bloody shore, and a long silence, followed by a second mighty roar of waves now mercifully far away. Silence again.

In the fog, just outside our vision, a woman laughed. Long, low and inexpressibly evil! Musically lovely, but oh, so wicked!

Just a laugh, nothing more, but in it was hinted the knowledge of something that we could not then know or guess; something that we should and must know, but which was withheld from us.

We looked at Myrdhinn. He shook his head without speaking.

Something had been done by the Lady of the Lake, to repay insults, to avenge Lanceloc (said to be her kin) and to injure us all, but what it was we did not know.

We went our way again, deeper and deeper inland, on into the fog. And behind us, till we had gone so far we could not hear it, rippled that lovely musical laughter, chilling the blood in our veins.

3

The Sleeper and the Seer

There is no need, my Emperor, to weary you with dry details of all we said and thought and did during the next few days. It is not for that reason I am writing. Briefly, then: We marched for several nights, through hostile country, picking up stragglers as we went, and hiding until we numbered forty men and could march by day. Twice we fought wandering bands of Saxons as we pressed on westward toward Arthur's homeland of Lyonesse, for he had often expressed a wish to be buried in his natal village of Avalon. But as we neared it, we met wild-eyed refugees, fleeing a more dire peril than the sea raiders—the sea itself! For, we learned, on the very eve of that fatal field of Camlan, the fertile and populous province of Lyonesse had sunk beneath the sea!

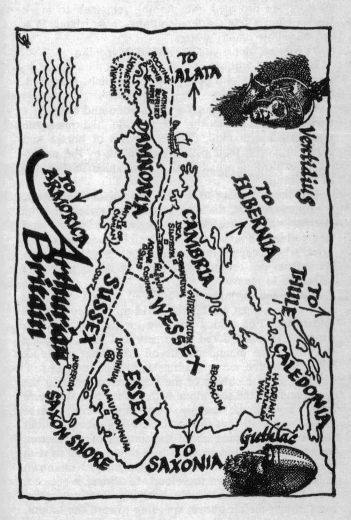

Yea, sixty villages and towns, each with its church and wealth and people, among them Arthur's own Avalon, lay drowned and nothing remained to mark the spot but a few scattered hilltops, now islands in a sea of yellow muddy waters.

"Vivienne, think you?" I asked Myrdhinn.

He nodded without speaking, but his nine bards, in tones as solemn as a peal of drowned bells, answered, "Aye."

We hurried on through a thick wood and came to a shallow place where the ebbing tide had filled the underbrush with mud, corpses, bodies of horses and cattle, fish with their bellies burst open by the underwater explosions which had accompanied the sinking of the land.

Myrdhinn leading to a goal he had decided upon, we followed: first, the nine bards; then myself and the charger which bore Arthur's body, very yellow and unbreathing, though warm and flexible; then the legionaries, who accepted me as centurion, though only two were from my century, and most of the others were unknown to me.

We passed through the wood and arrived at a great hoar rock, almost a mountain, and up this we climbed and rested. For a long time we looked out over the drowned land murdered by sorcery and spite, watching the tide come in and cut us off from the mainland, while Myrdhinn sat apart, considering the future.

Then, on the ebbing of the tide, we returned to the wood and left the seer alone with the sleeper. We made camp beyond the deathly wood and waited—three days. During all that time a thick black cloud, neither fog nor smoke, hung about the summit of the mount, unmoving in the fiercest wind, and those among us with sharp ears claimed to hear mutterings in an unknown language issuing from the cloud. Likewise, it seemed, they heard various invisible hurrying creatures, passing through the air above, speeding toward the mount, conversing as they came.

For myself, I heard none of this, and it was very

likely but the stirring of volcanic activity still busy near the sunken province.

Finally Myrdhinn came to us, and the cloud disappeared as had Arthur and the glory and honor of his reign. Where he had been laid with Caliburn, his famed sword, fast in his grip, Myrdhinn would not say, except that he was in a secure spot not to be found by man until the time was come for the waking of him.

Be not concerned for Britain's champion, oh my Emperor, for I have the sure word of Myrdhinn the wise that Arthur shall one day wake! There will be a mighty war in which all the tribes shall engage which possess the tiniest drop of British blood. Then Arthur will wake, make himself known and with Caliburn carry carnage into the lands of Britain's enemies. And war shall be no more and peace shall reign forever over all of Earth!

This, Myrdhinn told us. He told us also that he had writ this in enduring letters of Cymric, Ogham and Latin, about the walls of Arthur's abode, sealing the entrance thereto with a rock cunningly fixed and inscribed:

> HERE ARTHUR LIES. KING ONCE AND
> KING TO BE.

Lest, Emperor (if Britain has by now been reclaimed by Roman legions), they should be tempted to search for and enter this secret place, be warned. Myrdhinn has set watchers there. Arthur cannot and must not be awakened before the appointed time. The watchers will see to that. They are not human, they will not sleep or rest, they do not eat or drink, tire or forget or die! They are there to keep the entrance inviolate. Be warned! They are dangerous and will wait as Myrdhinn commanded, till Arthur awakes, be it one or three thousands of years. I do not know, nor does it concern us. They are there, the Guardians—the Watchers!

The next morning, again we marched, followed the coastline westward, and after some time we reached the very end of land, where beyond lay nothing but the boundless ocean. Here on the brink of a high raw cliff stood a monstrous boulder so cleverly poised that the touch of a hand might rock it, but many oxen could not pull it from its place, though bar and pry might dislodge it.

Myrdhinn drew from his robes a bronze plate already prepared and inscribed with an account of what we had done, instructions for entering Arthur's chamber and a warning to the unwary.

Again we left him alone; again we saw the black cloud gather and from a distance saw a marvel hard to explain. The massive and ponderous boulder rose in air to the height of a tall man!

This work, which would have taxed the powers of a Titan, was done noiselessly and with apparent ease. Myrdhinn merely touched it, so far as we could judge, and it rose.

He stooped, put the plate beneath it, and the rocking stone descended upon it, holding it safe there until such time as Myrdhinn described, upon joining us:

"When the moment is come for Arthur's awaking, the earth will shake, the rocking stone will topple down the cliff and Lyonesse will rise from the sea. Then, according to my vision, men will find my hidden words, will read, understand and obey. Then, when the drowned lands are fertile enough so that apple blossoms blow again in Avalon, in apple blossom time, men will enter his sleeping-chamber, waking him without fear of the watchers, and the era of peace on earth will begin."

You, my Emperor, may think this fantastic, but had you heard the words of the ancient, you could not have doubted. It may occur to you that Myrdhinn was a sorcerer, and it is true that at times he did use sorcery, as will be shown, but he dreaded it mightily. His Christian beliefs warred with his Druidic learning and he had the feeling that he was risking hellfire by the use of black magic.

He was an heir to all the lost lore of the ancients,

and much of his sorcery was marvelous tricks with quite natural explanations, but the basic facts which made them possible were hidden from the rabble. The world is hoary with years and has forgotten much.

Now, our mission accomplished, we must needs look to our own welfare and so held a council to decide our future, and found that we were of several minds.

Some were for striking deep into the hills and gathering other fugitives about us until we were able to strike again for freedom. Sir Bedwyr proposed this plan and many agreed with him, but I disputed, it seeming wiser to take ship and sail across to Armorica, where we might find kinsmen who would see us on the road to Rome.

Here, I suggested, a punitive expedition might be sent as had been once before from Gaul. Surely, I argued, Britain was too valuable a part of the Empire to be lost—and then Myrdhinn ended the bickering.

"You, Sir Bedwyr, and you, Centurion, think of nothing but the regaining of Britain, but believe me when I tell you this is not possible. The Empire itself is dying; the seat of power is shifting eastward. Britain has been lost for a generation and its only hope of Romano-British domination died when treachery and intrigue brought us to Camlan field. Gaul is going down the same road and soon will be lost forever to Rome.

"Britain belongs now to the strongest and will be dismembered among them. It is for us to flee, not to Rome, whose power is waning, but to another land of which the ancients tell.

"Suppose, now, that there was a land, beyond the western ocean, so far away that it is unknown to the Jutes and Angles, the Saxons and the Norse—known to Rome long ago, but forgotten by all except scholars. Would it not be worth visiting, exploring, conquering perhaps, to furnish for us poor exiles a new home, a new domain into which Rome might send fleets and colonies should the barbarians press too hard? I am certain that there is such a land.

"Firstly, it is said that King Solomon of the Jews obtained precious metals from its mines, brought hence by the men of Tyre. Homer, of the Greeks, speaks of a westerly land beyond the seas, locating, as does Pliny, the Western Ethiopians in this land. Plato tells us of a sunken continent named Atlantis, but this is not the same, for Anaxagoras also tells of a great division of the world beyond this ocean, dry and unsubmerged.

"The historian Theopompus tells us of the Meropians and their continent beyond the western ocean, larger, he says, than all our known world, and Aristotle says that the Carthaginian explorers discovered and settled a part of the southern country, until their Senate decreed that no one should voyage thither, killing all the settlers, lest it no longer remain a secret; for the Carthaginians wished this country to be kept as a refuge for themselves if ever a disaster befell their republic, but lost their shipping in the Punic Wars.

"Statius Sebosius calls this land 'the two Hesperides' and tells us that forty-two days' sailing will bring us there. Could you ask for better proof than all of this?"

"Ridiculous!" snorted Sir Bedwyr. "There is not a vessel in Britain that could be equipped for such a voyage! Far better to recruit, build up strength and have at the Saxons again."

"You are forgetting the *Prydwen*. Arthur's own dromon lies safe at Isca Silurum, if the Saxon dragon-ships have not raided and burned the city. If we find her whole, will you sail with us?"

"Not I," quoth he, stoutly. "I live and die in Britain. What! Should I venture to sea in a ship so weighed down with metal that a puff of breeze might founder her? Let steel kill me, not tin!"

Here he spoke of a novelty, which the Cornish tin miners had conceived. They had sent great stores of this metal, without cost, to Arthur for embellishment of his ship, and the Imperator had sheathed the *Prydwen* with it, from stem to stern, above and below water, knowing it to be protection against fireballs above and barnacles below. This made the *Prydwen* glitter so handsomely that many called her "The House of Glass."

"Your fears are unfounded. I feel it in my prophetic soul, that I and all who sail with me shall see this land which may indeed prove to be the Isles of the Blest of which you have all heard at your mother's knee. Why not? The wise geographer, Strabo, believed in it. Shall we consider him a romancer? It may indeed be that the Meropians have already sailed eastward and discovered Europe; for Cornelius Nepos, the eminent historian, says that when Q. Metellus Celer was pro-consul in Gaul, in 63 B.C., certain peculiar strangers were sent to him as a gift from the King of the Batavi. They said that they had been driven from their own land, *eastward* over the oceans until they had landed on the coast of Belgica.

"This may have inspired Seneca, one hundred and thirteen years thereafter, to prophesy in his tragedy of Medea, as follows:

" 'In later years an age shall come, when the ocean shall relax its bonds, a great continent shall be laid open and new lands revealed. Then Thule shall not be the remotest land known on the earth.'

"Four hundred and fifty years have elapsed since that prediction. If we sail and discover, we cannot now call ourselves the first, because we shall but follow in the footsteps of others who have traveled in less stout vessels than ours.

"Fishers from Armorica, our own kinsfolk, have visited its northern fishing-grounds yearly, in their ridiculous craft, while Maeldune of Hibernia, with seventeen followers, less than a hundred years ago, was blown to sea in flimsy skin currachs, and claimed to have reached a large island where grew marvelous nuts with insides white as snow.

"So you see there are such lands and they can be reached! Moreover, in our own times, Brandon, the monk of Kerry, the same one who recently established the monastery at Clonfert, has been there not once only, but twice! He had no great warship, such as we, but a merchant vessel with strong hides nailed over it, pitched at the seams, and it took him and his people forty days (almost exactly as related by Statius Sebosius) to reach this mysterious country.

"Now who among you will come with me and call yourselves men?"

"There is nothing here for us but a choice between death or slavery and degradation. I say let us all go and find this paradise on earth, this land of Tir-nan-og, this country of Hy Bresail, these Fortunate and Blessed Isles!"

Thus I, carried away with enthusiasm.

Then, indeed, began much arguing pro and con, which in the end resolved itself into a division of our force. Many, fearing monsters of the deep, demons and other fantasies, elected to remain, and choosing Sir Bedwyr as their leader they marched off toward the wild mountains, and whether they died before they reached the safety of the hills or lived henceforward a life of skulking outlawry, I know not.

At a little port we bought skin currachs, and, hugging shore, passed through the muddy waters, left them for cleaner, and in the end we reached Isca Silurum, without seeing a Saxon sail. And mightily glad we were to see the glitter of the *Prydwen*'s sides and the golden glint of Isca's guardian genius, high upon its pillar, for these things told us that we were sailing into a free and friendly province.

So we found it, a little section of free land, bounded by the four cities of Aquae Sulis, Corinium, Glevum and Gobannium—a little island of freedom in a barbarian sea, and we in its one safe port of Isca were loath to leave it for the dreaded Sea of Darkness.

Yet a month later we left it. One hundred fighting-men, besides a full complement of sailors, and thirty Saxons whose strong backs we thought would be useful when winds could not be found. These were prisoners doomed to execution, and we took them to make up a lack of rowers. Better for us if we had let them die by the ax!

So we turned our backs on Britain, never, any of us, to see it more.

4

A Little Ship—and a Great Sea

Now, it is not my concern to make a tedious account of our sea voyage, but a few items of importance must be told for your guidance.

When your fleet of conquest and discovery sails, lay in great store of provisions, for this sea is vast.

Once out of sight of land, let your shipmen sail into the face of the setting sun; they will find the land that is waiting for your rule.

If driven out of their course by storms, having sailed thus west for forty days or thereabouts, sail north or south along the coast of this land which the people here call Alata, and they will find a broad gulf, as we found it, into which empties a mighty river.

Let them search for this river, for there at its mouth lies a fortified town and in it wait guides who will conduct your men to my capital city.

Carry much water. It is life itself, for this sea is so vast that we tossed upon it near two months, and had we not had many rainy days we could not have lived, though four times we found islands and filled our casks, pails, pans, even our drinking-cups before leaving those hospitable shores for our westward journey.

Yet there was no bickering aboard ship, among us Romano-British, although on the tenth day at sea we learned the mettle of our slaves.

At first we had filled the port oar-bank with Saxons, thinking that rowing as a unit against a unit of free men on the opposite bank might breed within them a spirit of competition and bring about a better understanding. Enemies though they were, we respected them as doughty fighters and hoped to use their strong backs to advantage. But they sulked and would not work well, lagging in the stroke and causing trouble in many ways.

Then we separated them, fifteen to a side, and a free man between each two of them. This system, with use of the whip, worked better. There was no more lagging, and sulk as they might, the *Prydwen* plowed on through fair and foul weather alike, sometimes with sail and sometimes with oar-play, but questing westward with a lookout always at the masthead; for at that time not even Myrdhinn was certain how far we might have to seek for sight of land.

Before the dawn of this tenth day, these despairing homesick Saxons struck in the only way left open to them, preferring death to continued slavery.

I was roused from sleep by a yell, and my door crashed open. In bounced Marcus, my sister's son, with a cry of "Fire!" which brought me up standing. Unarmed, I rushed out in my night-gear.

Below decks, the planking beneath the oar benches was blazing, spreading fast along the inner sides, crisping the leathers over the oar-holes and flaring to high heaven, painting the sail scarlet.

It was more than one fire—it was many—started simultaneously, but running together so rapidly that we could hear the flames roar. A bucket brigade was forming, and as I looked the first water fell, but I had no eyes for that.

There was a greater sight, a thing so brave in its hopeless despair and determination that I cannot describe it with justice. Midway down the port bank sat three men already lapped in fire!

Two had already breathed flames and were dead or dying, for their heads had dropped on their breasts and their long hair was burning. The third saw me staring, laughed wildly in his torment and triumph and beat his breast with a charred and blistered hand.

Then he began to sing! I shall never forget the sight, the smell of burning flesh, the crackle of rushing flames and that fierce terrible song:

> *"Cattle die, kings die,*
> *Kindred die, we also die;*
> *One thing never dies:*
> *The fair fame of the valiant!"*

His eyes closed, I thought him spent, and then he raised his face upward—and cried (a glad call, inspiring as a trumpet blast!):

"Courage, comrades, let us go to Woden like men!"

And he rolled from his bench into the flames, stone dead.

Gods! How they fought us as we tried to quench the fire they had set, by saving through the days the oil issued in their rations, letting it soak into the planking, and, when all was ready, igniting it with live coals from a cresset handy to one in his chains, then passing the coals from hand to hand till all were supplied.

More than one of us bore marks of their manacles as they sought to hinder us until we all should burn together; but in the end, those living were herded aft under guard, not all walking there, being borne by those comrades who had not been clubbed into insensibility.

You may well suppose that after the fire was out, we were all in savage mood and with little inclination to be lenient to the rebels.

"Overboard with them!" was the main cry, as the men crowded round. Then Myrdhinn came forward.

"I have something to say to you all," he mildly interrupted. "Saxons, is your chief dead?"

"I, Wulfgar Ironbelly, am King, and alive," growled a flaxen-bearded giant, thrusting to the edge of his group.

"And I, his brother Guthlac, am alive," echoed one who might have been his twin, closely following. "Speak to us both, Gaffer, and we will harken."

"First," Myrdhinn began, "I am responsible for this expedition. I know my limitations, and having no experience upon the sea I have not interfered with affairs pertaining to ship life and operations. However, I have no intention that men brave enough to seek liberty through painful death and courageous enough to watch their kinsmen suffer in quiet and watch in quiet the fire creeping to envelop themselves shall now die a useless death, depriving this ship of near a score and a half of such doughty spirits. Saxons, ye are free men!"

An uneasy murmur rippled through the crowd. Was Myrdhinn mad?"

The Saxons looked at each other, unbelieving. Had they heard aright?

"You are free," Myrdhinn repeated, "on conditions. We obviously cannot put back at this stage of the journey, the purpose of which may have escaped you. We are engaged in a journey to the world's edge in search of new lands of which we have tidings. We do not know what we may find there or if we shall ever return. Knowing that behind us lies only ruin, war's desolation, and an unhappy future, we go west, where our faith has placed the Land of the Blessed. Possibly we may find it. Very likely, we shall not.

"Saxons, I ask you to fight beside us, to chance the decrees of Fortune with us, to accept hunger, thirst, the perils of a strange land, for the joy of discovery and adventure. In short, I would sail with you all as brothers. Saxons! Is it yea or nay?"

They talked among themselves in low voices. Then Guthlac struck hands with his brother and their eyes gleamed through the soot.

"What a tale we shall bring home with us, Wulfgar!"

"Count on us as free men under your conditions, Wealas!"

The gathering broke up and I followed Myrdhinn to his cabin.

"In God's name, are you mad? Can't you see, if we do discover anything, the news will reach the Saxons too? Those pirates will follow to ravage any settlements that Rome may make!"

Myrdhinn shook his head. "Do not concern yourself about trifles, Varro. Not one of those men will ever see his homeland. They are doomed men already."

I stared at him. Sometimes Myrdhinn terrified me.

"Just how much do you know? How about us? Will *we* succeed?"

"I know more than you think and less than I wish. I can foresee much, but not all—or enough. There are blanks in the future which are closed to me as much as to other men, and nothing I could tell you would be enough, or what you should know, the future being mutable and subject to change. But do not worry about Saxon pirates ravaging Roman towns in Brandon Land, for that they will never do."

I believed him then, and now I know that what he said was true.

Well, we fought on, beating our way into storms and out of them, storms so tremendous that we took in seas over the bulwarks and learned what it was to struggle without ceasing, through a world all water, with a ship that would scarcely obey the helmsman, so sluggishly she rolled. We knew the worry of broken oars, of riven sails, of a crew more dead than alive from loss of sleep and the battering of the waves, but bailing like fiends to keep the water down so that the next great water mountain might not in its falling finish the work entirely and send us all to Neptune.

But Myrdhinn kept us courageous and still believing in him; when it seemed as though we were to sail till our beards were gray, we kept on striving to cross this mighty River of Ocean, though beginning to despair of ever reaching its farther bank.

Finally the winds ceased blowing and not even a tiny swell rippled the surface, so it was "out oars and row," which we did for a weary week, and nobody became disheartened; for Myrdhinn told us that Brandon had come to this place and passed through it without harm, though hindered by floating weed. So we knew ourselves to be in the proper track and took this for a good omen, till fog came down and for three days we saw neither sun nor star to guide us, and our shipman was like to go out of his mind with worry and fret about it.

So Myrdhinn looked into his private stores and brought up a little hollow iron fish, which he placed with care in a bucket of water, treating it as a very precious thing.

At once, it turned itself about, pointing with its nose to the south and marking the north with its tail, so intelligently that almost our shipman was afraid to look at it, not having much trust in Myrdhinn's good intentions, and, I think, disbelieving in any other lands save those he knew.

"Remark, worthy voyager," said Myrdhinn, "how the side fins point out the points of west and east, and be guided by them. And guard this little fish that it be not lost, for I prize it far more than its actual value would indicate, it having been given to me by a yellow-skinned wanderer who by its aid had guided himself across the broad plains of Scythia, to the island of Samothrace where we met.

"Also, fear not the days to come, since Brandon has written that beyond this Sea of Calms lies a fair island inhabited by a wise people, and among them we may expect to find shelter."

We rowed, the sun and stars returned, our food gave out entirely; we drank our bellies full and rowed again, stayed by that thin cheer, until one day the winds came and bore us on, and all of us fell on our knees and thanked our various gods (Christian and pagan together); for there were now but very few still strong enough to move an oar.

I repeat, bring large stores of food, lest your men be in the state we now found ourselves, debating whether or no one of us poor hungry folk should die that the rest might eat. Myrdhinn saved us from that sin. In this broad watery desert he found us food!

I might mention here that in all our long journey we saw none of the sea monsters of which fables have so much to tell, though we did see strange sights that filled us with dread.

One night our lookout came below, squealing and white with fear, crying out that the sea was blazing and we were lost. Hurrying to look, we were startled to find that all around us the water was glowing and shimmering with light. But it was not fire, my Emperor, and it was harmless, though I cannot explain the mystery.

One must expect odd things if one travels. Not everything strange is dangerous, and who but cowards would hold back from great adventure because of odd, unexplainable events?

We took it for a portent, but it was not—unless indeed it foretold good, for no evil happened us. Fear not this trivial oddity, native to these seas, but boldly disregard it when found, and press onward. *We* passed from it unscathed.

We saw dolphins and mightier fish also, but none so huge as the unbelievable fish Jasconye, which Brandon describes as being the hugest fish in all the world, and writes that upon its back he and all his men celebrated the Feast of the Resurrection, not knowing but that they stood upon an island, until they lit fire to cook some victual, and their island sank and left them all swimming!

This I take to be a tale for children. Disregard it. We saw none so huge, though we were companied for some distance by a convoy of very large creatures who sported around us, watching us while they sent high spurts of water and froth into the air from their nostrils as they breathed. They harmed us not, being curious only, though by their very size and weight they might prove dangerous if maddened. Be warned in *this* matter!

After this we met another kind of fish, very evilly

disposed toward man, and we learned about it as follows:

Kinial'ch, one of our bravest, though without any Roman blood, being purely Cymric, had been wounded severely in our affray with the rebels. While we had food he lived and languished, becoming no better and in fact failing slightly each day, until in the end, when our rations grew scanty and coarse, he died.

We buried him in the only way we could. His Cymric comrades keened over him, gashing themselves with their knives. Myrdhinn prepared him for burial, marking his winding-sheet not only with a Christian cross, but also with a sickle which he painted upon the cloth in gold, while beside it he pinned a scrap of mistletoe, these things being symbols of the old Druidic faith never yet completely destroyed in the dark fastnesses of Cambrian hills.

So prepared for any future, we slid the body over the side, and witnessed a horrid sight. Scarce had it touched the water when a fierce fish seized upon it in a welter of foam, and fought for the fragments with other of its kin which instantly appeared.

We slew several with javelin casts, but finding these victims were speedily set upon, we ceased, for others smelling the blood in the water came and followed us. They kept in our wake for days, until, as I have written, we were dying for want of food. Then Myrdhinn came to our help.

We had tried to kill one of these fish before, for food, but when wounded each was rent apart by its companions. Now Myrdhinn bade us try again, saying that this time we would not fail.

He formed a length of rope into a circle, coated it with greenish paste from a small pot, gave three of us heavy mittens and warned us not to touch the rope with our bodies. Then, telling us what to do, he dangled his foot overside and pretended to slip.

As one of the man-eaters came to the surface we flung the rope around him. When it struck the water, the surface bubbled and fumed, hissing as though touched by hot iron. The fish flung itself about in a frenzy, but could no more escape than from a stone wall built about it. Then it stiffened out and lay belly upward, rocking in the enclosed space, while its kindred nosed about outside.

Before they could break in, though the rope was now sinking, we had hooks in the carcass and dragged it in, and it was not long before we were dining upon tasty steaks. So we escaped from the Sea of Calms, and feeding thriftily upon our fish-meat (for Myrdhinn warned us this feat was not magic and could not be repeated) we sailed on.

The skin of this great man-eating fish was hard to cut, and Guthlac spoke for it, shaping the thickest part, while moist, into a breastplate. This he studded with the bosses from an old worn-out piece of armor we found for him, and took also the buckles and straps.

With more of the hide, he covered a wooden buckler, and with small pieces made scabbards for sword and seaxe, binding also his ax-haft with narrow strips; so when this hide dried and shrank tight in the sun, Guthlac was possessor of as fine equipment as any on board.

And indeed, many of us were envious of him, for this thick, knobby hide proved to be nigh as tough as metal, though we could not then foresee the dire result of this day's work of his, which was to bring sorrow to me in later years.

5

Brandon's Isle

Close to a week later, a violent wind in company with thunder and lightning and hissing sheets of rain overtook us, and until dark and after we raced along in its grip. But it passed us before dawn, and as we lay rocking in the following swell, many miles from where the storm had found us, we in some curiosity peered ahead in the half-light of early morning, aided by far lightning flashes.

Every man of us knew a strange feeling, a sensation of an event about to occur, something pleasant or horrid, we could not tell which—but something which sent before it a warning of its coming.

Then the wind shifted, blowing toward us, and plainly was wafted the sweet hot smell of lush, rotting vegetation, so we knew then and one whispered to another, "Land! Land!" and the other, "What land, mate?" and the other, "What land, mate?" for Brandon told of many isles, some with friendly folk and some where dwelt enchanters to be feared, and some where worshipful priests dwelt, solitarily praising God, and clothed only in a weave of their long gray hair.

But, even as we whispered among us, a river of fire poured down the sky with a sound as though Heaven's floor were split wide open, and the lookout in the maintop raised his hands in the glare, crying "Brandon's Isle!" in a wild exulting shout, and again all was dark and we groped as though struck blind.

In that instant we knew that the Scot adventurer's tale was true, at least in part, for the little isles with the enchanters, either friendly or inimical, were all tiny and low in the sea, but this which reared itself before us was mighty land indeed, high and rugged, nor could we tell then in that brief flash if it be island or no.

And I may well say here that I think the stories of enchanters were creations of fancy, inserted into a description of travel too dry otherwise to appeal to Brandon's legend-loving folk.

So disregard anything you may be told in Hibernia or Britain of sorcery in these western seas. Vanishing isles there may be, but *we* saw them not; the folk are simple and friendly and the fruit of the isles is good and nourishing, like blood of life itself to hungry mariners, salted to a very pickle, as we were that night.

At this time, not knowing what lay before us, we took soundings, dropped anchor and waited for dawn, all very quietly after that first burst of joy, that we might see what was to be seen before our presence near this strange land was suspected by its dwellers.

As we lay there, slowly rocking on the long swells, listening to the low murmur of the surf upon that darkness-hidden strand, the sky slowly reddening above us, the smell of wood burning came over the water on the seaward-trending breeze; and this, increasing, told us more plainly than any words could that the land was peopled.

We stacked javelins and arrows in their places, saw to our bowstrings, cranked back the arrow engines, brought down the short wicked arms of the two tormenta and loaded each with a jagged rock from the ballast—all this in quiet so far as possible and we thought unheard, until the light suddenly strengthened and we saw that strand and upon it the figure of a man peering out to sea, brought there perchance by the strange sounds of creaking cordage or of ratchet and pawl clinking as we cranked one or another of the engines.

That he saw us we could not doubt, for at this moment the red rim of the sun burst up out of the sea and flooded us and him with light. A breathless moment we stared at him and he at us over the intervening rollers, until I hailed him, throwing my sword arm high with empty hand and outflung palm to show we came as friends.

Then, startled, he fled inland among the thick growth of trees and bushes, shouting as he went, and presently returned with a company of men bearing spears and clubs, each set with barbs very jagged and cruel to see. Before them marched an old white-haired man clad in a white robe beautifully ornamented around the hem and throat with painted figures, these at our distance impossible to distinguish clearly. He carried a green flowering branch and nothing else, so that the meaning was plain—we might have either peace or war!

Now these folk stopped a little distance out of the greenery, while the old man came on alone to the very edge of the water, and here he paused and called out to us in a clear pleasant voice that seemed the very essence of peaceful living and happy carefree ways.

Myrdhinn climbed up on the bulwark and tried several languages, gesturing at the sun, the sea, the sky and land, while for his part the other old man answered in possibly more than one dialect, but no common ground could be found for conversation, till at last each gave up his efforts and stood smiling at the other in humorous bewilderment across the intervening waters. Then Myrdhinn said:

"Put the boat overside. I am going ashore."

And this we did against our wills, fearing treachery, but Myrdhinn's mind was made up and his will was firm. So ashore he went, and we could see their arms waving as they gesticulated and strove to make themselves understood.

At length the old man pointed inland in silent invitation, and Myrdhinn nodded, and all in an instant, it seemed, the twain had turned and were gone from our sight, with many of the armed men following, though some were left. These were all big, strong fellows well able, it seemed to us, to cast a spear out to where we lay; so unobtrusively we trained the arrow engine,

loaded with a full sheaf of arrows, upon them and
swung also the port catapult in their direction. We were
now almost certain that, despite the rolling of the vessel, we could drop the boulder among them. Then we
grasped our bows behind the bulwarks—and waited.

The sun rose high and higher, until at almost midday Myrdhinn and the other old man came back with
their following of curious spearmen.

"Lay down your arms, my friends!" he shouted.
"Come ashore to me on Brandon's Isle, for this is
truly the land we seek. Leave a guard of fifty and come,
you others."

While he was speaking, the old islander harangued
his followers to somewhat similar effect, for each
stepped forward and threw down his weapon to form
a pile on the sand, after which they moved back some
twenty feet and showed us their empty hands.

All this time, since daybreak, there had been a
rolling mutter of small drums, neither loud nor very
far inland. This threatening sound now stopped and
the hush that followed pressed down upon our accustomed ears, as might a palpable noise.

In this deathly quiet, I gave low commands and our
other boat was lowered and sent ashore, where some
leaped out and joined Myrdhinn and others brought
back the two boats, plying between ship and shore
until all of us were there with the exception of the
guards, the tormenta men and the arrow-engineers.

"For," I warned, "these strangers may meditate
treachery; wherefore keep sharp watch and be ready
to cover our retreat if need be."

So, once lined in formation upon the sands, at my
signal we stepped forward three paces together and
cast down our bows, our shortswords, even our eating-
daggers, and stood facing the islanders' array across the
two piles of weapons—two unarmed companies, each
with its holy man in front.

Then Myrdhinn and the old priest stepped forward
and kissed each other, and as they did so, the drumming burst out with a great fury. We stared at one

another, almost tempted to reach for our weapons, wondering if this meant attack—and the bushes behind those facing us swayed and parted and through them came a large crowd of women, grass and flower clad, and many naked children—all smiling very prettily, chattering among themselves with merry laughter, while they proffered us gifts of flowers and fruits.

Very acceptable was this fruit to our salt-soaked palates, and marvelously good, though strange in taste and form. And thus the islanders took us to their hearts and we made a home with them for a month, a happy interlude in our stern lives.

So we rested, some making progress in the language, with a fair tutor to conjugate the amatory verbs; some hunting among the interior hills or fishing in the bay; while we all took turns in working a few hours each day on the *Prydwen*, which we had careened in a shallow cove, to scrape away the sea growths and recalk.

We stepped a new artemon and replaced some warped planking and two charred ribs amidships, making the ship ready for sea, though we had no thought of sailing so soon as we were actually to do.

One evening a hunting-party came back with a strange tale of an ancient man whom they had met upon the island's farther coast and whom they had known for white (these folk being rather golden in color), for he had spoken to them in the language of the Scoti.

One of the Cambrians was familiar with this tongue, having been prisoner and slave beyond the Hibernian sea; so he answered and learned that we were truly upon Brandon's Isle, for the oldster had been in company with Brandon upon the first voyage of that venturesome monk, and, liking the country well, he had taken a native wife and remained when the others returned to their own land.

Nor, thinking the matter over as we sailed in quest of him around the coast, could I blame him in my heart, for these island ladies, though thoroughly barbarian, are very lovely and dignified both in form and manner, and anyone might well do worse than remain in this Elysium, should occasion offer. But that was not for us. All unknowing, we sailed on toward our destiny—and war, excitement and change were waiting for us in the person of that one old man.

Arriving, we found him so aged that he was dying slowly from his load of years. However, his eye was bright and his tongue nimble through the joy of our coming, when in his age he had given up all hope and almost all thought of seeing a face from his native lands.

In the cool darkness of his grass house, Myrdhinn sat and talked with him alone; for the excitement of seeing so many of us fair drove him frantic with joy and at first he could not speak for the choking in his throat, but sat looking at us with slow tears trickling into his waist-long beard. But to Myrdhinn he *could* talk and make himself understood, though the Scoti words came slow and he fumbled among his thoughts to say the thing he would.

And a tale he had to tell us!

It seems (and now this is the part that directly concerns us, and you, my Emperor) that Brandon did not know there were still more lands westward of those he found, and Fergus the Scot had not learned of this for a long time. Then a party of young men looking for adventure had invited him with them on a plundering trip to a nearby island, and they in their log boats were blown far to the northwest, and out of their path, by one of the quickly coming storms of wind, common to these seas, called by the natives Hurakan, from the name of the god who they believe inspires the disturbance.

Finally they found land and explored it, sailing both north and south, but not penetrating far inland; for this it seemed to them was more than an island, and what people or monsters might dwell there they could not know. Before they left this part of the land they found that a warlike folk held the coast, for they were surprised one night as they slept beneath their boats and many killed; so that, although they had left in a score of craft, the survivors came home again in three, without loot or captive women, though they had a prisoner of those who had attacked them. I saw the skin, stuffed, of this being, and whether it is human or no, I hesitate to say. The skin is scaly and slippery with slime, the creature (in the living state) spending much time in the sea. The eyes are round rather than ovid, and lashless, the nostrils flat and inconspicuous as though meant to hold themselves in against the water. Below a broad lipless mouth filled with pointed fangs, on either side of the scaly neck, are marks very similar to the gills of fishes, but they neither open nor close, so that if they were once water-dwellers entirely, it must have been very long ago.

The legs are bandy, and in back, at the end of a ridged backbone, is a bony projection, varying with the age of the creature, from six to ten inches in length, so that when the individual sits, it must needs scoop a hole in the earth to accommodate this immovable tail or rest itself upon a log or stone.

The feet and hands are webbed, each digit tipped with a curved sharp claw; so in battle, though knowing the use of no artificial weapon except the hurling of stones, they are very formidable enemies, and Fergus and his companions were lucky to escape.

After that one excursion, Fergus roamed no more, but stayed at home and raised sturdy sons and daughters to comfort his old age. So after telling Myrdhinn of these things and what he could remember of the way thither, and showing us this stuffed trophy, and having held speech of this and that, with many questions of his homeland, on which Myrdhinn out of his long memory and many travels could well satisfy him, he dismissed us for that day, promising himself the pleasure of a further talk upon the morrow.

Then the people of that part of the island (Cubana-can they call it) made a feast for us, and we slept peacefully among friends, but on the morrow when

Myrdhinn went to visit this oldster, he was found to be dead on his couch, smiling with happiness.

So died this self-made exile. May I die as content—which, my Emperor, depends on you!

The eldest two sons of Fergus we took on board, for they were determined to be of us, and indeed we knew that from *that* family two only would not be missed. Also, we felt somehow that they might be of use to us, might bring us good fortune in finding this far mysterious land of the Two Hesperides.

Again we returned to our first landing, stayed about a week, though pressed to remain and dwell there with this friendly, well-disposed folk, and, not without sorrow and a little heartache at leaving, we sailed—this time companied with ten-score boats filled with our friends.

They led and followed and circled round about us, for a long distance, till a fine breeze sprang up and filled our sails, whereupon it was "In oars and rest," and we watched them drop away a few at a time, as the paddlers grew weary and the land faded from sight.

Then at last the land was gone, not even its highest point showing on the horizon, like a distant dingy cloud, and the last lingering boat had fallen behind with our promises to return soon, and we scarce could see the glitter of their highflung wet paddles in last farewell. And then even they disappeared.

"Taino's" they named themselves to us. "Good men." And finer people I have never met, for true cordiality and gentleness to strangers.

We sailed the sea all alone, not even a bird to company us, westward again, sailing to return to that peaceful, happy isle of Brandon's nevermore.

6

Castaways

Days went and came, with rain and sun, and we sailed—we sailed—a dreary round of days, threading through numbers of low islands, uninhabited and desolate, all very lonely to see.

Not long after we left, Myrdhinn found odd sea-treasure, which I may well mention here, for its results brought us as much good as Guthlac's fishskin armor brought us woe.

One day we came across a floating log with branches upon it, and in those branches perched a large land bird, green in hue, croaking a sad lament as the log rolled now this way, now that, so that this castaway was alternately submerged and raised, streaming from drenched feathers.

Mightily encouraged by the thought that we were sailing rightly, Myrdhinn would not let us pass by, though we had little inclination to do so, feeling our hearts go out in pity to this forlorn, helpless thing, and even more inclined to a rescue by the fact, as you may know, that green is one of the colors sacred to the Druids.

So Myrdhinn, sometimes Druid, sometimes Christian, considered this finding to be an omen of singular good fortune.

We steered close to pick up the bird, and as we drew near it spread its wings and tried to fly to us, but being so soaked with water it fell into the sea and was sinking when we arrived. One of the bards hooked out the bird, handing it to Myrdhinn, but even in his hands it gasped, fluttered, rolled an eye and became still.

Myrdhinn mourned, but magic could not help here—we had come too late. Though he could fan, through the years, embers of life to a healthy glow, when the last spark was gone he was helpless. No more than any man could he raise from the dead.

Perhaps foreseeing what importance his act was to hold, or from sentiment, he ordered the skin cured and of it he made himself a magnificent headdress, during the long days of exploring little islands.

In his ceremonial robes, mystically embroidered with strange symbols, and with this hat upon his head, the bird's head proudly raised, beak half open as though it might emit a clarion call, he looked to be what he truly was—a very Prince of Magic.

Deeper we penetrated into this maze of islets, but found no mainland till we had passed through into open water again. Unexpectedly the color of the water changed and became of a muddy hue, and not long after we sighted a low coast from which poured a wide turbid river, bringing much silt and floating rubbish down to the sea.

By this we knew that a broad land lay before us, and, cautious of exploring it, having seen one of its inhabitants, we coasted for some time, enjoying fair weather, and did not set foot on shore though we saw no signs of life, either beasts or human, only many, many birds which followed us for the scraps which our cook threw overside.

We sailed for so long that we began to perceive that we, in following the coastline, were turning back southward toward Brandon's Isle, and here our water gave out and we put in to fill our butts.

Everywhere here were abominable swamps and barren lands. The water was brackish and not fit to drink, so we sailed further on and still saw nothing but salt morasses, without smoke of fire or sign of any friendly folk.

At last we did see a section of coast that appeared

better than the rest, having clumps of green trees indicating springs, and a little cove for anchorage. So we put over a boat, and Guthlac being urgent to go ashore, we let him go, taking ten of his own Saxons with butts and buckets, and some of our own folk to help.

They being armed, we had no fear for them, having seen for so long an uninhabited coast, and so watched some scatter among the rocks hunting for shellfish, and others pass out of sight in the greenery looking for sweet water, and after went about our duties.

From these we were startled by shouts from shore, and our party among the rocks came running back, and hotly pursuing came a band of those fierce, scaly, frog-like creatures, hurling stones and croaking; lolloping along on their short bandy legs, sometimes erect and sometimes on all fours, as fast as a horse could run.

And there before our eyes they dragged down, tore to scraps, and devoured our comrades!

At this uproar, the others came running back from the trees, and paused in horror at the sight of carnage. I saw Guthlac form them, Saxon and Roman alike, into the Saxon shield wall, and then they were buried from sight in the croaking, snapping horde. How could we shoot? All were closely intermingled.

Once the throng opened and I saw Guthlac again, streaming with blood, split with his terrible notched seaxe a creature from crown to teeth, and losing then his weapon, he snatched out his ax and laid about him, until they closed in again and we could see nothing. But we noticed how those sharp claws slid harmlessly from his fishskin armor, whereas they tore through leather jerkins like cloth.

The end came quickly. Many more came pouring out of the swampy lands and Marcus, who had hawk eyes, thought he saw a prisoner hustled away in the press, and took him to be Guthlac, but could not be sure, for by this time our trumpeter had sounded "Battle Stations!"

Seizing bows, our archers were pouring arrows among the throng, but they, though never having imagined such a novelty, pressed forward thinking nothing of it, and indeed at our distance most of these arrows rattled harmlessly among them, though the stones they threw fell upon our decks, their strong arms being quite the match for an ordinary slinger in precision and distance.

Then our port arrow engine went off with a clatter, pouring a whole quiver of arrows into their front; and each piercing more than one in the horde, they fell by dozens, and the rest set up a hullabaloo of croaks and grunts and splashed into the water after us.

We cut the anchor free, never stopping to raise it, and with our oars whitening the waves we sped out of the cove, they pursuing like a dolphin school until we dropped a boulder into the thick of them; whereupon they dived and followed under water for a long way, until they saw the futility of pursuit, and turned back.

Now to turn tail as we did may not have been a Roman deed, yet it was most wise, though you at your distance may not think it, for had we stayed, surely our expedition would have ended without more ado.

Down the coast we went, lorn in our hearts for good fighting-companions we had lost, Wulfgar raging mad at the loss of his brother, anxious to leap over and swim back that he might kill and die, until finally his own folk seized him and carried him below, frothing in his beard, and put an oar in his grip and bade him row. And row he did, and heard the stout wood creak and lost his sorrow in work.

So, thirsty beyond belief until we found upon a bare little islet some pools of rainwater not quite dried, we went south along this unfriendly coast, rounded a cape and found ourselves going north again. Shortly after, rain gave us drink and filled our remaining butts. We continued up the coast, seeing lovely beaches and green-fronded trees, and were sure that this section would be more hospitable, but durst not venture a landing.

Far we sailed, taking turn about at the oars, the Saxons rowing port on their shift, in competition with a crew of archers to starboard, while the next shift pitted a number of sailors against the crews of the tormenta and the arrow engines; the third shift being composed of Romano-British against Cymry of pure blood.

Thus we made sport of labor, wagering that one would tire before another, rotating the crews so that the labor would be equal among all.

This long routine was broken at last by the skies growing like dark bronze, and in the heavens sounded a dreadful ominous humming. We knew by these signs, as your sailors must learn and be advised, that the fierce wind god, Hurakan, was abroad and raging.

We furled the sail we had been carrying in hope of a wind and rowed out to sea into the coming darkness that we might not be driven ashore. Here our shipman caused a sea anchor to be cast over, we running with bare poles, and keeping our course with oar-play as the wind struck.

The seas roared and raged, hurling us about like a helpless chip, while our two islanders, very sick for perhaps the first time in their lives, had no strength to control themselves, but were thrown about till finally we strapped them in a bunk for their own safety.

Night came and with it no relief from the furious wind. I beat my way against it into Myrdhinn's cabin and caught my breath, which was almost impossible outside.

"Almost exactly the way we found Brandon's Isle," smiled Myrdhinn. "Storm, night falling, a passing of the wind, and in the morning a happy, peaceful, friendly land. Shall it be thus, tomorrow?"

"Pray the gods it may be so! However, this wind shows no sign of passing; so let us beseech them in their mercy that they not bring us too close to land in this howling dark and wind—"

And during these words of mine, we struck!

We both were hurled against the side of the cabin;

I heard the artemon snap, and the mast break short off, and the thunder of the two halves of the mast, falling into the rowers' pit, carrying planking with it, and the screams of the dying men that Myrdhinn and I had brought so far through so many perils, famine, war and thirst—to die in the dark on an unknown coast at the end of the world.

The cabin door was jammed, but I hacked it open with my shortsword, feeling the dromon shudder at each tremendous wave which, striking us on the side, swept completely over us, rocking our *Prydwen* like a cradle. As it rocked, I could hear our planking crunch and splinter and the surge of ocean flowing free in our cargo and ballast, drowning out the rowers' pit and heard a great voice crying to the dead below:

"Witta! Bleda! Cissa! Oswulf!"

No answer came.

"Tolfig! Beotric! Oisc! Balday!" I knew the voice for Wulfgar's.

"I told you no Saxons would trouble Roman settlements!" shouted Myrdhinn in my ear.

The cabin floor became lost beneath the water.

However, by the time it lapped our knees, I had the way cleared and we rushed out.

It was dark as the bowels of Tartarus and the seas roared in at us, almost unseen until we were struck.

I heard a gurgling cry: "Health to Woden!" and hurled from my feet in the watery dark, together with Myrdhinn, knew that the last of the Saxons had gone overboard before me. At once I was separated from my companion and was gripped by a savage undertow that strove to hurry me out to sea.

I dived deep into it, swimming strongly in the same direction, to find myself free when I rose. As best I could, I turned back toward the coast, listening for the crash of billows to guide me through the screaming spume-filled night, and finally did hear the distant boom as our wreck pounded herself to pieces on this merciless shore.

Struggling toward the sound, I thanked God for His

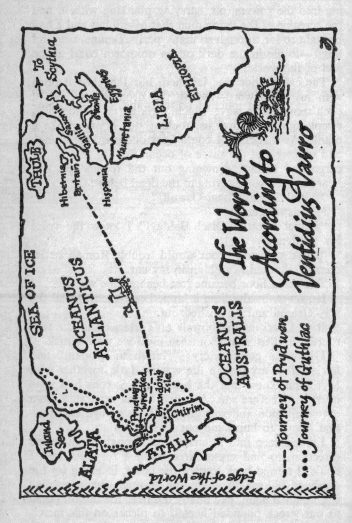

The World According to Ventidius Varro

—— Journey of Prydwen
···· Journey of Guthlac

SEA OF ICE

OCEANUS ATLANTICUS

OCEANUS AUSTRALIS

THULE

To Scythia

Hibernia
Britain
Gaul
Germania
Sarmatia
Greece
Egyptus
Hispania
Mauretania
LIBIA
ETHIOPIA

Inland Sea
ALATA
Prydwen wrecked
ATALA
Brandon's Isle
Chirim

Edge of the World

mercies, in that I could swim well and also for the fact that no hampering armor bore me down. As I approached the shore, I heard a strangled cry directly ahead and violently collided with a feebly thrashing form which at first gripped my shoulders, but we both sinking, he released me and struck out for the surface.

I rose beside him, my fingers gripped in his beard and knew from its length that I had found Myrdhinn. Before we had time to exchange a word, had such been possible, my feet touched bottom, and, crying encouragement into that ancient person's ear, I heaved mightily, and aided by a wave that rolled us like a pair of knucklebones, Neptune cast us, our legs and arms tangled, far up on a sandy shore.

All but spent, we yet clawed on a few paces from the fury of the water, and, exhausted near to dying, we lay down for a time. Then, my heart no longer pounding as though it sought to burst my breast, I got up, bidding the seer to remain where he was while I sought along the shore for survivors; and so went along the strand for a short distance when, feeling myself followed, I turned and found this dauntless graybeard close behind. I clasped him close, feeling his withered body shake with cold under his drenched robes, and the throb of his unconquerable heart, and without words we went on together.

Never before had I felt such a kinship with this old man as at this time, when, if ever, he might have been expected to take first thought for himself. The immortal spirit in him drove on the creaking carcass and laughed at distress, the storm and catastrophe.

Truly, whatever the unhallowed bargain with the Dark, whatever perpetuated his being beyond that of normal life, whatever his failings, Myrdhinn was very much a man!

We pushed on into the watery wind and had not gone far before finding a body. After some labor the man gasped and spoke, and we knew him for Marcus, my sister's son. He was grievously pounded and sore and complained of head pains; so searching there we found a gash and bound it up, as well as might be in a darkness so profound that, working, I could scarce see my fingers.

I left him in Myrdhinn's care and beseeched them both, if the lad were able soon, to return along the beach, searching, while I kept on in the original direction. I had not far to seek. Indeed, it seemed that everyone must have been washed ashore, so often did my questing feet stumble over bodies lying in or just above the surf, as I followed the shoreline just within the lap of the waves.

Whenever I came upon one, I dragged him high and worked upon him till recovery or until I was certain that further effort was useless, and eventually, among a little company of seven rescued, I heard my last-found survivor gasp, choke and breathe again, and looked around me to find that the darkness had appreciably lightened.

Now I could make out faces through the murk, recognize them, and beyond, through a spurt of the driving rain that still rushed over us in fitful bursts as though a tank above were overturning to drench us anew every few moments, I made out a dim mass approaching from the direction in which we had been searching.

This mass soon resolved itself into a little crowd of twenty, and learning from them that all progress beyond was blocked by a deep inlet, and that all living stood before us, we returned along the shore in the direction of the wreck. We scattered widely inland on the chance that some of our people might have been able to struggle farther away from the waves than I had searched.

No more living were found here, though we rescued two poor drowned bodies that the sea was sporting with in the shallows, tumbling them about like cat at play with mouse. We bore them along and added them to the growing company of the dead—two new members whose loss and whose lost experience we as yet scarcely appreciated. We were to grieve over them more bitterly in the days to come.

One was the shipman, and at his death we were already struck with an increasing dread. How, without his guiding knowledge of the sea, the courses of wind and wave, might we ever return to Britain or Rome?

It seemed ironical, as we sought among the dead, that Neptune had taken only his godchildren and spurned us landsmen. Those gathered about me were, without exception, fighting-men, and the dead on the beach were mostly the crew of the ship.

The other, whom we had just laid down, was the one man from all our company (save Myrdhinn) we could least have spared, though we did not realize that just then and mourned the shipman much and Morgo, the smith, but little.

Yet with the passing of Morgo likewise passed our knowledge of metals and their working, and though in later years Myrdhinn was able to help from his books, we had lost the practical knowledge needed to apply what he could tell us and suffered from this loss in many ways. Indeed, one of our most hazardous exploits sprang from this very lack of ability and brave men were done to death, as you will see at the proper time.

The gray skies brightened, though still overcast with scudding clouds. We left the dead for the time and hastened on toward the wrecked *Prydwen*. It was a sad sight which greeted us.

The dromon had broken in half under the incessant pounding, and only the forepart remained whole, lying in a nest of rocks, some hundred yards out from shore. The after portion was greatly crumbled away and lost, while with it had gone most of our gear, as we already knew, for the strand was strewn with refuse. Clothing was tangled with weed, as also provision chests, arrows, bows and planking; in fact, anything that would float.

So, with despair, we came to where Myrdhinn, Marcus and other rescued stood beside very many drowned and dead, among them Wulfgar Ironbelly, and all but one of the bards, looking disconsolate; and here we saw this bard trying valiantly to strike out an accompaniment to his keening, from a harp as drenched and tuneless as he.

His doleful clamor, fitting all too well the depressing state we were in, put us all in a mood to sit down, clasp hands, weep together and die there in the cold rain without an effort to help ourselves. I could not stand it, and dashed the harp from his hands, turning such a furious face upon him that he raised his arm against the expected blow and ceased complaining about "white-maned sea horses who trample the brave and daring beneath their hooves of silver!"

All stood aghast, for to those of British blood the person of a bard is sacred and to interrupt a keening is sacrilege. Whatever I did now must be done quickly or the moment of decisive action would pass and be wasted.

I spoke—to Myrdhinn—but loudly so that all might hear.

"Sir and leader! Under your command we have gone beyond the farthest bounds of the Scoti explorers. We are lost now. Our shipman is dead and also the majority of the crew."

Myrdhinn started. He motioned for me to continue.

"Sir! Unless you can lead us whence we came, out of this land where no Roman has come before us, in this land we must live and die. I see around me no more than fifty living people out of the ten score who sailed from Isca three months agone. We are all, save you, comparatively young men; our arms, our tools, our valuables and garments lie yonder in that wreck and the tide is ebbing. Even your tools of magic are there, without which a man be he however wise can do little. Should we therefore bide here listening to this lonesome caterwauling over those who, however well intentioned, can do nothing for us wherever they are now? The prudent man looks to his own welfare first, and mourns the dead later! Strip, men, and into the sea! We'll save what we can!"

As though some dark spell were lifted from the

hearts of all, they raised a hoarse cheer and we began to work and live again, the bard peeling down as nimbly as any, though spitting curses like a cat in muddy water, at thought of his interrupted dirge. But in the struggle of salvage, even he began to recover his spirits and shouted as lustily as any or grinned upon some lucky find.

Only Myrdhinn kept away, and though I had almost expected as much, he being old and not fit for much rough work in the numbing waters, it grieved me to see him going inland, head down as though in somber thought, until hidden behind the trees which grew not far away.

I felt that I had usurped authority, had rebelled against my superior, had made a breach between myself and one whom I respected and feared.

Yet it was not my fault if our natures conflicted. I am a practical man, a man of earth and things earthy. Myrdhinn was a man of the spirit, and although he had fought and upon one occasion taken the command away from Arthur, leading the troops to victory, it was foreign to his nature. To him, it doubtless had seemed most important to speed the departing spirits of our dead companions in the time-hallowed manner. To me, it seemed ridiculous. I could not help it. I was made so, and am of that mind today.

But, from the moment of that speech, I began to gain power over the minds of the survivors, and Myrdhinn to lose in proportion to my rising authority, though he always considered himself in command.

It was in my mind that he had gone away to be alone, but I saw soon how wrongly I had judged his character when, resting beside our goods, I saw a curl of smoke beyond the trees. I was about to seize sword and rally the men, thinking this an enemy fire, when Myrdhinn appeared and beckoned us. So thither we went and found that he had discovered a snug spot among the tree-clad dunes, where the savage shout of the wind was stifled to a murmur, and the smoke from a welcome blaze went straight almost to the treetops.

"There are a few things, Ventidius, that I can do without my tools of magic," he said in a low voice, and smiled.

I felt ashamed and could say nothing, though why I should feel remorse seemed strange. He pressed my arm and left me to dry myself, nor ever after did he refer to my outburst on that disastrous day.

And now I must admit to a very grievous fault in leadership.

Here we were, some fifty poor castaways, thrown up from the sea upon a wild, perhaps a hostile, shore. Yet I neglected, at the sight of warmth and comfort, to give the simplest order of precaution, and instead of commanding various men to gather up weapons that we might arm, dry our bowstrings, and be ready whatever might occur, I pushed lustily into the circle about the fire.

It was comfortable there, and the steam soon rose from our bare bodies. We twisted and turned, quite content in the glow, and then our chatter was hushed as we caught sight, upon the brink of an overlooking knoll above us, of a number of very peculiar people.

7

Captives of Tlapallan

It was a stern, well-armed gathering of human warriors who had come out of the pine wood above, and outnumbering us by at least a score, they showed no fear of us naked strangers, but stood and inspected us while none moved on either side.

Then their leader stepped forward and raised his right arm in salute, with his open palm toward us.

As he, with slight modifications denoting superior rank, was dressed like the others, his description will fit almost all.

His skin was the color of copper, and his accouterments harmonized, for he wore a shining copper breastplate from his shoulders to his belly and wide copper bracelets on wrists and forearms.

Upon his head a copper helmet glistened and in it were fixed stag antlers; though this being open at the top, so that an enemy might easier remove his scalp as a battle trophy, it was really not a galea, but more resembled a circlet, thirk, heavy and a palm wide.

He was cinctured with a copper band, broad and thick, beginning just below the breastplate, which protected his loins and supported a scant woven skirt, spangled with glittering circles of mica.

Around his neck he wore a broad collar of bear's teeth, jingling shell and pearls, while in his left hand he carried a copper hatchet, bound on a wooden handle.

Now on either side, surrounding us, came up other bands of barbaric fighting-men, dressed in the same manner, but less richly, their breastplates and cinctures not so broad or thick, and lacking the mica on their skirts, while centurions each wore a single string of ornaments and the men in ranks none at all.

Thus were we flanked, in a manner showing considerable military discipline. Some of our adversaries bore lances, others held throwing-sticks poised ready to hurl a featherless dart, while three in every group of ten men had swung behind them four-foot sticks with one end bent and hollowed like a ladle. These last, the engineers of this rude army, had placed heavy stones in the cup of the ladle, so that the whole apparatus formed a deadly, though small, catapult to menace our naked, unarmed band.

Before and on either side, imagine these grim, silent, copper men; behind us the raging sea. Do you think shame to us, given no chance except that of surrender or extinction, that we surrendered?

We were cold and not yet dried, our spirits low from the events of the night. A little way up the beach lay our friends and companions, stiff and stark in death. A snap of the fingers, a cross look, a careless motion, and we would have mingled our bones with theirs.

If our good bows had been dry and strung, our slingers ready, our swords in reach, then indeed there might be a different tale—but you, my Emperor, might have no subject king to write you of it and no kingdom to grasp in this strange country.

I spoke to the commander, who had come out to meet us. While the men behind us listened, I tried him with Latin, Cymric and Saxon with no result, bitterly regretting that our two islanders, who might have interpreted, had drowned, bound tightly to their bunks.

He replied in a soft speech, then, as that brought no response from me, used another which is spoken entirely without motion of the lips. I understood neither.

Myrdhinn came out between the lines, in his clinging, sodden robes, the only man clothed in our group, and began to talk in the language of the Druids, following this as he told me later with Greek, Hebrew and various Gaulish dialects—all without any valuable result, although occasionally a word would strike this barbarian commander as being familiar and he would interrupt and repeat the word, to find that it was not after all what he had thought it to be.

He stood and listened with a look of deepening bewilderment and indecision, then terminated the parley by turning his back upon us and waving in his men.

As they seized upon us, Myrdhinn cried, "Do not resist!" to our men, and we were led with the rest into the wood upon the knoll and surrounded by a company of lancers whose harsh looks and threatening manner gave us little hope for a successful outbreak.

We sat down or reclined, talking very little, watching from our elevated position our captor and his subordinate officers (easily picked out by their antler-decorated helmets) as they went through our rescued possessions, obviously marveling at some things and contemptuously casting down other articles.

Steel and iron especially fascinated them, as also to a lesser degree did our articles of cast bronze, which metal was close enough to their native copper for them to recognize, but whose hardness and temper they could not understand when one came across my case of razors and promptly sliced off his fingertip in feeling of the edge.

All these metal things they laid to one side, and made various piles of the other items, classifying by weight, size and estimated value; after which they all went down to the shore and stood looking at the remains of our ship for a long time.

Then they came back, and the officers replaced some of our guards, while those released men joined the others in stripping and plunging into the water. In a surprisingly short time they had stripped the *Prydwen* of everything movable: every bolt, clamp, nail and scrap of metal they could tear, pry or break away.

The after portion of the divided ship, being sunk, they did not bother with at this time, but the arrow engines and the tormentae lost everything, being dismantled, brought ashore and fire made from our campfire to burn away the clamps from the beams.

After everything possible was gathered upon the beach, we were led down and laden like beasts of burden with our own gear. They made bundles larger than I had thought man could carry; yet we carried them on our backs by means of a looped thong on each, which broadened to a band where it crossed our foreheads. This enabled the neck muscles to do a large share of the work, and truly this simple invention was of great help and I can recommend it to the large slave-owners in Rome who find mules and baggage animals expensive.

In this country, wherever I have been, there are no beasts of burden, except where dogs (little better than domesticated wolves) are used, and men have learned this handy trick to save their backs.

It did not save ours, however, for we were laden far heavier than otherwise we might have been, and in a long line we plodded down the beach in the direction of the inlet. We were obliged to pass the bodies of our dead, and here we saw a revolting sight.

These bodies had been previously stripped and robbed, but there was upon even a naked man one more thing to steal, and three ghouls were about that grisly business. We gazed in horror.

The barbarians lifted each head in turn, ran a sharp knife around the skull, dug fingers into the cut and tore the hair away. It was done in an instant, almost before we could utter a cry of protest, and followed by a quick scraping to clean off the fragments of flesh which still clung to the hairy cap which resulted.

We were sickened and revolted, knowing now for certain of the bitter cruelty and horror of this country's customs and feeling, too, a rising dread of the future which awaited us wherever we were about to be conducted.

Lance-butts drove us on. We staggered and weaved beneath our enormous loads following a fisherman's path into the wood.

Behind us lay our dead, denied a Christian burial, mutilated, naked and pitiful! They seemed a symbol of all we had lost, and if ever dead cried mutely for vengeance, those sad bodies on this cursed shore dinned it into our minds. I think all of us felt it deeply and were the more silent as we passed into and among the trees.

Myrdhinn was the only man inclined to speak.

"These folk must be kin to the Scythians. They have the same trick of denuding the skull to the ears. I presume they tan the trophies later or smoke—"

But he got no further. His nearest guard turned viciously and, without a sound of explanation, struck him across the mouth with the flat of his stone hatchet.

So we went on without conversation, Myrdhinn with a beard no longer white, but red and dripping on his embroidered robe.

At the time we thought this another proof of needless and malicious cruelty, but learned that they had good reason thus to command silence. We had not gone a mile when, without warning, one of the officers who stood beside our line of march, as we plodded, captor and captive, in single file along the narrow path, suddenly clutched his throat as though strangling, and coughing blood he sank to his knees and rolled upon his side.

Immediately there was confusion. Men grasped their atlatls (or throwing-sticks) and fitted darts to them; lancers charged through the underbrush to left and right, raising a shrill war-cry of "Ya-hi-ee-hee!" and in among us all fell a shower of stones, striking down impartially prisoners and guards.

At once the quiet wood became a howling Saturnalia. Back came the lancers, closely pursued by a press of savage painted men, so horribly daubed that they seemed scarcely human, and a struggle to the death began. On the outskirts of the fight circled a few dancing oldsters, too feeble to wield club or hatchet, screaming on their fellows to the attack, and frequently lifting long tubes of cane to their mouths and sending by their breath small darts among us.

It was one of these which had brought low the officer first to fall, piercing his jugular, though any prick would have been dangerous, each dart having been dipped in rotting meat until green.

Our captors were by no means idle, their armor proving a decided advantage, as time and again we could see them catch deftly some blow of hatchet, club or lance upon copper armlet or breastplate and quickly run their adversary through or split his skull in return.

For these savage attackers were driven mad by sight of carnage and would pause over some fallen man to rip off his hair, without considering the battle raging round about, so that another might easily strike *him* down all unperceived.

We poor captives scarcely knew which side to cheer for, being between two calamities, nor were we touched after that first volley of stones; so it seemed to me that perhaps we white-skins were that prize for which both red peoples fought. If this be so, I thought, far better that we stay where we were than flee to such dubious succor as these naked painted fiends could offer.

At very least, the accoutrements of our captors bespoke civilization in some degree, and thinking thus I chose sides in that screaming hell of blood and fury—and acted.

Near me fought the commander, beset by three. One he lanced, one he brained, but the third brought him low with a knobbed stick and howling with glee whipped out a stone knife and sprang upon him.

That was enough for me. I flung off my pack, and all naked and unarmed as I was, I sank my fingers in the savage throat. I could see the astonishment in the commander's face as we struggled over and upon him, but my antagonist gave me no time to think.

His body was oiled and slippery. He stank of rancid bear fat, smoke and fur, and in my grip he twisted like a serpent, drove his knife through my forearm and out again in a twink of an eye, and would have had it through my throat in another, had not the commander rolled from beneath us, seized his hatchet and split that ferocious visage from hair-roots to teeth.

I snatched the knife and sprang up, "Ya-hi-ee-hee!" I howled. The commander echoed it with the first smile I had seen since we had landed upon this bloody coast, and back to back we beat off those who still dashed themselves upon us.

Though too busy to look about, I heard others of my companions follow my example, and with good British cheers join in the affray. Suddenly the waves of battle ceased to break upon our stubborn line. Attackers and attacked stood listening. Faint and far a cry arose, long, ululating and eery—and was repeated.

Stopping not for dead or wounded, our foes slipped back into the wood and disappeared as a company of well-armed barbaric soldiery panted up and took control of the field.

We were now after a brief rest compelled to give up our weapons, and to resume our burdens; though all of us were treated with a measure of respect and not forced to hurry as before, for the feared attack was over and done and now the woods were safe.

After a little, the commander came back to me and, seeing that I was in pain from my arm wound, he signaled to one of his men to carry my pack and walked on with me some distance trying to find some manner in which we might exchange ideas. Finally he gave up, with a humorous quirk of the mouth, and eyed me for a bit.

Then he carefully pronounced the syllables, "Hayon-wa-tha," several times and tapped his breast, setting his necklace of teeth and pearls to rattling.

So that is your name, is it, my noble barbarian? I thought, and tapped my own breast.

"Ventidius Varro," I repeated, but this was too much for him, and after boggling over the V sound, he christened me "Haro" at first, and sometime later began calling me "Atoharo," this being the nearest he ever came to my true name.

"Haro! Haro!" he now said, holding up one hand with fingers spread. "Hayonwatha!"—holding out the other in the same way.

Then, with a rippling outpour of his labial language, he clasped his hands to symbolize the union of us twain. He touched his heart and held out his left hand. It was easy to understand that heart and friendship went with the offer, and I gladly proffered my left, pleased to have found a friend so easily, but he was not yet done.

Unloosing his knife, he made an incision in his own arm, clapping the bleeding place to my wound that the bloodstreams might mingle. So I gained a blood-brother who, though I could not then foresee it, was to become a staunch ally and a true friend in the years ahead.

While this had been taking place, we had all been pressing on with vigor through the forest, and now, without warning, debouched into a clearing of several acres, in the center of which was a palisaded fort of logs, strong and high-walled, as befitted a far outpost in a savage country held in peace only by constant raids and forays.

My new-found friend had me stop with him and we let the long procession go by, while we looked on and around the clearing. On all sides were thick forests of pine; but in the open was much tilled land in which grew a long-leafed tall plant which I did not recognize, and after some difficulty secured the name of teocentli for it.

The grain obtained from this plant grows upon pithy spindles, sheathed in tender leaf wrappings. Each kernel is a dozen times the size of wheat and when ground produces an excellent meal for baking, though it is good in many other preparations and is the staple cereal of the country. The civilization of the country is based upon it, for without its great yield from few seed, the enormous slave population along the broad river basins could not be fed, and this civilization depended upon slavery.

You will find seed of it among the goods I am sending. It is beyond doubt easier to reap, mill and cook in many ways than our other varieties of corn, such as wheat, rye, and barley.

The commander pointed out another field of coarse, rank, broad-leafed weed and made signs that it was very good, rubbing his stomach and exhaling deeply, but in what manner it was used I could not then imagine. Little as it may seem possible, these people dry this herb, crumble it into little stone cups attached to a reed mouthpiece and set fire to it, sucking the aromatic vapors at the mouth and breathing them out through the nostrils!

This has a medicinal effect and produces a giddiness and sickness in the neophyte, which after some time is followed by a general feeling of exhilaration, like a stomach full of mild wine. Among the savager peoples of this country, the practice is widespread and they will not open a council or consider an important matter without first blowing puffs of smoke to the four corners of the earth and going through a complicated and somewhat unnecessary ritual, to cause good spirits to favor their enterprises.

The folk I had fallen in with, however, have progressed beyond such crude superstitions, worshiping only three major gods, typifying Sun, Earth and Water, and smoke the herb for its virtues only.

Seeing that I was anxious to learn, Hayonwatha pointed out in his soft speech various individuals as they passed by, naming them:

"Chippeway, Yamasee, Otali, Nashee, Shawano"— with many another nation; and as they passed, with leisure to look closely I could see differences of coloration and weapon embellishment.

Then waving his arm broadly to include all the varied nationalities, he said, "Tlapallicos!" and fell into a glum, brooding mood, as though the thought irritated him.

I tapped him on the breast. "Tlapallico?" I queried.

He started, his eyes flashed and his strong right hand fell to his belted hatchet.

"Onondagaono!" he exclaimed, and struck his breast as though deeply insulted. Then he smiled and repeated, "Onondaga! Onondaga!" twice, to be certain I should not again fall into error, but left off the suffix "ono," which I inferred to apply to tribe, clan or race and not to an individual.

I pointed to my fellows and said "Romans," which he repeated several times to fix the word in his memory.

"Tlapallicos?" I questioned, pointing at some prisoners, mostly wounded, who followed under guard at the tail of the procession.

"Calusas!" he growled and spat on one as he passed, to indicate his contempt. "Chichamecs!"

As I might remark, "Saxons—barbarians!"

Yet it was against these natives of the region, and

their neighbors, the Carankawas, that the Tlapallicos, semi-civilized and disciplined to ferocity as they were, must sally or protect themselves in camp by walls of mounded earth spined high with a pointed log palisade.

The procession passed and we followed across the clearing—up the earthwork ramp, through a gate in the palisade, and we had entered Ford Chipam. Within the enclosure were a large number of huts, mostly flimsy constructions of wattled reeds smeared with mud, but some of pole frameworks erected over a sunken floor below the ground level, the whole sheathed with broad pieces of bark or the hides of animals.

At the exact center stood two log structures, one small, one large. The small one was the commander's dwelling, and the large one, with doors and windows that could be barred and made tight, the prison of the fort.

We were urged within. "Weik-waum," said Hayonwatha, and the openings were made fast. Here the fifty of us spent the night, receiving rations a little before dark: deer and bear meat cooked into a tasty stew with the yellow kernels of teocentli, and small black beans. It was good and plentiful and afterward some of us slept, but I could not, nor Myrdhinn.

During most of the night we peered out of the barred windows at the scene on the parade ground where the captive Calusas were being put to death to appease the manes of those Tlapallicos slain in the day's battle.

Mutilated, burned and scalped, they died to a man chanting defiance to their captors, and days later I saw their skulls set high on the pointed palisade to warn lurking forest spies that a like fate awaited any who dared resist the power of this farthest-flung fort of the mighty empire we had reached.

"Hue-hue-Tlapallan," Hayonwatha later named it to me. "The old-old-red-land!"

And red it was, every inch of it: red in soil, in habits, in spirit, drenched in blood, its altars reeking, its priests stinking with gore; ruddy the foliage of its northern boundaries, ruddy the ground where we lay and all along its southern marches.

The very thoughts of its people were tinged with red, their desires and dreams more ruddy than the color of their hides.

The sun that night tinged all the enclosure, staining huts and houses; the ramps on the red earth mounds, the firing-platforms of red pine—all took on a bloodier hue, which was retained after sunset by the leaping flames that consumed the enemies of that sun's worshipers.

Had we known more, we might have taken this as an omen affecting our further life in this cruel land.

8

How Naughty Children Were Frightened in Samothrace

Early in the morning, talking outside brought us to the bars again, where we saw several passing men, lightly dressed but well armed, equipped to run or fight.

We watched them as they were let out of the north gate and through the opening, saw them look about warily and enter the forest, separating there, and guessed them to be runners sent to apprise some monarch of our entry into his land.

Obviously these people held the outer barbarians in deep respect, for some time after the last man had gone a squad of men loitered near the gate on the chance that one might return closely pursued.

But nothing of the sort occurred, and after the fog and chill of the dawn had given way to warmth and after we had been fed, the guard returned to their quarters, leaving only two pacing sentinels on each firing-platform on the four walls, and high above them a stationary watcher, perched on a tower built above a mound between the prison and the commander's house.

Every hour, all day long, this sentry was relieved by another, and only once in the forty days we spent at this fort did we see any relaxation in vigilance or discipline.

Men were constantly leaving or entering the fort in parties of various numbers, but never less than four. Sometimes they brought wicker baskets of fish, both of the fresh and salt varieties; sometimes deer, black or brown bear, grown fat as swine on the berries with which these forests abound.

Often large birds were brought in, most succulent, bronze-feathered, red-wattled and strange to see, besides other species which we recognized—doves, geese, ducks, cranes, grouse, pheasants and many similar edibles.

And all day long baskets of salt came in and were stored away with the care befitting a great treasure, to protect which this fort had been erected.

The country abounds in all things necessary for good living. I have seen doves flying in flocks that hid the sun, so many that three days did not bring the end of the flock; while a man might enter the woods as they slept at night and not trouble himself to be cautious or even burden himself with a stick to knock them down, but pluck them from the trees and bushes for the stretching forth of a hand! And in the morning we would find every green thing gone from the wood as though it had been smitten with a blight overnight.

A rich and fertile country it is that I hold for you, my Emperor!

At this time, however, none of us expected much besides the day's food, living in uncertainty and dread as to when the runners might return and what orders they would bring.

So a week went by with no change in our surroundings or habits, except that we had been given back our clothing (but no armor), and a doctor had treated Myrdhinn's gashed lips, my arm wound and divers others of us that had suffered some small injury at the time of the wreck. One man in particular this doctor treated in a manner that should interest Roman physicians as much as it did me.

The second day of our captivity, he complained of head pains, later groaning and crying out in torment, while the next day he looked at us with fever-brilliant eyes, recognizing no one.

Myrdhinn could not help him and we gave him up for dead, but this doctor of whom I speak came to see him, and while a younger man (his son, I believe) looked on with interest, our companion was given dry leaves to chew and the doctor took some himself.

Then, with one of our company seated upon each arm and leg of our fellow to hold him steady, the doctor began his work.

First, with a razor-sharp knife of obsidian glass, which is here called itztli, he laid back a portion of the scalp, exposing the bone beneath, spitting juice from his own leaves upon the wound. Then he removed part of the bone, which, as we all could see, had been cracked and was pressing upon the brain. Working swiftly, he removed all specks of bone with shell tweezers, rounded the edges of the hole, smearing them with spittle, deftly cut a piece of thick sea-shell to fit and clapped it over the opening.

Straightway he applied more spittle, sewed up the scalp flap with sinew and bade us by sign to keep the man under restraint, which we did for two days, binding him face down upon a wooden pallet which they brought us, after which time he became sensible and could be trusted to care for himself, though still very sick.

Now the odd thing is this: although he suffered during the operation, yet his pain was almost annulled by the application of this spittle and by the effects of the juice he must have swallowed from his own cud.

Therefore I send you all these leaves I have been able to collect, they being rare and most precious, brought to us with difficulty and hardship from unfriendly lands far to the south, and hope that when they are before your learned men, they may be recognized and similar plants found in Europe.

After we had been incarcerated for a week, though more as respected prisoners of war than slaves or enemies, I was called and conducted to the commander's weik-waum.

Here we set about the business of mutual communication, and as we both were anxious to learn, at the end of the month we could exchange enough words in his own speech to get one another's meaning. Myrdhinn was also admitted to these lessons and learned far quicker than I, and in turn we instructed our companions.

In these talks we learned much which may well be set down here, the swift course of following events being understood all the better for the present interruption, although you should realize that I myself did not know all of these things for many years.

The country where we dwell is named Alata, as upon the map which I enclose you will see it drawn, partly from observation and a good deal by reports from the native traders, who cover vast distances on foot and water, there being no other means of travel anywhere in the whole land.

Far to the north lies an inland sea of fresh water and here live savage tribes, as also along the ocean seaboard. These speak many languages and war among one another, being utter barbarians, and are termed generally Chichamecs—their country, Chichameca—in disregard for whatever they may call themselves.

To the west, broad plains and valleys and gently rolling hills, likewise inhabited by wandering tribes, extend to the very edge of the world, which is marked by a titanic range of mountains not to be crossed by

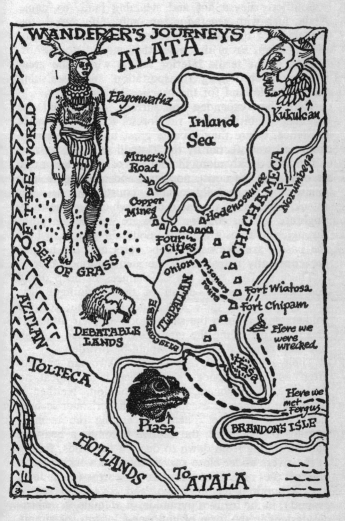

man, for they extend upward beyond the reaches of breathable air.

Southerly lies a hot and steaming land, by name Atala, lush with vegetation, uncomfortably moist, the homeland of the Mias, the ruling class of the country of Tlapallan. From this place they moved northward, settling in the fertile interior valleys where the great rivers run, providing transportation and furnishing much tillable land for the practice of agriculture.

Here they expanded and thrived, driving out the original inhabitants into the forests to lead a savage existence, where they became great hunters and warriors and were feared by the Tlapallicos and Mias.

Studded thickly along the borders of Tlapallan, more especially to the north, northeast and east, lies a long chain of forts, heavily manned, constantly ready for attack, holding all the main rivers which are the thoroughfares of this country. There are well-beaten paths through the forests and the mountain ranges, where the passes are likewise held by forts and the heights are constantly patrolled by the men stationed there.

These soldiers hold the Chichamecs in deep dread and some contempt—dread of their fighting-ability, and contempt of their arms and education; for the soldiers spring from the same stock as their attackers and those defending the marches of Tlapallan are but one step removed from the would-be invaders.

Their system of slavery is this. A woman or man after capture is at once a slave. There is no appeal, no exchange of prisoners, no manumission. Neither is there any chance of escape, since the prisoner is hurried inland at once. Then, lost among the teeming myriads of Tlapallan, the captive becomes a beast of burden, toiling from dawn to dusk in the fields, fishing in the rivers under close surveillance, or working upon one of the numerous mounds of earth (sometimes over a hundred feet in height and covering acres of ground), in the form of pyramids, of animals, geometrical designs in the form of hollow enclosures, or simple barrows to provide work for idle hands.

These many forms of mounds and designs are the chief pride and distinguishing mark of Tlapallan from other lands. Almost everything these people do concerns a mound in some way.

The ramparts of the forts are earth, with a palisade on top. The rich river borders are knobbed with mounds, upon which the people seek shelter at a time of sudden flooding of the alluvial lands, for these mighty rivers are apt to overflow their banks or change their course overnight. Other mounds cover the bones of illustrious dead, and these are huge. I was told that one alone had taken fifty years to erect, using the labor of two thousand slaves, in such times as they could be spared from the tilling of the fields.

Two people lie buried in this mound, but that was long ago and no one now remembers their names or anything of their history!

No such burial is given to the slaves. *They* erect the mounds where the temples are built, *they* see the watch-fires flame night and day, always tended, extinguished but once a year to be immediately relit, but they have only one share in the worship.

After they have grown old and feeble, their days of work done, having been transformed from valuable pieces of property into worthless mouths open for corn, they climb again those temple mounds their sweat and tears have salted and are savagely done to death upon the altars there to the glory of their captors' cruel gods.

Their children's fate is different. Torn from their parents at the earliest possible time, the young Chichamecs are educated according to the harsh principles of Tlapallan. Deprived of love and affection from birth, they grow stern and cruel. Most boys become soldiers, those of much promise being educated especially for positions of power, but the dull child or the cripple goes the way of his parents and may toil years later with earth-laden basket up some high mound and meet an aged crone tottering down, not knowing her to be his mother—or be in the throng below the temple when the high priest above, in the last rays of the setting sun, holds up his father's still throbbing heart to coax their departing god back again from his dark lair.

But however hard this stupid one's toil, however difficult and hungry the days, he has a hope his parents never knew. The son of slave parents, by any whim of his master, may be made free, take up land for himself and become a small freeholder of Tlapallan, living in hopes that his son in turn, third remove from the forest life, may become a merchant, a trader in obsidian, wrought metal, or paints to embellish the bodies of the Chichamecs—his cousins.

If so, this trader brings back all manner of precious things—furs, pearls, rare featherwork, gold or silver —unless indeed he be slain by those haughty, untamed people, as a true son of Tlapallan!

Although the coloration of the skin, the contour of the features and the proud, cruel expression of all the races are very similar, a Mia may be ready distinguished from a Tlapallico by reason of the skull's shape. Shortly after birth, a Mian baby has a small board bound tightly to his head, both front and back, compressing the soft bone shape, sometimes ridged along the top of the head like a bird's crest, but often rising to a peak.

This renders it impossible for a slave to ever masquerade as one of the ruling class, nor can he intermarry among them.

Hayonwatha was of the second generation, bred to war, but by the odd mistake of his own mother having been accidentally chosen as his nurse, he had learned something of forbidden mother love and, deprived of it early, had nursed all his life since a bitter hate for Tlapallan and the sons of slaves which made up in great part the common soldiery and garrisons of the forts. It was this rankling bile that showed strongly in his voice when he named to me on the march the tribes of various individuals as they passed before us—tribes of which those various individuals themselves were ignorant, being placed to defend forts far from their homelands, that they might remain ignorant of their own people and feel themselves as strangers in a hostile land, with their only friends their fellow soldiers and every tribesman, in the forest round about, their enemy.

So the individual lost his identity and became a Tlapallico, a citizen of Tlapallan, except in a few cases such as that of Hayonwatha when he, in a moment of crazy pride before a stranger to whom he owed his life and who he knew could not understand, denied his birthright of citizenship and called himself "Onondaga" after his mother's people, far north along the shores of the Inland Sea.

All this Hayonwatha explained fully, in private talk with myself and Myrdhinn, and told us how the Mias had fought their way up from the southwest where no forts were now needed, a desert country of poison wells and springs separating the borders of Tlapallan from the nearest large tribes of civilized people. He told us how the Tlapallicos raided across these Debatable Lands, having maps of the sweet waters on their lines of march, and brought back prisoners who were prized for their skill in featherwork and blanket weaving.

Also he told us that some of the various barbarian tribes looked to the southwest as their final resting-place, it being said that from these regions all men had come, and they regarded this as the terrestrial Paradise. Therefore, to the southwest their heads were directed when they were buried, lying face up with their valuables and their weapons around them, so that they might prosper and defend themselves in the Land of the Dead.

All this interested Myrdhinn greatly, for to him it seemed that this earthly Paradise might be the very Garden of Eden from whence all men sprang, and he could hardly contain himself with anxiety to be free and searching for this Land of the Blest, and also worrying for fear that we would never be permitted.

I do not know how many times he told me of various faiths and religions known to him which held that Paradise was in some mystical Western Land, or how often he dinned into my ears the fact that we had sailed southwest to reach this peculiar country.

He was genuinely interested and hag-ridden with this thought, and night after night when others were sleeping I watched him at our barred windows, scanning the stars for some phenomenon which would indicate a favorable end to our imprisonment.

But the stars were uncommunicative and disappointed him, some even being strange to us and not the same as in Britain, which suggested to me that possibly Myrdhinn's magic and divinations would not avail us in this land of Alata—its gods being against us.

Myrdhinn smiled at this and said that though divinations were obscure, his magic was powerful anywhere, resting upon basic facts of truth, unchangeable anywhere on earth, most of his feats depending upon earthy materials common to anyone, supposing them to have the knowledge to perceive and extract the virtues within.

"Give me," he said, "my books, my materials, and I could get us all out of here with white magic; but what can I do as I am, being stripped of all but my robes?"

"Black magic!" said I. "Use that. The worthy end justifies the dirty tools."

Myrdhinn shook his head.

"Aye, black magic would avail. I could blast this fort with a spell, and imperil my mortal soul in doing it, but I have taken too many trips along the murky borders of Hell! Long ago, I saw too much and was warned by it. Never again will I use black magic except as a last resort which must be worth the peril involved. Yet, lest you doubt that I have powers at my beck which can protect us—watch well from the window and be not afraid, for this is neither white nor black magic, but a simple thing that once all Samothrace knew and elders there frightened unruly children by it."

He went to the window and chirped into his beard, and suddenly from the half-dark a flittermouse came flapping. It clung to the bars and eyed us all, and Myrdhinn with a forefinger stroked its silky back, chirping—and the little creature chirped in response!

All in a twink it was gone, and Myrdhinn raised his arm.

"Watch!" he said, "and be still!"

Round the sleeping fort flew the flittermouse, round and round again, three times in all, flying widdershins, and vanished again.

Then Myrdhinn dropped his arm and stood listening.

"Do you hear it?" he asked.

I shook my head. All was as it had been, save that a light breeze had begun to blow.

I said as much, and Myrdhinn chuckled. "A breeze? Listen."

The breeze became a stiff wind, increasing to a gale which buffeted our stout prison and made the timbers creak.

Cries rose from the soldiers' quarters, as the light huts and tents blew over and exposed the sleepers to the stars.

Still the gale increased. All of the prisoners were now awake. Our prison shook and trembled. In the forest we could hear the crash of falling trees. We were forced to shout to one another to be heard, then could no longer do that. And still the tremendous wind swept the fort like a besom, piling the loose flimsy wreckage of the weik-waums against the southern palisade.

Suddenly we saw overhead the black sky and the aloof stars, and caught a glimpse of our roof flitting away before hearing the crash of it on the parade ground and smelled the smoke where embers of campfires had been whipped against our log walls.

"Stop it!" I screamed to Myrdhinn. "You will kill us all!"

Myrdhinn raised his arm and all at once there was
no more wind.

Now we could hear a multitudinous groaning and
lament from the injured, followed by a mighty flare of
light. The wreckage against the palisade was flaming,
driving back the night, and our hut wall burst into
furious tongues of fire, licking up our door and surging past the window near it.

On one another's shoulders we got over the wall and
looked around at the damage. Myrdhinn's "little spell
to frighten naughty children" had done its work well.

The whole enclosure was bare of huts. Here and
there staggered injured men, carrying or aiding others.
Fully a third were dead and none save ourselves, incarcerated in the strongest building in the fort, were
entirely without scathe.

The watch tower was down and crashed through the
commander's quarters, though I saw him limping about,
trying to restore order.

The palisade was burning furiously, and so stupe-
fied with calamity was the camp that it burned on
unheeded. Had the Chichamecs struck then we would
all have been killed.

Weapons, provisions and trade goods were inextricably mixed into the mass of burning wreckage, and only
a few things, among them our gear, had escaped
(having been placed in a root-cellar beneath the commander's dwelling), though the building above was
ruined.

Myrdhinn turned to me.

"Will Druid lore work in Alata, Ventidius?"

I had no words to deny it.

9

Kukulcan

The remarkable discipline of this people was quickly manifested after the first shock had worn away. Crackling orders from the commander started the work of salvage, and before sunrise the fires had been extinguished, the wreckage searched for weapons, valuables, and everything else which could be saved.

For my share, as commander of my party I had given orders that we help wherever possible, thinking that a show of good will might help us all, even as my help to Hayonwatha had resulted in friendship and personal favors.

This, although a further usurpation of Myrdhinn's authority, aroused no antagonism in him, he heartily agreeing; and I thought he seemed secretly relieved that I had taken command, for he had no liking for the duties of war, though he had fought in Britain.

We offered our help in caring for the wounded and soon had them segregated in our former prison with Nicanor, a legionary with some knowledge of medicine, and Myrdhinn in charge, until the physician of the fort relieved them.

During this work we had come across the pit in which lay our gear, and in the confusion we managed to arm ourselves with bow and buckler, sword and dagger. Thus arrayed we marched to the commander.

"Sir," I announced, "receive us as friends and allies in this emergency, I pray. You are in dire peril from the forest men. We will hold the breach until the palisade be rebuilt."

Hayonwatha looked at us strangely.

"Do you understand what you are doing, Atoharo?

You could easily escape. We could not prevent you now."

I laughed.

"Whither should we go? Flee to the Chichamecs? Nay, let us earn our freedom by proving ourselves friends. Give us the post of danger and if the barbarians attack you shall see how white men fight."

Again that odd look.

"Let it be so. I have warned you. If you choose to stay, we value the aid you bring. Whatever may arise, this day makes us truly brothers. Count upon my future help in anything I can do. But remember, your freedom depends not upon me, but upon Kukulcan!"

So I told off twenty, who marched to the smoking ruins and stood guard, scanning the forest while the rest of us donned full armor. Then we relieved the guards, who likewise armored themselves, and afterward we all scattered along the walls, each with bow and quiver ready.

For the time being, the fort was ours—as peculiar a twist of fortune as might be conceivable to anyone. Would we had profited by it!

Just after sunrise, runners went out, scattering in the forest, and by midday a detachment from Fort Wiatosa, our nearest neighbor, came in on the double, heavily armed guards and baggage-laden slaves who struggled along panting and spent.

Then you might have seen those copper-colored warriors scramble for atlatl and darts, lances and javelins, bone and flint and shell knives, and, again properly armed, go strutting, feeling themselves men of valor. As their elation increased, our spirits went down.

Sentinels came up and replaced us on mound and parapet, and we formed ranks on the parade ground and waited.

Soon Hayonwatha approached, in a group of his chief officers. We watched them tensely. What would be the orders? Behind me, the men murmured. Would it be prison again? Sooner than that, they would fight, as I well knew.

Myrdhinn and Nicanor came running from the prison to listen. I stepped forward five paces, unbuckled sword and scabbard and held them out. Hayonwatha raised his hand in dignified refusal.

"Replace your weapon, Atoharo. This day has earned you a place among us. Let us be as one people, with no talk of prisoner and captor, until I receive the orders for which I sent upon your arrival. Receive also this token of our friendship."

An officer handed him a necklace similar to that which he wore: many-stranded, glittering with pearls, elk and bear teeth, gold and mica beads. I removed my helmet and the commander placed the costly thing around my neck.

I saluted. Myrdhinn went back to the hospital, smiling in his beard, and our company disbanded.

That evening was one of merriment, for not a man, whether of Tlapallan or Britain, but felt better with the feel of weapons at his side, and if our former captors swaggered, think then of us, far longer deprived of the touch of good steel and trusty bow!

And imagine us striding like gods on earth, glittering and jingling among the many campfires, welcome at any, the heroes of the day—and Myrdhinn, the man to whom we owed it all, discreetly in the background, handsomely robed, quietly observing, scheming, considering the future and the stars.

It is no part of this story to detail how, in the following days, we amazed these fighting-men with our bows, whose deadly precision they beheld for the first time in their lives. I warned my men to be careful to keep a loose string, in order that the full power of the bow might not be manifested, and by no means to shoot beyond the farthest range of the atlatl—thus not displaying our greatest strength and keeping secret our reserves.

Also, when they wished to make bows and emulate our weapons, we carefully selected only moderately desirable woods, and were none too particular in showing them the correct grip and finger release.

After a while they went back to their atlatls, satisfied that they were our equals in distance, if not quite so in precision, which was what we had intended.

Together, bands of my men and bands of the Tlapallicos mingled in the forest, where their slingers competed with ours in the hunting of small game, and beat us roundly too.

We visited Fort Wiatosa, and found it identical with Fort Chipam; went a-fishing and saw again the wrecked *Prydwen,* the stern lying ten feet under, glittering and beautiful, though a ruin that made us grieve for her past splendor.

Belatedly the Chichamecs learned of the damage done to the fort, long after its repairing, and they hurled themselves upon us in utter disregard for singing arrows and darts and forced an entry, only to die on steel and stone, the survivors seeking the forest again like wounded bears who slowly back away, growling horridly and licking their wounds, but not beaten or daunted.

One morning, nearly two months after our arrival, the vigilant watcher in the tower signaled that there was movement in the forest. Soon a troop of a hundred armed men marched into the clearing, formed in columns of fours and hailed the fort.

The gates opened at once and they marched in, their officer presenting a belt of beadwork, as credentials, to Hayonwatha. This announced the bearer as the new commander, and his orders were that two thirds of the former garrison, under Hayonwatha, be detailed to guard us on our way to the capital of Tlapallan.

I did not know this and was surprised to find Hayonwatha surly and curt, for to me he had not been the stern hard-bitten commander with which his men were familiar. Nor could I learn much from him, his attitude showing that secret orders had changed our relationship.

"At last," I said, somewhat nettled, "you may tell

us whither we are to go, if you cannot tell me what is to be our fate."

"You march at daybreak. We go to Kukulcan. You are to be judged."

"Who or what is Kukulcan?"

He did not seem to hear me, but sat on his bench with his head in his hands, and in a tone of uttermost despair, repeated:

"Kukulcan! Kukulcan!"

So I left, wondering greatly, for whether Kukulcan might be a city, a country, or a ruler's name, I had not the least idea.

10

The City of the Snake

There was the tingle of frost in the air as we set out the following morning. Autumnal days were rapidly approaching and as we marched on northwesterly, following well-marked and hard-beaten paths worn a foot or more below the surface of the forest mold, we began to feel the chill and were glad of night shelter.

This comfort we found at forts. Night followed night, but always during the waning daylight we arrived at yet another in this gigantic scheme of mounded fortifications which protects the long frontiers of Tlapallan from invasion. Though connected by no Wall of Hadrian, this system was fully as efficient as Britain's, at this time, for the Mias had no organized attack to fear. The Chichamecs were always at war among themselves, being split up into many tribes with various languages and dialects, though strangers managed to talk with some ease by movements of the hands.

From one fort to another we were passed along, supplied with food, laden with goods to carry on: pipe bowls from the stone-carvers, hides from the trappers and hunters, jewelry and loose pearls from the creek fishers. And as we were routed by the great mica mines in a nearby range of mountains, men were attached to our procession who carried, on litters soft with grass, closely wrapped disks and slabs of mica, beautifully polished and worked.

Some of these were three feet across, intended for mirrors to embellish some noble's home, for riding on the backs of the lesser peoples were three distinct classes of noble folk, descendants of the old Mias and fit for nothing but to oppress and persecute.

With the addition, as we pushed northward, of slaves and their attendant guards, our array reached the final total of near three hundred, a monstrous tax upon the provisions of the forts at which we rested. Finally our original party split away from the latter accretions, who were to follow as a separate band, and we went on rapidly, having nothing to carry but our own armor and gear though the slaves with us labored under heavy loads of metal from the *Prydwen*. In all this time, we had been permitted to keep our weapons and this gave us cheer and set our fears at ease.

Colder, shorter and more dreary grew the days. Occasionally a light sifting of snow whitened the ground during the night, and at last we were given stout bracae of deerhide to wear and slept in bearskins quite comfortably.

Over mountains, into and out of valleys, fording streams or ferrying them, we marched through the forest country, passing across such broad expanses of tree-covered lands that Anderida, Britain's mightiest wood, with all its goblin-haunted ruins, could have been dropped into one of these immense valley plains and totally lost. At one time we traveled up a wide stream more than a hundred miles in coracles made of bark, and in all that distance saw from the water no natural openings in the crowding trees, and no smoke or other signs of humanity, except as we neared the forts which kept this watery highway safe for Tlapallan's citizens.

We grew thin and muscular, never really hungry or satisfied, and at long last arrived at a river, immensely broad, and were supplied (at a fort, of course) with sufficient craft to take us to our journey's end, and were told that our forest marches were behind us.

Our paths had been made easy for us, and we moved through this almost trackless wilderness as a post-rider might confidently ride the highways of Rome, sure of a change of horses as needed or a place to lay his head or a relief to take and carry on his message.

We white men learned to respect the manner in which the country was managed, especially when we saw the large number of coracles that rocked in the shallow cove on the morning of our embarkation.

"Ohion," Hayonwatha named this river. "Yonder, upstream, several days journey—lies the City of the Snake and Kukulcan."

We splashed through the tinkling ice fringe and pushed out into the deep water. Vigilant scouts shot ahead, and more slowly we commenced the final step of our long journey.

At times we saw creatures drinking unalarmed: wolves, bear, large wild cattle with humped backs, shaggy hair and short sharp horns.

Again we saw giant elk, broad-antlered, or the maneless lion who preys upon these creatures, long tail switching as he snarled at us glaring his hate before bounding into the forest.

We now observed among these far stretches of timber, maple, oak, birch, beech and pine, leafage mostly seared by frost, some few yet violently scarlet, and were offered at our resting-places nuts of kinds that were strange, yet very sweet and good, with dessert to follow of the smoky-tasting wild grapes which abound everywhere.

A rich land, my Emperor, running over with riches for its owners!

At last the forests fell away, for we had left the frontiers behind us. Clearings showed along the river-banks, each with its mounds, its forts, its tilled lands, and many, many servile people who eyed our white skins with dull, stupid curiosity, until the whips cracked over their own scarred backs.

Then, with hardly a glint of rebellion in their black eyes, they took up their burdens, building more mounds or making higher those already built.

Clearings broadened into meadows and moorland, forts became enclosed towns or cities defended by citadels, all without any stonework, done in heaped earth walls crowned by palisades, yet quite impregnable against any force that existed to menace them.

One day we left this Ohion, and entered a tributary stream. Not long after, we arrived at the chief, though not the largest, city of Tlapallan. It was the impressive and bloodstained City of the Snake.

In progressing up the nobler river we had observed smoke pillars rising ahead of us, their columns broken into long and short puffs, and were told by our friends that word was going on ahead that we were coming, from village to village.

Along the lesser tributary, we noticed that the centers of population were undefended by fortified enclosures, and concluded that we had arrived at a point where danger from barbarians was improbable. Now we decided that we were wrong, for we saw a long mound wall stretching along a narrow ridge at the junction of a small river with that which we were following along-shore.

As we first caught sight of it, we were struck with its resemblance to a serpent, the image being greater than any serpent that ever crawled, for it extended fully a quarter-mile. If the far-flung loops of its un-dulations, which formed fort-like enclosures, had been straightened, it would have been much longer.

The body itself is thirty feet across, though only the

height of a tall man above the ground level. In its enclosures, all the people, in the unprotected communities up and down the little rivers, could find shelter in case of invasion. The tail was near one stream, its head near another, and upon its back were built log houses, connected by palisades, in order to form a continuous wall at all points not less than twenty feet high. At the three gates were fortified outworks, almost impregnable.

As we marched along the outside of this imposing fortress, we saw every available spot, upon roof or palisade, filled with people. They watched us, but there was no word of welcome, nor did they follow along the wall, but remained where they were until we were out of sight. This chill greeting seemed ominous.

The feeling was not lessened when, at Hayonwatha's command, the Tlapallicos took up a position to the right and left of each of us. In a column of threes we approached the gateway at the Serpent's jaws. These were widely spread, and beyond the outworks we could see another mound, oval in shape, crowned with a roof or pavilion of logs, and noticed that another pair of jaws at its opposite end opened to surround this oval completely, though the head of the other snake was bodiless—as the river, which flowed nearby, interfered with any extension of the earthworks.

Not knowing whether we were prisoners or honored guests, we fifty Romans approached the gates, wide flung and waiting. One hundred feet from the entrance, our long column halted. The company trumpeter sounded his shell trumpet, and with measured stride a procession came forward to meet us.

Company upon company of fighting-men, they met us and split to left and right, impassively taking their places. We were surrounded!

That foreboding of mine grew stronger, and I quietly passed the word down my line to be ready for trouble. I heard behind me the snick of steel in sheath, the thrum of bows being strung taut, the rattle of arrows, and felt easier.

We might be doomed, but we would die bravely, I thought.

Slaves bore a litter through the gate, and we saw reclining upon it a grossly obese man, middle-aged and cruel of countenance.

Physically he was a giant, for when standing he was nearly eight feet in height, and at one time he had been the champion of his race. The solid copper antlers upon his head made him look much taller, though creeping age and vices had blurred the originally fine lines of the face and body. As a scepter, he carried a finely worked spear, the copper head of which weighed more than a woodcutter's ax.

His robe, we were later told, was woven of human hair!

Spear butts thudded in salute. Hayonwatha murmured, "Kukulcan!" All the red men bowed low in servile salutation.

Then Hayonwatha touched Myrdhinn's arm and led him forward to the litter, where he sank to his knees and bowed his forehead to the ground. Myrdhinn proudly stepped back, and the monarch's face purpled.

Instantly, slaves leaped upon Myrdhinn, tore the robes off him and hurled him to the ground. I turned to my men, felt a tremendous blow, and, reeling, saw my comrades falling from blows from left and right, heard the armed men rushing, closing in, leaping upon us!

With that picture before my eyes, the war-cries of friend and foe ringing loud, I felt the warm blood running down my back beneath my armor and the grit of dirt in my mouth. *This is Death!* I thought. In my mind I cursed the false friend who had pretended to be my blood brother in order to trap us more completely. I knew myself trodden upon, but felt no pain from kick or blow, just a sensation of earth opened beneath me, and myself falling into the abyss.

11

The Snake—and the Egg

The next I remember, I lay in utter darkness. Beneath
me was a puddle of cold water. I tried to roll out of it
and heard groans. I was conscious enough to know that
the groans were my own, and then I must have
swooned again, for without any apparent interval of
time it was light and I could see. But it was not the
light of day, nor the good sweet air of upper earth.

Like moles we lay, I and my men. They huddled
dispiritedly by themselves while other groups of prisoners, copper-colored folk, kept also to themselves,
though casting curious glances at us. Stark naked, all
of us, shivering with cold in the dank air, winter close
at hand. I wondered as I lay there if this was the mode
of execution we were to expect.

Distant noises, and my aching eyes focused properly
upon a glare of torches, which shone through a grille
of stout oak bars laid transversely across the entrance
to this large underground chamber. Then, as these
bars were removed, an officer and two guardsmen
came in with torches, lighting up the place more clearly.

The officer passed among us with disdain. One could
see that he regarded us as a farmer might his sheep.
Without fear, he made the circuit of the walls, looking
for evidences of digging.

Satisfied that no tunnels were under construction,
he returned to the entrance, snapped orders, and slaves
entered with steaming buckets, which they emptied
into long troughs and retired.

The bars slid into place, the locking pins drove
home and we were left in our den. Sickened by the

sounds of feeding swine, where men fought and gobbled at the troughs, I rolled on my face in the water
and hoped for death.

A kindly hand stroked my head and a kind voice
said, "My poor friend!"

I rolled over again. It was Myrdhinn. Gaunt and
bony, clothed only in his beard, he still retained his
dignity.

"Rouse and eat. Gather strength and courage. This
is not our end!"

Then I first saw who stood by him: Hayonwatha,
who had led us into this trap—my blood-brother!

"Traitor! Judas!" I croaked, and tried to raise myself to strike him down, but was too weak to throw
off Myrdhinn's restraining hand.

"Eat!" he repeated. "Our friend is prisoner and
condemned to death with us. We will explain while
you regain strength. Trust him as true man, for his
future is tied with ours."

And so, trusting Myrdhinn at least, I ate thick stew
of corn and beans from the cupped hands of Hayonwatha, whom I wished to kill, and reclined on my
elbow, listening, feeling the good food bring back life,
and my aching head throb less mightily.

I learned that law among these barbarians was
rigidly followed, its transgressors punished by death,
its ironbound code unchangeable in the slightest degree. This code ordering that prisoners should be
brought in bound, naked and unarmed, had been
wantonly broken by our coming—free, clothed and
armed!

Hayonwatha, who had conceived that because we
had gained *his* friendship we should be treated as
friends, had been bitterly astonished to see the treatment meted out to Myrdhinn.

Myrdhinn had brought it upon himself by his refusal to demean himself before one whom he considered an inferior, but whom these people considered a
deity incarnate, lord of sea, sky and earth.

By giving us kind treatment, Hayonwatha had forfeited his precarious citizenship (being of the second generation), and with him all his men, because they had not risen to strip him of his office and ask for a new commander. This word had gone ahead of us by smoke pillars, and unknowing we had marched toward a planned doom, though Hayonwatha had suspected that trouble was coming when the garrison of the fort had been replaced. His orders had been to bring us in as prisoners, and for that reason his men had formed to seize us without injury, without knowing *they* were to be prisoned with us.

Here in the pit, for three days, while I had lain unconscious, my men and Hayonwatha's had been at odds, but the fight was about worked out of both factions and apathy had set in, for there was little hope for escape and a grisly end in view for all of us.

"So you see, Ventidius," said Myrdhinn, "that he really did more for us than we had any right to expect, and his own friendliness has brought him misery such as ours."

I tried a smile. It hurt. I took Hayonwatha's hand. "When I am more recovered we will see what we can do."

"We are friends, then?"

"Friends," I echoed. "Myrdhinn, order it to be so."

He stalked off, and through half-shut eyes I saw the groups intermingle. *At least,* I thought, *if there is any escape, let us fight as one people.* Then I became very sick and, I believe, delirious; not so much out of mind, however, that I could not tell that the light from very high, small openings was waning, or so much that I did not know when the food was brought again.

I heard Myrdhinn say, "Another gone." I roused from my torpor to see a Tlapallico dragged away by burly guards.

Out he went, fighting grimly, protesting while a good seven-score men stood by and watched him go without offering resistance. The bars sealed us in again, the light waned, and it became almost completely dark in our miry pit.

Then far, far away, heard dimly through the many feet of earth above us, a roar of cheering fell and rose, and fell again; and with it came night and deeper cold and things which slithered and crawled over our shrinking bodies as we slept.

Such, repeated again and again, was to be a typical day of our life for many days to come.

"Here," remarked Hayonwatha, "is the river up which we came; here, Nachan the City of the Snake; and here is the Snake herself, Ciacoatl, the Devourer, the Earth-Mother, defender of the city by means of her own earthy body, being rampart and object of worship also."

We three leaders were squatted around a dry spot. Hayonwatha drew his finger along the dirt floor as he spoke.

"Such a monster should have a suitable mate," I said.

He looked up. "She has. About fifty miles away is her mate, situated properly to close off a bend of another river, in similar manner to Ciacoatl. They lie looking at each other across the land. His name is Mixcoatl, the Storm-Serpent, god of the water and the rain. A large city, Colhuacan, City of the Twisting Mound, is protected by his body. About ten miles up this river lies Miapan, the greatest citadel in all of Tlapallan, for in it sixty thousand people, with provisions and chattels, may find shelter in case of siege, while down the river is a fortified town, Tlacopan, shielding the people of the lower valley.

"These three strong places are the main strongholds of the Mias.

"Now, to the northeast, lies a great inland sea of fresh water, where are the hunting-grounds of my mother's people. It is not many days' journey and if we could reach them, along this road where the miners travel from these four cities to the copper mines near the inland sea, I am convinced that we would be welcome.

"Through the uncounted moons these Mias have held the land of Tlapallan, they have driven back the

Onondagaono, persecuted them, raided them for slaves and loot, but my people are still free and could they control their own fierceness and unite with their neighbors they might meet and drive back any invasion."

"Who are these neighbors?" I queried.

"Once there was one people, fierce, terrible fighters, independent and brave. They lived in this country before they were driven out by the superior strength of the trained and disciplined Mias. Moving north, they became hunters and fishermen, living wild in the woods in small communities. The struggle for life was hard and, losing touch with one another, various persons came to blows over the hunting, or women, and so factions were created. As time went on, these factions became separate nations who now agree on scarcely anything and are as ready to take one another's scalps as they are to take those of their real enemy, the Mias."

"How many nations do you reckon them?" asked Myrdhinn.

Hayonwatha checked them on his fingers.

"There are five powerful nations of the woods. First, the Onondagaono, my own people, strongest and bravest of all, then the Gwengwehono, the Nundawaono, the Ganeagaono and the Onayotekaono."*

"Would they unite, think you?"

Hayonwatha chuckled grimly, his nearest approach to a laugh.

"Certainly—in death! Nothing else will unite them. Not even Tarenyawagon, the Master of Life, could do that!"

"Tarenyawagon? It is he whom you worship?"

But Hayonwatha, so loquacious on some subjects, was suddenly struck dumb, and brooding, he moved away and sat by himself, while we (understanding that we had unintentionally pried into a mystery) remained where we were and discussed the future.

* These correspond with the Indian nations we know as the Onondaga, the Cayuga, the Seneca, the Mohawk and the Oneida.

From what he had told us, we knew that should we be able to escape we would be exchanging one dreadful fate for another, unless by our own prowess we might make ourselves so feared that we would be let alone in the forests where we must lead the lives of outlaws.

Among all these Chichamecan tribes, these five nations appeared to be the most intelligent, having kept their independence during their wild life without sacrificing everything else to the hunt for food, although their code of warfare, we were told, was no better than the very wildest of the painted prisoners we had seen in the many forts we had visited on our long journey.

The Mias fought to secure slaves. All their enemies fought for captives to torture, having no need of slaves in their system of living. The practices of the forest nations seemed to us bitter and unnecessarily cruel.

Each war-party that set out tried to do the very utmost of injury to its enemy. Women and little children were butchered, and because of this fact these five nations, especially, were headed for mutual extermination.

Yet, as Hayonwatha explained the code, we could see that it was not without a rude sense. Each woman might fight or be a mother of fighters—ergo, each child might grow to be a fighter or a woman! They were killed, as warriors, for the killing of them was a powerful blow to the enemy. It helped to weaken his power and it struck, theoretically, terror to his heart.

But to us, it seemed that this element of terror was overrated, for the killing of a man's wife or child must naturally drive him ever after in search for revenge. So the Chichamecans made themselves weaker and an easier prey to the slavers of Tlapallan.

Still, could we escape, our best haven was north, beyond the frontier, among Hayonwatha's people, where more than anywhere in Alata we might reasonably hope to make friends.

We had learned that our deep prison lay under the

Egg, held between the jaws of the Snake. Could we dig out, which was impossible owing to the rigid daily inspection, we would come out among the buildings of the city or upon the level plain outside the rampart. In either event, we would be discovered, for so large a body of men could not escape the notice of the sentries.

There was a possibility that we might escape by the door had it not been continually guarded. We had rushed the log grille so many times that a whole company of guards accompanied the inspecting officer on his triple daily rounds, and most of us bore wounds from their spears.

None of my men had yet been taken above ground, but Hayonwatha's command had been reduced more than three score.

Each day, at sunrise, high noon and sunset, a man was selected and taken away. We heard the crowd roar and knew that he had been sacrificed to the Sun, but how we did not know, for the natives shuddered with horror when asked, and we did not press the argument, for the one we questioned might be the next to die.

Once I asked Myrdhinn to save us by sorcery, but he sadly refused. Below ground, he was out of touch with the powers of the air. Being stripped stark, he had no tools of magic, except a small cross which our captors had left him, as they had allowed the rest of us to keep amulets and rings as personal ornaments of no value. Even black magic, he explained, depended upon certain materials, and here was absolutely nothing with which he could work.

So it seemed that we all must die, and we had become almost resigned to it, seeing comrades among the copper people taken away each day, the end seeming so inevitable that they scarcely resisted.

Above ground the year was waning. The light that seeped down to us was gray and sometimes there was snow on the furs of the inspector.

One night Myrdhinn called me to him, just after the

food had been brought (food for my fifty and for ten of Hayonwatha's men, and now we knew we had been underground a full month and wondered for what dreadful purpose we whites were being saved until the last).

"Ventidius, can you tell me the day of the year?" I laughed. The idea was ridiculous.

"I can. I have kept account of the days during all our wanderings. Pass the word among the men to join us in solemn celebration of the birth of our Lord. Although I am a sinful person, I am the only one among you who can perform the Christ's Mass. Therefore let us fast and spend the night in solemn thought, and let each man look into his heart and make himself ready for the greater life, for I think we shall not spend another night in this prison."

So we worshiped in the dark chamber, while our fellow prisoners looked on, trying to understand, and the guard beyond the grille commented scurrilously on our behavior, and during his remarks said something which Hayonwatha caught and remembered. So when we were finished, he hurried to me and said:

"Have you been preparing for death, Atoharo?"

"If it must be, my brother."

"It must. There is no doubt. Tomorrow is the Feast of the Sun!"

"What is to take place?"

"During tonight every fire in Tlapallan will be extinguished. Tomorrow is the shortest day of the year, the day when the Sun is most apt to leave us and never return. To prevent this, the H'menes, the wise men, command a great sacrifice in order that the Sun may smell the blood and, delighting in it, may return to gladden the hearts of his worshipers.

"Tomorrow will be spent without fire on any hearth. In the morning there will be no sacrifices, nor at midday. Instead, the secret brotherhood of the Sh'tols will dance, beginning with an appeal to the Sun to remain for another year, and then appealing to Mixcoatl and Ciacoatl to influence their fellow god.

"Then they will dance the dance of battle, lasting most of the day. There will be games of skill and blood to inure the Mian youth to gore, and to inspire them to become leaders of Tlapallan.

"Shortly after, the sacrifices will begin. When the Sun touches the hills, the eldest H'mene will ignite with the Sastun, a magic crystal, a flame from which all others in the city will be relit. But we shall not see that!

"Today is our end!"

Myrdhinn said, "Never despair. We have another day."

But he would not say anything more to encourage us, and knowing that he could have no more hope than we, there was no cheer among us and we spent the night in meditation, self-communing and prayer.

In the morning, Myrdhinn, to the best of his remembrance, repeated the Mass. Our Host was coarse teocentli cake, our precious Drink was muddy water from river seepage in a low hollow in our floor, but we felt spiritually encouraged and ready for our fate.

And our companions made ready to die, singing harsh tuneless chants, and combing and braiding one another's hair as well as might be without oil or any comb but their fingers.

Thus we waited, receiving no food, seeing no inspectors, during most of the day. We heard distantly the many noises of an assembled multitude and a continual thudding of drums; for all the scattered peoples of the valley had congregated in one or another of the four cities, though more had come here than elsewhere, this being the capital city and the religious center of Tlapallan.

In every village, town, city and fort, wherever the borders of Tlapallan extended, similar ceremonies were taking place, and the "old, old red land" that night would be reddened in many ways!

12

Sacrifice—and Sorcery

We, deep in our dark pit, heard the accustomed
tramp of sandaled feet and saw the grille black against
the ruddy torchlight, like a barred entrance to Hell.
The barrier was removed and we were beckoned forth
singly. As we came out, each of us had his arms forced
back and a clamp of wood hooked around each upper
arm.

These clamps were made all of one size, so that
upon a large man, skin might be nipped in fastening,
but on a youth they were loose. Each clamp was connected to its mate by an adjustable hair rope, which
was drawn so tight as nearly to dislocate our shoulders
and make every little motion painful.

They held our Marcus not too tightly, for he was
slight as a girl, and at this I was gladdened, for we all
liked him, being youngest of us all, and in a sense our
charge.

In this situation, filled with mingled satisfaction,
pain and dread, we were hustled above, encouraged
with kick and spear-butt, to stumble finally into daylight, where, blinking and bewildered, we were greeted
with a thunderous roar of voices.

We stood upon the top of the Egg!

All around us, people were thronged—on the ground
below, packed thick along the palisades and rooftops,
and thicker yet where the favored ones were closely
pressing along the jaws and throat of the Snake. There
fell a great silence.

In the center of the cleared top of the Egg was a
pavilion without walls, so that we could look within
and see a stone altar where were gathered certain high

members of the nobility, their ruler the obese giant, Kukulcan, and the H'menes, or priests of the Sun.

From the H'menes, a horrid specter detached itself. It advanced, dancing, whirling in a flutter of feathers and strips of colored fur. Its body was painted black, with the bones of the skeleton outlined in red. It came closer still before we could be certain that it was true man and not some lich.

In his hands he shook rattles of human fingerbones strung upon cords, and about his waist he was cinctured with a belt from which hung and dangled the scalps of men, together with dried lumps of flesh that could be no less than human hearts.

He came at us—gobbling and yelping like an animal in pain.

We, held firmly by our armored guards, could do nothing; he passed by, yanking savagely at my clamps. I was forced to groan, and went down on my knees. The agony in my shoulders was intense.

He yelped and passed me by. I saw him pass from one to another, till he came to Marcus and, pulling mightily, tugged the clamps away.

He held them high and cast them down and all the people shouted.

"The gods want this one first!" he gobbled, and, seized by his guards, Marcus went forward at a stumbling run to the stinking altar, where red-robed butchers waited with their obsidian knives.

And there our Marcus was foully done to death by those red-handed sons of hell, slowly to satisfy better those evil gods of darkness!

First they tore the skin from back and shoulders, and watching under bitter compulsion by our guards we saw Marcus faint and saw him wake again, bravely trying to keep quiet while they mutilated him to the glory of their gods.

We watched—heaven forgive us!—and felt our hearts leave us and lumps of iron take their place, and we heard him at last, with all strength gone from him —heard him cry and moan and scream for mercy or death—and we watched! We watched and could do nothing!

It was after midday when they began. The sun had perceptibly lowered when they ripped out his quivering heart and held it to the sun as an offering. He had but just died, for upon his lips still lingered the smile he gave me, his only kinsman, when he caught my eye and foresaw the near sheltering wing of merciful death, racing fast to fling over him its peaceful shadow.

Myrdhinn was muttering, "Had I but my tools! Almighty Creator, why am I separated from my tools?"

The others cursed or prayed or wept, as the mood swept them.

I alone, dry-eyed, watched the sacrifice of my own nephew, and in my heart I knew that nothing could permit such a foul deed to go unavenged. I swore an oath that I would live, I would escape, and I would raise a power in this merciless land that would sweep this civilization, and all it stood for, from the face of the earth.

One might think that we could see no further indignity perpetrated on the dead, but they had not yet finished their cruel rites. With heavy stone choppers, the body was cut into tiny fragments and the lesser priests scattered the bits far and wide among the folk, who partook of these morsels as we might partake of a sacrament.

Next, Myrdhinn was hustled forward and bound to a post of the pavilion, and Nicanor, Tiburcus and Agrestis (would I could write their names in gold!) were unbound, given bows and arrows and commanded by Kukulcan to display their skill with these weapons.

Myrdhinn closed his eyes and his lips moved as though in prayer. I saw the Three confer briefly, tighten strings, fit arrows and raise their bows. Then I looked away.

Strings thrummed, there was a frightful screech and I saw that gross beast, Kukulcan, staggering with an arrow in his belly, saw him tug and quiver and fall; heard arrows whistle into the group around the altar, beheld the H'menes scatter and run, and drop; saw the chief butcher who had selected Marcus, bounding about, cackling, an arrow in his eye; heard my own voice and that of my comrades raising a good Roman cheer; and watched the Three fall, pierced through and through with fifty lances.

Thus ended the ceremonies of execution.

Myrdhinn was unbound and returned to us, and because dark clouds were gathering, as if the elements were angry at the enormities done upon that wicked altar, the surviving H'menes hurried to relight their sacred fire, before the clouds covered the face of their deity and made this impossible.

So, after all, against Hayonwatha's prediction, we did see the Sastun, a perfect crystal, used in focusing the sun's rays upon tinder, and saw the flame rise beneath the shelter of that pavilion, where attendants watched always, protecting the sacred fire.

We saw, as we were being clubbed ruthlessly back into the pits, a fortune in pearls being cast into the blaze to atone for our sacrilege, and remembered with a shock that Myrdhinn had seemed confident that we were not to die this day. Again I wondered, as often before, just how much he could foretell the future, and wondered why sometimes he appeared to know so much, and other times apparently no more than the rest of us.

Later, as we squatted, naked and cold, on the damp floor of our prison, with night come over the lands above us and the sure promise of a mighty sacrifice of us all, beginning with sunrise, Myrdhinn bemoaned again the lack of his tools, of magic, saying:

"Bereft of everything, what can I do? Had I but a leaf of oak, of ash and of thorn, I could free us all and with weapons we might make such an account of ourselves that these folk would not forget us!"

"Say you so, indeed?" eagerly cried Kulhwch, brother of that Kinial'ch who had died at sea. "I have on me, in this amulet, at this very moment, not only a leaf each of oak, ash and thorn, but also a leaf of vervain and three berries of oak mistletoe. These barbarians left me my amulet, thinking it worthless! Tell us, Myrdhinn, how can it help us?"

"First," said Myrdhinn, "we must have light."

Almost with the words his face began to shine with a glow worm's light—a most uncanny sight in that dreadful, oppressing dark.

After, he held his palms upon his cheeks, and as he stroked them, his hands likewise began glowing, while we stared in utter fascination at the head and hands shining bodiless in the black.

"Tell me," said Myrdhinn, inspecting the amulet, picking out the stitches with his thumbnail, "how do you come by this charm? If dishonestly, it will not avail!"

"Honestly, O Seer," proudly proclaimed Kulhwch. "I was told by my father that I had faery blood in my veins and when I was born in the mystical city of Emrys, elfin horns blew for three days everywhere in Tirnan-Og. 'Twas sent me by my godmother (reputedly a faery), who dwells in the Four-horned Castle at Caer Sidi. Kinial'ch had also one, but it did him little good, nor is like to do me more."

"You are mistaken there," said Myrdhinn, "for this charm, given to you to insure foresight and good judgment, gives me the ingredients we need for escape. Yet—" He hesitated. "It means a plunge into black magic. I have shunned that for fifty years. There are dangers for the soul."

"There is a sure and certain danger here for the bodies of us all, Myrdhinn!" I cried impatiently. "By all the gods, if you can get us out of here, do so. We are rats in a trap! Get us out and let us fight for our lives. Remember Marcus!"

"Aye, Marcus. I am not forgetting Marcus. There will be vengeance. But this thing—Varro, you little know what you ask!

"Yet I will do it, for I see no other way. I will do it, let come what may. Our Lord be my judge, it is a good cause. Be silent all, nor speak a single word, whatever you may see."

Under his breath, I heard him patter a mumbling prayer; heard mention of Hên Ddihenydd, the "Ancient and Unoriginated One"; heard the name of Keridwen and her hideous son Avaggdu—and then no more, the whisper was so faint.

His head fell backward as though he had fainted; he lay upon the floor, seemingly without life. The shining hands raised as though they belonged to another than Myrdhinn; they lifted the contents of the amulet, a mingled powder of crumbled leaves, and dropped a pinch upon each closed eyelid and the bearded lips.

The light faded from the hands.

I saw a shining mist, the breath of life, leave Myrdhinn's nostrils.

The light faded from the face.

The shining mist thickened and grew smaller than a man's fist. It fell to the floor.

The light faded from the mist.

I heard the sucking and clatter of little, pulpy, clawed feet running over the floor. They reached the grille and went on.

The very sound was gone.

I cannot say how long we waited, though it seemed very long. Footsteps sounded in the corridor and torchlight gleamed in upon us. A guard entered. His eyes were wild and staring. He looked straight before him and spoke no word.

He walked directly to Myrdhinn and swept the crumbled bits of leaf from his face. Myrdhinn sat up.

"It is done," he said to us; then to the guard, "lead us from this place, and to our arms."

The guard turned, still wildly staring without a motion of eyeball or eyelids, and with no reply he stalked stiffly out the door. We followed.

Halfway down the corridor, we saw a guard standing stiffly, holding a torch, and we shrank into the shadows, but Myrdhinn, laughing grimly, said:

"Come, fainthearts, and follow. No man lives below ground in this heathen temple. Quickly! Quickly!"

So we followed the walking dead man to the chamber near the entrance, where in a storeroom was piled our property and much tin.

I reached for my lorica, donned it, and heard a thud near me. The guard had fallen and his torch filled the chamber with wild light.

"Quickly!" urged Myrdhinn, thrusting it into a wall cresset. "The man is dead, and will be rottenness and corruption in a few moments. His soul has descended to Annwn, the lowest abyss of Cythraul, and his flesh cannot long abide the separation. Soon he and the other sentries here will be bare bones. I cannot repeat this, or my soul is also lost! Haste, lest we be discovered!"

Before him fell naked Hayonwatha, beating his breast, abasing himself, kissing Myrdhinn's hand, and crowding around came the other ten Chichamecs.

"Great Tarenyawagon!" moaned the stately Hayonwatha. "Sender of dreams! Master of Death! Forgive us that we did not know you!"

"Rise, friend. Let us be away."

And he helped the red man to rise, who looked at him with the eyes of a worshiper.

We got into our armor, shouldered our articles of greatest value, made packs of everything in Myrdhinn's chest, that he in future might lack for nothing, and eyed wistfully the clamps and gears for the tormenta and arrow engines, but could not carry them.

So, armed and willing to kill, we came above ground.

At the pavilion, watching the sacred fire near the unhallowed altar, sat three H'mene neophytes.

We wrinkled our noses, for the altar stank dreadfully. Then, with a horrid shock, it came to us that it was not the altar we smelled! The neophytes were dead, bloated, and burst open!

Truly, Myrdhinn had said aright that the body could not abide the separation of the soul!

We passed down the side of the Egg. Houses on

each side were blank and dark. No torches flared at the outworks, but we could see a sentinel leaning against the gateway, barring our path.

Myrdhinn led on. We followed, to find that the man was not whole. His bones were dry and rattled when he fell.

And so we left that accursed city.

Now behind us, before we were far, began a shouting, but we were already nearing the wooded land beyond the tilled fields, and as we reached them, at Myrdhinn's signal, a little flittermouse came flapping, eyed us evilly and went squeaking toward the city.

In the dusk we could see it take a direction that would bring it around the waking City of the Snake, and as we disappeared among the trees, hurrying for our very lives, we heard the wind from nowhere, coming over us in a gentle breeze, the first airy outriders of the fearful cavalry of the storm which would follow to devastate and destroy.

And this time there would be no Myrdhinn to call off those trampling cataphracts of the gathering windy legions.

13

The Stonish Giants and the Flying Heads

All that day we pushed toward the north, through the forest, beneath a gray sky from which, toward evening, a light snow came sifting down. By this time we had left the large towns well behind us, though we could see smoke rising in many places, questioning and answering, as the word was passed along to the scattered villages and the lonely outposts, in hard-won clearings.

But these very messages defeated their own purpose, for the broken, puffing pillars of smoke showed us the position of our enemies, and Hayonwatha read the signals and told us of the almost total destruction of the City of the Snake, and of how we were thought to have gone down the river toward the south, many coracles having been found to be missing.

This mistake was the saving of us, for the forts along the northern frontier were lax in their night watch, and we passed between them, so closely that we saw the dying embers of a signal fire, with no one near it, and slipped within the borders of the free Chichamecan wilderness, five and fifty fighting-men in single file, making no more noise than so many foxes. And few as we were, Myrdhinn was with us, a host in himself!

Toward morning, having marched twenty-four hours without food or sleep, with short pauses for rest, we began to feel that we should be far enough from danger so that we might stop and recuperate. But Hayonwatha led on as tireless as ever, and seeing that our aged seer did not demure, we were shamed and followed on, though all our muscles complained, having softened during our imprisonment.

Just at daybreak, we came out upon the shores of a small lake with a wooded island in it. Here, under instruction from our leader, we made rafts and piled upon them all our armor and gear.

These things we ferried over to the island, while Hayonwatha and his ten men returned into the forest and were gone a long time, wiping out our tracks. Then they made false tracks and returned on the opposite shore, blotting out their latest marks before they entered the icy waters and rejoined us, half dead from the cold.

Nor could we make any fire till after dark, and then only the merest spark among a nest of boulders where every ray of light was deadened—and this of certain

woods carefully chosen which gave no smoke that
might carry an odor to the shore. So, without supping,
we slept, and in the morning found that any traces we
might have left were now securely hidden, for snow
lay deep upon our brush shelters and continued falling all that day.

This was followed by severely cold weather in which
the lake froze over, except upon one side of the island
for a space of about twenty feet where an underwater
current rushed black and bubbling to the surface. Here
the fishing was very good. There were also hares in
the groves and fat, warmly feathered birds which could
be easily captured after they had roosted for the night.

Yet, food for all of us was not to be had in sufficient
quantity, and had it not been for the fortunate coming
of a noble stag, with all his retinue, to our retreat
(having been pursued by wolves across the ice from
the mainland), we should have been forced to seek
elsewhere for our living and this might have been our
deaths.

Twice we saw antlered Tlapallico scouts, and once a
raiding-party going southward with scalps and Chichamecan prisoners.

Before our meat was quite gone, Myrdhinn and
Hayonwatha came to a decision and we moved onward
into Chichameca, crossing the deep snows by means of
flat, oval boats fastened one upon each foot whereby
we did not sink into the drifts, these being made of
interwoven withes and thongs and very light, though
hard to learn the practice and use, and the cause of
much cursing and sore muscles.

At this period of the winter season, the northern
peoples seldom engage in any great amount of warfare,
owing to the difficulties of travel; so it seemed our best
time for making a peaceful contact.

We met a small party of Tlapallicos and shot them
down from among the trees while they lay in camp.
We lost none and released several prisoners, all women,
who fell upon their dead captors with reviling and
would have mutilated the bodies had we not interfered,

although Myrdhinn ordered the heads to be cut off and brought with us.

This was a lucky meeting, for these women were of the People of the Hills, Hayonwatha's tribe, and some remembered his mother, Thiohero; so they willingly guided us to their people and saved us two days' journey. We made friends, became temporarily a part of the tribe and wintered there in stout log houses, the village enclosed by a stout palisade though not as well as others in Tlapallan.

We gave daily instructions in the use of the bow, and these tall forest men became good archers, which improved their hunting and their chances of survival in the grim fight for life against Nature and the many enemies which surrounded and beset them continually.

As winter wore into spring, Myrdhinn became more exclusive and harder to see.

He had smoked and preserved the Tlapallican heads; now at nights he studied the stars, and daily he busied himself in a house reserved for his private use, from which came many evil smells and sometimes colored lights and heavy choking smokes.

Often he held talks with Hayonwatha and the head men of the tribe, learning their legends, superstitions and fears—planning his plans.

We became deeply attached to these People of the Hills and found them reverent of us at first, then companionable and jolly when we knew them better, though we had yet to learn of their natural ferocity in battle.

We thought, one day in early spring, that time had come. The men began painting themselves for war, the young boys and youths emulating their elders, and kings sent word from the other settlements to this Onondaga village that the nation was to make ready.

But Myrdhinn interfered with this plan, and after a long conclave to which he alone of our company was admitted, a short time elapsed and a party set out, well armed, but not painted for war, toward the nearest community of traditional enemies.

I, with ten armored Romans, was among them.

After days of travel, we approached with great caution the largest village of the Possessors of the Flint. When far enough away to be sure that our activities would not be observed, we stripped the bark from a large birch and made a speaking-trumpet longer than a man. Then, in the dusk, we came to a spot near the edge of the clearing where this village lay. We set up the trumpet on a tripod, and waited for complete darkness.

When we could no longer see into the clearing, two of the swiftest young men seized four of the preserved Tlapallican heads by their long hair and made swiftly toward the village. Here they hurled the heads, each grinning most ghastly because of its shrunken lips, over the palisade and ran back to us very quietly.

This caused a faint buzz which was rising to a hubbub when our trumpet bellowed in the night.

"Ganeagaono!" Hayonwatha's voice rumbled like an inhuman monster.

"Possessors of the Flint! I am a Stone Giant! Harken to my council! Long have I slumbered in the hills until my people should need me. I am your friend!

"The Flying Heads are gathering in the forests and the mountains to devour the once mighty nation of the Onguys. Tharon and the Sender of Dreams bade me rise and scatter them like crows from your cornfields. They are too many for me alone!

"Ganeagaono! Continue to listen. I rose among their chattering council. They fled after breaking their teeth upon my limbs of stone! They are meeting to eat you up, one little nation at a time, for there is no longer a powerful people to fight them away.

"Possessors of the Flint! Harken! Look upon the Flying Heads I struck down as they came to spy upon your weakness and to listen on your rooftops as you plan to kill your brothers! Send your runners with peace belts to the People of the Hills, at earliest dawn.

Set a date for a peace council. I go to warn the other nations. You will meet them all at Onondaga!"

The thunderous grumbling stopped. Myrdhinn gave me a long tube and held a coal of fire to its upper end. Immediately sparks cascaded from it like a fountain. I strode out into the open, and a moan of terror, like wind among bare branches, swept that crowded palisade, and a ball of red fire shot from the tube, high into the air, coloring me the hue of blood.

Strong men groaned in awe. I was dressed in full armor, and, being well over six feet, must have appeared in that uncertain light far beyond natural stature.

I stood there a moment in a shower of sparks. Then I gave them the full Roman salute, turned as the tube spat out a clot of green flame, and in that ghastly light re-entered the forest.

The fire-tube at once was extinguished.

Myrdhinn hugged me in his joy. "Fine! Fine!" he muttered. "Listen to that roar of utter terror! Now if the others are only as successful."

Hayonwatha was already snapping orders, and guided by him we made our way back to our forest town.

Other expeditions came straggling in. All had proven successful. The other four nations were in panic, and by daylight runners came in from those we had warned. A little later came emissaries from the Great Hill People, and later still came messengers from the Granite People and the People of the Mucky Lands, while the Onondagas, well schooled in their lessons, met these panting peace-bringers with well-simulated terror of a night visitation which they pretended to have experienced themselves.

Back went the runners with a date for a conclave, and less than a week later all met at a lake which all desired, but which had been a battleground ever since the breaking up of the Onguy nation.

And there they were met together, a great multitude, their smokes studding all the hills around the lake, met in mutual fear of an imaginary enemy although their one real and dangerous foe had not been enough to cause them to combine.

From concealment, we Romans in full armor marched forth, with Myrdhinn at the head in his ceremonial robes, his sea-found headdress trailing long green feathers far down his back.

Now, at this sight a murmur of dismay ran through the host confronting us. Yet we could see that though they were afraid (for at first sight we must have appeared like true sons of those rocky hills) at the clank of our armor, they quickly recovered their natural dignity and stoicism, for they are a people who take great pride in preserving their composure, even under great bodily suffering.

Already they had so commanded their features that no look, even of surprise, betokened that our coming was a thing beyond their experience. But nervous clutchings of hatched handles and knife-hafts, and gloomy stares, showed us plainly that their interest was precarious and the beautiful glen of Thendara might once more become a battlefield.

We approached the assembled Onondaga nation. Fifty paces away, We halted. Myrdhinn advanced and Hayonwatha came forward to meet him, bearing a long, feather-decorated pipe, lit and smoking.

They went through a ceremonious ritual, during which we felt that those piercing eyes focused upon us were rapidly learning that we were far more human than we had at first seemed.

We all became uneasy. At length, Myrdhinn spoke loudly:

"Men of the Onguys, order your women to put out your campfires!"

They eyed him in wonderment and he repeated:

"At once. To the last ember!"

Through the host, the striplings sped to the lake shore, to the hills. The many plumes of smoke thinned and vanished.

"As you, on earth, blot out the many scattered fires that mark each separate family of the once powerful

Onguys, I, Tarenyawagon, blot out the Great Flame. Behold!"

He gestured toward the sky and a running sound of woe swept the throng. A black shadow was impinging upon the edge of the sun!

Before their fear could turn toward thoughts of saving the sun by killing us, Myrdhinn raised his voice.

"Men of the Onguy Nation! I see before me many men. They look at one another in hatred and suspicion, yet they are brothers. They are of the same color, they speak the same language; among them are the same clans, the same societies; they like similar foods, they play similar games—they are brothers.

"My sons: should brothers kill one another while the roof above their heads is burning from the sparks of an enemy torch? Should brothers fight among themselves when their father, their mother, their little children are being led into captivity, or already suffer under the whip of their merciless captors?

"Continue to listen, my sons:

"You have an enemy at the door of every lodge— more treacherous than the tree-cat, more savage than the bear, more to be dreaded than the hungry wolf pack. One man is helpless; one clan may strike and run, but if all the brothers hold together, they may drive the enemy from their doors!"

All the sun was now darkened but a tiny edge, yet no one murmured or slipped away.

"People of the Granite, of the Great Hills, of the Mucky Lands! Look about you! Possessors of the Flint, regard! Your enemies are not the Flying Heads, nor are they men gathered here! Beside each of you stands a brother to fight for you, to guard your back in battle. He will help and protect you, if you will do the same for him. Throw down your old black thoughts and let them mingle with the blackness that shrouds us now."

For all the sun was completely blackened!

"Let one darkness blot out the other. Clasp your

neighbor by the hand and let me hear you call him brother!"

That was an anxious moment. Myrdhinn had only short moments to complete his long-considered plan and it seemed that it was bound to fail, as that assemblage stood peering at one another. Everything must be over before the light reappeared or the people would realize the event to be only a natural phenomenon of the skies.

At length an old feeble king of the Nudawaono tottered toward the equally ancient king of the Onondagaono and took his hand.

A great shout went up and the ferment of fellowship began to spread through the gathering. Hayonwatha's shell trumpet cut through the uproar and Myrdhinn spoke again.

"My children: Do not forget your present emotions. There will come to your minds grievances, old sores not yet healed by time, new differences of opinion. Pass over them or let them be settled by your councilors. You have one great enemy—Tlapallan!"

A mighty roar of fury interrupted him. Pale and anxious, counting the remaining seconds, he waited for order.

"Continue to listen, my sons: Revere the aged, abandon them no longer to the beasts of the forest. Consider them to be your charges, even as your infants. Are you not better than the Mias, who regard an aged person as merely a body to be mutilated for the glory of a bloody god?

"Be kind among yourselves, merciless to your one enemy. So shall you find peace and become great. Thus you shall form a league in which you will know power, and in so doing you unite in planting a four-rooted tree which branches severally to the north, south, east and west. Beneath its shade you must sit in friendship, if it is not to be felled by your foes.

"Beneath it also you must erect a mystical Long House in this glen, in which you all may dwell, and over it will stand the mighty tree of the League as your symbol and your sentinel forever!

"I give you new fire for your hearthstone."

He rapped the coal from the ceremonial pipe upon the ground. It sizzled, a running serpent of fire darted along the ground, a cloud of white smoke rose, there came a noise like a thunderclap, and a few feet away from the center of the cleared space in which seer and trumpeter stood, a bright red blaze sprang up out of the ground.

And at that exact instant the bright edge of the sun reappeared!

"Light torches, return to your weik-waums and know this spot henceforth as the Place of the Council Fire. Be Onguys no more, but call yourselves Hodeno-saunee, People of the Long House.

"I have spoken!"

He returned to our company, and in perfect unison we retired to quarters previously arranged for us by the friendly Onondagas, while as we went we saw the throng pressing forward to secure the magic fire, clutching brands, strips of clothing, or reeds.

Now, you must not think this speech changed in a day all the harsh feelings of many years.

It was, however, the beginning of a long council and there was wrangling and bitter words, but before these bickerings could develop into real trouble Myrdhinn would thrust himself into the talk and suddenly argumentation was over before the participants rightly knew how difficulties had so suddenly become simple.

The council lasted four days. Myrdhinn was formally adopted into the Nation of the Flint and given important office in its councils, Hayonwatha also was given the rank of Royaneh, or councilor, and had I wished, I could have also been honored.

But I wanted none of this barbaric adulation, and indeed, Myrdhinn received it unwillingly, fearing it would hinder his own plans for the spring traveling. For he was very anxious to be away toward the south-west, in search of the Land of the Dead.

Eventually the council broke up, with the result desired by all. Five nations, each feeble by itself against the overwhelming might of Tlapallan, had now combined into a great forest power.

The lusty young giant stretched its muscles and desired war to test its strength, but its brains (fifty Royanehs elected by the people) bade it wait and bide its time and grow stronger.

So, during the spring, the People of the Long House learned the use of the bow and became proficient and dangerous. And in the last days of that season we determined upon a raid upon the Miner's Road and possibly an attack on the frontier of Tlapallan.

14

The Mantle of Arthur

Now, this so-called Miner's Road was not really a road at all, being (from the habit of these people in walking single file through the thick forests) at no place along it more than a foot in width and narrowing very often to become no wider than a few inches. Its depth also varied, depending on whether or not it passed over rocky ground or soft soil. Yet its whole length was well marked, well patrolled, and studded with forts; for this hard-beaten path connected the four central cities, before mentioned, with the rich copper mines near the Inland Sea, and along it, during the summer months, passed a stream of heavily laden slaves.

To us, this seemed like a long arm of hated Tlapallan thrust deep into the treasure chests of Chichameca, and we resolved to break that arm, and if possible to stop this systematic looting.

So a war party marched: myself, Hayonwatha, twenty Romans, eighty Hodenosaunee, all conscious that upon us rested the duty of proving to Tlapallan that a power has risen in the north. Myrdhinn, with the rest of the Romans and two hundred of the People of the Long House, marched to seize the mines, while other detachments headed, in strength commensurate with the size of the fort they were to attack, for each of the holdings along the Miner's Road.

My party had orders to intercept and cut off, below the last fortification, any party which might slip through the line of communication with news for Tlapallan. We were to kill or take prisoner any small party of troops coming to the aid of the forts, should Tlapallan be warned. We hoped that by night attacks, all forts might be taken before smoke signals could spread the news, for our strength was great, the woods full of our warriors.

As a mark of favor, before I left Myrdhinn called me aside and pressed a small package upon me. I opened it and thought he was joking, for the little box inside was empty.

He laughed. "Feel within."

I did so and was surprised to feel the fine texture of fabric, in which as my fingers quested they seemed to become lost and my eyes blurred as I looked at my hand. Nor could I see the bottom of the box, which puzzled me, it also being blurred and wavering.

"That," said Myrdhinn, "is a priceless relic—the Mantle of Arthur."

Then I understood. We all had heard of the robe which rendered anything beneath it invisible, but I had not thought until then that it might be in our possession.

"Myrdhinn! You have brought—?"

He nodded. "Aye. The thirteen precious things were in my great chest. Would you have had me leave them for the Saxons?"

I smiled. "I suppose this is not magic?"

"What is magic?" he said impatiently. "Only something which the uninitiate does not understand. There is nothing evil about it. You need have no fears. You will not be blasted. 'Tis but a simple linen robe covered with black paint."

"Black paint? Nay, seer, you jest. There is nothing black about it. It is without color."

"Precisely. Without color, because it has robbed the light which falls upon it of all color, and in doing so the various colors contained within light have canceled one another out, leaving nothing. Thus, it follows that one can no more see the robe or what it covers than one can see light itself as it passes through the air; for light and the colors which compose light are absent, being fully absorbed by this absolutely perfect black."

I could not have shown much comprehension, for he muttered:

"Why waste words? You are a man of war. I am a man of thought. We have nothing in common. Be off therefore to your killing."

So with that for farewell, I took the soft cloth which I could not see or understand, stuffed it under my lorica and marched away.

Now, for three days we lay in the hills overlooking the Miner's Road, at our appointed place, and nothing larger than tree-mice did we see, and our duty began to pall upon us all and grow very irksome. On the fourth morning, it seemed to me that further inaction could not be borne, for beyond the hills southward we could see the smoke arising from the City of the Snake and we yearned to strike some blow that would hurt and harm.

I lay thinking. What could a company so few as we do against such a multitude? Too, we must not disobey the orders of Myrdhinn and the Royanehs. The Miner's Road must not be left unwatched.

Then I remembered the Mantle, where it nestled

warm beneath my lorica, and suddenly a plan, grand and dazzling, came to me.

If we were to attack Tlapallan we needed strange and powerful arms, which would terrify our enemy with their might. In the pits beneath the Egg lay the things we needed to create those arms—the clamps of the arrow engines and the tormenta! The bronze clamps we could not make, owing to the death of our smith and the lack of tin. (For even yet, we have found no tin in this land.)

But I, under the Mantle of Arthur, could enter the gates and steal those clamps out of the pits, unseen and safely too!

So, with five Hodenosaunee, I left the ten Romans in charge, and we six went over the southern hills. At the edge of the forest nearest the city my followers hid themselves while I donned the Mantle. The sight of their erstwhile stern and impassive faces as they saw me fade from sight was worth remembering. I thought they would turn and flee when they heard me speak from empty air, but though they wavered as they would not before enemy acts or lance, they held firm and I left them there to think on the godlike mysteries of white men and their ways.

After nearly an hour's brisk walk, I passed by the outworks and entered through the open gates, though I was obliged to wait a little time, for there was a coming and going of many people, as the fields were being put in order for the planting season.

Secure in my invisibility, I strolled among the buildings, many of which were newly built, showing the damage done on the night of our escape. I spied out the strength of the city, and while I was amusing myself by calculating the thousands of people which it contained and mentally marking the weakest spots in the palisade which spined the back of the Woman-Snake, an accident imperiled the success of my adventure and nearly cost me my life.

Around the corner of a building ran a little naked reddish boy, his face all one large grin at some prank he had just played on some pursuing comrades. Head down, he hurled himself into my middle, all unseen as I was to him, and we both went rolling.

My robe flew up above my knees, my hood came off my head and had he not been well-nigh stunned by the impact, I must needs have killed the child or have all my trouble go for nothing.

I had barely time to scramble to my feet, adjust my robe and hood, and stand out of the way when a shouting pack of boys came and fell upon their fellow and bore him away, dizzy and sick.

After this I had no more inclination to roam aimlessly, but made for the Egg, found the entrance to the pits unguarded and soon came out again with three of the heavy clamps beneath my robe, which were as much as I could handily carry.

When I arrived among my followers, I was hungry and ate a cup full of teocentli meal stirred into cold water, which is all we carry for rations when on a journey, it being light and very nourishing, and it would be a valuable addition to the army commissariat.

Then I returned and made two more trips with clamps and on the third trip brought the last of them and some tin from the *Prydwen*'s sheathing.

It was now darkening and I knew I could not make another journey before nightfall, but wished to bring more tin while my luck still was good. The tin was worth more than gold to us, if we could discover in what proportions and in what manner we were to use it with the great supplies of copper which Myrdhinn and his men must have taken in their assault on the mines. So I tempted Fortune, and found I could not depend upon her fickle smile, as you shall see.

Returning, I had entered the crypt in almost absolute darkness and was feeling about for the pile of sheet tin which I knew was there, when suddenly I felt myself seized by unseen hands. I surged away, heard a ripping and suddenly I was free, but with the Mantle of Arthur stripped from me, without even a knife to protect myself against the armed men who crowded the place.

Luckily I was near the entrance. I dashed out, knocked over two men with torches who were hurrying to shut the corridor gate, and was loose in the city, with the people aroused and hunting me, every gate watched and with nothing open to me for a hiding-place.

At first I made for the river. Its high bank was lined with torch-bearers, so thickly gathered that an ant could not have slipped through. I headed back to climb the palisade.

Sneaking in the shadows, I came to a large unlighted house of logs, toward the center of the city. Behind me were a number of people, though not intentionally, for I knew I had not been seen. Another group was coming toward me, a short distance away.

What was I to do? Another moment and I should be within one of the two circles of light, or be seen by either group against the flares of the other as I tried to escape from between them.

I could not burrow into the ground or fly into the air. Then, as I looked up, an owl quitted the roof with a screech, dazzled by the many torches, and sailed into the forest. The owl has been a bird of evil omen to many, but I will forever bless that one!

The hint it had given me was enough. In an instant I had climbed up the chinks in the log wall, with toe-tips and fingertips, and was comfortably ensconced upon the roof by the time the two groups met, conferred and went upon their separate ways.

For the moment I was safe, but my situation was most precarious. At best I could remain there only until daylight, and there were no indications that this relentless search would die down by then.

I was thinking what would be best to do, when a man came out of the house beneath me and walked unsurely toward a bench, groping about beneath it, till he came upon a jug of water, from which he drank avidly as though parched with thirst.

Again he groped, his hands before him, back toward the entrance. This was strange in itself, for there was light enough from the stars and distant torches for me to see his face, so that he should be well able to see where he was going. Then I saw with surprise that he was walking with his eyes closed. The man was blind!

Perhaps, anywhere in the rest of the world, this would not have been peculiar. Even in Chichameca, there were people who were blind, deaf or dumb. But here in Tlapallan he was a freak, for Tlapallan had no use for, or mercy upon, anyone who was handicapped by any affliction. Even among the ruling class of the Mias, an individual with an incurable disease was marked for death upon the altar of the Egg, whose priests had never enough sacrifices stored below in the pits to satisfy Ciacoatl, called the Devourer.

You can imagine what chance this blind man, a Tlapallico of the third generation removed from his original slave parents as his garments proclaimed him, would have had if his blindness had been known to the priests, whose pits were completely empty just now.

"Anywhere that is safe for you is safe for me, my friend!" I muttered to myself, as I swung off the roof edge and dropped beside him. He whirled with a little cry. I clapped my hand over his mouth and shoved him inside out of the light.

"Old man," I said, fiercely, "your people are hunting me. If they find me here they will take you too and we shall both be skinned alive on the altar. Do you understand my words?"

He nodded with vigor.

"Then hide me wherever you are yourself hiding. Quickly!"

He led me to an opening in the floor and went down a short ladder. I followed, snatching a stone hatchet from the wall. My life was in his hands, but he was equally at my mercy and I was younger and stronger than he. As I reached the dirt floor, he ran up the ladder like a youth, and I was about to hurl the hatchet when he pulled a trap-door into place and by pulling a cord drew a bearskin across the floor above.

And then we sat in the dark together and became acquainted.

He had not always been blind. In his youth he had been a trader, until captured by Chichamecans and tortured by being forced to run between two long rows of barbarians armed with switches of thorn.

He had escaped, leaped into a river and floated to safety with his head hidden in a clump of floating weed, though grievously hurt. From a stroke of thorn-bush across the eyes or poison in the river water, his sight later had begun to fail, and he had stayed within the city with his family, his wife and their one son, likewise married.

His family had dug this refuge beneath their dwelling and here for five years he had lived, quite blind, in constant dread of discovery, going outside only upon the darkest of nights to taste the fresh air, when no one he met could go about easier than himself.

Tonight, being left alone, the women helping in the search for me, his thirst had tormented him into going after water.

As we talked, I learned that he had little love for Tlapallan and had enjoyed the free life of a forest trader; so I made him the proposition that he should help me to escape and I in turn would secure him a safe home among the Hodenosaunee, whose population was growing through their practice of raiding lesser tribes, taking captives and adopting them into their own nation with full rights of citizenship.

It appealed to him, and later it appealed to the women of his family, and two days later, his son, returning from a forest expedition, bringing furs, elk-teeth and shell beads, likewise favored the plan. He had heard talk of a growing power in the north and was clever enough to see that an ambitious man might help himself mightily if allied to a nation whose sun was rising.

The following morning was set for another trading-expedition, and with it this whole family planned to go, the blind man and I to be robed as women who were passing through the gates to walk a little way with their men before bidding them farewell.

This was the seventh day since the raid on the Miner's Road had begun. No copper had come into the city and there was much talk and alarm because of this. Therefore a punitive expedition was being planned, and hearing of this I was filled with fear lest trading-parties should be forbidden the forest. I changed the plans to that night, and about the third hour after sunset, the young trader gathered his slaves (who were totally ignorant of our identity), and the blind man, his wife, myself and the son's wife, all four of us closely muffled, approached the small gate at the Snake's tail.

We might have known that there was little hope of success, when both the city within and the forests without crept with suspicion, when a spy had been known to enter the city, steal valuables and escape safely, when no copper or messenger from any of twenty forts along the Miner's Road had been seen or heard from for a week.

We should have realized that a muffled person would be obviously marked for inspection, but we did not, until as we were passing out through a triple guard the blanket was twitched from the head of the young wife at the same time as my own. My height, I suppose, gave us away, but the cry of the guard told us all was lost.

He swung at my head. I dodged, and my own hatchet split his skull.

Then we were all running, we five, through the stupid slaves who were screaming beneath the knives and clubs of the guards, without the least knowledge of why they were being killed.

We would certainly have been cut down had it not been for the heroism of the old blind man, who, after we had passed unscratched through the gate, stopped and turned back, standing deliberately in the way before five guards who were pursuing us with leveled spears and coming with great bounds. His body barred the gate, and he fell there, dragging with him those fearfully barbed spears which could not be withdrawn, but must be cut away.

And in that moment of horror the whole sky burst into livid green and bloody scarlet! The women shrieked and dragged at the hands of the young trader and mine. We looked back. Above our heads drove a whistling arrow flight into the fighting mass at the gateway. All the world seemed alternately fire and night. We staggered like pallid corpses in the bloody rain of Judgment Day, and then ran on, they obeying my sharp commands, straight on into the darkness from whence the fire-tubes hissed and spat. Myrdhinn had come!

Some two hundred yards from the gateway we met a host of archers, kneeling and firing, by order, flights of arrows which soared over the palisade into the city, barring any egress from the gate. Myrdhinn strode forward from among them and took my hand.

"I have lost the priceless Mantle," I said ruefully. "I am ashamed. I have acted like a child."

Myrdhinn clapped me on the back. He seemed in the best of spirits.

"Think no more of it," he said jovially. "You have given me something far more valuable. I was the child that I did not insist that we should bring the clamps and the tin on the night of our escape. I should have foreseen their value, but that night they seemed no more than so much metal, and a hindrance to our progress.

"My friend, we have them now to design others by! We have the tin for bronze-making, we have the mines in which we can obtain the copper, and in seven days of fighting, Chichameca has taken twenty strong forts of Tlapallan and the Tlapallicos within are either good reliable Hodenosaunee or are dead meat.

"If necessary, we will go to the coast, make a ship, sail to the wreck of the *Prydwen* and get enough tin to outfit with bronze clamps enough tormenta to build a fence around Tlapallan.

"These folk are fighting-men. We can do anything now. Anything!"

He beamed upon his archers, like a hoary patriarch among his many sons.

"Very well, for the future," I said. "But let us look to the present. Shortly the Mias will be sallying out at another gate. They will cut off our retreat."

"Not so. Hayonwatha holds the gate at the Egg. The outworks are his. The other gate is held by ten companies."

"But we are not strong enough to take the city! They number thousands. The outlying villages will be surrounding us with men, if we do not make haste. We are deep within Tlapallan. For a real conquest, the small villages must first be taken and destroyed, their people driven into the main cities or cut up and absorbed into our armies. They are filled with slaves, who fight now for the Mias, but who would gladly fight for us if they had a chance of winning. We have here one city. If we take it too soon, we lose everything. The other three cities of Colhuacan, Miapan and Tlacopan will march upon us and swamp us with men! Where are our engines? Where can we find reinforcements?

"Chichameca is not united, but divided into hundreds of tribes who hate the Hodenosaunee as much as they hate Tlapallan. They must be with us also.

"Remember the extent of this Empire, the greatness of their holdings, their thousands of temples, their many forts, the myriads of men who march at the command of the Mias! Be satisfied, Myrdhinn, with what you have accomplished.

"We are little people. Let us become great before we seek our just vengeance!"

"You are a man of war, Ventidius. Your thoughts are wise. Trumpeter, call in the men!"

Harsh and loud the shell trumpet brayed across the frantic city. Far beneath the other darting fire-balls which marked the attacking-points, other trumpets answered. The din lessened, the fire-balls ceased their dropping, though burning huts still reddened the sky, and Chichameca started home like a glutted bear, leaving Tlapallan to lick her wounds and mourn her lost copper mines.

Only once on the long trip back did Myrdhinn and I hold any conversation. During it, I said curiously:

"Of course, I realize that the five men of my company, who were guarding the clamps, sent word back to their post, and I understand that their messenger met your men that were sweeping down from the upper forts, so that, uniting, all the companies came down on the city. But how did you know I meant to escape tonight, and how did you know at which gate I would be and at what time?"

Myrdhinn chuckled. "I knew."

"But how? How?"

A soft swishing passed overhead. I looked up and saw great yellow eyes peering down upon me.

"Maybe the owl told me. Owls have a reputation for omniscience, haven't they?"

And that was all I was ever able to learn. Myrdhinn always loved a mystery.

15

We Seek the Land of the Dead

So we let time work for us, and constantly messengers ran the woods, carrying beaded belts cabalistically embellished, each bead and little figure with its own important meaning, the only real language these many various tribes of Chichameca have in common.

One by one, the tribes agreed to pacts binding them

to strike when we struck, to wait until we were ready, and the League that should one day strike Tlapallan to the heart grew stronger and more dangerous.

The summer came and went, and Myrdhinn, I knew, was fretting to be off on his will-o'-the-wisp hunt for the Land of the Dead.

Days grew colder; a tang came into the air. Everything was peaceful and happy. Nothing happened to disturb us. There had been no effort to capture any of the lost forts we held, nor had any expeditions been sent out to obtain copper or to punish Chichameca.

Then, one day, Myrdhinn's youthful heart got the better of him and he rebelled openly against the monotony of life.

He *was* going in search of the Land of the Dead! He *would* solve the eternal mystery of Death! He would call for volunteers among the men. Those who had not taken native wives would surely come. As for him, he was going *now!* And he did.

Out of thirty-seven Romans (thirteen had been killed during the various assaults upon the mines, the forts, and the City of the Snake), twenty-one marched with Myrdhinn in search for new adventure. The number would have been even had I not made it odd. The rest had married among the Hodenosaunee, and were valuable where they were, to further the work of the League.

You can follow our route on the map, and you must not think that because I dwell not on the journey itself, that it was a little thing. We covered enormous distances that winter. We even went beyond the grasp of winter itself and found green grass and flowers when the season called for snow, but that is in advance of the tale. First, to march southwest, we were forced to take coracles and paddle north! We crossed a broad arm of the Inland Sea.

We climbed mountains, we forded rivers, we hunted and fished. We left mountains far behind us and came to broad moorlands, veritable countries in themselves, peopled only by tremendous herds of wild, humpbacked cattle, which might take a day or more to pass a single point. The sound of their trampling hooves makes the air quiver and the ground tremble. Before them is grass, growing often taller than a man; behind them nothing but hard-beaten earth is left. Everything green and soft has been stamped into the ground!

Their flesh is good.

These vast moorlands, greater in extent than Britain, we christened the Sea of Grass and journeyed on, led by Myrdhinn's little iron fish, floated occasionally in a cup of water.

Now and then we met people, dirtier, less courageous, more dispirited than our sturdy allies we had left. Small wonder, for these lands were the original highway of the Mias when they came north from the Hot Lands, and during their long wanderings the Mias had nearly depopulated the whole grass country. Only scattered individuals had been overlooked who had since coalesced into families and groups, and were trying the hard business of becoming tribes and nations again. The ambition seemed hopeless, for they told us the moorlands were often raided.

But to the southwest (Myrdhinn started) was a nation which had never been defeated, they told us. Attacked in their lake country of Aztlan, beyond us to the north, by a vastly superior force of Mias, they had refused to become Tlapallicos, had beaten off their attackers and quitted their beloved country to go south.

What had become of them? No one knew, but raiding parties of Tlapallan had gone after them and had returned fewer in numbers and seeming discouraged. Some parties had never returned.

Could we go westward? Certainly not! There lay mountains, high, unclimbable, where no man might go and breathe. Beyond them the sun went to sleep each night, there he would one day go to die.

And there, if there is a Land of the Dead, it must surely lie, for we have searched everywhere else that we can and have not found it.

We went within sight of the mountain foothills and

turned south, thinking that we might come to an end of the immense range and go around it. Possibly there is such a route, where one may stand upon Earth's Brink and look over the edge, but we were turned aside.

We came to a land of sand, heat, no rain, few springs, filled with thorny, leafless trees, bulbous and strange. We saw reptiles, by one of which a comrade was bitten and died in great pain. We fought out of it, almost dead for want of water, decided we could not cross it and turned eastward to go around it, afterward returning south.

Then we arrived in a forbidding land of rocks and great gullies, eaten deeper than one can see into the bowels of the earth by rivers which flow so far below the observer that although he can see the glint of sunlight upon a wave if the time of day be right, he can hear nothing of the tumult which rages below.

A strange land, this land of Alata. In it are many marvels.

Yet even here in the scrap heap of all the world, the black threat of Tlapallan lay like a curse over the doughty folk who had the hardihood to carve out homes in the very rocks.

For some time we had been following signs that told us of a large company of men ahead, and had thrown out scouts to protect us from a surprise.

Now, one in advance hurried back with the word that far ahead he had heard sounds of strife; so with bows strung and ready we pushed cautiously on, following along the bottom of a deep, dry gully.

Before we expected to discover anything, we heard war-cries and around a bend in the gorge saw a fierce conflict at some distance.

We beheld, carefully concealed as we were, an encampment of Tlapallicos at the dead end of the way, and high above was an odd fortress-home—a great house set in a deep recess of the almost perpendicular cliff. Smoke was curling from its jagged rooftop from many kitchens within its more than two hundred rooms.

Its terraced parapets were dark with people, shouting
and brandishing spears.

Above them, an outthrust of the upper tableland
overhung like a broad lip of stone, shielding them from
any boulders, though the Tlapallicos had made this
protection a menace, for now it held back vast volumes
of choking smoke, from fires of green wood and wet
leaves below, which the wind blew directly into the
hollow.

Through this choking cloud, massive stones were
plunging down from battlements and towers and the
Tlapallicos climbing the cliff were having trouble. The
besieged had drawn up the ladders connecting sections
of the path, leaving scarcely a handhold between.

Indeed, some of these intervening segments had been
previously polished to a glossy smoothness by those
who constantly stayed at home—the cripples, oldsters,
children and women.

Furthermore, the warriors stoutly contested the way,
hurling spears and doubleheaded darts, while their
women poured down boiling water, sand, ashes and
hot embers to torment their enemy.

Yet, far to one side, untouched and hidden by smoke
from those above, a line of Tlapallicos was creeping
up from cranny to cranny, connecting various shelves
and footholds with ladders, the whole string of them
glittering, with their accouterments of mica and
burnished copper, until it seemed that the symbolical
Snake of Tlapallan had come alive and was slithering
up the cliff wall to engorge those hapless dwellers. And
we could see that if matters continued as they were,
fight as sturdily as they might, the end could be only
slavery and death for the cliff folk.

Secure for the moment in our concealment, we held
conclave and decided to interrupt, for as Myrdhinn
stated, "We could not live by ourselves forever, but
must find friends or make them, in this inhospitable
land, and whom better could we trust than implacable
enemies of our own foes?"

Then, we all agreeing, I cried, "Let us prove, first, that we are friendly!"

And we stood up among the encircling boulders, in which we had lain like chicks in a nest, and our long bows twanged.

As though this had been a signal, the wind changed and drove the smoke swirling down upon the attackers, and above, on the highest ladder, we could see the antlered men toppling, falling, impaled by arrows, striking the ladders below, sweeping their comrades to death.

A great cry of amazement burst from the defenders and they saw our armor glitter, and beheld for the first time the swift execution of arrow play. But we had no time for them. Without hesitation the Tlapallicos in the encampment wheeled about and rushed upon us.

We gave them three flights into the thick of the ranks, but with no dismay they leapt the bodies of their dead and came on. Further shooting was impossible. We threw our heavy lances, and hurling their hatchets in return, they drew long knives and we closed.

Luckily for us that we were armored men! Fortunate we, to have learned our work in a stern school.

Back to back, we twenty met seven score, even Myrdhinn laying about him manfully. Their only shields were the soft copper breastplates and the many copper bracelets upon their arms from shoulder to wrist, fit protection perhaps against atlatl dart and stone knife, but our good edges cut through them like cheese.

An officer hurled himself upon me. I slashed through his bead insignia, when my shortsword struck between neck and shoulder. He fell. Others came, and others. My fingers were slippery with blood. I struck till my arm wearied. I could not see how my comrades fared.

Faces came at me, howling. They went down. More faces, furiously contorted, behind them, came forward. The sword twisted in my hand. I could not tell if I was striking with the flat of it, or the edge.

My muscles were cramped with killing, and still they

came. It seemed that all Tlapallan was hurling itself upon us.

Suddenly the faces were gone. I blinked. My helmet was gone, my forehead was wet, my head one great ache. I wiped the moisture out of my eyes. It was red. Half my right ear was shorn away.

Then there were howling faces before me again. I raised my sword, like as a twin to those that carved out the Roman Empire, and would if the gods willed carve out another here. It flew from my wet fingers. I heard a legionary cry, "Friends, Varro, friends!"

My vision cleared. I saw the Tlapallicos running like deer, saw them leap, and bound, and fall, saw cliff dwellers meet them with ax and club, and hurry on. And I beheld the fighting women of the rocks finishing those that still moved, dying, but too proud to moan for mercy, glaring without fear into the eyes of those who wielded the knife; and I said in my heart, *Britain could be retaken with bravery like that.*

And Myrdhinn went forward in his white robes, all dotted with red crosses, and made friends for us with the Elders of Aztlan.

And they named him in their language Quetzalcoatl, the Feathered Serpent, because of his beautiful feathered headdress, and also for his guile, giving him credit for causing the wind to change which was choking them with smoke; and we entered into their airy castle with all the pomp and adulation which deities might receive.

Now we had another language to learn, this time without much difficulty, for they were eager to teach that they might learn what manner of people we were. Although the words were dissimilar, the sentence structure of the Mias was much the same as their own, which was a help to us. Also, during the various impacts of Tlapallan's culture upon them, they had learned a few words that we also knew.

Besides, their women, who in their society had equal rights with the men, took us over and made us comfortable in their homes, treating us like kings, and we learned more than a few words from them.

The first I learned of the Azteca speech was the name of the very lovely and lovable little lady who eased my pain and brought me food as I recovered quickly from my head wounds in that dry, clean air.

Gold Flower of Day, her parents had christened her, or as we might say Aurora, not half so musically right for this delightful girl.

In a short time I was up and about, and by then among us all we had learned considerable, which we had shared as we'd learned it.

We were in the city of Aztlan. Less than five miles away was another city, Azatlan. But between them was a hideous country, all up and down over naked rock and deep gullies, so that one city was very little help to the other in case of trouble.

"We must change all that," I said one night to my companions.

"Why?" asked Myrdhinn. "We are not planning to stop here long, are we? Shall we not push on to the land of our search?"

I turned to the rest.

"What shall we do, comrades? Waste our lives in a fruitless hunt for a mythical land, or make a nation here?"

"Remain!" they chorused.

"Myrdhinn," I said, "with magic and guile you made a nation in the north. The destruction of Tlapallan is my one aim in life. Let the Gods listen! I solemnly vow never to rest until I have built a nation in this southern wilderness, that working in unison with your own nation will crack Tlapallan like a nut between hammer and stone. And here is all the magic I shall use!"

I leapt to my feet, swept out my sword and kissed the blade.

"I swear it on the cross of the sword. Who takes that vow?"

"I!" "I!" "And I!" They all gathered around.

Myrdhinn smiled—half humorously, half ruefully.

"And I, I presume, must bow to the will of the majority? After all, I suppose it is the better way."

So the search for the Land of the Dead ended with our advent among the cliff dwellers, though, as Myrdhinn learned, they too had legends concerning a mystical country, Mictlampa, "where the sun sleeps," from whence (a land of seven dark caves) they believe they originally came "up from below" to air and sunlight and happier life, but to which, after death, the souls of good and bad alike must return.

Almost every tribe and clan, at least in this section of Alata, has its own distinct legend, but all agree in the important belief that they came "up from below." And we too have come to believe that somewhere, possibly in this vicinity, lies an entrance to some inner world far beneath our feet. Perhaps the ancients were right in locating Hades at the core of earth.

But we have not hunted, nor have we any intentions of doing so.

Instead, we built a new Rome, in little, among the rocks, building it in spirit and ambition instead of marble and gold. All that can come later—was not the real Rome once a huddle of huts?

After my illness, first looking about me, this is what I saw:

A collection of some thousands of barbarians with only the beginnings of a culture and practically no religion. They revered the spirits of slain animals and saw in themselves a kinship to the beasts! Also, their implements of agriculture were crude and few, and their very weapons almost worthless in comparison with ours.

Tlapallan had stunted their growth, stultified their culture, hindered their natural abilities and kept them high in the rocks lest they should utterly perish—but like an eaglet in its eyrie, whose flashing eye proclaims its proud heritage, the bold, free manner of these Azteca spoke of dauntless courage that laughed at fate and any that might attempt oppression.

Tlapallan's hatred for free communities had bred in this small people a determination to fight until death for their freedom. They needed only the right leaders—and we had come!

Looking on them in my illness, I dreamed and planned, and when I had mastered their tongue and had obtained the consent of the Elders I began to go among the young men of both the cities, selecting, marshaling, drilling—training them with the bow and shortsword.

Before us, in Alata, the sword had been an unheard-of thing, its place being taken by long knives, short javelins or the massive club; though the throwing-hatchet was no weapon to be despised.

But now came a new and ghastly weapon, a sword in name, but what a sword! Of wood it was, short, heavy, saw-edged on both sides with sharp jagged fragments of volcanic glass, a merciless weapon. I chuckled to myself when I considered the feelings of a foe which for the first time saw a sword-using people, fired with ambition and the lust for empire, rushing to close in upon the field of battle.

To each of my companions I gave the command of a company and one proud day saw march in review before the gathered Azteca wives, families and Elders, ten centuries of martial youth, fully equipped.

The next day wives and sweethearts, dry-eyed and brave, bade farewell to their men as they marched out into the wastelands upon the long road to conquest, assimilation of the conquered and eventual empire.

The eaglet chick had broken from its shell!

Simultaneously with the people in general, from priests ordained by myself (who know nothing of priestcraft), was being preached a new religion, worthy of a fighting people, the children of Destiny.

I gave them Ceres, Lucina, Vulcan, Flora, Venus, Mars—all the gods of old fighting Rome that I could remember, and said no more about Rome's later decadent faith than I could help.

Myrdhinn preached them love, charity, altar offerings

of fruits and flowers—all the weak things that made
Rome lose Britain.

He introduced the Mass, to the best of his ability,
using a paste of meal and milk as his best substitute
for the Host, but for such folk as these were becoming
such thoughts seemed too mild, and at the offerings of
jubilation upon our safe return with captives, converts
and booty, I saw blood mixed with the meal instead of
milk, though Myrdhinn looked elsewhere and pretended
not to see.

The folk took my remembrances of early faiths as
new and divine revelation. They found their own names
for the deities I had given them, and soon each had his
or her own following, tended by priests who apparently
rose from the ground, so soon they came into being.

Since my little legion had learned the new technique
of making war, the world seemed too small for it and
any enemies, no matter how far away these enemies
might be. They had won a battle on unfamiliar ground
and they thought themselves invincible. Constantly they
begged me to lead them against new foes, and I confess
I was very willing. Fighting was my profession, my
very life.

We marched again. Again we returned in triumph
from foray after foray, incorporating into our growing
empire communities which had dwelt apart for hundreds of years scarcely knowing one another's names.
As old enmities died, the little communities lost those
names and became brotherly under compulsion under
Aztec banners and governors.

The priests were busy from sunrise till late at night,
proselyting, converting, ordaining missionaries for far
villages, describing their new deities from colorful,
fantastic and fertile imaginations. My poor powers of
picturing heavenly attributes were far outstripped.

I shall not forget the surprise I had when, returning
from a long campaign in the Land of Burned-Out Fires
(a hideous, twisted country of ancient volcanic lands,
cursed with eroded lava and almost devoid of comfort),

I was met at the edge of our territory by a deputation of priests, bearing an effigy, easy to recognize.

It was myself life-size, clothed in mimic harness, with lorica, shortsword and helmet all complete in featherwork, cleverly and beautifully done. I chuckled to myself when I was alone, to see how worship was being shyly tendered to me in person, a grizzled, scarred, leather-and-iron centurion of Rome. Was I to become a living god—I, who had brought into being so many imaginary ones?

Gold Flower of Day (I dwelt with her family) brought me as offering, after the next morning meal, a handful of humming-birds' feathers, highly prized among these simple folk, for they are rare in the rock valleys owing to a scarcity of flowering shrubs.

Touched by this evidence of thoughtfulness and devotion, I looked upon her with new eyes, and to preserve her gift I tucked the quills under one of the metal strips on my lorica and for some days wore them there as I passed among the people. Often I caught sly glances upon my decoration, but thought nothing of it until one day Gold Flower of Day came and humbly begged me to permit that she sew on, with new thongs, some of the plates that had been partly torn away in the last campaign. Naturally, I gave my consent.

Judge of my surprise to find, on its return, every tiny particle of that old battle-nicked lorica completely hidden by a gorgeous and shimmering shirt of featherwork, sewn upon a backing of soft doeskin, in the most fantastic and beautiful pattern, and entirely done in feathers of the humming-bird.

All the villages subject to the twin cities had been raided by fast runners to produce feathers for that offering. It was my reward for making men out of those secluded cave-dwellers and it was a gift fit for a Caesar! Surely not even old Picus himself ever beheld such a garment! I walked resplendent among the people, and was very proud, but not nearly as proud as the devoted eyes of Gold Flower of Day told me that she felt, when

I thanked her and taught her the meaning of a kiss, for I knew that the thought was hers.

Then one day a deputation of the Elders waited upon me and with solemn ceremony in their pit-temple below the floor of their cavern home they christened me anew "Nuitziton" or Humming-bird, a name which slipped far more easily from their tongue that it did from mine; but I grew accustomed to it after a while and came to favor my Aztec name, though never did I forget that I was a Roman.

Inaction irked me, and I was plagued by the goad of ambitious dreams. We marched again, in search of new conquests, but before I left I slipped the gorgeous tunic over the head of that effigy of mine, making the other featherwork look tawdry in comparison, and I promised the priest, whose care it was, that the circle of conquest I had begun should be broadened until we had scured enough feathers of the Nuitziton to cover the effigy completely.

That began the long-protracted War of the Humming-birds' Feathers against the southerly, powerful, Toltec nation, which campaign lasted two long years, covered uncounted miles of territory and added thousands to my rule.

At the end of the war, my power was more than Myrdhinn's. The Aztec nation was drunk with the bloody wine of repeated success. They all but forgot the teachings of the one they had first revered as their savior, and whom in gratitude they had christened Quetzalcoatl. With never a single appeal to sorcery, I had become their one undisputed leader.

Our people, by absorbing subject villages, had enormously outgrown their cliff homes and many dwelt below on the floor of the gorges, wherever could be found sweet water and tillable lands; for much of the water hereabout is oddly colored, and death to the drinker.

At last came a day of celebration for the vast multitude which called itself Aztecan. It was the day upon which, in a temple erected for the occasion, I placed the last feather upon the head-band of the effigy, and saw that upon the entire figure there was no particle, however small, of the original substance that could be seen.

From the assemblage rose such a shout that all the mighty cliffs roundabout echoed and re-echoed.

Then advanced Myrdhinn himself, kindly enough, but awe-inspiring in his white robes of ceremony, crowned with his ritualistic headdress of the Quetzal bird.

He placed his withered, wrinkled hands on my head in benediction, and said:

"Ventidius Varro, soldier of Rome, shipmate, leader, hope of this budding Aztec nation, in accordance with the expressed desire of their chosen religious leaders here gathered I give you your new name before all the people. Forget the name of Ventidius and that of Nuitziton, and henceforth be known to all men as Huitzilopochtli—God of War!"

He paused, smiled a little wryly, then:

"Hail, living god!" said Myrdhinn to me (standing there, abashed, knowing him to be far the better man, and feeling myself a traitor worse than Judas, in the respect that I had stolen his power and authority), and bowed his hoary head in salutation. And all the people shouted!

16

Myrdhinn's Messenger

Not as yet had I breathed to these people my hope of hurling the consolidated tribes against the might of Tlapallan, the hereditary oppressors of a vast country, so far as history goes among men who have no written language and preserve memories from one generation to another by painted pictures on skins or a paper made from reeds.

Nor, since our coming, had any raiders attacked the cities of Aztlan, though occasionally our war-parties had met theirs, in the Debatable Lands, a country of hunger, devoid of water and nourishment, which formed our best barrier against Tlapallan's power.

Here, warriors fought to a finish, and sometimes survivors came to us with news of victory, and sometimes the news was borne to the Four Cities of the Mias, but neither side carried word of defeat.

The defeated party enriched the bellies of the wolves and wild dogs, for on that side were no survivors.

Tlapallan knew of our growing power. The Debatable Lands swarmed with their spies, who now and again came sneaking among us. Some went back and took with them the news that everywhere we were arming; took with them, too, our knowledge of the bow, so that had Tlapallan been ruled by a man with vision instead of the lecherous son of the former Kukulcan, who now held that title in his father's place, the end might have been very different. But stubbornly clinging to tradition, he kept to the atlatl, and when the time came, we, far out of range, laid his soldiers down like rows of teocentli.

After three years and a half of battling in the southwest, I now began to see my way clear to the fulfillment of that vow I had made in the filthy reeking enclosure upon the Egg.

I could look about me from the tableland, far as eye could see, and all about stretched a land I might call mine. Mine by conquest! Southerly, near a broad shallow river, was allied to us by force the country of Tolteca, which I knew would march anywhere at my will, were I to point into the grinning mouths of Cerberus.

At last, speeding toward me with every sunrise, every sunset, I could sense the coming of that day when upon the ramparts of Azatlan I could give the word, and

Aztlan would march, in unison with Tolteca, upon the last great foray which would settle for all time whether Aztlan or Tlapallan should rule this continent.

Yet I was not happy as I had expected to be. I brooded, life seemed miserable, I did not know what I lacked. Great aims had lost their fascination. Had I spent too much time in war? Had killing hardened my heart so that all else seemed worthless to me?

I leaned one night upon the rampart, looking easterly, thinking of the countless miles of land and sea separating me from my British home, feeling weary of life.

The light of noonday, by reflection, floods the walls of these ramparts, penetrating the deep recesses of the cave, but as the sun sinks, a dark shadow creeps across the cavern front and the interior is in gloom. A similar blackness had come over my spirit.

Toward what were my struggles tending? Could any part of my dreams come true? Could I seize a bit of these tremendous lands to call it permanently Roman, and carve out a haven for the stricken empire Myrdhinn pictured to me from his greater wisdom?—a haven for Rome to occupy and colonize and create from ruins of empire, a greater Rome that could never perish?

I had dared to dream that I could mold the future; that I could create a far-flung kingdom, knit together by roads after the pattern of Rome, crowded along all their length by marching men, traders, priests, merchants, pilgrims, with fast runners threading the throng, bringing news, taking messages, and somewhere at the center—myself, a little Caesar who might grow huge enough to stretch a helping hand across the seas to succor my homelands in some hour of great need.

Now that it seemed success was almost within my reach, ambition had died in me. What did I lack, when everything was mine?

Lost in my dismal musings, I felt a timid touch upon my arm. I looked down. Beside me, eyes demurely downcast, as behooves a maid, stood my dainty Gold

Flower of Day, and smiling upon her I knew beyond
doubt why my life was empty and gray.

I threw my robe around her shoulders and kissed
her, long and sweetly, and lapped in the protection of
my robe we went in to her family. Thus simply were we
betrothed, and on a day of feasting and jubilation she
became my bride.

No luckier man than I ever trod the earth, I know,
and none ever knew a lovelier lady. For lady she truly
is in her own way, nor need give one inch of precedence
to talented, cultured Roman matrons. She is a very real
help and encouragement. I respect and honor my ruddy,
warm-hearted Gold Flower of Day—barbarian!

To her belongs the credit for the rest of my achieve-
ments. Power had turned to ashes in my mouth. She
gave life new zest. I went on. She had faith in me that
never failed, and I could not betray it.

A long peace followed the subjugation of Tolteca,
during which I made known my plans for the invasion
of Tlapallan, which plans were polished and considered
in many assemblies. Then it was drill, drill, drill, until
the lowliest legionary understood the work he was to
do as well as any veteran might. Instead of centuries,
my fellow wanderers had come to command cohorts,
sturdy and strong, armed with spear, bow and sword,
protected by shields of stout wood and hide, their
bodies covered by thickly padded cloth armor, a good
substitute for metal when used only against atlatl darts.

It was thus that they passed before Myrdhinn and
me in review upon a day of joy and celebration, and
Myrdhinn, gazing at the stern host marching by in
perfect unison, every man's accouterments exactly
like his fellow's, every stride in time with a booming
snakeskin drum, every spear slanted alike down the
whole line, said, "Your Eagle of Aztlan has whetted
his beak until it is sharp." And then, reflectively: "Have
you decided what you will name the boy?"

Just then, the signifer passed, holding on its pole
the old and battered Eagle of the Sixth Legion, Victrix,

and staring hard at this relic bobbing proudly above the strangely resurrected ghost of the old legion, I thought to myself that this new legion might yet know the glory of the old, and answered:

"You yourself have named him. Gwalchmai, he shall be called—the Eagle. And may he have an eagle's spirit!"

So he had, for he crowed and smiled in the arms of his mother's mother, to see the martial panoply of two legions marching by on the long road to Tlapallan. At last we were on the way, marching out under banners, leaving the old and the halt behind with the women, to care for the children who were too small for war.

Everyone else followed the bronze Eagle of the Sixth—seven thousand Aztec fighting-men, and closely behind came almost as many from Tolteca.

We won through the moorlands, in early springtime, very sweet and beautiful with flowers, and I led my little nation, for although it was meant to be a fighting unit, we were laden with packs of provisions, and many large dogs (our only beasts of burden) were also laden with packs of dried meats and other foods.

Also, most of the able-bodied women had refused to be separated from their men during a struggle for freedom which could end only in the total destruction of one or the other side, and had accordingly chosen to come with us to live or die as need be. So the array looked much more like a migrant people than an army, and in it was my own Gold Flower of Day.

The journey was far more difficult than our westward crossing had been, for now we were many mouths and the season was too early for the large herds of wild cattle. Such scattered game as we sighted had generally scented the strong odor of the coming manherd and was in flight before we were near enough to shoot.

Yet, by frequent halts, camping until hunting-parties could press on ahead and kill game, we managed to keep life in us. We were helped by those lonely moor

wanderers who skulked in the high grass, in constant
dread of Tlapallan's slave-raiders. When they were convinced of our friendliness, they joined us with all their
knowledge of hunting-grounds and hiding-places. Without their guidance, we might easily have failed to win
through unperceived, as we did almost to Tlapallan's
borders, without the loss of a single soul.

A week's march from dangerous territory, in a
pleasant place of small lakes and marshes, giving us
hope of good hunting among the beasts and waterfowl,
besides excellent fishing along shores quite unfre-
quented, we threw up an earthen fort, its ramparts
crowned with an agger of stakes and thorns and circum-
vallated by a dry ditch.

We dug wolf-pits in every direction surrounding, all
carefully covered, with sharp stakes at the bottom; and
leaving me and my nation in safe seclusion, Myrdhinn
with a fighting-force of twenty picked men, five Romans
and a moorman guide set out on a long journey around
the frontier of Tlapallan, in order to reach the Hodenosaunee and find out how that folk were faring after
our long absence.

Now I was sole ruler indeed, and my first orders
were for the construction of a firing-platform for a
ballista at each corner of our four-square fort, and
these were built and placed in position.

Admittedly they were crude, being built entirely
without metal, the absence of clamps being rectified
by many wrappings of green hide, well shrunken into
place. I had little hope of any efficient marksmanship
with any such rickety engines, but I did count heavily
upon their astonishing effect upon an enemy, for they
were a novelty in the warfare waged in Alata. I surmised that before the ballistas were racked to bits the
enemy would have fled.

My crews of engineers became proficient in their
duties and we combed the country for suitable stones
without sight of enemy scouts, finding the days very
dull, for three long months. Our occupations were ex-
ercising, hunting and drilling, for every day we ex-

pected to be discovered and besieged, and here were many mouths to feed and undisciplined tempers worn raw by constant association inside strait walls.

However, we remained concealed, thanks to broad and nearly impassable forests which separated us from Tlapallan, though our position was especially happy, in that none of their highways (the large rivers) ran very near to us.

While we regained strength, great events were taking place in the North. Myrdhinn and his tiny force skirted safely the farthest outposts, again crossed the Inland Sea, and came to the log towns of the Hodenosaunee, where he was warmly greeted by that stern but honorable people, who never forgot a friend or forgave an enemy.

Once more they met our Roman companions, now true sons of the forest, skin-clad, painted in the manner of their nations, most of them fathers of little Hodenosaunee, but still Roman enough at heart.

While we adventured, our friends had not been idle in preparations. Myrdhinn found the copper mines still held by the forest men, and learned that the twenty forts which protected the Miner's Road had never been retaken. A great store of copper had been dug and hidden away and was available for use. The frontier had moved south!

Myrdhinn's first action was the setting up of smelters and forges, where, after bitter failures, a fair bronze was at last produced, though not of the quality to which the Sixth had been accustomed.

Once they had determined upon the proper mixture of the copper and tin, molds were made from the old clamps taken from the *Prydwen,* which had cost so many lives and so much toil to recover. Then other clamps were made, enough to outfit a great battery of ballistas and tormenta; and with the remaining tin, pilum-heads were made, with bronze points and shanks of soft copper, so that in use the shanks would bend and droop, weighing down whatever shield the lance-head might be fixed within.

So departed the shining glory which had made the *Prydwen* a queen among ships, and her spirit entered the ruddy metal of Tlapallan to make it strong enough to bring new glory to Rome.

The heat of early summer lay upon our fortified camp. We lay and panted and tried to sleep in our close quarters. At intervals came the challenges of the sentries, with the usual answer, "All is well."

Yet something in the dark of the moon came over the walls, avoided the sentries and came into my bed-chamber. I saw the movement of it against the dimness of the door opening. I heard the scrape of its claws running at me over the hard earth. I first supposed it to be one of the dogs that frequented the camp; yet in size it was smaller than any of those. Then, thinking it to be a tree-cat from the forest, mad for food, I cast a short javelin which always was close to my hand in those days. I heard a savage yell, like nothing of earth; something struck me violently on the chest and the opening was darkened again as the creature spread broad wings and soared away.

Then there was a clamor from the wall! One of the sentries, a tall moorman, came howling down. "Puk-wud-jee! Puk-wud-jee!" he cried, in great fear, and told how its round yellow eyes had shriveled his very soul as it had sailed above him while he'd walked his round.

Questioning him, I learned that in the belief of his people, a Puk-wud-jee was a small woods-demon, sometimes friendly, but more often inimical to man. It was always upon the alert for an opportunity to steal a man-child from its cradle board, that the baby might be fed enchanted food to cause it to shrink in size and grow to become a denizen of the wood.

He assured me in all seriousness that such things were of constant occurrence, and furthermore should this mischievous elf be seen in its true shape (for it often simulated the appearance of some common animal to further its evil designs), it inevitably brought death to the beholder. Nor would he describe it to me, being in great terror lest what he might say would also bring the curse upon me that he felt would assuredly be his bane. So I sent him to his quarters and had another guard posted in his place and returned to my own couch, smiling, for the thought now came to me of the great-eyed owl which I had seen before on two critical occasions—once as I had lain in peril upon a roof in the City of the Snake, and once after my rescue as we'd retreated, though in a manner victors, from that place of blood.

And I suspected that this visitor of the night had brought some news from Myrdhinn, or betokened his nearness, and entering my own quarters I found that the former was the truth. Before a rushlight sat Gold Flower of Day, in her cotton nightwear, puzzling over the unfamiliar Latin letter which she had removed from a bronze cylinder that this creature had hurled at me before it had fled.

So I hurriedly smoothed out the scroll, and forgot the sentry and his fears, which was unjust, for at that moment he lay with his own stone knife embedded in his heart, though no one knew it till dawn.

It read:

> *To Varro, Legatus of Aztlan, from Merlin Ambrosius, Imperator; greeting.*
>
> *The People of the Long House await the new moon, to march upon the City of the Snake. Runners have spread the word among the tribes of Chichameca, to roll down upon the frontier forts, from the Inland Sea to the Mica Mines. The kings have agreed to attack on that date. Follow the plans we arranged. Take the fort at the junction of the rivers, garrison it, and push on to meet us. We strike with all strength. God with us! Let us avenge Marcus!*
>
> *Vale.*

17

The Eagle and the Snake

Now, after this message from Myrdhinn, we all were elated, for we had not known if our friends were alive or dead, in which latter case our plans were ruined and we must make haste to evacuate and return whence we had come. Indeed, for the last month complaints had been growing at our inaction and the first enthusiasm was long since dulled. The people of Alata are peculiarly without patience. They can win a battle, but find it difficult to win a war. They are not willing to wait, but would rather settle everything by a headlong rush, which is the reason that Mian discipline had so long held the country.

Had it not been for my constant drilling on the parade grounds and the discipline that irked their savage spirits, but which was recognized as necessary by the most intractable, I believe my force would have been halved by desertion.

However, the chief credit must go to their women, whose unquestioning faith in my aims was of much importance; for they argued to themselves, as they watched the eternal marching and weapon-play, that such long training could not be for nothing, and under their criticizing looks that warriors vied for supremacy over their fellows.

Here, too, while encamped, I originated an order of knighthood, with a graduated scale of honors, colored mantles and badges which they might wear to show their rank, and much solemn ritual to be used in initiation of the chosen. I dubbed these selected few "Valiants" which became in the common talk "Braves" (though now, in these latter years, the idea has spread

148

far beyond my people, and all over Chichameca the barbarians deck themselves with feathers to denote honors attained, and any male, of age and below a king's rank, calls himself a brave).

All these things kept them under my order, until the day when we learned that the Hodenosaunee awaited only the day to pour over the borders with ax and fire. All Chichameca was seething with unrest and could the voices that rose from those dark forests have been blended into one, it would have been a cry of hate to freeze Mian blood to the last drop.

We bode our time to the appointed day. Then, leaving a guard of five centuries, the engineers, and the women, we quitted our forest home and entered the trees again, our destination being the fork where Tlapallan's two greatest river-highways met.

A strong fort was situated here, but not strong enough to resist us. Its defenders were not used to our method of fighting; the savage tribes roundabout did not have the perseverance to stay with the attack and consequently they had always been thrown back.

We invested the fort, and for two days and nights shot arrows into it, many of them flaming—nor did we allow the defenders to reach water, their earthwork connections with the river being constantly pelted with a dropping patter of missiles. On the third morning, the fort surrendered.

Not a building remained standing. Everything inflammable was burned to the ground, and those defenders remaining alive were none of them unwounded.

They must have expected torture and death, but no Tlapallico flinched as they marched forth into our ranks and cast their weapons into a pile.

We fed them and set them free in their coracles, to scatter into the land and spread the tidings of our coming. We hoped that the inhabitants would seek the shelter of the forts. We could deal with forts, I felt certain, and those people left outside, by reason of cramped quarters, must of necessity be the enslaved part of the population, which I felt would hasten to join us.

Leisurely then, we rebuilt the gutted fort, sent a force back to help dismantle the fort we had encamped in and bring the women and engines here, to help make this place doubly strong. After they had arrived I increased the garrison by five centuries more, and shortly after set out up the lesser river toward the Four Cities.

While we were active in this section, to the east, north and south all Tlapallan's frontier was rocking to the impact of the Chichamecan hordes pressing forward upon every fort in all that far-flung chain, holding the Mias and Tlapallicos inside while the federated tribes rushed on in their thousands between the embattled fortifications.

None inside could sally forth to hinder, and drums beat unanswered and smokes talked from pinnacle to peak without any result.

Alata was a shrieking arena, and Tlapallan was becoming more of a red land than ever its christener could have dreamed!

We, Aztlan and Tolteca, were farther advanced than any, being well within the gates and nearing day by day the Four Cities, Tlapallan's heart. Little villages and settlements were rolled over and absorbed. Weeping women, stern-faced, broken-bodied men bony from animal toil in the fields, armed with anything which might cut an enemy's throat or smash an oppressor's skull—so many desperate ones joined us to strike a blow for freedom that toward the last days I gave them separate commanders, formed them into centuries and used them as shock troops, for they fought as though they had no desire to live.

From the frontier we entered the forest belt which lies between that and the tilled lands. At night our many fires reddened the sky—by day we marched on, unchecked, but not unhindered.

Occasionally a man would drop, pierced by an atlatl dart from some tall tree. Sometimes a boulder would fall from the heights and rebound among us. But never a battle, nor even a skirmish. I began to suspect that we were hurrying into a trap.

Once, loose stones set a whole hillside sliding, killing many of us below, the rubble flying like rocks from a battery of ballistae. Our scouts hunted down the assailants and slew them. Our ranks reformed. We marched on—deeper and deeper into the hostile land.

Then back from a dark, close wood of pine came a tattered and dying scout, last of his band, with the word that within it a host lay in wait, of trusted Tlapallicos, and beyond them was encamped the flower of the Mian nation, ready to cut up what remained, should we struggle through.

We paused and debated. I called a council of my tribunes (they had been kings in their own right before I had come to Aztlan) and admitted several centurions from the most trusted companies of our recent additions. Many suggestions were advanced and discussed, but one of the former slaves originated the thought that saved us, and I gave that centurion the power to order and to act.

This battered, whip-scarred warrior, named Ga-no-go-a-da-we, or as we might say "Man-who-burns-hair," was of the Clan of the Bear, and had been greatly surprised to learn of his kinsmen's prowess in the north— he being of the Great Hill People, and a slave of the first degree, ten years in unremitting toil and heartbreak for his people. Never was a man more fittingly named.

At his command, the seven centuries, under him, entered the trees, taking advantage of every rock and shrub. They made that wood theirs, as water fills the interstices in a cup full of pebbles. They fought and killed, and were killed, and a few came back. Behind those who returned, the forest flamed to high heaven— and they defiled before us, waving aloft long belts and chains of bloody scalps, armed with the finest of Mia weapons, which they brandished at the barrier of fire which held our enemy from us.

Then it became a race to circle the spreading flames, find a defensible position and be there in time to forestall the Mian army which we knew would march at once to cut us off. But they, not knowing in which direction we would be most apt to break by the burning forest, divided their forces and committed suicide.

By the time the first division, which vastly outnumbered my two cohorts even though it was only half of the original array, was ready to attack us, we had thrown up earthworks, fronted by a deep ditch, and were almost ready for them.

They camped, night being upon us, and being out of atlatl-shot they thought themselves safe; but by the time they were well settled, our bows rained death among them, some lucky shots setting fire to dry grasses near their supply of food, causing them much damage.

The fear of hunger was responsible the next day, though their camp was now out of bow-shot, for deciding their commander to risk an immediate attack instead of waiting for the other section.

Just at daybreak they rushed our works.

Beyond atlatl range they began to drop by scores, then by hundreds.

They littered the meadowland; they struggled into a little swamp and made solid footing there with their own dead bodies; they choked a brook that gave us drink, till the very course of it was changed and it ran red and wild like a mad, living thing across the meadow, drowning the wounded who lay in its course. They came nearly to the works, faltered, reeled back and fled. Down upon their heads and backs drove pitiless arrow-sleet, piercing plates of copper and mica, harrying them, scattering them, far as bow could reach.

They re-formed and came again. Gods! What men they were!

This time they gained the rampart, but it was a feeble stroke they dealt. Ax and knife and spear could not down my matchless swordsmen. From afar the Mias had died, struck down by the new weapon their Kukulcan had been too slow, too niggardly, to furnish them. Their ruler was a man of little vision, a lecher, uxorious with his women, and because of it his country died!

Now his betrayed soldiers met still another new weapon—the pitiless, mutilating maccahuitl, the sword with glass fangs, which smashed down and tore flesh apart in a single stroke.

They had never dreamed of an instrument like a sword. They threw their lances, closed to finish with ax and knife, and were hurled away, maimed, mangled, beaten, and when the ramparts were clean the terrible bows behind them sang death to the runners again.

So the Eagle of Aztlan bit deep into the Snake of Tlapallan!

It was a red day and we longed for rest, but we knew the woods were full of wanderers, and somewhere an untried, unafraid army of Mias and Tlapallicos was hunting along our track.

We searched the meadow for arrows and other weapons, ate and drank and were easy in our camp, but our sentinels were alert.

The day ended, and in a black night, hidden from spies among the trees, we dug till skies began to lighten, making wolf-pits to trap the enemy we expected. And it was well we did, for by the third hour of light they were upon us.

They could hardly have allowed themselves much time for rest, after their long journey, for some staggered with weariness as they debouched into the clearing.

Yet, as they saw us there entrenched, new spirit came to them, and without a cry or cheer they charged across the bodies of their dead.

Nearer they came and nearer, and not an arrow flew.

"Steady!" I passed down the word along the line. "Steady! Wait till they strike the pits!"

Closer still, they surged upon us in a wide crescent with leveled lances. Upon their grim faces we could see stern determination and we knew they meant to end the affair at once, without mercy.

To them we represented all that was evil, savage

and vile. We were to be obliterated, stamped into the ground.

Behold them as they charge! Their bodies glisten with sweat and oil. Their long conical heads are flung back in pride. The stag antlers upon the helmets clash and rattle; mica scales and burnished copper glitter in the morning sun. The ground rumbles to their tread.

They are coming! The undefeated hosts of Tlapallan, the terrible disciplined array that conquered the irregular scattered tribes of Alata and stole the best lands in a continent! They come, and Aztlan, the despised, but also undefeated, is waiting with arrow feathers close against the ear.

Man-who-burns-hair raises the shout of the scalp dance:

> *"Ha-wa-sa-say!*
> *Hah!*
> *Ha-wa-sa-say!"*

Someone stops him.

Now they rush into the thick of the heaps of dead. A young officer leaps from the ranks, copper plate upon his antlers betokening high rank. He bounds into the air, brandishing his lance, and howls like a wolf.

He waves on his company, now ululating their war-cry, "Ya-ha-ee-hee!"

He leaps again and hurls his lance—an empty threat—they are yet too far—and drops to earth which opens and swallows him whole, gulping him from sight, and the roar of wonder from his men is threaded by his cry as the stake below tears through his entrails.

Then the whole front rank, pushed on by those behind, drops into the wolf-pits. The drumming thunder of the sandaled charge dies down, and into those left standing our winged arrows bite.

I give credit to brave men.

They re-formed amidst the arrow-flight and came on, filling the second row of pits level full of dead men over which their comrades advanced. Atlatl darts buzzed and whined over our wall. They struck the third row, faltered and were checked but not halted.

The fourth row was too much. When almost touching our earthworks they broke and ran, and our arrows cut them down as hail lays flat the corn. Their officers beat and beseeched them, but being flesh and blood, not iron, they would not stand, and behind them as they fled I saw officer after officer, the highest and the low, fall upon his lance and go to his gods with honor untarnished by defeat.

I could hold my fierce people no longer. With exultant cries of "Al-a-lala! Al-a-lala!" they poured over the earthworks, streamed among the empty pits and dashed after the Mias, I leading, lest I be left entirely behind.

As we neared the wood, out burst the remnants of that mighty Mia army in close array, like a wounded bear, blood-blind who smites about him in every direction, hoping to kill before he dies.

Shame was burning them and they meant to make their mark upon us!

Then our long days of discipline told. Peremptorily my trumpet sang through the shouting, answered shrilly by the war-whistles held by tribunes and centurions, and instantly our whole ragged advance stiffened from a mob into an army, whose even ranks separated, giving room to those behind that they also might shoot. Now, facing the Mias, stood the harrow formation of the quincunx, from which poured such a devastating volley that the attackers shrank back upon themselves.

"Stand fast!" I shouted, expecting a rally, but they were beaten. They broke and ran, scattered for the last time.

A great cry went up from behind me. Man-who-burns-hair plunged past, his face like a fiend's, dabbled with paint, distorted with hate and fury. Following him, the slave centuries entered the forest, out of formation, obeying no command, hunting, each man for himself like a hungry pack of wolves harrying the fleeing deer, chasing the panic-stricken antlered manherd.

Not many returned. In the forest they fought and died, counting death a little thing in the avenging of so many wrongs. A few came back while we were hunting out the bodies of our dead and piling them into a mound for mass burial, outfitting each with weapons and water bottle to be used in the long journey to Mictlampa, Land of the Dead. Others appeared while the priests were writing out the passes which each must have on the journey, in order to go unhindered by precipices and dangerous monsters. All the dogs in camp were killed, that they might precede their masters into the underworld and help them across the last barrier—a broad river.

How Myrdhinn would have been shocked, could he have seen it!

I myself was more than a little dismayed at the treatment of our numerous captives. Many were flayed, to the glory of the gods, others killed in unfair combat, being tethered by one foot to a stone, and pitted singly with toy weapons against four fully armed men, while a large basket called "The Cup of Eagles" was completely filled with the hearts taken from those who had been fastened to scaffolds and filled with arrows there that their blood might drip upon the ground as a libation to the gods. And I was one of the gods!

I was glad that Myrdhinn was away.

At length these dreadful rites were over, though night came upon us before the heap of bodies was smoothly rounded with well-tamped earth.

We made tamalli cakes of meal and supped; but there were many, I knew but could not prevent, who had red meat, though it had been long since we had hunted for game.

In the night I heard a whisper at my hut-entrance. "Tecutli [Lord]." I did not answer, but in the morning found Man-who-burns-hair lying across the opening, the last to return from the harrying.

He was no longer commander of many, nothing now

but a simple centurion, for no more than that number of slaves were now alive to march behind him, but when we moved out of that glade of death and vengeance he bore himself with as proud a carriage as any Caesar at the head of a triumph. One could see that never more could he be a slave. He had bought back his manhood with blood.

18

The New Kukulcan

The strength of our enemy in the field was broken, but their spirit was not, and as they fled through the forests singly or in small groups they snarled back their defiance and turned to fight like cornered tree-cats when we came too close.

We crossed the fertile valley and entered a trackless wilderness between the rivers where we were constantly tormented by unexpected attacks. We never crossed a ford uncontested, never entered a forest opening without hearing atlatl darts whistle across it at our scouts.

They distressed us immensely and we believed that we were well rid of them when we burst eventually into the cultivated country. It was a disappointment to find that the retreating bands of Mias had devastated the fields of growing grain and vegetables, burned buildings and stores of provisions, and stripped the sections of country in our path bare of anything which might be of use to us.

Occasionally a slave, skulking amid smoking ruins to grub for a morsel of charred food, came and attached himself to our force, hoping for better rations, but we were in bitter plight. There were many hungry days when no one ate and when the weakest lay by the way to rest and follow, if the gods willed, or to die and burden us no more. Thankful then were we that our women were secure in their strong fort at the junction of the rivers.

Our one thought was to push on and on, to drive through the heart of this country, make our connection with Myrdhinn and the Hodenosaunee, and to rest and eat again. We looked upon the new recruits as thieves, stealing the food out of our mouths; yet had it not been for one of these unwanted men, we might not have been so successful.

He directed us to a large underground winter storehouse of teocentli, put up in barrels in earthenware, hollow tree-trunks and bark baskets. It had been overlooked by our enemy, and we seized upon the grain with joy, ground it and made tamalli cakes, surely sweeter than ever food had tasted before to any man. Some ground it between stones and, without cooking, mixed the meal with water as we used to treat wheat when marching with the Sixth in Britain, drinking it down to ease the pain of their shriveled insides, before treating that space to more solid food.

We had enough for both cohorts—yea, and something left over for the next two days, though it was sparingly used.

From this man we learned that those we followed were massacring all slaves who were too old or too young to fight. Women and babes at the breast had been cut down by these red-handed sons of the Red Land and only those were left alive who swore allegiance to the Empire of Kukulcan. Thus a steadily enlarging force was preceding us in the direction of the Four Cities, though into which one it intended to enter and make a stand against us, we could not guess.

We could do nothing but follow in its track, so wide a strip of desolation was being made, and we did follow, hoping to come up with them and destroy them; but we never quite managed this, though often we saw flames burst out of buildings just ahead, or came upon butchered slaves still warm, though gone to the Land of the Dead.

Now we could guess that the Mias felt themselves in desperate straits, though they knew their own plight better than we. We learned from refugees that most of the frontier forts had fallen before the roaring fury that aroused Chichameca had, in its uniting, flung upon them. To the east, we were told the land was overrun with war-parties, acknowledging no master, burning, slaying, looting wherever occasion offered, so that no man's life was safe, except in the great towns, and fortified cities of refuge.

And there were rumors that in the North, the Holy City of the Snake had fallen, and no more would the Devourer there engorge herself on hapless slaves; but this I discredited, for I did not believe that all the Hodenosaunee could gather enough power to take that stronghold, providing the countrymen had sought shelter.

We did not know that Myrdhinn *had* taken the City of the Snake, gutted it, sparing only women and children of the Mias, though giving quarter to all Tlapallicos who flung down their arms and sought mercy. The People of the Long House had slain the H'menes, torn down the pavilion and altar on the ill-famed Egg and erected there a twenty-foot cross, at Myrdhinn's orders, and afterward had quitted the city and were now coming to meet us, in all haste.

Before we found out these things, we came to the southernmost of the Four Cities, the strong walled city of Tlacopan, and sat down outside the walls to make ourselves comfortable in the siege of it; none too soon either, for my men were beginning to murmur at the long wandering and empty bellies and no foe that they could meet to satisfy their numerous grudges upon since that one forest battle.

Truly, I think that had it not been for my reputation as a living god of war they would not have followed me so far—for, after all, they were only barbarians who were being forced by my will to actions foreign to anything in their previous experience. It is a perilous thing to be the midwife when a nation is born.

If any among us had thought that the reduction of this fortified city would be a simple thing, they had the idea knocked out of them when we first stormed the palisades on all its four sides.

We learned then what a vast difference there could be in siege-fighting, depending entirely whether Aztlan or Tlapallan was on the inside of the earthworks.

They let us come on, much as we had enticed *our* pursuers, then all along the parapets we saw heads popping up, and slingstones began to whiz and whir. Very accurate they were, too, and deadly.

Most of the front rank went down on my side, I know, and the mortality was high elsewhere, but the battle was carried in close to the walls in the face of a stinging storm of darts, and we tried to set fire to the logs. However, everything being wet from a three-day rain, fortune did not favor us, and being without shelter of any kind we fell back to let nature fight for us.

Like most of these towns, a double earthwork and palisade led from the fortifications to a nearby river, for the procuring of water. This was a good protection against atlatl darts, which are thrown with an overhand cast and fly in a straight line, but was worthless against the dropping fire of our archers. We made life so miserable for the defenders by maintaining a steady drop of arrows, and by patrolling the river entrance to this path, that finally we were enabled to drive out those holding the gate, and seizing the earthworks we cut the city entirely off from its water supply.

Days went on, and we knew they must be suffering from thirst, if not from hunger. We, too, were famished, for the fish and game available was not nearly enough and we were living scantily upon grain that the scouts brought in from undestroyed villages and farms.

Then, one day when we all felt certain that surrender must be near, a wild-eyed scout came hurrying in with the news that a large army was marching upon us to relieve the fort. I knew that at all costs we must be behind the shelter of those walls when the new enemy came up, so I gave over the command to the tribunes, with orders to knock together a number of light ladders, to storm the walls, and make ready to receive us as we fell slowly back upon the town. I sallied out with ten centuries from Aztlan, five from Tolteca, and most of the freed Tlapallicos to be used as light wood-runners to find the enemy, engage him and entice him into a nearby pass where he would be at our mercy beneath falling rock.

With the works suffering the fiercest attack of the siege, we left them, and not long after, high in the air, lying behind piles of hastily gathered boulders, hidden and waiting all tense for the fight, knowing that after the one sharp blow we must flee, we were praying that we would have a shelter to feel secure in.

We saw the naked bodies of our savage allies slipping silently among the underbrush in the pass below, and from our eminence could see the van of the enemy closely in pursuit.

What was this? Here were no antlered Tlapallican helmets! Nowhere slanted the repugnantly flattened brow of a Mia! Instead I saw the single dipping feathers of the Hodenosaunee, Myrdhinn's own nation! Friends, not foes!

"Hold your fire," I shouted, and tumbled headlong to meet them. In no time I was hugging my old comrades—Valerius, Antoninus, Intinco the Caledonian, Lucius—and gravely shook Myrdhinn's hand. I felt a strong palm on my shoulder.

"Atoharo, my brother," said Hayonwatha.

And I hugged him in my glee till his ribs creaked against my lorica and I saw that stern face tighten into a grin, for once. Oh, he could laugh, that hero blood-brother of mine, but none but his friends and family ever knew it!

In haste I brought down my companies, and, mingling, we hurried back to lend a hand in the battle but found that Tlacopan had fallen to my tribunes,

who had immediately denied their pledged terms when
the Mia weapons had been thrown down. They had
allowed all Tlapallicos to retain their weapons and
bidden them settle accounts with their former masters.

The payment was about completed when we arrived,
but I had the pleasure of demoting those tribunes to
the ranks and raising six of my Valiants to their
places, and I would have made Man-who-burns-hair
one of them and given him authority over our new
Tlapallico recruits, but when I looked for him he was
gone from his place, and could not be found among
the slain, either within or without the city.

He did not turn up the next day, so I was reluc-
tantly forced to believe him dead in the forest, but
could not hold the march for one centurion; so we
razed the palisades and burned the buildings, marching
the following day.

Three nations were we, and numbered over twenty
thousand lances, counting our not very dependable
Tlapallico allies who were too new to us for me to
trust their loyalty if they became too hungry.

Our destination now was Colhuacan, the City of the
Twisting Mound, where Mixcoatl, the Storm Serpent,
was worshiped, second only in holiness and sacrifices
to the foul City of the Snake. Thither the priest-king
Kukulcan had fled, before his city had been taken, and
only ten miles away lay the greatest citadel of Tlapallan—Miapan, whose earth ramparts were higher and
thicker than Hadrian's Wall.

We might take Colhuacan, but would it be possible
to enter Miapan in another status than that of captive?
We marched. We would see.

Again we were obliged to fight our way, and again
we were annoyed in all the familiar manners.

The season now being far advanced, we dreaded
that we might fail because of snows if we were too
long delayed, and Myrdhinn and I knew well that if we
did fail, such a force would be impossible to bring
together again. I wondered if I dared ask the help of

sorcery and was on the point of it many times but did not, knowing Myrdhinn's views upon the matter.

As we approached the country where Colhuacan lay, we were surprised to find that resistance was growing less instead of greater, and pushed forward cautiously, expecting a trap, but soon resistance died down altogether and we came out of the glades into the cleared land and saw the walls of the city.

The gates were open and there was an affray there.

Men ran out and were followed by others, who cut them down; there was rebellion in the city, and the Mias were fleeing from the Tlapallico slaves!

"Forward, Aztlan!" I cried, and led the way at a run.

A scarred man I knew came out to meet me. It was Man-who-burns-hair! "Tecutli! Lord Huitzilopochtli!" he hailed exultantly. "Behold your enemy!" And he flung a bleeding head at my feet.

One glance at the flabby cheeks and pouched eyes was enough, without the ornate golden circlet and antlers for corroboration.

The family resemblance to the ruler who had once sentenced me to death was strong. It was indeed the Kukulcan, the Mian ruler.

"How did you do it?" I asked in joyous wonder as we entered the city through a cheering host of armed slaves.

"Deserted, had myself taken prisoner, talked to the slaves when I was put with them—told of massacred Tlapallicos the Mias left on the road to Tlacopan, told of heroes, of living gods, of the men I led—told of the master who cut the flesh from my back with a copper whip—bade them rise when we knew you were near. Lord, may I lead men again?"

"You may indeed, and soon shall. It is well done."

And that day, in the sacred city of Colhuacan, he was raised to the post of tribune, delighting him greatly, though his glory was overshadowed; for that day, by popular acclaim without a single dissenting

voice, Myrdhinn was unanimously chosen the new
Kukulcan, and Tlapallan for the first time in all history
had a white ruler.

19

How We Came to Miapan

As we lay in the shelter of Mian walls, resting, and
replacing broken weapons with new, our scouts went
out spying upon Miapan and the reports they brought
back made me thoughtful. It was almost impregnable.
The city-fortress is divided in three parts: the North,
Middle and South forts.

The whole is situated on a plateau three hundred
feet above the nearby river, and deep gullies and
ravines surround it like a moat at all points except in
the northeast, the only point where the land joins the
plateau in a level manner. Here is a great plain, with
every tree and bush removed, so that no besieger can
find shelter. Here the Mias were wont to hold their
sports, as you shall learn.

Fronting this plain, the walls of the North Fort are
at their strongest, being seventy feet thick at the base
and twenty-three feet high. On the plain side is a wide
and deep moat, filled with water to protect this most
exposed portion of Miapan. There is also a moat, more
shallow, just inside the wall. This was also filled with
water, and sharp stakes were planted in it.

From this point, the gullies form natural defenses,
and the walls are not so high or thick; yet they continue, zigzagging to protect every foot of level ground
upon the surface of the plateau. They form a total
length of more than three and a half miles, though a

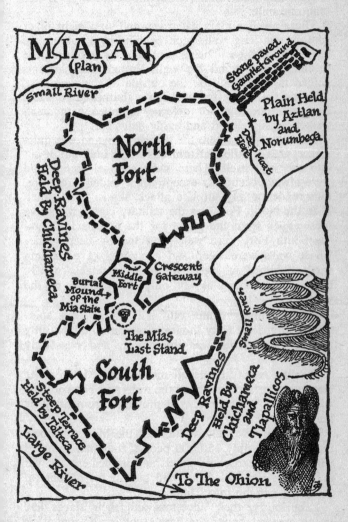

straight line from the north to the south walls is less than one mile.

There are five main gateways, and sixty-eight other gaps in this long wall, each opening being about ten feet wide, and each being protected by a blockhouse reaching out beyond the wall. From these bastions, defenders could enfilade the outside of the ramparts.

Along the top of the wall ran a sharpened palisade, also with openings for defense, supplied with small wickets, easily closed and easily defended.

At many spots where the declivity beyond was quite inaccessible, a little platform was either built out or cut into the wall itself. These were sentinel stands and were always occupied, except when under direct fire, thus rendering any surprise attack almost impossible.

In the North Fort was the military camp, which we must attack from the plain, for the Middle Fort and the South Fort were well protected by deep gullies whose walls were steep and composed of crumbling earth. Trapped in these, we must inevitably perish, even though above us lay only the families of the warriors.

In the military camp, our first interest, our spies estimated at least forty thousand men awaited us; fully armed, very active, was the report, and constantly drilling.

Possibly twenty thousand more occupied the other connected forts and manned the walls and blockhouses, while in the South Fort, well protected from us, their families dwelt.

Here then was the last stand of the Mias. Numbering, in all, possibly 150,000 people, they had gathered with all their household goods and implements of war in this, their citadel. They had built it for a home at their first coming into Tlapallan.

Laboriously, their ancestors and their slaves had borne on their backs the baskets of earth, containing from a peck to a half-bushel, that in the end had created these formidable ramparts. Here they had found a home and from behind those walls they had expanded and grown into a nation.

Now, back they had come, reaping the fruits of their cruelty, to find all their world in arms against them, and once again, so great were their losses, they found the sheltering walls of Miapan broad enough to enclose the entire Mian nation.

"Conquer Miapan," said the spies, "and you have the whole of Tlapallan!"

So we lay in Colhuacan three weeks and a little more, and every day brought recruits. By twos and threes and scores they came flocking in—savage moormen, wifeless, childless, ragged, fierce and destitute. They never smiled or laughed, and spent most of their time sitting alone, sharpening their knives or hatchets, or learning the trick of archery. Scarred and maimed Tlapallico slaves, slinking in like cowed dogs. They cringed when spoken to sharply, but there was a fierce, furtive look in their eyes, like the yellow glare in the orbs of a tree-cat.

They brought their own war-paint. It was always black.

"Have you no gayer colors in your medicine-bag?" I asked one group.

One oldster, savagely marked with running weals which would never quite heal, looked up and said grimly:

"We will find red paint inside the walls of Miapan!"

A cold feeling came upon me and I walked away, hearing behind me the guttural grunts which pass for hearty laughter among this iron-hearted folk.

More loquacious and friendly were the newcomers from the free forest towns. Emboldened and cheered by news of successes, they trooped into camp, from Adriutha, Oswaya and Carenay, from Kayaderos and Danascara. Engineers, trained by Myrdhinn in his own town of Thendara, brought heavy loads of sharp copper arrowheads, bronze swords and fittings for siege artillery.

We distributed these smaller articles at once, but

postponed the building of engines till we should be
before the walls—for without beasts of burden we
could only with difficulty drag such heavy pieces
thither.

Little bands of Chichamecans came in and swore
fealty, and one day we were joined by some very
curious strangers drawn with weariness of forced
marches. They came from a far northern city, built
entirely of stone they said, which they called Nor-um-
Bega.

They were not swarthy like others we had seen in
this country, but seemed whiter than any, though brown
with tan. They were dressed and armed no differently
than other Chichamecans, but there the similarity
ended, for their faces were freckled, their eyes were
blue, and their hair and beards were a bright flaring
red!

Never before have I heard of a red-haired people,
and from what country they came I know not, nor
could they tell aught, save that they came here in the
morning of time, in stout ships. Behind them they left
a land which had sunken beneath them, drowning a
populous country.

They had never been bothered by the Mias and they
had no interest in our cause, other than that it promised
fine fighting. They asked no reward, and wanted nothing but to fight beside us, for fighting seems to be their
religion and only pleasure and it seems likely in the
end to be their bane.

In the beginning, their legends say, they were many
as the forest leaves, and the north country was theirs,
even beyond Thule, and many were their cities. Wealthy
they once were, with great store of jewels and fine
things, but now they are poor through warfare, and so
few that one city holds them all with room to spare.

Every male able to march, from stripling to oldster,
had come at the news of war against Tlapallan, yet
the total was less than four hundred; so I suppose in a
few years, as things are going, Nor-um-Bega will live
only in the legends of its neighbors.

But they fought stout-heartedly beside my Valiants, for they have no love of life and no care for it.

Now I must speak of a shameful thing.

We had found some crocks of wine beneath one of the houses sacred to the Kukulcan and his women. It was thin stuff, but heady, and the first wine I had seen since the wreck of the *Prydwen*. I made a fool of myself without any trouble at all.

On the eve of our proposed march upon Miapan, I gathered my tribunes and centurions in my quarters for celebration and we all got pleasantly drunk.

I was trying to teach them a drinking-song of the Sixth and having a terrible time, for very few could understand the words and none had any idea of how to carry a tune. Music, as we know it, is strange to them. I was roaring out the chorus, trying to outshout my leather-lunged friends, who were all singing to a rhythmic clashing of cups:

> *"Drink! Drink! Let the cannikins clink*
> *And with wine let us make merry!*
> *For with the dawn we must be gone*
> *And there will be some to bury!"*

Suddenly I found that I was singing alone and looked stupidly at my fellows, who were glaring at the door with expressions of awe and dread, and twisting about, I saw Myrdhinn there, eying us with a look of furious disgust, much as Moses must have looked upon the revelers around the Golden Calf.

"Swine!" he roared. "Wallowers in filth and iniquity! While you take your ease, your friends and fellows have been fallen upon by the Mias and are dying in torture. Swilling fools, your end is sorrow and destruction! I lay a word upon you, Ventidius. Your nation shall wander in search of a home and shall not find it for six hundred years. They shall be wanderers upon the face of the earth, until they find an island in a lake. Upon this, marked by an eagle with a snake in its mouth, let them settle, but they will not thrive.

"Their ways are bloody, they are beyond regeneration, they have cast aside my teachings and perverted them. I repudiate them, and Ventidius, yourself shall never see Rome! Now bestir yourself and follow me!"

"But how do you know?" I asked, a bit stupidly, still fuddled with the drink.

"Oh, hurry, dolt! Hurry!" he cried impatiently. "While you talk brave men are dying. The woods are full of my messengers.

"You know I understand the language of the birds. It was folly for Hayonwatha to go scouting. I had already told all officers what lay before us, and how we must attack. Hayonwatha was at that council fire. Poor headstrong fool! He must see for himself, and so he has got himself taken and thirty others with him!

"Well, brave souls, they knew how to die, and most are already dead, but if they have followed the usual Mian custom and saved the leader for the last, there is yet a chance for your blood-brother if we are quick. Haste, then. We will talk as we go."

My head had been rapidly clearing.

"Give your orders, Myrdhinn, but I fear it is useless. The host cannot reach Miapan in less than six hours."

Myrdhinn smiled a tight-lipped smile.

"No, the host cannot, but you and I will be there in that many minutes."

And as I gaped at him, wondering if my humming ears had heard him right, he snapped out an order to a staring tribune:

"Bid a trumpeter sound. March at sunrise." (The eastern sky was already pink.) "Say to all the host that their commanders have gone ahead and will meet them on the road to Miapan. Let nothing stop you."

He saluted and turned away, and as Myrdhinn and I slipped into the forest, I heard a hundred shell trumpets braying their harsh reply to the clear sweet notes of my own trumpeter, with his instrument of bronze, and I knew that soon, perhaps for the last time, the old bronze eagle of the Sixth would look down on marching men.

Once in the seclusion of the trees, Myrdhinn seemed to forget the need for haste. He sat down upon a log and motioned me beside him.

From his breast he drew out a small vial and held it to the light. I could see a few small dark pills rattling within it.

"With these, Ventidius," he said reflectively, "we shall conquer time and space, and in a few brief moments cover the miles that stretch between us and Miapan. I cannot tell you what is in them, nor how they are made. They were given me by a desirable Thessalian witch, with whom I dallied away a summer's days—long ago, when I was young. We used them to halt the swift pace of Chronos. We spent years of delight together, in one golden month of the time that others knew. She gave me a few that remained at our parting.

"Well, well, she is long since dust, and if there is black magic, or sin to account for, it lies in the compounding, not in the partaking!

"Come then, Varro. Let us each swallow a pellet. Perchance it will bring me memories of red-lipped Selene—and wicked days."

He rolled one out into my palm and I placed it on my tongue.

It was faintly bitter, I thought. Then, as it dissolved, my eyes became blurred. I rubbed them, but they remained misty for what seemed a long time; then, as they cleared, it seemed that I had become stone-deaf.

Directly before me, a little bird had been singing to greet the sun. I saw him there upon this twig. His mouth was open, so I knew he still was singing, but I could not hear a note. I stared, trying to understand, and noticed also that the wind, which had been strong, had stopped entirely.

Myrdhinn was eying me wtih amusement.

"Come," he said, and I knew that I was not deaf. "Let us haste now, to Miapan."

I rose and followed him, in that strange and death-like hush which had come over the forest.

Behind us, at the gates of Colhuacan, a company was surging out, or had been. Now they stood as though frozen, some with one foot raised in midstride, but immobile, while above them floated a pennon, oddly twisted, but not fluttering. It was as though it had been suddenly changed from a flapping bit of cloth and feathers to a replica of itself carven from wood or metal.

Myrdhinn led on. I noticed that when he pushed a branch out of his way, it did not fly back and strike me, but remained where it was.

We forded a shallow stream.

"Look down," said Myrdhinn.

I did so, and was amazed to find that the water did not rush in to fill up the holes that our feet left as they were withdrawn from it. Every footprint was to be seen as we looked back from the other shore. We might have walked in soft mud instead of water, so slowly did the liquid flow back.

We walked swiftly on. A wind began to blow in our faces. It was cool at first, then warm, and soon uncomfortably hot. I saw Myrdhinn pluck at his robe and draw it knee-high. It was becoming brown, as though crisped by the heat.

"We must go slower," he said, finally, "or we will be burned by the friction of the air."

Then I understood! It was not the world that had suddenly become quiet about us. Our sense of time had been speeded up!

All at once I felt desperately hungry. My bodily resources were being exhausted by the unaccustomed demands upon them.

Time passed. We walked on and on. Hours apparently passed, yet the eastern sky grew no rosier. Morning, it seemed, had stopped and would never come.

"Look at the dawn, Ventidius. It is almost the same as when we started. Do you realize how far we have come in little time? Yet we have not hastened beyond a quick stride. We are not breathed. We have but walked briskly along, yet have covered miles in moments. Now you can understand how the legend arose that witches were wont to anoint themselves with a foul salve and fly through the air in the form of a bird. No one guessed that the secret lay in a tiny swallowed pellet, and the witches never told."

"Look yonder, Myrdhinn," I interrupted. "The smokes of Miapan!"

"Aye, and thither are we bound."

"Had we the Mantle of Arthur, which I so foolishly lost, one of us might effect a rescue."

Myrdhinn looked at me oddly.

"Think no more of it. We shall pass the guards in safety."

We walked, slowly it seemed, though the wind blew hot against us, around the ravine which bordered the South Fort. The sentries on their high platforms looked out at us like wooden men, without blinking an eye or shifting their position.

Then quickly Myrdhinn drew me behind a rock. I felt a swimming of the senses and like the bursting of a bubble in my ears, sounds began again. Somewhere near the smoke, a multitude was shouting.

Stiffly, Myrdhinn shook out a pill for each of us The sounds died as time froze around us again, and nothing moved but ourselves.

We resumed our journey along the ravine.

We came abreast of the Middle Fort, only five hundred feet wide, but very strong and well built. Here, too, the sentries looked out at us and let us pass without alarm.

Now we could see that the smoke arose outside of the walls of the North Fort. A great crowd of people were gathered there, upon the broad flat plain I have previously described.

Myrdhinn calmly led the way, almost into the crowd, and I followed with some trepidation. If the effects of this drug should wear away unexpectedly, being old and perhaps uncertain in duration, we would be torn to scraps before Myrdhinn could reach for his vial.

We came to a little eminence and looked down upon horror.

Directly across from us, about sixty feet away, was another little mound, likewise unoccupied, as if for some religious reason. Beginning there, as also from our mound, a low earthen roadway ran, elevated a foot above the level of the plain, and about twelve feet wide. These two roadways ran parallel to each other for a little more than a quarter of a mile, where they were joined by a curve.

The roadways and curve were thick with people, facing the enclosure. Here the ground was hidden by a pavement of limestone slabs, upon which many fierce fires were burning, a little distance apart.

Between the fires were two lines of men, armed with sticks and whips. We could see that our captured comrades had been compelled to run between these lines, exposed to the cruel blows of their tormentors, until from weakness they could no longer leap through the many fires and must of necessity fall into one and be destroyed in great pain.

It was obvious that even the strongest of men had little or no hope of surviving such an ordeal, and indeed we later learned that if a captive should manage to cover the entire circuit of the enclosure, he did not earn release thereby, but was forced to run and leap, again and again, until the inevitable end.

Looking where a knot of men were clustered, whose slow, slow squirming motion showed us that there was, for their own time, violent movement, we saw the stern, heroic face of Hayonwatha.

We had come in time, but not a moment too soon!

"Stay you here," I muttered, and unsheathing my sword I bounced down from the mound.

At first I cut at the men before me, but I soon found that their passive resistance was not to be overborne. Though I might hew the arm from one, or slash the viscera out of another, it did no good, for the example did not frighten those about in time for them to react and withdraw from my path. I might waste all of the power of the drug and yet not hack through that statuesque gathering.

So I took the shortest way and leapt through a fire. In the time of those about me, it must have been a roaring, terrifying blaze.

On the contrary, I could see each pointed flame very distinctly. I was not burned or scorched as I passed through it. There was no smell of fire upon my clothing, nor was I more than faintly warmed.

So I came to the cluster around my blood-brother, and hurling them right and left, I sheathed my sword, threw him across my back and returned by the way I had come. In all that way, he did not twist or writhe in my grip.

As I reached the mound again, I saw faces turned toward the mound and knew that Myrdhinn had stood in one position long enough to be observed by those around him. The men I had attacked were beginning to fall toward the ground, but had not quite reached it, and upon their faces expressions of pain had just begun to form.

Those who saw Myrdhinn appear (suddenly to them) must have been astounded. I chuckled at their dismay at the unaccountable disappearance of their last captive, simultaneously with the advent and equally sudden disappearance of a white-robed, white-bearded ancient man, who for a moment trod their sacred mound and vanished into thin air. How could they construe this in any other manner than to suppose that the gods were displeased with them?

Such an occurrence must necessarily dishearten them and weaken their courage.

So it proved. We lay in seclusion, where we could see the multitude, during the time we were waiting for the effect of the drug to wear away. It squirmed and seethed on the plain, like a disturbed hill of ants, scurrying panic-stricken and aimlessly in search of an intruder. It streamed, infinitely slowly, toward the entrances of the North Fort.

Occasionally we pressed Hayonwatha back upon the

soft turf, and he strove to rise, though after we had done this three times he stopped his sluggish struggling, and the beginnings of a smile, very curious and horrible to see, could be discerned. Then we knew that we had remained in one position long enough for him to recognize us and to understand that all was well.

Before he had finished his smile, the power passed from us with a rush.

Quickly Myrdhinn explained, forced Hayonwatha to take a pellet, and we did likewise.

Instantly we started back along the road we had come. Somewhere, far behind us, thirty thousand lances were marching upon Miapan, and their commanders must hasten to take their proper posts!

20

The Fall of Miapan

"I once knew a wise woman of Caledonia who had the gift of seeing," said Myrdhinn thoughtfully, staring out over our earthworks across the plain at the lights of Miapan and the stars above.

"It was her prophecy to me that should I seek to the westward when the time was ripe, there should I surely find the Land of the Dead. Well, I am in a western country of which she could have had no knowledge, and we have wandered far in it, yet there is nothing here to indicate the proximity of an earthly paradise. Other things which she foresaw have come to pass and I hesitate to believe her misled in this matter.

"But all my studies of the stars do not confirm her statements. Perhaps the time has not yet come."

"What do the stars say?" I asked, shivering in the cold wind.

"Too little. I feel that something is being concealed from me. All that I can learn is that something evil is about to befall, and soon."

"I know that myself. Look you, Myrdhinn. Two weeks we have been here, and to what good? First they meet us on the plain in pitched battle and we lose a thousand men. Then we attack the walls and find that they have developed bows and arrows since the death of their Kukulcan who forbade them to use such an innovation. True, their bows are not good and their arrows unfeathered, but with a strong pull even their archery finds a mark at the distance they shoot at. The fact is, Myrdhinn, that another two weeks of this will bring snow upon us and our army will disband in spite of all we can do.

"We can't carry on a long siege without proper provisions in this harsh, unfriendly country, and we have no reserves to fall back on. We are fighting an agricultural people who are well provisioned. On the contrary, our allies are a hunting people who have little thought for the morrow, if they are fed today. Our resources are used up, Myrdhinn. Snow means defeat. That is what *I* read in the stars."

Myrdhinn shook his head.

"Nay, this is a personal evil, meant for me alone. See yonder. There floats the Ghoul, the dark star—in my house, and in the ascendant."

"I know nought of mystic lore, nothing more than finding my way north by the Plow. I cannot help you."

"True," he said, somberly. "You are a man of war. Well, let us to thoughts of war. How are the ballistae coming?"

"Forty and six are ready to move up tomorrow. Fifty more will be complete within a week. Of arrow engines we have three score. That total used up all of the clamps. I have had enough boulders dug up to last three days. Arrows are plentiful and fire-lances are being made. I should say that day after tomorrow we may

commence such a rain of missiles into the North Fort
that they will be forced to evacuate."

"Good. Let us hope for a speedy conclusion to this
bloody affair. What is that?"

A high wail began to our left, rose to a shriek and
soared above us like a screaming ghost.

"A whistling arrow from a sentry," I snapped,
startled and angry because of it. "Something is wrong
in the artillery enclosure. Look, there are flames! An
attack, Myrdhinn, a night attack! They are burning our
engines!"

I set my bone whistle to my lips and blew a mighty
blast.

Aztlan shot out of its sleep in a hurry. Three companies formed on the plain, and as I led them off at
the double, the clouds, which had been scattering, came
together again and rain pelted down upon us as though
the heavens were weeping to watch us.

We met the raiding-party in the hollow of the eastern ravine. It was a dreary battle, with nothing in it to
warm the blood. Darkness became complete, save when
occasionally broken by very distant and unseasonable
flashes of lightning. Nothing was right about this war,
even the elements had turned against us, I thought, not
realizing then that but for this unexpected and untimely
shower we would most likely have lost our entire park
of siege weapons.

The rain was cold and froze upon our weapons and
clothing. Many wounded died that night from exposure,
or were drowned in the loose mud which washed down
from the walls nearest the fortress.

They had ladders out against the walls, and hoping
to cut off their retreat, I led a charge to capture these,
but most of them were already drawn inside and we
were destroyed by the stones which plunged down upon
us as we clawed vainly at the slippery sides of the ravine
in an attempt to follow. Three hundred men died use-
lessly that night, with nothing gained for so many lives.
Fifty of them were Valiants.

And the taunts from the wall next day burnt our brains like fire.

Crazy with rage, I besought Myrdhinn for help. Twenty engines were totally destroyed, and more than half the ballistae were so weakened that they must be rebuilt.

The others were placed, some on the plain, others so that a steady downpour of stones could be kept up across the various ravines at the sides of the North Fort. But although we knew that we were doing execution, we heard no sounds of pain or fear from within, only jeers and mockery.

Again I begged Myrdhinn to use sorcery, but he refused as usual.

"No. Let it be a clean, honest war, with no magic mixed into it. However," he said, "now that you have learned that you cannot butt down these walls like a brainless aurochs, I will show you how the People of the Long House took the City of the Snake with little loss.

"Set up three ballistae for me, at the edge of the wood fronting the eastern wall, and tonight we will give them a surprise. We made some eggs in Thendara that will hatch out the Thunder Bird inside of Miapan!"

Just before dark we lit fires at the edge of the wood. Then up came the engineers trundling barrows laden with dark spheres, each of twenty-pound weight and about nine inches thick. Under Myrdhinn's direction, one of these was placed in a fire convenient to the nearest ballista. I could see then that its composition was partly of metal, for the hue changed with heat, from bronze to golden and then to shimmering pallor. It glowed, and little crackling noises could be heard inside as rainbow colors raced across its surface.

Finally a glowing cloud surrounded it as the fiery vapors pent within began to issue forth from its pores.

Myrdhinn's assistants then removed it from the fire with tongs, placed it in the ballista pan and knocked out the chock.

It seemed to sail from us slowly, a train of glowing

vapor following it as it soared over the ravine and fell into the city.

A deep rumble followed, the ground shook, an awful flare of light made the stars dim, and in the ensuing hush we heard the sounds of lamentation and of fear within the ramparts of Miapan.

Now another flew, shining even more brightly with the heat of its passing through the air.

Over the walls and out of sight it went, and instantly burst with a dreadful *splitting* crash, as when lightning rends a large oak from leaves to roots. Again the uprush of ghastly light, shining through the chinks of the log palisade and the wicket gates. Then utter darkness and the long screaming of the wounded and burned.

"What is it?" I gasped. "Hellfire?"

"Nay, son, naught but the fiery principles of earth, combined and blended, heated to bursting-point and ignited by the further friction of the air as each container rushes through that medium and is heated more than its walls can stand. Weakened, it bursts and drenches all with unquenchable fire.

"Have you forgotten how Ovid, in speaking of the leaden missiles used by slingers, writes:

> *Hermes was fired, as in the clouds he hung;*
> *So the cold bullet that with fury slung*
> *From Balearic engines, mounts on high,*
> *Glows in the whirl, and burns along the sky.*

"That gave me the idea, but the composition of the fiery material is old. Archimedes used this same preparation in another form to inflame the Roman ships at the siege of Syracuse, and Hannibal used it in still another form when he split the rocks of the Alps and let his armies and elephants through. No, it is not new, only forgotten and that is well: else war might be too terrible."

Other missiles were now coming out of the fires, and the engineers began a persistent dropping upon the

North Fort. One by one, they flew and fell, these awesome dangerous products of Myrdhinn's lore—terrible, hairy stars, soaring in the black night sky, bringing death, terror and destruction in their train.

The ground shook constantly, houses were blazing within, but the Mias steadfastly refused to give up, and dawn came and found them still in possession and strong enough to hurl our attack into the ravine again and pile it up there in confusion and utter rout.

At the same time, Aztlan, Nor-um-Bega, and a large force of Chichamecans charged across the plain and reached the walls, but were forced to retire in a shower of arrows, atlatl darts and slingstones, leaving many dead and most of their courage behind them.

Tolteca held the river safe and did not break ranks to attack, there being an almost perpendicular earth wall before them which it would have been suicide to scale.

Now that daylight had come, we ceased throwing Myrdhinn's awesome missiles, though the ballistae kept on pounding the works with boulders, knocking great holes in the palisades, through which those arrow engines that could discharge phalaricas managed to place those flaming javelins with fine precision into both the North and Middle Forts.

We left the South Fort mostly untouched, hoping to take the other works first and drive the defenders out into the lower section where they would be compactly crowded and at our mercy.

Again night came, and again the fire-balls flew and burst and scattered death. Sometime during those hours, the North Fort was quietly evacuated and at dawn of the second day of this new horror of war, I launched a half-hearted sally, with what remained of my Valiants, giving Man-who-burns-hair the command and allowing him to carry the bronze eagle of the Sixth, that they might know courage.

I really expected it to be thrown back again, but an attempt had to be made or the whole siege must be given up. Myrdhinn's fire-balls were gone!

On the contrary, it reached and went over the wall without facing a dart or stone. I saw the eagle wave violently as its bearer danced on the firing-platform of the wall.

My trumpet caroled. Answering brays went up, and Aztlan and Nor-um-Bega poured into the North Fort!

By midmorning we had all the force which had held the plain placed to best advantage inside the walls, had set up a pair of ballistae to batter away the resistance ahead and were ready to advance along the isthmus.

As you can see by the map, two crescent-shaped mounds had long ago been built to barricade the narrowest section of the isthmus and protect the Middle Fort. These had been recently joined by a log wall several feet thick, its components inextricably tangled together, and sharpened stakes pointing out at us from every cranny.

Here the Mian warriors defied us and our artillery. After an hour of stone-throwing which did little good against this heap of splintered logs, we advanced, fought and retired with considerable loss.

Then I had a battering-ram constructed, but this only beat the logs more tightly together and our adversaries laughed at us while they cut our engineers down.

I was wild at being held back by this paltry agger, and calling a meeting of tribunes, I asked for suggestion.

Vicinius suggested using the testudo to reach the barricade and then a sudden sally. It seemed the only thing to do. Nothing but a direct assault would carry it, for the position could not be flanked owing to the steep declivities of loose and slippery earth which fell away on either side into the deep ravine.

So I instructed my picked Valiants, and in phalanxes three companies moved forward with shields in front, over our heads and at each side, all closely overlapping.

Above us, as we trotted, the boulders from the ballistae hummed and thudded into the twin mounds, black with fighting-men.

Their darts and stones rattled on our tortoise sides

like hail, but did little damage. Then, as we neared the log wall, the engineers ceased firing lest we be struck. We charged, flinging down our shields upon the spikes, and over this protection we reached the top.

Then the cry from our men might have been heard in Rome, as they broke ranks and, leaving cover, came charging down to support us.

We desperately needed help, being greatly outnumbered. The fighting was furious. It was hack and kill, pull out the blade and dodge, recover, poise and stab with pugio and gladius against the thrust of long lances. Reeling under a rain of blows, we fought and fell. Vicinius died there, and Intinco the Caledonian killed his slayer and fell dead across his friend's body—and women were to mourn them both in Adriutha.

I had less than twenty men around me when our men came up the wall like a wave and, cheering, surrounded us and drove the Mias back, back, fiercely contesting the way until they were pressed against the Great Gateway of the South Fort and could go no farther.

The commander who had been in charge of the resistance sank to his knees with weakness from loss of blood. All his men were dead and he the last to defy us. Twice he strove to shorten his lance and fall upon it, but could not.

Then, through our press, came leaping Man-who-burns-hair.

"I know him!" he howled. "My master who scourged my back to rags! He is mine!"

He whipped out his knife. The kneeling man looked up dauntlessly.

"Ha, slave. Wolves yap at the dying cougar!"

With a last quick motion he swept the antler circlet from his head and leaned forward that his scalp might be the easier taken, and as his remorseless enemy snatched away the bloody trophy, we knew the Middle Fort was ours.

Across the Great Gateway the defenders, though they must now have been fighting entirely without hope, had flung up a barricade of their house furnishings, dead bodies of animals and people, to make three parallel walls which we must take one after another. It being nearly dark, we made no attempt to essay this system of defense, but occupied ourselves in moving up twenty ballistae and catapults to command their forum, which was situated in the center of the South Fort, around a dewpond, their only remaining water supply.

The defenders were engaged during most of the night in strengthening their defenses, though loud voices and much waving of torches were reported by our stationerii and I took this to mean that there was some dissension among them.

What it might be we could not conceive, unless some counseled surrender and others would not agree.

We learned in the chill before dawn, when a savage sally broke out on the river side of the fort and at least five thousand men hurtled down the embankment, across a terrace and came howling upon the sleeping, poorly picketed camp which guarded our fleet of 250 coracles. And Tolteca, whose charge they were, broke its ranks like cravens, and let the Mias through!

So this fighting-force, still free and united to rally and attack again, made off down the river in search of allies from some of the tiny hilltop forts if there were any yet untaken by the wild rovers.

At dawn, a hawk-visaged man clambered over the barricade of corpses, to the sound of Mian trumpets. He was clad in the white doeskin shirt, embroidered with pearly shell beads, that is the emblem of a herald in Alata. In his left hand he bore a green branch as a request for a parley.

The stationerii let him through to me.

He bowed, but not humbly, and I could almost hear that stiff, proud neck creak as he bent his head and asked for terms.

"I have no terms to offer you," I said, "but immediate laying down of all your arms, removal of your defensive walls and preparation for an evacuation to take place by midday."

His eyes flashed, but he answered not a word as he turned to go.

"After that is done, I will give you my terms," I called after him, and chuckled fiercely to myself as I smote my armored chest with my clenched fist. *Marcus! Marcus! Look down and see this day!*

21

The Passing of Myrdhinn

I sat in my booth near the edge of the wood, looking out across the plain, while shaving. Along the isthmus and out of the North Fort were marching companies bearing tied bundles of darts, arrows and lances to be stacked above the piles of hatchets and knives, that all might be burned together.

Somehow, my pleasure in the sight was waning, knowing what was to follow, and knowing it to be foul treachery by any rules of war.

Myrdhinn came in and sat down. His face likewise was gloomy.

"Have you made plans for the evacuation, Ventidius?"

"Amnesty for all Tlapallicans who change their allegiance. Death to the rest and death to all Mias!"

Myrdhinn started from his seat in horror. I calmly went on shaving.

"That is massacre!"

"Extermination," I corrected.

"Ventidius, you have become too hard," Myrdhinn said softly. "You are no longer the eager fellow who sought adventures and new lands with the zest of a boy. Is nothing left of the old Ventidius? Does nothing remain but the man of war?"

"Nothing," I said quietly. "Did you expect more? I was born knowing of war's alarms. My mother fled from a burning city to save her life and mine. My father died there. I have been bred to war; it is all I know.

"There was one soft spot in my heart. Marcus had that. I loved the boy. You know what happened. On the Egg my heart became all hard.

"Have you forgotten the vow we made in that reeking pit? Have you forgotten that we swore to avenge Marcus?"

He looked at me steadily.

"How many lives do you need in repayment for one? Have you not heard the saying of Hernin, the Bard of the college of Llanveithin: 'The brave is never cruel'?"

"I never knew him. His words are words for others, not for me!" I crashed my fist down on the bench and stood up. "My last word, Myrdhinn. Death for all Mias!"

He took my hand and gently urged me down again.

"Ventidius, listen. I have just come out of Miapan. They are burying the dead there, son. If you were to see it, I think you would be moved to pity."

"What do I know of pity? What *can* such as I know of pity? Many times you have called me a man of war and I have not felt offended, for truly that *is* all I know —all that I am. Here in this new country I have carved out a dominion that is mine. My people worship me as a living god of war who delights in blood and offerings of bleeding hearts. I tell you, Myrdhinn, I am beginning to *enjoy* the sight of suffering!

"There is no love in my heart for anything—except perhaps for my wife and son. She very likely will soon be facing death at the hands of those Mian refugees gone down the river—and I idle here. No pity, no mercy, Myrdhinn. The earlier these folk are exterminated, the sooner I shall be free to set off to the rescue of my wife and the women of my nation.

"The civilization of these Mias rests on a foundation of corpses. Blood soaks the ground of every foot of Tlapallan. The cry of those oppressed by the Mias rises to the stars for vengeance. Better that they be blotted out forever than be permitted to go and rebuild again their cruel empire. They showed us, strangers and castaways, no mercy, no pity. That was left for their slaves to do!

"At midday, Myrdhinn, I turn Aztlan upon them, and if the Hodenosaunee hold back, let them also beware!"

"That would be a civil war."

"Call it that. But there is no danger. Your men are as eager for blood as are mine. Nothing could hold them back from revenge for which they have so long waited. Not even you!"

"If I can," he said quietly, "will you call off your hordes?"

I laughed.

"*If* you can. But that would be a miracle, and the day for miracles has passed. Unless—"

A thought gave me pause. "You intend sorcery?"

"Not sorcery. I have told you I have forsworn it. Nothing could tempt me to use sorcery again and lose my soul. I will plead with them, reason with them."

That was funny. *As well,* I thought, *plead with the wolves that have just brought down a stag, but have yet to rend him and fill their bellies.*

"Tell me," I asked curiously, "why this change of heart? You loved Marcus. You wanted to avenge him."

"I have been in the fort and heard the moans of the dying, seen noble ladies tenderly caring for their wounded, mourning their losses, weeping over dead babies."

"That is war. It has always been so. A rat protects its children, cares for them! Should not other vermin, such as Mias, do the same?"

He looked at me in horror, but spoke sadly:

"Rats do not bury their dead, Ventidius. The Mias have thrown up a great mound of earth over the bodies

of those brave men who held the two crescents of the
Middle Fort and there they are praying to the Sun to
receive those souls. Elsewhere the dead are being in-
terred separately by their surviving loved ones. The
warriors are being buried with their hunting-gear, the
women place in the ground among their household
articles, their grain, their cooking-utensils.

"The little children—

"I saw, Ventidius, one little chap, a fine boy of whom
any father might be proud. He was lying in his little
grave with his toys by him. His right hand had been
placed in a jar of food that he might not be hungry
in the other world. You see? The men can hunt for
their living, the women work for it, but the wee things
can do neither and must be able to help themselves.
So the food jars are set close! In his left hand he had
a little red ball stuffed with feathers."

He gazed at me keenly.

"A little red ball—stuffed with feathers?"

I repeated the words in my mind. My brain seemed
dull, my head heavy. All at once I felt old. Such a ball
had I given my little son, and it was the pride of his
heart. He had waved me godspeed with it when I had
marched away from Aztlan.

And Myrdhinn, the old gray fox, had seen and remembered as he remembered everything!

It was true, of course. All that he had said was true.
These Mias were not demons, not inhuman—at least
not more than other men—they knew loyalty and
courage. I had met them in war and I knew that. Their
women were beautiful and lovable in the eyes of their
own men, and their children were beloved by both. We
had smashed the system; must we exterminate the race
as well?

A hard lump seemed to melt in my breast. I no
longer hated anybody and I wanted to weep, but did
not know how—I had forgotten long ago.

"Go and speak to the men. Aztlan and Tolteca, too.
If you can win them over, we will let the people go."

Gladness came into Myrdhinn's eyes. He gazed at me fondly and went out.

I did not follow, but sat there alone. I wanted to think upon my little son so far away. That is why I did not hear what Myrdhinn had to say to the army, but a great clamor and shouting brought me to my feet and with sword in hand I ran out to defend his life from the men he had roused to fury. I stood there with open mouth and must have looked like a fool. They were cheering him!

Cheering! Aye, the men from Adriutha and Caranay, side by side with my warriors of Aztlan! Even the red-haired killers from Nor-um-Bega and the savage Chichamecan barbarians! All were cheering.

And that, I think, was Myrdhinn's greatest triumph!

By midday, Miapan was evacuated, and on the plain the people, mostly women and children, but still a great host, stood between our armed ranks and received my orders.

"March fifteen days' journey straight westward," I commanded, "then directly south to the Hot Lands of Atala, whence you came. Laggards or deserters will be killed." And I detailed ten companies of moormen to follow a day's journey behind, for that purpose.

One man in each hundred was allowed to keep his arms for hunting, otherwise all weapons were burned at the time of their exodus.

These instructions, I estimated, would take them into the open uninhabited grasslands, where the hairy cattle would feed them and they would meet no enemies, and looking upon them as they marched away without lamentations or backward looks, still proud in defeat, I could not but feel that after all this was the better way and Marcus, somewhere, would be pleased.

That day ended organized Mian resistance. The Eagle had conquered the Snake.

Although on widely separated hilltops throughout the broken Empire a few thousands of refugees still held out, I knew that their forts, however well built, were doomed to fall, for without exception they were watered only by dewponds and occasional rainfall, and being constructed only as temporary refuge for people living close at hand, they could not stand a siege. Indeed, they had never faced a prolonged siege before our coming, for that was not a Chichamecan habit. We felt that we could safely leave these islands of Tlapallan to be overswept by the sea of Chichamecans around them.

Accordingly, in five coracles, all that remained of our fleet, I, Myrdhinn, my tribunes of Aztlan, and other doughty men, totaling over a hundred, set out toward our river fort, which by now must be in danger from those still unsubdued and merciless men who had stolen our fleet. Short shrift could our women expect from them!

Following along the shores pounded the Aztlan legion and behind them the unruly hordes of Tolteca, now burning to wipe out their shame.

Hayonwatha came with us, but his people invested Miapan, to wait for Myrdhinn's return, and the Norum-Begans, fewer in number, set off for their far city, laden with loot.

Down the little river we went, entered the larger stream, finding evidences of those who fled before us, and days later came to the junction of the two waterways where lay our fort—and none too soon.

It was attacked by the Mias, but not taken. On the walls, from our distant view, we could see the short wicked arms of ballistae, and catapults, jerking stones and javelins into the mass of coracles below, while clouds of arrows, darts and slingstones were flying from both sides. We raised a mighty yell, plunged our paddles deep and almost flew down the broad Ohion.

As we came near them, we were seen from the fort and greeted loudly. Tumbling into their flimsy craft, the land force fell back and were coming up to meet us when our following legion burst out into sight.

Dismayed at the sight of this pursuing force and

greatly outnumbered, the Mias swung their prows about and made off downstream.

Our coracles shot into pursuit, hailed wildly as we passed the fort. I made out the dear form of Gold Flower of Day, waving a fluttering scarf. I swung my paddle in response and was seen.

Before we had left the fort far behind, we began to overhaul the last of the coracles, which now turned about to meet and destroy us. I stood up and fitted an arrow to my bow, well dressed with gray goose-feathers, but before I shot I made out from my greater height above the water an almost impossible sight.

Up the river was coming toward us, slowly against the current, a craft which I had never again expected to see. It was a Saxon dragon-ship!

Without an oar out to give it headway, it forged toward us with a bone in its teeth, swiftly coming nearer as we flew, pursuers and pursued, down the stream toward it.

Now it was seen and recognized as a new menace by the fugitive Mias. A trumpet recalled those who had fallen back to meet us, and the whole mass of coracles drew compactly together, bristling with armed men, ready for whatever might occur.

As we drew almost together, an armored man sprang into view on the ship's tiny deck. He steadied himself with a hand on the dragon's neck, while above him its movable red tongue waggled viciously as though it were hissing at all of us. He shaded his eyes and peered at us as we rushed toward each other.

All at once I recognized him.

Guthlac! Guthlac, last of the Saxons! Guthlac, whom we had thought slain by the fish-people of the swamps!

I raised a long hail across the narrowing waters.

"Turn, Guthlac, turn! These are enemies!"

He knew me and swung his ax wildly to signify that he had heard.

"Well met, Wealas!" he shouted, then seized a shell trumpet that hung there and blew an echoing blast.

At once we saw what had towed the ship so strongly up the stream, for breaking through the surface in a shower of spray came dozens of the hideous and scaly Piasa, who cast off their towing-collars and ropes and hurled themselves into the vanguard of the Mias.

Frantically they backwatered and tried to turn aside, but the Piasa tore wide holes in their bark craft and they sank in the rushing waters.

We withdrew, guessing that these creatures could distinguish little between friend and foe among the various races of man, and contented ourselves with maintaining an arrow fire into the confused mass of struggling enemies.

Now more Piasa tumbled over the sides of the dragon-ship and with exulting croaks took to the water, while from downstream came churning up a frothy shoal of others.

It was soon over. Not a coracle floated on the stream, and from the bank where our little flotilla had taken refuge we saw the waters of the Ohion slipping redly toward the sea, while the monstrous man-like creatures, glutted, rolled playfully in the greasy ripples, supping up the floating scraps that bobbed about in the eddies.

At a series of notes from Guthlac's trumpet, some of these caught upon the trailing ropes and drew the dragon-ship upon our shore, just as our panting followers came hurrying up, to recoil in horror at the frightful beasts that stood up in the shallows and strode grimly toward them.

Guthlac leapt nimbly down and came laughing forward among his horde, forcing them back with rough cuffs which they did not resent, but fawned upon him like hounds upon the master. Then he came up and seized my hand, shaking it stoutly.

"A good killing, Wealas. Woden loves such tribute. Long since, I thought you in Hela's halls."

"And I you, Guthlac. How is it that you have made yourself king among the Piasa?"

"The Piasa?" He looked blank, then laughed. "Oh,

you mean my fish-folk. That may be how they are named by the red men, but they call themselves Gronks."

"Then they have a language men may learn?"

"Oh yes! A good language, mostly grunts, croaks and hisses, but they do not talk to men very often— usually they prefer to act."

Looking at the sinister refuse floating in the river, I could well believe him.

At Guthlac's command they took themselves out of the way, to a narrow strip of sandy shore, where with their long talons they scooped out shallow holes to accommodate their short unbending tails.

Presently they squatted above these holes and gazed at us coldly and, I thought, with appetite.

"After you deserted me to the tender mercies of the swamp denizens," Guthlac began ironically, "I considered myself a dead man. They hustled me off over quaking morasses to an odd dank huddle of cluster hovels deep inland. Here they thrust me into a moss-grown hut of wet and rotting logs and brought me raw fish to eat.

"There I remained for a long time in dread of death, until I plucked up courage and ventured out. I was greeted with every sign of simple worship, and it was not long before I realized that they were in awe of me. When I made them understand that I wanted my ax, it was immediately brought to me, and my seaxe as well. Obviously, then, I was not to be killed. I have been treated very well by them.

"It was almost two years before I finally learned enough of their speech to understand why I was preserved and all my companions torn to pieces.

"As you can see, they are on the way toward becoming men. That is their ambition. They imitate men, and they believe that by eating the flesh of people they will sooner become men. Some time ago, one of their eldest announced that from the sea would appear a divine being, partly man, partly fish, who would become their ruler and teach them how to become human.

"When they saw my armor of fish-hide and found that their claws slid off it harmlessly, they took me for this deity, and I have profited by it.

"I have taught them a good deal, given them simple weapons, tried to give them fire, but they would have none of it. Fire makes them vastly afraid; so I have learned to prefer my own food raw in consideration of their feelings.

"I was another year building the ship, doing it mostly alone, though they carried the timbers for me and set them in place according to my orders. When it was done, I sailed along the coast, thinking to follow you, for in that direction you were sailing when we parted.

"We came to open sea, still following southerly, and arrived at a land of little brown people, who call their country Chivim. I taught them the worship of Woden, but could not be happy among them.

"After I had abode there a long time, hearing no word of you, I realized that I was searching in the wrong direction and that you must have rounded the cape I left behind me, and instead of going again to sea, you had probably turned north, following the sea-coast. So, the next spring, my subjects towed me away from Chivim.

"There was never any lack of food. The Gronks can follow a fish under the water, doubling and darting till it is caught. We lived well, both at sea and searching along the coast.

"We went far north. You would scarcely dream how vastly far this land must stretch. We came to a point where the water numbed my subjects, and ice mountains floated in the sea. We turned back without any news of you, and that was another year.

"Back along the seacoast we went, sometimes capturing a fisherman too scared to tell us anything, until one day we saw wreckage in a cove and I knew it to be the *Prydwen*. We had passed close by on the north-ward voyage, but high tide must have covered it, for only a few timbers projected even then among the waves.

"So I landed there. We spied upon the outpost and took it, the Gronks feeding upon the garrison but before all were dead, I learned what had befallen you, that there was war in the interior and that my friends" (he stressed the word in a sardonic way, I thought) "were fighting a powerful people. So, as my subjects cannot live long away from water, we hastened back to that river mouth and, searching up the stream of the Misconzebe, found the right tributary at length and came hither as you see, and almost too late to join you in the fighting."

"But not too late to join us in peace," said Myrdhinn enthusiastically. "Give up your savage subjects and dwell with men once more. We are kings among the heathen now."

Guthlac shook his head.

"I also am a king, and my subjects are no less faithful than yours. My place is with them. Yet I will bide with you a time, for I have work that must be done."

He grunted an order, and all of his followers, except a dozen to pull the ship, splashed back into the river and made off downstream.

Myrdhinn and I were carried back to the ship by two stout Piasa, and when Guthlac resumed his place in the prow, we were towed upriver to the fort, convoyed by our five coracles and followed by the warriors on the shore.

Royal was our welcome, as loving arms enfolded us, and though many of the women were lorn and husbandless because of the fighting, there was no keening for the dead.

Happy faces met us and tears were reserved for the privacy of the weik-waums.

At night I observed Myrdhinn glumly eying the stars. I clapped him on the shoulder.

"How now for your prophecies of disaster? You said the stars portended doom for you, but the war is over and all is well. Come! Admit that even you can sometimes be wrong!"

"Often I have been wrong, Ventidius, but never the stars. There is a destiny yet to be completed."

And he would say nothing more that night.

In the morning a festive day was declared. During our absence the women had pounded flat a broad surface of hard ground to be used as a ball court. The Azteca are very fond of this game, sometimes wagering everything they possess upon the sport. It is played with a bouncing ball which must pass through a stone hoop, set perpendicularly in the wall of the court, to score a point.

As the opening is but little larger than the ball itself and because a large number of players are striving to secure the ball for their own side, goals are difficult to make and people have been known to wager even their clothing against the possibility of one, which, being made, drives them naked from the spectators amid laughter.

Guthlac, seeing several bet upon points which were not made and leave thus in shame and nudity, declared roundly that the trick was impossible. I laughed at him.

"I can do it easily," I said. "Even Myrdhinn, aged as he is, finds no difficulty in it."

"Do it, then, and I will believe you. I have a jar of wine on board my ship that says the feat cannot be done."

Myrdhinn smiled. "That wine *I* shall earn, Ventidius."

Pressing back, he strode into the ball court.

A herald shouted:

"Make way! Make way for the Tecutli Quetzalcoatl!"

And the people bowed low before him as he took the ball.

He tucked up his long robes, ran, bounded, and in midair (as it must be done) threw the ball through the hoop without touching the sides, scoring a perfect point. How the people shouted!

He returned to his seat near me, and the game was resumed while Guthlac sent one of the Piasa down to the river after the wine.

Myrdhinn took it, sniffed the aroma with appreciation and laughed. I handed him my drinking-horn.

"You must pay me a drink for the use of that!" I cried.

Guthlac said nothing, but smiled a strange smile. Whether it was the sudden gleam of ferocity in his eyes, quickly masked, or perchance only a wild suspicion, I know not, but all at once I distrusted the Saxon.

"Hold, Myrdhinn!" I shouted.

Too late! He had drained the cup to the dregs. His face went pale and haggard and he looked ancient beyond the power of words to tell. He struggled to speak, choked, then said thickly, "So this is the dark destiny the stars withheld!" and sank into the arms of Cronach Hên, the last remaining of his nine faithful bards.

Before we could gather our wits, Cronach Hên let his harp fall, laid Myrdhinn gently down and spitting curses like a cat, he dashed at Guthlac.

One of the Piasa was quicker than any of us. He caught up the bard, sinking his long curved talons deep through the flesh, hooking them among the ribs. Then easily he tore him asunder as a man might rend a roasted pigeon.

Women screamed in the crowd, and Guthlac croaked a command to his monstrous following as he backed warily among them.

"Now I have satisfied the souls of my brother and my men! Now I have avenged myself upon the murderer who led us here, who sacrificed us all in a mad search for a worthless land. Come, Wealas, take me if you can!"

The Piasa sprang at us, long scaly arms spreading wide to grapple, talons hooked to tear.

Though the sight of these horrors chilled the hearts of my men, none refused the battle, but would not at first close in, hurling hatchets and spears from a little distance, which they kept easily, for these creatures were agile only in the water.

So, during our first surprise, his group won almost through us to the river gate. With twenty Valiants about me, hastily rearmored, we fell upon him there.

"Stand back, Wealas," he bellowed at me, as he retreated deeper among his Piasa, swinging his short ax to fend off spear strokes from three Hodenosaunee who were pressing him close.

"Stand back, lest I cleave ye to the teeth!"

The three red men rushed recklessly in, shouting their war-cry, "Sassakway! Sassakway!" The Piasa seized them. I heard bones crack and crunch and three brave souls were fled without a groan or whimper of pain.

I felt immortal. I ran at them.

Guthlac's eyes lit with savage joy. He snapped an order to his creatures. They gave way and opened a lane, through which he strode, buckler to the fore, ax whistling in a glistening circle.

"Take it, Wealas," he roared, and flung it at my head.

It flew harmlessly by. I hurled my pilum.

Now, he understood spears and lances, but he underestimated the difference between them and the Roman pilum.

He laughed and caught the point deftly on his buckler. The bronze head penetrated and clung, the soft copper shank bent, the heavy shaft trailed on the ground and dragged his buckler low.

I leapt forward and stepped upon the shaft. He had one breath of time to realize that he was a dead man, before my shortsword beat down his defending seaxe and shore deep between neck and shoulder.

He fell. Myrdhinn was avenged!

At that instant, I felt myself seized from behind in an agonizing grip.

A Piasa raised me high above his head, and hanging there for an instant I saw Myrdhinn lying in a little open circle in the crowd.

He opened his eyes and caught my gaze, strangely and lovingly as a fond father might follow with his look a willful and erring son who had foolishly plunged himself into danger.

His lips moved. The grip relaxed and I was flung down. Surprisingly, I was not stunned by the impact. I scarcely felt the ground.

As with Antaeus, the earth seemed to give me superhuman strength. I *knew* that I was invincible! The Piasa snatched for me. I laughed at him, brushed his grip away like a feather. I seized him by the scaly throat and broke his neck like a bird's.

All the multitude flung themselves upon the remaining Piasa, forcing them down, overwhelming them by sheer numbers.

I hurried to Myrdhinn and bent over him. I must have been a horrid sight, all dabbled with gore, my armor clawed away and my hands dripping red on his white robes, but he smiled faintly.

"I did it, Ventidius, for you. That time, it *was* sorcery! I gave you all my strength, that you might not die. I have loved you like a son—I never had a son—how could I let you die? God forgive me, I used sorcery again—"

"God will, Myrdhinn," I said softly, but his eyes had closed and I do not know if he heard me or not.

I thought him sped. Then he spoke again, very low, and I bent to catch the words.

"So this is what was meant by the saying that I should find the Land of the Dead—beyond the sunset—at the end of the world. Come then, show me the way! Must I go alone?"

He stared about, but it was plain that he saw none of us.

Suddenly he sat upright and his face glowed with joy.

Out of the west came flying rapidly a great white bird such as I have never seen before. It approached, circled us thrice without alighting or giving voice, and flapped away again, speedily as it had come.

The aged body relaxed. I laid him down with care,

and kneeling there, I buried my face in my hands, for I knew him gone at last.

Over me swept a dreary loneliness. I had lost a dear friend, a revered man whose wisdom had saved me often from my follies. At last, I realized that I had loved him like a parent, but it was too late—too late—I could not tell him now.

Through tears, I saw those around me kneel in parting reverence, and very far away, a white bird flying on and on—into the western sky and far beyond.

So we buried his body, and over it we made a tesselated pavement of colored pebbles, showing a picture of a man treading upon a snake, symbolic of his destruction of the Mian Empire, for his was the glory, seeing that without him all our efforts would have come to naught.

Above his grave we built a large mound, in the following days of our encampment there, but that night the Royanehs of Myrdhinn's young nation demanded the persons of the few remaining Piasa left alive.

I shrugged as I turned away, and the cold-blooded scaly monsters gazed after me, staring with an unblinking fish-look.

What were their thoughts, I wonder, as they saw the people gathering brush and fixing stakes in the ground?

Fire was a mystery to them, strange, cruel water creatures. But they died by it and were long in so doing.

"Houp! Houp!" shouted the dancing warriors, mimicking their death croaks, prancing high, circling the flames.

"Houp! Houp!"

And there were no scalps to take, for nowhere upon their bodies was there any hair.

22

Twenty Years Later

In the northwest, far from Aztlan, near the mountains which fence off the Edge of the World, there dwells today (twenty years after the death of Myrdhinn) a miserable people, called by their neighbors the Flatheads. If they be Mian refugees, I know not, for I have learned of them only by rumor, but their skulls are similarly shaped by binding against a board when the infant is very young.

And in the moorlands, every lonely wanderer got himself a wife, so that many a noble, gently reared Mian lady has drudged away her life in tanning hides, bearing burdens and savage children for a cruel spouse.

From some of these, we know that many perished wandering to the moors. A few may have got through to the Hot Lands of Atala, but most were scattered and slain by those I sent to guard their journey.

So perished the haughty and valiant Mian nation, and with them their far-flung Empire of the Mounds.

Back once more in the cliff dwellings, we have known peace. We led war into the swamps of the Piasa and well-nigh exterminated them.

Tolteca, south of us, is newly turbulent and the time is coming when there must again be war.

In the north, I hear from Hayonwatha, who still lives, though all my British friends are dead from age or battle, that the nation of the Hodenosaunee is growing yet more powerful. My soldiers, or allies, hold all the forts that once represented the Mian frontier. The Chichamecans, too, are friendly.

Your legate, then, wherever he may land, oh my Emperor, will receive a welcome, for all expect the

coming of white men again and the word is out everywhere to receive them kindly and in peace as sons of
the Fair God, Quetzalcoatl, the man who spoke of
peace, but could be stern in war to end it quickly.

Treat my son, Gwalchmai, Hawk of Battle as Myrdhinn once called his godson, kindly I beg. He will be
unaccustomed to great cities, though he has read of
them in Myrdhinn's books and has learned, I fear,
other more dangerous things. He has performed some
peculiar feats that smack of sorcery to me.

Come, then, at once while I still live. I dream of
Roman keels grating on the shingle of Alata. I long to
hear the sounds of Roman trumpets. I have conquered
a continent for Rome, but there is none that will hold
it undivided after I am gone.

Already they forget the Christian prayer that Myrdhinn taught his worshipers, forgetting the meanings of
the words. My Azteca grow restless with liberty and
long to wander.

Come before it is too late. Come and take your
empire!

Vale.

Epilog

I laid down the ancient pages and turned to my veteran friend. "That is the end of the writing," I said.

"But not the end of the story?"

"How can it be? Why wasn't the message carried farther than Key West? What happened to the son of Ventidius? How was the message lost?"

"I think I can guess. Do you know how Key West got its name?"

I shook my head.

"When the Spaniards discovered the island, it was covered with skeletons where a battle had been fought. So many were there that they called it Cayo de los Huessos (Island of the Bones), which was Englished as Key West. Suppose that those bones were the remains of the ship's crew, sent with the message, and killed by the Piasa who had been driven from the Florida swamps by Ventidius' men!"

"Then that perhaps was the real end of the Piasa?" He nodded.

"And the end of Kwalchmai, Ventidius' only son?" I hazarded.

"I wonder," thoughtfully said my veteran friend. "I wonder.

"After all, he was Merlin's godson. If any came out of that battle alive, it must have been he. But that was a thousand years ago, and we shall probably never know."

BOOK TWO

The Ship from Atlantis

1

Merlin's Godson

It was the Year of the Rabbit, in the chronology of Aztlan, and the day-sign being fortunate a great festival was taking place a few miles above the spot where the Misconzebe, Grandfather of Rivers, mingles with the salt waters of the Gulf.

For a month the invited guests had been arriving at Fortress Tollan, which held the entrance to this broad highway to the north and the rich lands of Tlapallan. The reeds which gave that district its name were gone, trampled into the mud by thousands of feet or woven into temporary shelters by the visitors. The shore was lined with watercraft.

Hide bull-boats, birch-bark and elm canoes or those carved from a single log rocked at anchor or lay bottom up until they might be needed. Decorated in fanciful patterns, they lay in colorful rows near the crowded city of weik-waums, wickiups and tepees which had sprung up around the palisade spined, earthen walled fortress. Few of those who had come to this mightiest of peace councils gave the fleet more than a passing glance. The novelty was beyond.

Drawn up in the shallows, well fastened against the tugging current, lay what any Briton would have recognized as a Saxon pirate ship. In this Year of our Lord 616, they crowded the rivers and estuaries of Britain, but in Alata (as North America was known at that time), there was only one. Built almost twenty years before of stout oak planks, caulked with pitch and bison hair, it had been well cared for awaiting this moment.

It was seventy-seven feet in length and clinker built. At the prow and stern the decks were raised. In between, considerably lower, was a partial main deck or fighting platform, but the rowers' pit was open to the weather. Here were rowing benches, fifteen to each side, with a gangway down the center. Rows of wooden shields, emblazoned with the totems of those young Aztecs who had been chosen to wield the carven oars, were fastened to the sides to protect them from arrows or waves.

It was a well found ship and it needed to be, for in it the son of the King of the World's Edge was to set forth eastward to discover the world. From the dragon's head with golden mane at the stem post, to the tail at the stern decorated with glittering mica plates, it blazed with color. The hull was striped with red and white, fox tails hung for standards and weather vanes and a burnished copper band encircled the single mast.

The oar holes were provided with shutters to keep out the sea when under sail, as were the tiny windows in the commander's cabin at the poop and the arsenal and stores hold just forward. To the crowd, which continually milled and shifted along the shore, the *Feathered Serpent* was a great wonder.

They were as motley in appearance as their dwellings and their canoes. Many tribes and nations were represented here upon this gala day. Yonder strode caciques of the Azteca with saw edged, obsidian toothed swords hanging by their sides. Feather fringed shields adorned their arms and plumed helmets graced their heads. Among them walked scarred fighters from the western moorlands armed with stone knife and tomahawk, short horn bows upon their backs. Some of these wore bison headdresses; others wore warbonnets betokening the taking of many coups.

Those who had come north from the great swamps bore blowpipes made of cane and carried slings and a pouch of stones, while the representatives from the Long House of the Five Nations looked with arrogance

upon their smaller brothers in arms. These were tall
men, distinguished by a single eagle feather fastened
into a central roach of hair, and they had come far
south from their homeland to attend the gathering.
They were a fierce people, these Hodenosaunee, but
none wore war-paint for they had brought peace belts
into the red land of Tlapallan where once they had
marched under the battle standard of Merlin the En-
chanter, to aid in the destruction of the hated Mian
mound builders and their cruel empire.

Policing them all, the Dog Soldiers kept order in the
camp, but there was little for them to do. It was a happy
throng. There was laughing and feasting for all. There
was smoking in council and storytelling for the old,
using the universal sign language common to the many
nations. The young men strove together. In competition
they wrestled and leaped and threw the tomahawk,
lance or atlatl dart. They bent the long bow at the
archery butts, darted like fish through the river or
hurled the racing canoes along its surface.

Many a maiden's dark eyes glistened with enjoyment
and pride at the sight and many a moccasined foot
would tread a new trail to a new home when the celebration was over. As ever, happiness was mingled with
regret. Slim girls looked toward the high stepped mound
near the river and sighed in vain desire, gazing upon
the unattainable, and would not be consoled.

Here stood a strong young man whose brown hair
and lighter skin set him apart from the others of his
age. He was dressed much as they in doeskin loincloth,
beaded headband, leggings and moccasins, for the
weather was warm and he had recently competed in
the games. His face was serious, for this was the final
day of the feastings and the important business of the
meeting was at hand.

The chief priest of the War God stepped forward
and intoned:

"Oh, Tlaloc, He Who Makes Things Sprout, and
thou his wife, Foam on the Water, look favorably on

the mission of this young man, the son of your brother Huitzilopochtli, the Raging and Terrible God!

"Huitzilopochtli came among us when we were weak. We hid in the rocks like a rabbit. He gave us weapons, he taught us to walk in pride, he ended our fear. He created the nation of Aztlan. Behind him we marched upon our Mian oppressors. With the help of his brother god, Quetzalcoatl, Lord of the Wind, and our northern allies of the Hodenosaunee, we killed the Mian Kukulcan and drove his people back to Atala.

"Now Tlapallan is at peace as Quetzalcoatl would have wished, for he loved peace as he was loved by us, though we are men of war. Today we are met in peace and there is no war anywhere in Alata. Our God and leader, Huitzilopochtli, has called us together to do honor to his son, Gwalchmai, the Eagle, who sails upon the Great Waters in yonder serpent-ship. He will take the tale of our battling and valor to his father's people.

"We ask you, Tlaloc, to grant him favor and fair winds, a swift passage across the seas and a swift return to us who wish he need not leave us for even a little while."

He raised his hands in blessing and bowed his head and stepped aside. Another man came forward. His polished steel armor glittered in the sun. He raised his copper braceleted right arm in the Roman salute and although his hair was gray at the temples beneath his crested helmet, the strong muscles rippled under his bronzed skin. The crowd roared a greeting. He motioned for silence.

"This is my son and my messenger. His godfather was Quetzalcoatl, who is gone from us to the Land of the Dead, but who may yet return. Today we remember the Lord of the Wind and how his magic aided us all, both you of Alata and we Romans shipwrecked upon your shores. We knew him as a man of great knowledge. He was unafraid to do battle and unafraid to speak of mercy when battle was done. That others may know of his greatness, my wife and I send our only son back to Rome that he may carry the tale of his godfather's wisdom and bring other of our people here. Gold Flower of Day—"

A dainty woman came forward, smiling fondly upon her husband and son. She wore a beautiful cape of hummingbird's feathers over a hualpilli, or shift, of gauzy white cotton. Her black hair was glossy and long, coiled in the squash blossom fashion over and around each ear. On her wrists were bracelets of cowrie shells and around her neck hung a plaque of matched pearls. Her waist, still slim, was cinctured with a belt of coins which could not have been duplicated elsewhere in Alata. These were joined Roman denarii of silver and copper sesterces, linked together by gold. Divers had brought them up from the wrecked *Prydwen,* the warship of Arthur of Britain, in which Merlin Ambrosius had sailed across the Atlantic to find a new land. With him and his nine bards, Ventidius Varro, the centurion of the Sixth Legion, had also come to make himself a king and be worshiped as a god.

Gold Flower of Day kissed her son and took the sword and belt which Ventidius removed and gave her. There were tears in her eyes as she buckled the belt upon her son, but they were tears of pride. She hugged him tightly once and released him. The crowd roared approbation and there was a great shaking of gourd rattles and blowing of bone whistles.

Ventidius raised his hand again. She stepped back and the tumult stilled. He held up a bronze cylinder so all could see.

"In this is the record of all that has been done here. Our battles in Azatlan, the joining of the Onguy nations to form the Long House, our march on Miapan, our crushing of the Tlapallican armies, our destruction of the Mian Empire.

"I send it to my Tecutli, my Lord across the sea, who will be happy to know that brave men dwell here as there. That it may not fail to reach its destination, I now place it in the keeping of my son, who, with his companions, will by strength of arm and his godfather's wisdom see it safely there. May fair winds and calm waters aid him and bring him safely back."

He gave it into the young man's hand. Gwalchmai slipped it into his belt and the two men gripped each other's forearm and gazed deeply into one another's eyes. There was no other word spoken nor other leave-taking.

They slowly descended the steps of the teocalli and passed through the kneeling quiet crowd, followed by the priests. The thirty young Aztecan rowers who were to man the sweeps had already thrust the dragon-ship a little way out from the shore. It was necessary for Gwalchmai to wade out thigh deep to embark.

He stood on the steersman's platform, with his hand on the whipstaff of the tiller as the ship swung out into the current. He looked back at his parents standing on the shore. They were as impassive as he, Roman pride matching Aztec dignity, but if hearts could weep unseen—there would have been tears.

Thirty oars dipped in salute to the temple. Up rose the heavy cotton sail called "The Cloak of the Wind" with its winged serpent in red and green, ramping ready to strike. As the wind took it, the oars lashed the water and the ship picked up a bone in its teeth and borne by the stream went down to meet the rollers of the Gulf.

Ventidius and his wife stood watching as the ship grew small in the distance. There was no sound from the crowd. For once, even the children were quiet, sensing the moment. There was a fleck of color far away. Was it a glint of sunlight upon an oarblade or a gleam upon a wave? A seagull's veering wing as it plunged into the water or the flicker of the dragon's movable tongue? No one could be sure, but it was gone.

They turned from the shore and went back through the waiting crowd, Ventidius' arm now about his wife, who walked leaning unashamedly against him, her eyes half closed, but dry.

Two men stepped out of the throng and walked beside them, without speaking: Ga-no-go-a-da-we,

Man Who Burns Hair, the mighty emissary from the People of the Flint, and Ha-yon-wa-tha, Royaneh of the Onondaga.

Ventidius looked up from the ground and saw them and his face worked. Gold Flower of Day smiled, reached out and touched them affectionately. "Old friends, dear friends—always there when we have needed you. Now that we are two again, we need you most of all."

Ventidius bent and kissed her. "Nay, dear one, we will always be three. Amavimus. Amamus. Amabimus. We have loved. We love. We shall love. We cannot know what he will find at the end of his journey. At the end of mine, I found you."

And the little group passed on, through the crowd, toward their own quarters; and the feasting began again.

Once out of the muddy channels of the Misconzebe delta, the dragon-ship turned eastward. The wind lay fair behind and the sail strained away from the mast. There were small islands and shoals to avoid and other river mouths to discharge trees and floating debris. As their way lay coastwise for some while Gwalchmai gave the tiller into the hands of the steersman and directed him to hold away from the shore. So they sailed for a long day's run, keeping the distant greenery just visible to their left.

At evening they bore in under oars and beached upon a coral strand in a pleasant cove. A rill of sweet water emptied here into the sea and tracks dimpled deep into the mud tokened that this was a favorite watering place for deer. While some of the crew sought for oysters, mussels and crabs, others took their hunting gear from their chests under the rowing benches and slipped into the forest. It was not long before venison was roasting over a bed of driftwood coals which shimmered with heat and color.

After a tremendous meal in which none of the ship's stores had been used, most of the men lay down to sleep near the fire. The night was warm and no shelter was needed, although, as with most Saxon warships, it was possible to unship the light mast and drop the tip of it into the forked jackstaff at the prow.

Under this slanting ridgepole, when the sail was drawn over it and made fast, the rowers' pit would remain dry and the crew could sleep in comfort, either when drifting with a sea-anchor out or drawn up on a beach till morning.

The night passed uneventfully though sentries had been posted and regularly relieved. The next day Gwalchmai, following the instructions given him by his father, directed the course steadily southward to parallel the coastline of Florida, although at that time it had no name.

This had once been a country of dread. Even now it held few human inhabitants in spite of its beauty and plenitude of game. It was noisy with birds of all description during the day and the swamps boomed with the roar of the bull-alligators. Occasionally the scream of a hunting panther shrilled, but there was nothing to disturb the crew of the *Feathered Serpent*.

The weather remained fine. The god Hurakan slept, it appeared. They passed through a multitude of islands and coral reefs, still living off the land, putting in only to sleep, hunt and maintain their water supply carried in large earthenware pots. Then as they were about to round Cape Sable adverse winds blew them southwesterly out of sight of land.

Had it not been for the little iron fish of Merlin's which, floating in a bowl of water, had guided the *Prydwen* westward across the ocean to Alata, they would have been well lost. As it was, when the seas quieted they were glad to see land and feel it under their feet again. The vegetation was lush and there was much fruit. On the beach they trapped a giant turtle and feasted upon it.

After the others were asleep, Gwalchmai studied his maps in his little cabin. This island was unmarked upon them, but so were hundreds of others they had seen and the coastline itself had not been as the maps presented it. He was forced to conclude that he could depend upon them only in the most general manner and in the end he rolled them up again and put the painted cotton strips back in Merlin's great chest.

Other magic things which he knew were more potent were kept there. Merlin had called them his tools and they were as familiar to Gwalchmai as his own right hand. Here were his witching herbs, his philters and his amulets. In a casket, covered with carvings which did not always remain the same, were powders and pills not to be used without prayers and spells. Here, in a little tray, was his wand of power and the wizard's ring which he had always worn. Gwalchmai weighed it thoughtfully and slipped it on his finger.

He dimly remembered sitting on the old man's lap and pulling on the long white beard which had entranced him. Merlin had laughed and called him Hawk of Battle. He had been very small. Now Merlin was gone and Gwalchmai possessed his tools.

Here were his books of spells limned on fine parchment, and volumes of recipes for explosive powders and colored fires. Below them, in the bottom of the chest, were the Thirteen Magic Treasures of the Island of Britain, which he had brought away to preserve them from the Saxon pirates. Gwalchmai had just unwrapped the Cauldron of Plenty from the Cloak of Invisibility when an outcry from the shore startled him. Snatching up his father's shortsword he ran out, into a scene of horror.

A little earlier, strange scaly heads had poked up out of the sea, near the spot on the beach where the turtle had been butchered. The creatures paddled out of the water and snuffed the blood. As they did so, spined combs rose and fell on those heads like the crests of cockatoos, and under their retreating chinless jaws wattled pouches flushed an angry purple with blotches of red.

Enraged, they dug into the blood soaked sand and flung it about with webbed clawed members which could only be called hands. They glared about with their round lidless eyes and air hissed in and out of rudimentary gills.

Ventidius Varro had not thought to warn his son against these fearsome beings. Known to the nations of the southeast and the Illini as the Piasa, they called themselves Gronks. He had fought them and thought them exterminated. Only these few had found a refuge on this far island, to bear witness to what horrors Nature was capable of creating in a moment of madness.

As they caught sight of the ship a few started toward it on their bandy legs, their long sharp fangs clicking in anticipation. Most of the others fell to all fours and advanced upon the sleeping camp. Avoiding the fire, which was the only thing which these cold-blooded monsters held in dread, they circled and surrounded the unfortunate men. Although their bodies quivered with desire for the feast and their short stubby tails twitched as though they would lash like the tail of an infuriated alligator, they waited for the given signal.

While waiting they muttered together in low grunts and hissings, thus proving that they were more than beast if less than men. Then the leader roared, and as one, they hurled themselves into the camp.

The drowsy sentry fell instantly before that rush. It was a hopeless encounter from the start. No man of Alata ever slept apart from his weapons and confronted now by the horror their fathers had known these warriors of Gwalchmai's grappled with their terrible enemy. Torn limb from limb, their warm flesh eaten while it still held life, they struck out while they were able and died where they had slept.

The fierce cry of the Aztlan Valiants arose: "Al-a-la-la! Al-a-la-la!" But it grew weaker and fainter as those who sounded it fell with no time for death songs.

By the time Gwalchmai reached the shore it was almost over and he saw that he could not reach his men. He turned and ran back to the ship. The only help they could hope for must now be found only in sorcery.

Unnoticed by him as he cut his way through the smallest group for the second time, the bronze cylinder with his father's message slipped out of his belt pouch and fell into the sand. He attained the deck again, but they were close behind.

At the sight of the monsters clambering over the rail and the death-cries of his friends sounding in his ears, his heart failed for an instant. Avoiding the clawed embrace of the first pursuer, he plunged his sword to the hilt in its thinly armored underbelly. Then, as the overlapping scales clenched upon it when the attacker doubled up in its agony, he found he could not withdraw it.

He darted into the cabin, slammed and barred the door against the ponderous bodies which plunged against it. Again betraying an intelligence approaching that of man, one Gronk picked up an anchor stone out of the water by its rope and hurled it against the door, smashing in the stout oak planks.

By this time hordes of the scaly creatures were swarming over the camp, from which came no more war-cries, nor any sound indeed but those of an obscene gobbling. Struggling to enter, those on the ship crowded one another to enter the cabin, but Gwalchmai had reached Merlin's chest and seized a talisman of great power from the little tray.

It writhed in his hand like a living thing as he pronounced the cantrip which activated it. Smoke curled up from his seared palm, but he clung to it grimly until he had finished the spell. The Gronk picked up the anchor stone again and felled him with it, but it was a dying reflex action. The creature dropped dying, decaying as it struck the deck, the flesh falling away from the skeleton in moments. All over the island the same thing was happening. The feasters perished in the act. Those hurrying to the feast never reached it. Even those who dwelt at the far ends of the island died without knowing what had struck them down.

Gwalchmai lay unconscious in his blood in the ruined cabin. Skeletons lay with him and on the deck, but there was nothing left alive to harm him. He lay there, murmuring incoherently, and when his eyes opened he looked about without knowledge. By and by he slept.

The tide came gently in, lifting the prow of the *Feathered Serpent* from its trough in the sand, and because the other stones had been lifted from the sea by the other attackers, there was nothing to hold it upon the beach.

The breeze blew softly that morning from the shore and the dragon-ship drifted away, spinning slowly with no hands at the whipstaff. Later an easterly wind gave it speed and direction, away from the coast, out into the open ocean.

After long hours the edge of the Gulf Stream caught it and hurried it on, away from Alata, away from his homeland and away from the island of death. Centuries later the Spaniards landed and christened it Cayo de los Huessos—Island of the Bones. Today we call it Key West.

2

The Golden Bird

Gwalchmai woke, but he did not know that his name was Gwalchmai. He knew that he was a man and that he was on a ship, but what manner of ship it was or how he came to be there was lost knowledge. Yet nothing looked strange to him.

He knew that this was a mast and that was a sail. He swung the tiller and the *Feathered Serpent* answered the helm—sluggishly, because the sail was furled. He climbed up and cut the lashings and made the sheets fast. Now the gentle breeze bore him eastward. He felt that he was traveling in the right direction, but could not have said why it seemed right to him.

The reason for his satisfaction was buried deep in his injured memory. He frowned, trying to remember, and the wrinkling of his forehead pulled at the stiffened hair where it was stuck to the wound above his right temple. He explored the damage with his fingers and winced. The cut was wide and swollen. He let down a leather bucket overside and brought up water and bathed away the blood. The salt stung and burned, but afterward he felt better.

It came to him that he was very hungry. He seemed unusually weak and when he discovered the ship's stores, it was hard for him to open a tightly knotted sack of pemmican. He remembered having seen a long knife lying on the deck among some bones and went after it. It seemed a long journey and after he had retrieved it and brought it down into the hold he sat in front of the sack which smelled so good trying to recollect what he had meant to do with the knife. After a moment in thought he stabbed the sack and the rich food gushed out.

He gorged with both hands until he was satisfied. The lean pulverized sun-dried antelope meat, mixed with fat, dried wild cherries, marrow and fish eggs was almost instantly digestible. It was not long before he felt stronger. Placing the shortsword in the scabbard which still hung at his belt, he opened a jar of water and drank deeply. Instinct told him he must not drink the water in which the ship floated.

Afterward he slept again, the rest of that afternoon and all through the night. While he slept, the wind continued to blow eastward and at dawn it still pushed the ship on, though by intermittent light waftings, until midday when it ceased entirely and the ship drifted in the doldrums.

It was very hot without the breezes. Pitch softened and ran in the deck seams. The sail hung limply from the mast. Drifting, he noticed that little patches of weed were coalescing into larger mats, upon which crabs and insects crawled. The days went by with little change. He managed to clear the deck of the skeletons, but he became infected with a fever which exhausted him and he lay in his cabin for a long time, sick to the point of dying.

It was a fight to crawl to the water jars and back again to his pallet. It was only sullen determination to live that enabled him to choke down food. Weeks passed. The *Feathered Serpent* worked its way out of the Gulf Stream current and entered a calm expanse of sea. No rain fell. The weed mats became islands. The islands joined and locked the becalmed ship fast.

His strength became again as it had once been, but still his past was a blank. And then one day as he sat on the afterdeck with a cup of water in his hand, looking reflectively at the horizon across a sea of weed, he saw that it lay everywhere that the eye could search. Close to the trapped ship, lanes of clear water could be discerned, but farther away, in the direction whither ship and week islands were slowly drifting, there seemed to be no breaks in the thickly packed mass.

Nothing disturbed the surface, except a long even swell which came irregularly as though some huge denizen of the undersea went privately about its business far beneath. There were no waves. No rollers surged to break upon the coast of that seaweed continent, neither had the winds any power over it. This was the Sargasso, dread haven of dead ships, and only the sun and silence here conspired to drive men mad, before famine was to strike the mercy blow.

Far away the rays of the setting sun were reflected from some glistening object of ruddy golden hue, deep in the weed pack, and at this he stared while he sipped his water and wondered what it might be. Darkness hid the mystery and he retired. On the next day it was a little nearer.

Other days came and passed, dragging out their monotonous round. There was nothing to mark their passage but the sinking of the level in the water jars and the closer matting of the weed masses as the constant sluggish urging of the distant Gulf Stream forced them together. Then, as was inevitable, the last of the jars was emptied and all of the water was gone.

The brassy sky gave no promise of rain and his only relief now came from the moisture deposited upon the sail during the night, but the few drops he was able to gather tantalized him more than they satisfied. He searched through Merlin's chest for something to drink and found a small vial which held little more than a spoonful of clear syrup. It was pleasantly sweet and pungent and he drank it all.

Merlin had kept himself hale and hearty with it for many years, doling it out drop by drop, and Gwalchmai, in his proper senses, might have planned in other circumstances to do the same. It was a priceless potion worth all the gathered treasure of many a king. Gwalchmai was only aware that he no longer felt thirst, not knowing that he had emptied the only bottle in all the world which had ever contained the Elixir of Life.

Now he did not crave water. His cracked lips healed and he felt strong and exhilarated. Each evening he marked that the remote gleam had come a little nearer and it seemed that a form was almost visible in that far shining object—a form that as yet he could not recognize.

Once, when marking the downward progress of the sun, he saw upthrust against its half-hidden disk a protuberance from the sea. Tall, snaky, with huge horse head and shaggy mane, dripping water and weed, it poised there looking out over the surface in search of prey, but did not spy the ship and sank again, the sun descending with it.

Weary of the weight of his sword, he had given up the wearing of it some weeks before. Now he went thoughtfully below and strapped it on again. From that time, waking or sleeping, the sword never left his side.

Gwalchmai slid down a stay, through the rotting sail tatters of crimson and green, and pondered for a moment. From his lately accustomed post at the mast he had discovered that it was now possible to come closer to the mystery which interested him.

The moon had waxed and waned since any perceptible movement had taken place in the ship's position, but this morning that oddly enticing glimmer had come much closer to him. Near now, scarcely a mile away, it looked like a glided long-necked waterfowl, asleep with head bowed upon its breast. Could there be birds of such hugeness in the world?

Rain had fallen some days previously and now while he ate and drank he studied the route he might take to reach it.

As though to coax him on where his wishes led him, a lane had opened in the weed overnight where there had been no sign of one when he had retired. Passing within a hundred feet of his vessel, it veered eastward directly toward the curious bird.

Could he open a passage to the channel for his small boat? Surely it was worth a trial. An inner feeling insinuated that yonder something fine and desirable was waiting, but if he was to leave it must be soon.

An hour of watching had shown him that the channel was already narrower than it had been at early dawn. The same close inspection should have brought to his attention the fact that the banks and edges of the lane were heaped and torn. Rotting vegetation had been brought up from below as though some mighty rushing body had pushed through the weed, forcing a passage, piling up the debris of its passing. This had escaped his notice. He saw a road to his desire and nothing else.

After placing the small boat overside, he pushed away from the dragon-ship. He did not raise the sail, for there was no wind, and he took no food or water, though he felt certain that he would not return. In his still mazed mind this did not seem an unusual thing to do. Mystically, he felt himself guided—he could not have said by what or whom. It seemed that a quiet voice was talking to him without actual words. It instructed, commanded, directed his actions. He gave himself up to the voice.

At first, progress was difficult. Weed gathered against the prow and hindered him. He was obliged to stop frequently and press these clumps below the surface with an oar in order to pass over and on. After a half-hour he broke through into the channel and it was then a simple matter either to row or scull.

The clear water ran straight as a canal, directly toward the distant glowing swan. Very soon he came close enough to see that although it was not a living creature, it was as nearly perfect a replica as man could make.

The position of the head and neck remained unaltered. The beak was partially open and there was an eye above it which was closed. The lid appeared movable. As the young Aztlanian drew closer he could see that the nearer wing was feathered, by skillful carving and molding, but damaged. Half the pinion was gone and where the remainder trailed in the water the edges showed no signs of corrosion, but were torn and jagged.

He paddled closer. Now that it was evident that this phenomenon was indeed a ship, Gwalchmai felt little surprise. The craft he had quitted possessed the figurehead of a fabulous monster, with fangs and a wobbling tongue. It was conceivable that other ships might be constructed to resemble birds.

But where was the open part of the vessel? Was there an entrance? Could there be within it another lonely voyager like himself? He must inspect the opposite side and find out.

Then, before he could move, a little ringing voice tinkled inside his brain, like a tiny tocsin pealing out danger:

"Look behind you!" it warned, and he turned. Coming, and swiftly, was the maker of the path upon which he had intruded.

Thirty feet above the water towered a head, green with weed, leeches and parasitic encrustations. Eyes larger than his own head glared down upon him as paddle-like flippers thunderously smote the water and a white wave creamed the long neck high with foam. The beast would be almost instantly upon him and although Gwalchmai had no name for this menacing creature, he knew that here swam Death!

He stood up in his rocking boat and tugged out his shortsword as the jaws above him opened wider than those upon the figurehead of his own ship. He caught a glimpse of a pointed tongue, sharp fangs driving down and a blast of stench-laden air choked him. His ears were stunned by hissing louder than a scream.

Gwalchmai smote once, with all his strength, and felt the sharp steel bite through gristle. Then, over-balanced by the blow, he fell into the prow and the hideous bony head came down like a thunder stone upon the stern.

Up, up, high into the air he shot, clinging grimly to the sword hilt. Twisting there, unconsciously directed into a perfect dive, he fell again, piercing cleanly through the deep weed which lay hard against the golden ship.

Deep down, in clear water, still retaining his sword, he swam beneath the ship, noticing even then that the bird similarity continued under the surface. Feather carvings covered the metal and passing one huge dangling leg and then the other, he saw that each broad foot was webbed with a metallic membrane which quivered and waved as he stirred the water.

Driven by his own strong legs, he came to the surface, the matted weed offering little resistance to the keen edge he opposed to it. Now he found himself close to the other wing, which was undamaged though also hanging down and partially extended. By the rough corrugations and body carvings he climbed to the broad back. A quick glance showed him that the monster had submerged. An immense commotion beneath the surface rocked the golden bird and brought up bubbles of gas from the decaying weed. A wide scaly tail slapped the open water in the channel and the boat bobbed like a chip against it.

Instantly the hideous head reappeared beneath the boat, seized upon it, shook it, crunched it into splinters and spat out the remains.

Gwalchmai lay flat upon the sun-heated metal, covered with dry salt dust. He could see that one side of the great creature's head was oozing tears of slime. Upon that side, the horror was blind. His one wild stroke had sliced away the cornea of its eye!

Again the long neck shot up out of the choppy waves, turning, twisting to catch sight of the enemy. Gwalchmai knew that he was seen and sprang to his feet. He tapped the sword point upon the bird's back. The metal rang delicately beneath him.

"Come! Help me fight!" he cried and swung the blade over his head to deliver a mighty blow, which would certainly be his only one.

But what was this? A thrill beneath his moccasins, a tingle which coursed through his whole body—a quiver which ran through the ship, *if it was altogether a ship!*

There was a movement like that of muscles tensing. The dripping wings half lifted and struck the surface. The long beautiful swan neck swung up and lay back. The eyes glared open. A brilliant white light shone through from behind crystal pupils and it stared like a living creature into the countenance of the onrushing Titan.

Then, as the young man felt the perspiration start out upon his body in anticipation of the rending fangs, the bird's beak parted wider and from it issued a torrent of crackling flame, followed by a thunderclap so close that, dazzled by levin bolt and dazed by the stunning report, he was hurled to the metal beneath him.

The serpent's head whipped back, tattered rags of flesh, seared and charred, fluttering about the gushing neck stub. Then, guided only by its secondary brain at the spine's base, the dying survival from the primeval tore through the weed, blindly hurled itself against the deserted dragon-ship and sank in the splintered ruins.

When Gwalchmai became conscious the sun was low and he still lay where he had fallen. His fingers were cramped tightly upon the sword hilt. He rose and looked about him. The sea was very quiet. The channel banks had closed and left no marks of their separation. There was nothing floating to show where the *Feathered Serpent* had lain.

He turned his attention to discovering an entrance to this peculiar craft. He sought for a long time and found nothing.

A little before dusk he concluded that a rectangular hairline, just abaft of the neck and between the shoulders of the artificial fowl, might be a doorway to the mysteries below. Still he could not conceive how he was to get inside. He tried to force the point of his sword deeply enough to pry up an edge of this space, but although the substance gave to the pressure he could not scratch or move it.

At last, in darkness, he gave up the trial and lay down to sleep upon the queer metal which could not be damaged yet was soft beneath his body. It now seemed resilient and warm with a curious *aliveness*. He could not free himself from the thought that the great bird was aware of him, pitied him, and would care for and protect him through the hours of the night.

Although Merlin's magic potion had preserved his life, it could not forever eliminate the needs of the body. Hunger and thirst lay down with him and rose with him under the fiery morning sun. At dawn he attacked the supposed entrance again, but without fortune. By midday his misery had become acute.

The ruddy golden metal, so comfortable during the night, became a torturing grill under the tropical heat. He had lain upon his bunk in the drifting dragon-ship, when the pitch stewed from the deck seams above him, but although the air had been close and hard to breathe there had been shade, and water to drink. Here there was neither and he suffered.

Beneath his unprotected skull, his brain seemed to be cooking. He spoke or swallowed with great difficulty. He immersed himself twice in the tepid brine and obtained some relief, but the third time he found it almost impossible to climb back upon the broad wing and dared not try again.

At last, despairing of any help, he croaked, "Open! Open!"—and stopped, astounded at the effects of his command. Before him the door which all his efforts had been powerless to force was raising lightly without a sound. A short flight of steps led downward to a cool place of half-light, and a tinkle of purling water came up to greet him. There was no one on the stairs and no sign of whoever had opened the door.

Without hesitation he descended and as his weight left the bottom step the door above dropped into place as quietly as it had arisen.

3

The Image in the Alcove

It was like descending beneath the surface of a still, clean pool. Through the translucent sides of the ship, sunlight streamed in, made more golden by the medium through which it passed. The reflections at the waterline, which was plainly discernible, mingled and blended into gradations of amber and jade, shading off by degrees into aquamarine as the water deepened.

The floor was chequered with black and white squares and the interior of the ship was very quiet until he strode forward, searching for that welcome sound of trickling water.

Instantly a chiming of fairy bells rang sweetly, in chords and pizzicato runs. He stopped, perplexed, and when he did so the music also ceased. Obviously there

was a connection between his movements and the elfin
sounds. He noticed that, at the moment, he was standing upon a white square.

He pressed gently upon a black square with one
experimental foot. A faint trilling run of silver notes
replied, which repeated itself more loudly as his full
weight came upon the square. He stepped away to an
ivory block. Silence followed. At this explanation of
the mystery, his brow cleared and he walked boldly
on, while every step meant harmony.

There were the sounds of harps and dulcimers as
he progressed further, enraptured by beautiful scenes
and vistas upon the walls, neither painted nor graven
there. These seemed like magic windows through which
he gazed upon lifelike displays of marble cities thronged
by handsome, sturdy men and lovely women, so real
that it seemed the breath of his passing should ruffle
their flowing robes.

Thrumming woodwinds provided an undertone, as
he walked on, to the higher notes of violin and mono-
chord, blending and sinking away to a sighing murmur
of waves when he stopped before a harbor view. Great
ships, similar to the one he was exploring, breasted the
water or were drawn up beside long quays where
throngs of dark skinned slaves were about the business
of discharging cargo.

High in the air soared other ships, equally at home
in the clouds as on the ocean, while at the entrance to
the bottlenecked port, another was landing, its wings
half-furled, broad webbed feet thrust wide like a gull's,
to meet the impact of the waves.

He passed on. Trumpets brayed and clamored, drums
growled menacingly as he strode by a scene of war.
From the sky the swan-ships shot down levin bolts to
meet the jagged lightning streaming up from the squat
cities below. With seared off wings the warring craft
fell wheeling, to be lost in clouds of fire and rolling
smoke above the crumbled walls and towers.

Gwalchmai turned away. It was only a picture. Thirst
again drove him on. At the end of the long room, two

passages opened and diverged. He trod upon a white rectangle and while he hesitated the music died away.

The left-hand corridor curved sharply, as though it led back and around the wall of the room in which he stood. Its floor and walls, once white, were now the sunwarmed hue of old ivory, for dust lay thick upon them. The other passage bore straight ahead toward the neck and head of the giant fowl, but its end could not be seen for vision lost itself there in blackness.

Somber were the walls and ceiling, and the floor, once shining like polished ebony, was also dull with dust. Yet in this obvious evidence of long years of disuse and neglect could be seen unmistakable proof that somewhere within its eery depths was—life!

Here were tracks, recently made, human footprints and quite small, pointing in both directions. He bent above them, studying them, calling upon his experience in trail tracking. The tracks had been made by bare feet, delicately shaped, and the person who had made them had been in haste. Coming out of the dark corridor, the toe-prints were clear and distinct. Only occasionally had the dust been scuffed by a heel. Overlaying some of these were clear outlines of the whole foot, created as that person, walking, had returned. There were two sets of these spoors, made by the same feet. Twice, then, someone had come running out of that passage and re-entered it more slowly. Could it be the one who had opened the way for him?

He hesitated only a few seconds, though he could feel that some indefinable menace lay waiting in the dark way, like a beast of prey lurking beside the path which its hunter must eventually tread. Gwalchmai smiled faintly, a little nervous trait which marked him and which some men had learned to dread—but only with his lips.

His sword slid from its sheath. Surely it was better to reckon early with whatever he might find and either render it harmless or learn in what manner he could dwell with it in peace. He entered the passage. Immediately he felt that the crouching beast had pounced.

Drums and brasses crashed deafeningly against him, threaded by a clarion trumpet cry as counterpoint. The uproar drowned out the sound of the fountain he sought. Almost at once, he found he had approached a ramp. He set his feet to it in the threatening dark and began to climb.

As he advanced further down the narrow way, a curious menacing note crept into the sounds. A discordant violence was disrupting the harmony, almost seeming to become an articulate bellowing, warning him against further daring. Did something forbidden lie ahead?

Once again, the feeling came to him that this great bird-like ship was something more than a mere fabrication of metal. *Was* it a living creature after all and these sounds its voice? Did harmony denote approval of his actions—and violent discordance indicate its disapproval and anger?

He felt himself being absorbed into the very gullet of the creature, but with his lips grimly set he stumbled on, probing into the almost tangible blackness with his swordpoint. He pressed deeper into a deafening clamor of desperately crashing kettledrums and roaring serpentines, excruciatingly off-key; farther still into the stunning uproar, the jarring assault upon his ears and being. The very bones of his head thrilled and hummed with the painful vibrations which deafened him. On then! On with throbbing temples and fire-filled skull—to burst suddenly into another room, smaller than the first, peaceful, quiet, and drowned in pale green light.

The brilliance dazzled him and an instant hush, somehow ominous, rocked him like a blow. Intuitively, he felt that he was where he should not be, that this sanctum was the spot from which he had been meant to be turned aside by the strident voice of the ship. The commotion ceased, it was true, but now he sensed that he had made an implacable enemy. There was a feeling of hatred around him, never to leave him while he was on the ship. He was constantly to be aware of this sensation of something inimical, the "genius loci" perhaps, which he had offended and which, being deadly, powerful and patient, bode its time.

Without present thought of this, he now saw the fountain whose liquid invitation had drawn him thither, and running across the room, he plunged his aching head beneath the surface of its clear sweet pool. Limpid as the water was, the temptation to indulge immoderately proved very strong and only with a distinct effort could the young Aztec force himself to withdraw from it.

Not until then did he see the girl who watched him.

She stood upon a little dais, raised slightly from the floor, set in an alcove in the farther undecorated wall. She was completely nude; no clothing could have enhanced the glory of her form, nor did any embarrassment appear upon her perfect but expressionless features. With both hands extended slightly in a beseeching attitude she seemed to invite him nearer.

For a few long seconds Gwalchmai stared across the face. Neither spoke, nor was there any interrupting sound except the musical plashing into the pool.

Sunlight poured through the translucent emeraldine ceiling, upon a rose-pink floor, reflecting upon the fair body before him, rendering it lovely as a dawn-colored pearl in its nacreous home. Time stood still, waiting—

Then he rose to his feet, skirted the pool, moving forward not recking where he trod, bemused with beauty. Something crunched and splintered dryly beneath his moccasined feet and looking down with no great surprise, for everything here was strange, he saw that he trod in a tangle of human bones. He stepped over them with more care and confronted the girl. She did not move or show fear of this strange intruder into her lonely home.

Half timidly for one who had so bravely faced the sea-snake, he laid his hand upon her shoulder—and with a short laugh of disillusionment, he recoiled. Here was nothing human, to be companion for him in the wastes!

It was an image only, formed from the same odd metal as the ship, ruddy as his own skin, warm, stronger than bronze or steel, yet softer to the hand almost than living flesh. Was there life here—of a sort?

He could not be sure. Again he touched her—cheek, throat, breast. Her hair lifted lightly in his palm and stirred to his breath. The substance of her body dimpled to the pressure of his fingertip, but so did the very wall behind her! Yes! She was metal. It was a strange, marvelous, uncanny metal, but she was unhuman.

There was one more test that he could make, though he felt that it was desecration. His blade was still unsheathed. He touched the point to her side and drew it down from breast to thigh; then, as she did not wince or change expression, he set it against the delicately rounded hip and twisted vigorously.

No scratch, no impression marred the diamond hard surface of her shapeliness—she was metal and an image, nothing more!

Deeply disappointed and lonely, he felt this tantalizing mystery and inspected the bones to learn from them whatever he could. Dry, desiccated, crumbled away almost to dust, they powdered when he touched them, proving indisputably the hoary antiquity of these remains.

One skeleton was that of a woman, for it was adorned with a richly wrought golden necklace, but the other bones were certainly male. A short dagger lay at one hip and a small bell-mouthed instrument at the other. If a belt had once joined and supported these there was no sign of it now, nor any threads of clothing, but the metal was uncorroded by time.

He picked up the unfamiliar implement and examined it curiously. Could it be a weapon? Too light for a war club—perhaps a missile thrower of a sort? But the bell mouth was closed over by a thick curved piece of heavy crystal. No missile could be ejected through that! Life had suddenly become full of mysteries! He observed that the bones of the warrior's legs were broken between knee and ankle and knowing he had not trod in that direction, he bent to look at the fractures. As he did so, his finger slipped into a loop near the handle of the thing he held, unconsciously twitching it tight.

The next instant a dazzling flare of light almost struck him blind. The weapon, definitely proven to be such, leaped in his loose grasp and the concussion filled the room with dust.

When he could again see plainly, both skeletons had vanished, as had the golden necklace and the dagger sheath. The blade itself, molded from that mysterious sparkling metal, was not injured and the floor it lay upon was unharmed, though blackened by char and soot from the bones.

Respectfully, he eyed the powerful and deadly thing he held. Something like this, much larger, had killed the beast he had fought! If this needed an agency to set it off, then clearly the other weapon had been fired with intention—to save his life. By whom?

The question could not be answered at present, but he determined to make a thorough search of the ship and find his unknown benefactor who so shyly avoided the thanks due him.

Three days later he was still searching, but without much expectancy.

During that time he had poked and pried into every dusty nook upon the ship, from the galley situated in the tail of the bird to the tiny chamber back of the great goggle eyes, still unlidded as he had seen them from outside. Here he had peered out and over the yet partially opened beak, and, by pulling a lever attached to an enormous replica of the belt weapon which he had appropriated, had seen the lightning crash into the sea, lashing the stagnant weed with crackling flames.

This was the manner of it, then, but where was the operator, his unknown savior? Not in the laddered neck which led down again to the room of the fountain, nor in the larger room he had first entered. He took the other corridor to the left, which wound down and around that room to a lower level.

Here were darker chambers, though illumined by a lambent shimmering inherent in all the walls. Forward, in the breast of the bird, was a large cargo compartment crammed with chests of flexible paper-thin metal which would not tear or be cut by sword edge. They opened easily when he tugged gently upon a small tab which he found was always situated in the upper right-hand corners. Air hissed inward when he opened them, proving that they had been hermetically sealed.

These stores were the saving of him. In some chests he found dried fruits, in others a thick meaty paste, almost like pemmican. This was savory and good. Whatever the chest might hold, it needed only water to make the food swell into a tasty meal. In those three days he had learned to recognize the symbols which distinguished the two articles of food and although he felt sure that other edible substances were yet to be found, these alone were ample for his needs.

He discovered heat in the galley, by accidentally leaning against a wall stud; almost at once, a grid of coils set in a metal box against the wall had begun glowing red. Above this radiant heat he did his simple cooking, in pots of unfamiliar shape, eating with his fingers and knife from dishes such as he had never seen.

Water came from pipes in the wall, fed, he was sure, from the reservoir upon the floor above, where the little fountain constantly played without ever filling the catch basin to overflowing.

Centrally, below the water line, were machines, and here Gwalchmai was entirely bewildered. He guessed that their purpose was to propel the ship through the water, for he could trace massive rods and levers from their first connections to the legs of the immense swan. Suspecting that, before the wing outside had been injured, this craft might have flown in the manner he had seen in the murals, he had verified this thought by further research. Other rods eccentrically wrought and bent to meet the shoulders from which those pinions hung proved his theory correct, but he remained mystified, unable to guess what power motivated the ship.

This room of machines was a room of dread. It was filled with a buzzing, a humming, which occasionally took on the very timbre of a snarl which issued from deep within the maze of wheels, levers and cogs. When this happened, Merlin's ring, which he still wore, became warm upon his finger. He did not know the cause, but he intuitively felt it to be a warning of danger and felt himself threatened. Occasionally also, fat blue sparks spat between metal and metal, without apparent reason, shaking his edgy nerves as he tiptoed cautiously about the room. He saw beneath his feet the little fish darting beyond the plates of metal, which here were quite transparent. He touched nothing, though his devouring curiosity compelled him to slide between the levers and pry into every cranny without success in his search for other life.

There *was* life here. He could feel it surging about him, prickling his skin, causing his scalp to burn and itch, his hair to rise, his feet to tingle—but it was not life as he knew it.

There was nothing human in the cold ferocity which he felt constantly regarding him. He was not daunted by it. His courage had never been questioned, but he felt uneasy in this eery place of power. Gwalchmai doubted now that anything even remotely approaching human emotion could be assumed as a part of this terrible hatred which he felt weighing upon him, close as a second skin.

On the third evening, almost firmly convinced that his search was useless, he sat again in the room of the fountain, dabbling his hands in the water and glumly regarding the beautiful image. The green light, paler with the descending sun, bathed the room with peace and beauty. There is a healing quality in this color. It

is the hue of living things, the lifeblood of the Earth
Mother, and there is a benison and a blessing in it. In
this room he felt that he was welcome and in this room
only.

His loneliness seemed more than he could bear and
suddenly memories came rushing back. Aztlan, his
father and mother, his mission and his vow to complete
it, the faces of his dead companions who were to him
like brothers—all these and more he remembered as
the light streamed down upon him and he buried his
face in his hands and groaned at the hopelessness of
his situation.

Lost and a prisoner on a mysterious ship locked
tightly in a sea of weed! Alone and helpless to fulfill
his vow. Here was the only companion he had found:
an unseeing, insensate fabrication of metal, lovely as
the dreams of an angel, but without voice, without
emotion, without soul.

The silence bore heavily upon him also. No bird
lofted in these skies, no fish could leap through the
weed, no bee droned heavily by. After he had entered
that sanctuary upon the first day, no sounds but the
water in the fountain and the menacing fury of the
room of power had broken the deathly stillness of
the ship. He had stamped upon the black and white
squares, pounded upon the floor of the dark corridor,
but no chime, either harmonious or dissonant, had
answered and he heard only the noise of his own
making.

As he sat and inspected this cunning creation of
some long-dead artist, he felt that even his solitude in
the lonely dragon-ship was preferable to this, for there
he had no simulacrum of life to torment and tantalize
him. He remembered how his old white bearded godfather Merlin had amused him when he was very
small by causing a man-shaped mandrake root to leap
and prance before him to make him laugh. He smiled.

He knew the spell. Should he try it now? And then,
like a whisper in his ear, the thought came to him that
there was no need of magic, either white or black.

Upon this ship he had but to command to be obeyed. There was nothing to suggest this idea; it was but a random fancy. There was no one, no thing, to command; yet it set him thinking further.

On the back of the swan-ship, awaiting the stroke of the monster, he had not asked for help. He had commanded it!

"Help me fight!" he had ordered and the unknown benefactor had responded.

Smiling a grim, twisted smile at his own ridiculous folly, he looked straight at the beautiful statue and muttered:

"Come here and talk to me—if you can!"

And with a tread that was feather light, the metal girl quitted her pedestal, advanced toward him and, when two strides away, sank upon her knees with bowed head, murmuring in soft tones like a muted golden bell:

"I am here! What does my lord require of his servant?"

4

The Ship from Atlantis

To say that Gwalchmai was not surprised would be untrue, and he did recoil, as any other man might do, but he replied readily and after the first start he felt no thrill of fear. She was too lovely to be anything but kind and gracious, and the sweet voice, though metallic in timbre, charmed his senses.

"Tell me of yourself," he requested. "How did you come to be here and from what land? Are you the one who blasted the monster? Are there others of your kind and will they be friends with me or must I fight?"

Her expression did not change, nor did she move from her knees as she began to speak.

"When I was human and warm with life, my name was Corenice. With my father, Colrane, a star-seer, I dwelt upon a mountaintop in the drowned land of Poseidonis. Is the name familiar to you?"

The Aztlanian shook his head.

"I feared it," she mourned. "Even the memory of my lost homeland has passed away and I alone remember. Know this then, man: Poseidonis, an island continent, broad and powerful as it was in my youth, was but the tiny remnant of a mightier land, Atlantis, which perished for its sins.

"Because the people were wicked, in each of their generations the Spirit of the Wave sank miles of seacoast, giving meadowland, farms, villages and cities to the finny people of the sea.

"Still they did not give up their sin, for they did not recognize it as sin, at that time, and the dry land dwindled during the centuries."

"What was this wickedness?" Gwalchmai asked, curiously.

"Murder, the unforgivable sin! The wanton slaying of man by man—the sin which men call war!

"Atlantis was the mistress of the world. Her colonies and tributary nations covered the globe. She had won them—and what she termed glory—by the sword, and in the eyes of the Gods she was no more than a loathsome sore, polluting even that which remained clean. Through the ages she was punished by earthquake and fire, by volcanoes and the encroaching sea, until only Poseidonis remained.

"At last, though late, a new generation forswore the ways of war. They developed beyond the simple worship of the visible and its symbols and came to adore the Spirit of the Wave. Immediately they began to thrive. The sea took no more land. As they learned to live peacefully, waging no more wars, demanding no more tribute, Ahuni-i, the Spirit of the Wave, took human shape and came to live among men, in the form of a beautiful woman."

During this recital, she had not altered her expression or her position in the slightest and her voice, though melodious, came in a monotone. Gwalchmai interrupted.

"Will you not rise and be at ease? You should not kneel to me."

She did not move. "I cannot, in this body, do aught else than obey a direct command. It was created to serve and its actions were determined by the patterns built into it by the constructor. If it is your pleasure that I rise, you must command me to do so, or give me the power of independent action, thus letting my mind control this artificial body as it suits me."

"How can I do this?"

"There is a stud between my shoulder blades. Turn it thrice to the right and I will be able to act at my own volition."

The stud was not hard to find, for it was the only blemish on her exquisitely perfect back, but it was difficult to turn, being circular and very smooth. Finally he managed the required number of turns and the metal girl rose.

Now she was no longer a statue, but a person. She turned her face toward him and smiled. He found her now far lovelier, being animated, than he had thought when she seemed to be only an image. Corenice walked away a few steps and returned to him, a soft musical chiming accompanying all her movements, as the metal parts of her body functioned in the manner for which they were intended.

He concluded that in Atlantis great artists had once dwelt.

She took his hand and drew him down beside her, to sit at the edge of the fountain. Her hand seemed live and warm and her fingers were soft, but in them he sensed a power and strength which could crush stone to powder. Her voice had cadence, expression and a tonal quality as she resumed her narrative. She was alive!

"Ah! Could you have seen the holy beauty of the long green rollers entering the sacred harbor of Colicynos, you too would have worshiped, as did all Poseidonis, the Spirit of the Wave. Here, the legend, old long before my time, tells us that Ahuni-i stepped out of the creaming foam and showed herself to mortals who, still dark in spirit, fell upon their faces and adored her. Here she dwelt until her mortal body grew aged and feeble and could not answer her desires. Here she returned to the Wave, walking down the strand, deeper and deeper into the receding tide, until she could grasp the white mane of a silver-footed sea horse and be carried to the halls of coral. There, forever young, she still dwells until the time comes once again for her to encourage good in the hearts of a favored race of men.

"The priest whom she had instructed for so many years filled her little footprints with molten gold and built around them a walk of rainbow marble, extending from the green-sward to a point far beyond low-water mark. It is the most beautiful sight in Colicynos—or was, for Poseidonis is no more!"

"No more?" echoed Gwalchmai. "And why?"

Deep grief tinged her voice. "A curse came down from the sky upon our ancient world. Men had been taught to abhor war. They had become gentle and peaceloving, learned in the arts. One day a hot dry wind blew upon the City of the Golden Gates and folk went mad. They fell upon one another in the streets, striking out without reason, tearing at friend or stranger like beasts, cursing, killing, in a fever delirium of lust and hate. Suddenly the wind waned and with it passed the insanity.

"Halfway around the world it appeared again, blowing straight down from the zenith, like no other wind that had ever been known. It breathed upon Bassalonia and the people rose, raving, and hurled themselves over the border. Shandagone burned in the night, and Phorphar and Ninazar, that mighty city! Ash, and ruin and tombs, all of them! Their folk put to death by sword and club and strangling hands, and none of them had hated one another before.

"Zimba Buei, the City of Gold, felt its hot breath, more burning than the tropical sun above, and the blacks came down, with ax and spear, leaving nothing but bones and crumbling walls to mark the site of our mining colony.

"Drums beat in Shamballa. Valusia divided itself into factions and roared with the pain of civil strife. With distrust and hate worldwide, almost in a single night Poseidonis rearmed!

"Vimanas, our swan-ships, meant for peaceful trade, were fitted with the dyro-blast and a fleet which darkened the sky soared northward into Cimmeria to meet the fleet which we knew would soon be driving down upon us. They met near Congor and the historians relate that the sea boiled with the heat deflected down upon it from exploding ships. Neither fleet came home.

"All around the world similar scenes were taking place, but not until the strength of all nations was exhausted was the cause of the widespread dissension revealed. Then—above the White Island, in the Gobi Sea, the sky seemed suddenly to change into a vast inverted bowl of flame, filled with clotted masses of fire. Before the astounded people below were incinerated they saw a gigantic black ship descending.

"It was the accursed Lord of the Dark Face! Coming from the Morning Star, he had invisibly poised above the great centers of population and with his subtle arts caused strife among men. When all nations were weakened, their materiels for resistance spent, his spaceship descended to conquer enfeebled Earth.

"He rode upon fire! Stunning reverberations of heat and sound beat down upon the Gobi Sea, drying it to a desert of salt and sand. The White Island became a cinder with all human life extinct, but the Lord of the Dark Face peopled it with his followers.

"Most of them were artificial thought-forms of his own depraved mind, but they possessed a life of their

own, a life that was altogether evil. As emissaries,
taking on the semblance of the natives wherever they
visited, they went out into all countries, preaching the
dark gospel of the Kingdom of Pan. Down the long
steep grade that leads to atavism all the peoples passed,
lusting after the sins of the flesh and the greater abominations known only to the spirit.

"Only in Poseidonis was there any real resistance.
For a long time a secret worship, led by the Priest-
hood of the Midnight Sun, had existed in dark earth-
caverns which led down into unguessable depths. Here
black magic was practiced under the favor of the Gods
of the Nether World and the lore these priests had
attained was put to stern use at this bitter emergency.
With one accord, at this time, the people of Poseidonis
sought whatever weapons could be found to war against
Oduarpa, the Lord of the Dark Face.

"The shining temples of Ahuni-i were left vacant
and deserted, even by her priests, as the news came
that the deluded hosts of all Earth, led in battle
rank by the invaders from space and commanded by
Oduarpa, were marching to embark from the coasts
nearest to our country. At that despairing hour, men
forgot to look into the square and pitying eyes of the
Spirit of the Wave for wisdom and courage. They even
denied that Ahuni-i could save them. They surged
down into the unthinkable abysses below the Siluane
Hills and there in the eternal night they found what
they sought.

"None who descended would later tell of that which
lay below, but they found the strange and horrible land
of the Dark Sun and became in form very similar to
the inhabitants of that land.

"Up and out of the long tunnels they returned to
the clawed, long-armed monstrosities. On others,
leathery wings had sprouted, and many were no longer
biped, but were horned and spined and doubly dangerous. In the mad eyes of all there gleamed the lust to
kill. In the under land the bodily form of each had
taken on the semblance of his inner spirit and that

spirit had been warped by blasphemous arts until, no matter how mild previously, it had become the contaminated soul of a murderer!

"The host, men and women once, crossed the sea and met the would-be invaders at Gebira. In their Vimanas they fell upon the assembled armies, scattered and destroyed them. Flakes of fire fell from the skies like snow. Whole lands became as ash and cinders. Oluarpa was killed and upon his death his lieutenants vanished, for their pseudo-life was an extension of his. Mercilessly, the murderers wandered to and fro upon the tortured surface of the Earth, ravaging, wantonly slaying, stamping civilizations flat, destroying the long work of eons.

"The White Emperor recalled them, but many would not come. Those have gone down in the pantheons of the other lands as fearful deities to be propitiated with blood and tears. Hawk-headed, dog-faced, baboon-shaped—lion- or bull-bodied monsters. Our loved ones of Poseidonis who fought and suffered and lost their souls to save our endangered country!

"Some thousands came back. White magic warred with black magic that they might be cured in the healing temples—our protectors who were at the same time our greatest criminals. Some were beyond redemption and were mercifully exterminated. The remainder resumed their human shape once more, but their kindly nature had been warped. Their behavior was unpredictable and it was found that the slightest irritation caused them to fly into fits of ungovernable fury.

"Yet, though they had been blighted by their experiences, the mass of the nation regarded them as heroes. In order that they might still continue to live and enjoy life as fully as possible, an island off the coast of Alata was set apart for them.

"This was surrounded by a wall of force through which they might not pass to continue the infection from which they suffered. It was a gentle exile and they were granted every luxury. Whole families went to dwell with those they loved and here through the ages that followed they found happiness as they and their descendants fulfilled their destiny. It was a fertile island and now and again new blood came to it when convicted murderers were sent there, for who can slay a murderer without becoming one himself?

"Supplies were sent them for many years until they became self-supporting and then, the need no longer existing, they were almost forgotten by Poseidonis. My country, now the only civilized land upon the globe, suffered terribly during the passing centuries.

"All the rest of the world had lapsed into deepest barbarism. Again men returned to the caves and the forests. In a few places they even forgot the use of metals and the value of fire. The Spirit of the Wave, not holding Poseidonis guiltless for its part in the general ruin, caused the glaciers to melt and retreat into the north. The rising waters of her disapproval overwhelmed the large islands of Ruta and Daitya, remnants preserved from a former inundation.

"In other places there were encroachments, dismaying the people. Again they renounced war, and the last few happy years began for the dying continent of Atlantis. During this period, I was born.

"Several centuries before, an exploring expedition had crossed the dead sea bottom of the Gobi, searching for the fabled White Island. Its glories were gone, but they found Oduarpa's spaceship there and stripped it of its secrets. The metal of its structure was foreign to Earth and they called it orichalcum.

"This is the only metal in existence which lives. A tiny grain of it, added to a large quantity of lead, transmutes the lead into mercury, mercury into gold, and gold finally into orichalcum. This is the metal of which my artificial body is composed and all the substance of this Vimana!

"From that time onward, any body or movable thing constructed from orichalcum draws energy from sunlight and docilely submits to man's direction.

"When this discovery was made, aided by writings found on the spaceship, life was made easier for the inhabitants of Poseidonis. Artificially made men and women, scarcely to be recognized as non-human, carried on all the disagreeable work necessary without complaint or recompense. Swan-ships sailed the skies, never tiring, beautiful and swift, wafting the human population about in accordance with its frivolous will. Life became too easy. It no longer had purpose. Boredom came.

"As I have said, Colrane, my father, was a starseer. I helped him in his work in his observatory, high in the Siluane Hills, searching the sky night after night as thousands of others were doing, lest another visitation from the stars take us unaware.

"Little we suspected, with our eyes turned heavenward, the land slumbering peacefully about us, the nearby harbor of Colicynos a crescent moon of soft light upon the bosom of the dark sea, that destruction was creeping upon us from the realms beneath the ground.

"After the defeat of the nations, our people in their fear had tumbled in the entrance to the Land of the Dark Sun, sealing it with talismans, shutting it off, they thought, forever. But now, in their boredom and idleness, fools opened the unhallowed road and passed within, while back along the way they had trod came the inhabitants of the Dark Land to seize upon upper Earth.

"From our observatory my father and I felt the concussion and saw the flare as Mount Gartola split wide open. Father swung around the small scanner and focused it upon the rent, but with the naked eye I could see black winged things tumbling out of the mountain, hurling themselves down upon the plain and the sleeping city below.

"His face was white with fear as he dropped the tube. He clutched my arm, hurried me out upon the landing and into our Vimana. Earth shocks almost threw us from our feet. The Vimana rocked and fell from the landing, but caught itself without attention from us. It sprang into the air and spread its pinions.

"Father willed it to Mount Gartola and as we soared above the seething abominations he seared them with the dyro-blast. The Vimana flew back and forth just in front of their line in advance. I think he hoped to drive them back below ground, but if so there was no time. The Spirit of the Wave was at last enraged beyond forgiveness with the folly of sinful Atlantis.

"Far out at sea we saw the wild white line coming at us, while we wheeled and fought. The crest of the Wave was higher than any mountain I had ever seen. It pounded down upon Colicynos, and when it fell, flame leapt from the hills to meet it. Water rushed down into the Dark Land, Poseidonis blew itself apart in thunder—something struck against the Vimana's wing; I heard the crash and the crumpling—I knew we were falling but I do not remember the shock of striking the water.

"When I again became conscious, I was in dreadful pain. My back was broken and I felt that I had only moments to live. My father was near me, also suffering intensely. His arm was broken, both legs and several ribs. I could see that his condition was most desperate.

" 'Daughter,' he whispered, 'our bodies are dying, yet we need not die unless we will it. Shall we take the bodies of the servants?'

He referred to two bodies of orichalcum made to serve—one permanently placed upon a dais as an object of art and to be available if needed, the other packed away for future use. These were usually made in the likeness of living persons in the family which owned them. It was possible for an adept to will his or her astral self into such a body, becoming its ego. This was often done when a person's fleshy body was weary of living and it hampered a spirit still restless to complete a problem or an experiment. It was not a difficult matter to adjust oneself into one's new home and it is only a little harder to take over a real body for a short time and look out of its eyes at strange surroundings."

"I know about that," Gwalchmai interjected. "My

godfather, Merlin, spoke of it in his books of magic. He called it possession."

"Yes, it is possession, and it was then that we meant to possess the orichalcum bodies, activating them to take the place of our own. The heaving of the Vimana upon the turbulent ocean, as it swam half-submerged, gave me excruciating pain. I gasped, 'Anything, father, but do it quickly!'

"He gazed steadily at this female figure and I added my thoughts to his. I felt a sudden cessation of pain. I opened my eyes, which I did not remember having closed, and found myself standing, looking down upon two distorted figures on the floor. The experiment had been successful. Father said, faintly, 'Come here to me.'

"I walked toward him, feeling alive, human as any normal girl, which was odd to think about, although this metal body was modeled from my living form. He raised himself, high as he was able, trying to reach the stud on my back. The experiment was never performed without an assistant close at hand to do this when the interchange was completed. I could have lifted him, but he did not command it and this servile form responded only to commands. I could not help him or myself.

"His good arm reached upward to my knees, my waist—his breath whistling with pain. He touched the small of my back and I felt his fingers fall away. I heard the thud as he fell and I knew he was dead, but I could do nothing. Oh, Ahuni-i! I could not even cry.

"Then the body, receiving no other order, returned to its original spot on the dais, as it must always do upon the completion of a command. In it, I was imprisoned. I could never escape from it through any act of my own will. Here, magnetically held, I have stood for untold years. Waves cradled the ship, winds have rocked it, weed has gripped it fast, but nothing has stirred me.

"I have projected my astral body far. In spirit I have roved the world. For moments I have looked out of other eyes and heard with other ears. I have known of love, of hate, of death—all the emotions of others, never of mine.

"I have seen great nations rise from barbarism and sink into oblivion, and other nations, a score of times, build proud new cities on the ruins of the old, whose very names had been forgotten. I have seen the land rise and fall like the waves of the sea and forests become deserts and lakes become dry land and lake again and I have stood here waiting.

"I have learned languages for my amusement, of which no word is now spoken upon any living tongue, but rove as I might, learn what I would, I could not escape from my prison.

"Then, looking down upon the sea out of the eyes of an albatross, I saw your little wooden boat being borne to me into the weed by the currents and the breeze. I studied you. I knew that I must draw you to me and I influenced the sea worm to make a channel through the weed, a path which I hoped your curiosity might urge you to follow. You have a strong mind, when it is not sick. I could not move you to my will and it surprised me.

"You know the rest, but know this too: I could have done nothing to help you had you not given this unruly body of mine definite orders for it to obey. In my deep gratitude, you may command anything in my power to fulfill and it shall be done. At last *I* am mistress! Mistress of myself!"

"I have no commands," said Gwalchmai. "I do not know who I am or how I came to be here, and I am weary of loneliness."

Corenice studied the young man's face. She took his head between her hands and pressed it to her breast. Her touch was warm and soothing and her hair fell upon his shoulders as gently soft and trailing as that of a girl of flesh and blood.

He felt a sense of healing pouring into his mind and suddenly the blank spot there was filled. Again he had an identity. He remembered his parents and his mission. He recalled his promise to fulfill the duty he had vowed to complete whatever might intervene—

Now it was the man who fell to his knees in gratitude, telling her his story and giving thanks that it would, with her help, be possible to complete his vow. Surely it was for this that he alone had escaped alive from the island of the thirty slain.

Surprisingly, she agreed and smiled upon him. It was a young, gay, girlish smile. He was good to look upon. Gwalchmai saw it and wondered. Could her story be true? Was it possible that she was not human? He studied her. In every aspect, except for little golden glints which twinkled just under a translucent skin, if it was skin, and her golden color, she was as other girls that he had known in Aztlan.

Her nudity, to Gwalchmai, was nothing to be concerned about. With his upbringing in a hot climate and his background, clothing of any sort meant only an opportunity for embellishment, or a protection against the weather. This was normal and as it should be, yet as Corenice twisted her metallic hair into a coiled coronet, dimples sprang out in her elbows. As she stood before him with her head thrown back, her every gesture was so purely feminine that the breath caught in his throat.

Her tiniest motion was grace and beauty. He was stirred as none of the girls in his father's capital of Miapan had ever affected him, and they were the pride of the empire.

"When you were as I am, Corenice, did you seem as I see you now?"

"Would you like to see me as I was then?" she asked, almost shyly.

"It would please me very much, if I could; but so long ago, you say—?"

She opened a compartment in a desk and took out a transparent block. Two little figures stood within it.

"My father and I appeared thus upon my last birthday. Hold it to your eye, so—and press this corner hard."

Now, to Gwalchmai, the figures seemed life size. They moved and smiled at each other. The man said something. The girl laughed and pirouetted before him in a swirl of white silk while he stood back and admired her. There was great love in his expression. She kissed him on the cheek.

Then, with their arms about each other, they stood and seemed to look directly into Gwalchmai's eyes. He gasped. The girl in the cube looked exactly like the living statue.

"That is you and this is you! You are the same!"

"I told you the image was molded from my living body. Now, thanks to you, I live again."

"How old were you then, Corenice? How old are you now?"

But Corenice was rearranging her hair and although he repeated it, she obviously did not hear the question, for she did not answer. When she had finished, she looked upon him seriously.

"Your vow I will help you keep. I shall be most happy to do anything for you that you can ask and I can do, but I am, in my own way, as firmly bound to a duty as are you. There is a vow I made to my ancestors during the long centuries I stood alone in yonder alcove, looking out upon the wickedness of the world. There is a danger coming which I alone can ward away, lest other lands be destroyed as was Atlantis and for the same reason. I swore to somehow thwart that danger if I were ever set free, and Ahuni-i listened and sent you. That promise binds me now.

"My observations of you and of the sword you carry, and perhaps also the ring you wear, lead me to believe that your help would be valuable to me. If you would not come with me, I will take you now upon your way, aid you to complete your mission, and bring you back to your own country, but I would have you gladly at my side when I do what I must, for I may need help and time runs short."

"Where will your vow take us?" Gwalchmai asked.

"North! North to the coast of Alata. North to Atlantis' last surviving colony on all Earth's surface—to Nor-um-Bega, the Island of the Murderers!"

"I will go, Corenice of Colicynos. My sword hand upon it and my sword when you need it!"

Perhaps, since man first learned the binding power of a handclasp, no stranger pact had ever been sealed in that manner, nor one fraught with more far-reaching consequences.

5

The People of the Dawn

They had again seated themselves at the rim of the pool while they were talking. Corenice sprang to her feet with a harmonious chiming of mechanism.

"Follow me!" she cried, like a peal of elfin bells, and led the way below to the engine room. As before, the fishes swam beneath the transparent floor and green-gold light flooded over the humming power boxes and the weed fronds waved lazily below in the slow currents. As on his other visits, the excess energy spat and snapped, as for uncounted centuries it had done, exhausting itself into the sea. At last, it was to be directed by an intelligence and work again for man.

Gwalchmai noticed, for the first time, that the ominous feeling of being watched by an enemy had passed away. This room seemed no more to be dreaded than any of the others, except for a sense of caution which bade him keep his distance from the machinery.

"We cannot fly, as I should like to do," explained Corenice, "because of the broken wing. However, as you can see through the observation panels, the feet are uninjured. Our trip will be longer, but we shall reach our destination as surely, by swimming."

"How about this crowding weed? Can the swan-ship force a way?"

"We could burn a channel through, but all our power may be needed before we are done. There is yet an easier way."

She depressed five of a bank of keys upon a horizontal panel board and the Vimana woke once more from its long rest. Air raced out in swift bubbles along the translucent sides. The weed fronds lashed and swung as shadows danced against the walls. Water rumbled into hidden tanks. The long arching neck and head dipped like a diving bird, and leaving only a clear spot in the weed-carpeted sea to mark its passing, the swan-ship plunged beneath the surface.

Down, down in long easy spirals, driven by the powerful thrusts of the webbed feet. Deeper yet, while the sunlight dimmed and the interior of the ship grew twilight dark and the eternal cold of the great deeps drove away the long stored warmth of the upper air.

Other keys being depressed, heat returned from glowing grids in the walls and brilliant shafts of light shot downward from the eye lenses. Briefly illuminated, as they wheeled and circled lower, marine creatures darted to safety, some huge and monstrous, fearsome, tentacular, with powerful snapping beaks which might easily rend metal.

Gwalchmai repressed a shudder, but the girl, unmoved, sat peering down through the floor, waiting patiently as the searchlights cut broad swathes through the dark water.

Suddenly and with a sharp ejaculation, she snapped down another key which released the first five from their previous positions, and, leveling out, the ship hung at that level with lights still showing. The bottom, which had become as visible as a beach on a misty day, rushing up at them abruptly, now slid easily by with the yet unexpended impetus of their descent. For some moments he could see only ooze and broad furrows made by crawling things, though it was apparent by her interest that Corenice was aware of something more.

Then, as though by a trick of changing vision, a mound of mud assumed a more regular form and a rectangular outline could be distinguished surrounding a central dome. The hand of the metal maiden quivered upon the key bank. She pointed down.

"Atlantis!" she murmured. "Behold its people!"

Upon the dome sprawled a long ribbon-like form, coil upon coil surrounding something more than half hidden by the windings. Pulsations ran through the lax body as it fed. The horrible head lifted, sensing the unfamiliar light, and they could see the bones it was mumbling, nearly stripped of flesh, still mingled in the wreckage of the Saxon ship.

Gwalchmai was about to inquire if the wreck could be searched for Merlin's chest of magic treasures, but the creature poised only an instant in indecision. Then, with jaws agape to show row upon row of fangs, it came swimming with long undulations to investigate the edibility of this strange visitor.

Fast as it came, the Vimana was faster. Upward again, in a long steep slant, they rose to a point where light beat down upon them in thin rays through the tangled weed. Hour after hour, just below the longest streamers, they sped along. Gwalchmai tired, but would not give in to sleep. Finally, the girl, whose metal body could not know weariness, perceived his need.

At the time, they were in the room of the murals depicting the past glories of Atlantis. Without saying what she intended to do, Corenice rose and began to dance. Softly as thistledown, lightly as a windblown leaf, she leapt and spun and swung from one black square to another, waking melodies no human ear had heard since the seas had marched over Poseidonis.

Softer and more sweetly yet, the mystical harmonies sounded, interrupted by not a single discord. Gracefully the lithe figure swayed and postured, every movement a poem of beauty. His eyelids grew heavier and, drooping, finally closed. He lay back upon the soft metal of the bench and the music stopped.

Corenice smiled to herself and crossed the room. She stepped heedlessly from square to square, but now there were no answering sounds. Even the chiming bells of her mechanism were muted.

A concealed spring in the frame of the harbor scene let down a soft folding couch from the wall, the existence of which he had not suspected. She lifted him in her metal arms, easily as a mother lifts a baby, and laid him gently and tenderly down.

Long ago all fabrics had disappeared from the Vimana. Age had seen to that, and the sea air, but the couch was still comfortable as a bed of feathers, made from that wondrous orichalcum which could be either down-soft or diamond-hard.

She left him there and went to the control room in the bird's head. Frowning with concentration, she willed, having set the controls for mental operation. The speed increased. The broad, webbed feet beat the water with redoubled power. The ship tore on, fifty feet below the surface, toward the North. The strange girl stared out through the lenses, tireless, strong, more than human, unwinking and watchful. Only she knew what her thoughts might be and what the thoughts of the Vimana—for it did think, as no other creation of man had ever done, since the beginning of the world.

He did not awaken when, far beyond the borders of the weed, the ship slanted upward to the surface of a calm, smooth sea. Morning came, finding him still sleeping, and another night.

Upon the surface, the swan swam faster. Its broad breast skimmed over the waves, and its wings, even though one was crippled, were spread enough to give a slight lifting power which increased the speed. With its long neck laid well back and its head down between its shoulders, it hurtled along.

As though the steady rumble of shafting had a soothing, soporific effect upon his exhausted body,

Gwalchmai slept on and on. The vibration did not disturb him or the gentle rocking of the giant bird as first one and then the other paddle thrust against the water.

Again, through the second night, the swan-ship swam steadily northward, but slower, for it followed now a rocky, well-wooded coastline. When he finally awoke, a little after sunrise, the bed no longer vibrated under him, though he felt a slight lifting and falling and could hear a lapping of baby waves against the sides of the vessel.

To dress was the simple matter of putting on his moccasins, and, leaving his weapons where they lay, he went above to the upper deck in search of the girl. The air was chill as he emerged upon the back of the Vimana. He was surprised to see that early autumn had laid coloring fingers upon the leaves of the maple and oak trees which fringed the shores of the little cove, where, sheltered from the outer breakers, the ship lay at anchor. He had not realized until then how far the year must be advanced, nor how long he must have been drifting.

The seasons had passed unnoticed during the time he had been locked in the southerly sea of weed, but now he knew that months had elapsed, many precious days stolen from his life, in which he might have gone far upon his way.

A hail from the shore interrupted his thoughts and he saw Corenice waving to him.

"Ohi!" she called. "Are you really alive again? Accouter yourself and come to land."

He waved back, laughing, and in a few moments reappeared fully armed. One broad wing of the Vimana lay fully extended over the water, its tip touching some scattered rocks. It was easy to leap from one to another and gain the shore where she was waiting.

Her merry mood had passed when he reached her and pausing only for a brief clasp of hands she turned to serious business, hurrying him away from the edge of the beach, into the edge of the wood.

Here she paused and, pointing toward the ground, indicated to him the faint beginnings of a narrow trail.

"Many times I have passed along this way, in the spirit, following the makers of this path and helpless to warn against the wrongs they intended. Now I am here, in the body, and here my vow begins its fulfillment! You must say now, man, if you are with me. From this place, once we begin, we shall not turn back."

"Lead on," said Gwalchmai. "I follow."

She smiled. "I was sure I could depend upon you, but first there is a thing to be done. While you were sleeping I followed up the path a little way to be quite certain that there was no mistake in my recognition of the locality.

"As we may have far to go, we cannot leave the Vimana here to be seen and perhaps taken by an enemy. I will send it away, over the horizon, to await our return."

"You will do what?"

"Watch and see."

She turned toward the water. Through an opening in the tree clusters, the cove was plainly visible, and also the floating Vimana. Without making a discernible movement and without speech, she looked intently at the ship.

Gwalchmai thought he heard a faint clicking somewhere within her beautiful frame, a sound unlike the usual musical sounds accompanying her movements. At once a harsh rattling was heard from the cove. The Vimana, by itself, was taking in its anchor!

The widespread pinion furled tight against the shining body, the long neck swayed high and the powerful head turned purposefully about, as though the swan-ship was looking for its mistress. She waved her arm in a commanding sweep and after an instant of hesitation, almost human in its indecision, the great bird turned in a welter of foam and raced out to sea.

"Now, just how did you do that?" the young Aztlanian asked, deeply puzzled.

Corenice laughed, a chiming peal of melody. "Perhaps I have instruments within me to direct it from afar. Perhaps"—her voice was low and mocking—"it may have understood me! Are not we two of one flesh?"

He grunted in disbelief. Still smiling to herself, she led the way into the wood. They had not gone far before a little brook of sweet water crossed the path and here he lay and drank, long and deeply.

She stood and watched him, knowing his need. Somewhat wistfully she recalled that once, ages ago, she too had drunk and eaten with enjoyment of the good things that life in a body of flesh desired.

"You are hungry also?" she asked. "I did not remember. My energy comes directly from the sun, not by eating the things which the sun causes to grow. I made no provision for you, but yonder in the trees are vines and upon them grow purple grapes. If they would do for the moment—?"

She waited while he plucked ripe, heavy clusters, frost sweetened, eating avidly, selecting bunches to carry as they walked on.

"Are they juicy and good?" she queried, a bit ruefully. "I remember I used to enjoy them very much, long ago, when I was alive."

He nodded, mouth too full to reply, and they passed deeper and deeper into the forest, along the trail, leaving the cover far behind.

Nunganey, the Abenaki, lay flat as the rattlesnake he resembled, with his death-paint of yellow upon his belly and brown and black blotches on his back. Wood ashes smeared his cheeks and he was softly chanting his death song as from a lofty oak limb he looked down the forest trail.

Along this way came always the red-haired killers from Akilinek, the Island of Demons, somewhere on the tidal sea.

He did not know just where it might be situated. Once thirty canoes had gone to seek it. A great war party, the strength of three tribes. None had ever returned, taken either by the sleek green wolves of Squant, the square-eyed sea-goddess, or Hobbamock the Foul, who dwelt upon that island to be the curse of men.

Twice each year the hairy killers came ravening through the forests of the Abenaki—when the snow was one moon gone from the hills and again shortly before it returned. Never had they been conquered. They came as they pleased, with their heavy axes and their shirts from which the arrows bounced and their war-bonnets upon which stone tomahawks broke.

They plundered, slew, ravaged and were gone to sea again, paddling over the horizon in their curious stone boats (for Nunganey knew nothing of metals) with their weighty loads of maize, furs, meat and captives.

When they had gone, Nunganey's people were destitute. Still they clung to their homeland and hunting-grounds, loving their country savagely, refusing to be driven away or to fall permanently into the position of a subject nation. They always fought, though they never won.

Nunganey thought moodily on these things, striking softly into the thick bark with his stone hatchet as he waited.

Orono, the chief, had derided his plans for vengeance after the last raid, when Cosannip, his blood brother, had been taken captive, for what purpose no one knew. Nunganey had refused to become discouraged. He kept on, climbing daily into his high tree with bags of pebbles on his back.

Now, forty feet above the ground, there were suspended two ponderous sacks of stones, each made from the hide of a large black bear. Between them hung a latticework of saplings, studded with foot-long stakes, sharpened and burned stone hard. A single cut of his hatchet upon a single thong would release the cunning fastenings which held the whole suspended over the trail below.

He would see if these stonish men were proof against *that,* as they were against dart and spear! Then he would follow swiftly, sliding down the rawhide rope which lay ready to his hand. He would drop among them to kill and kill and kill again, until Cosannip was avenged and he himself lay dead.

That he would be slain he had no doubt. There was no man of the People who could stand singly against a demon's ax. He could not help marveling at the return of the killers, so soon after their raid. Generally one trip was all at each season, though the old men told that, in their grandfather's time, three visits a year had been the custom, and N'karnayoo—of old time—even oftener. He had only hoped, without reason, that they might return and fall into his trap.

Always, it would appear these demons, these Chenoo, had persecuted the Abenaki, the Children of the Dawn. Now here they were and he was waiting. Wan-pe, the fisher, had seen them on the shore and fled into the village to warn the people and Nunganey had sought the great oak and was ready.

Here they came at last, striding noiselessly over the forest floor. Were they so confident, these Chenoo, that two alone thought that they could walk among the wickams to choose and take as they would? Nunganey growled deep in his corded throat. He would see!

But what in the name of Kiehtan were they?

The man was dressed in somewhat similar manner to the invaders, but his hair was brown, not flaming red—his skin bronzed, not pallid like the Chenoo. Nor was his companion like any Abenaki woman. Entirely naked, her very flesh like the hard integument which the Chenoo put off or on at will, she was a beautiful demon who must die.

Both were strangers, however strangely armed, and they came from the sea. That alone marked them as enemies, in Nunganey's mind.

A score of strides more—ten—five—! The Abenaki's dark eyes glittered and his hatchet fell upon the restraining thong.

Gwalchmai and Corenice had come a long way without speaking. The forest was very still, but neither suspected danger until a blue-jay squawked. Then a whir in the air and a dark blur crashing down caused the metal girl to whirl quick as a tree-cat against him. Thrusting him violently aside and crouching, she received upon herself the full ringing impact of that mighty blow.

Flat on his back, Gwalchmai jerked out the flame gun at his belt. A blast of livid light crashed into the tree and Nunganey, already swinging from the rope, fell thudding from bough to bough, followed by a rain of debris as that rope was clipped above him.

Down smashed the entire treetop with a splintering roar. He saw the painted body strike the earth in a coil of rawhide, to be instantly covered with swishing leaves. He plunged into the foliage, yanking out the stunned Abenaki, and, stepping back, was about to cut down upon him with the flame swathe when Corenice called:

"Save that man alive! I want speech with him!"

Glowering, holding his surly prisoner rigid under the menace of that crystal lens, he turned upon her. Unscratched, unharmed, with her golden hair flying loose, she stood in the wreckage of the lattice. Its many prongs were driven deep around her, broken and askew. The two weights had fallen on either side, to burst the bags and send stones flying afar, splashing up the turf like soft mud.

Bewildered at her odd shortness of stature, he could at first only grin as, all woman in the midst of ruin, her first care was to wipe away a splotch of black loam from her face. She smiled back at him, quite undismayed, and easily cleared away the lumber in front of her, snapping stout pieces of seasoned oak with those dainty hands which looked so small and frail.

Then, still knee-deep, as she had been driven into the forest mold, she took seven steps through the soft earth as though it had been snow. The knees of Nunganey quaked as she approached him, warrior though he was. For an instant he sagged against the tree at his back as he wailed, "M'teoulin! Magician!" But then, stiffening proudly, he began to chant his death song. Desperation was in his eyes, but no more fear.

Gwalchmai looked at Corenice as she spoke to the Abenaki in his own language. "Man! Say now! Know you me?"

"Ho! Bumole the Night Woman art thou! Whom spear cannot touch nor hatchet harm! Slay me quickly and be done!"

Corenice thought swiftly. She was familiar with Abenaki legends. Upon many winter evenings of storytelling, she had invisibly haunted the wickams and long houses, when lonely for humanity she sought to learn—and forget her sterile existence. If she could use those legends to her own advantage, so much the better. So much easier her task would be.

"Right, Netop, Bumole am I, and this is Glooskap the Mighty, master of the thunder! Long ago, I swore to aid the Abenaki against their enemies and at last the time has come to dwell among you for a space. We would be treated by you as an ordinary hunter and his mate might be. We wish to live with you, play with you, perhaps fight for you if you prove worthy!"

Nunganey fell to his knees before her to prove his shame, but Corenice laid her little hand on his shoulder like an accolade, saying:

"Numchalse! Arise! Let us all be equal together, for if we are to help you, I also need your help. To enter your village, I must be clothed after the manner of your women, lest I be recognized as no human and thought no friend. Say, Netop, can you find me garb befitting a maiden of your people?"

Nunganey stammered in his joy and surprise, proud to be addressed as comrade by one so mighty, but finally answered:

"My sister, Keona, was to be a bride. One full year she worked with soft doeskin and porcupine quills to make herself beautiful in the eyes of her lover, but the Chenoo took her and she is no more. A boy then, I have grown to become a man, but still my mother cherishes the garments that she made. If satisfaction to the Night Woman, these shall be hers, though they are not lovely enough for her!"

Corenice beamed upon him at the unexpected compliment. "Wurragen!" she said. "It is well!"

Gwalchmai lowered his weapon, at her nod, and Nunganey sped without other permission into the forest. The young Aztlanian had followed most of the conversation as the language was somewhat similar to that of the Hodenosaunee, where Merlin had held court in their forest towns, and the wearer of Merlin's ring could understand the languages that Merlin had known.

"Do you think he will come back?" he asked. Corenice did not trouble to answer, merely signing him to follow as she walked on in the direction the Abenaki had taken.

They had covered perhaps a mile when they heard the padding of a runner approaching. Nunganey appeared, panting, bearing a pack upon his back. He shrugged it down and cried:

"My people await you with dancing and a feast! I have told them the Chenoo shall come against us in vain, now that the gods love us! They anxiously wait!"

"Then let it not be I to keep them waiting long!" gaily remarked Corenice, as she disappeared into a dense clump of low hemlock. In a few moments she reappeared and the two men gasped at the change.

Her soft shirt of white doeskin, lined with the breasts of woodpigeons, displayed her perfect throat. Careful embroidery, of colored porcupine quills and shell beads, could be seen beneath the open tunic worn outside the shirt and two narrow belts of tiny beads crossed between her breasts. Her tunic, short skirt and leggings were also ornamented and were deeply fringed with seagreen thrums. Moccasins of caribou skin covered her small feet and over her gleaming braided hair she had drawn the pointed hood of deerhide which was attached to the blue-gray fur cloak of wolfskin which she wore over all.

She was pleased at the admiration of the two men and was delighted further when Nunganey timidly proffered to the grim Aztlanian a broad belt of Siwan and plastron of the same, with a handsome beaver fur blanket. In the south, Gwalchmai had been more accustomed to wearing ornaments of feathers than these heavy beaded articles. He took the gifts, but grumbled aside to Corenice:

"I'd trade the whole outfit, fine as it is, for the hind leg of a dead deer, well roasted, and a baked squash with it!"

She laughed and Nunganey smiled anxiously, not understanding.

"You men! A rag would suit you all your little lives, had you but your bellies full twice a day! Now these are the first fine new clothes I have had for ten thousand years and I think such a marvelous present was well worth the waiting!"

So, with quip and answering jest, they took once more to the forest road, which led now at long last to friends.

6

The Island Under the Sea

In the days that followed they were taken to the hearts of the simple kindly people, who gladly gave them welcome. Gwalchmai learned to admire them as a dignified and noble race. Accustomed to a higher level of civilization among his own people, he at first thought of them as savages, but he soon realized that although they did no stone carving and had no system of writing, in their own way they were as skillful in astronomy as himself. Their eyes were as keen as his to pick out the tiny star in the Little Dipper which they called "the baby on the mother's back" and they could see things upon the moon which he could not discern. With their fine memories to aid them, they could recite lineages much farther back than his and quote them from ancient speeches or tell stories in rolling lines equal to the finest compositions of Merlin's bards. They had an instinctive sense of drama and would act out a tale with such expressive gestures that a deaf man could have followed and enjoyed it.

As a fighting-man, he was impressed by their ability, physique and courage. He joined in their hunts against wolf, bear and wolverine, testing their courage as they were observing his. When he killed in singlehanded encounter the great cougar of the North, he earned their respect as a man, though they were in awe of him as Glooskap, the mischievous mountain god.

Winter came and the youths played in the snow, wrestling, sliding on hides down icy slopes, snowballing one another. Gwalchmai vied with them as they strove for skill in the swift uproarious game of the

Snow Snake, hurling darts at the crooked peeled stick sliding so erratically down the slope. Laughing, young and joyous, they slogged through the woods on snowshoes, and groaned together kneading out one another's cramps.

In the wickams, Corenice, world old, lived after long years the life of humans, mimicking their ways as much as her metal body would permit. No eyes as quick as hers to find and thread the needle some old feeble hand had dropped; no fingers as soft and gentle as hers to comfort an aching body racked with pains of the winter cold; no arms that could rock a baby weary of the cradle board more quickly into quiet slumber.

The muted tinkling of tiny bells which accompanied her slightest movement fascinated the children. The elfin sounds charmed the adults also, confirming their knowledge that she was far from being as other women. No one feared her; they feared only the coming of the day when she and her mate must leave them.

Both listened to the elders in council and did not presume to give advice, considering themselves as transients. Gwalchmai's sympathetic heart burned to hear of the wrongs they had suffered from the Nor-um-Begans and though he said little, he was becoming fixed in the mood Corenice had wished him to develop. It was not without purpose that she had planned to spend the winter with the People of the Dawn. Although he had already agreed to be Corenice's man, until her purpose was accomplished, he felt drawn to them for it seemed to him that their ways were much similar to the ways of his own far distant land. It was this feeling that she had wished to foster. Now there would be no drawing back.

He and Nunganey became firm friends as the winter wore on, being nearly the same age. When the snow disappeared from the woods and the river was free from ice, the village began to prepare for the inevitable spring raid which was fast approaching. The young maidens made tearful farewell to their families and left for a secret place deep in the hills and the men and boys made ready to fight their usual hopeless battle.

Now Corenice was ready also to try to forestall that coming attack. As the two announced that they must depart, neither was surprised that Nunganey insisted upon going with them to aid in the furtherance of the plans she had secretly made.

So, on a bland day in the Sugar Moon, they dropped down the river in Nunganey's stout log canoe, fighting the incoming tide, until it turned and raced backward with them, leaving their warm-hearted friends lining the riverbank, calling farewells.

Nunganey raised his paddle in one final salute to the disappearing land and then all about them lay only the boundless sea. He, for one, had no expectation of ever returning.

In his own mind, he was already dead.

As they headed into the eye of the rising sun, the direction in which, so many times, the invading fleet had been observed to vanish, Gwalchmai's keen eye caught a golden glint winking low on the horizon. Corenice followed his gaze and nodded.

"The Vimana? In truth, it is coming to meet us and I must send it back. I have been in touch with it all these white months, guarding it from drifting in too close in storms and helping it to avoid floating ice. It wants to be with us, but that is no purpose of mine at present. There are other plans."

She looked steadily in that direction for some time and he could not tell when it disappeared, but looking up later from his even paddling he found that the gleam had gone.

They labored on and on, farther than the bravest fisherman had ever dared to go out into the waste. Nunganey was silent, teeth clamped tight, looking ever and again at his strong new bow to give himself courage. Gwalchmai had helped to make it, but the Abenaki had strung it with a bowstring twisted from his mother's hair, that it might avenge his sister and never miss. He thought of her often, but deepest in his heart, stronger even than family ties, were thoughts of Cosannip, his comrade and brother by the rites of mingled blood.

Corenice still wore her stout hide garments and the hood which covered her resplendent hair. As an additional disguise she had stained her face and hands with dye of berries and roots until now she seemed sister in hue to the men.

So they appeared to be what they hoped to be taken for, three native fishermen, blown out to sea against their will.

The canoe rose and fell upon the hills of ocean as the stately rollers marched under on their lonely parade from the far coasts of Europe. A little after midday, Nunganey raised his paddle and pointed ahead.

The prow dipped and the others could not see what he had indicated. On the next high wave a tall thin pinnacle of black rock showed plainly, though far away, like an upright needle almost buried in crumpled satin.

"Akilinek!" muttered Nunganey.

"Nor-um-Bega!" Corenice corrected softly.

An hour later, favored by a following wind, they were close enough to see foam clots and streamers drifting by—born, Gwalchmai thought, where waves crashed against that stony obstacle. But as they drew nearer, he could see that the dashing spray did not actually touch the rock at all. Instead, the waves went creaming up and up toward Heaven, flatly and high, some little distance away, bubbling back, sliding down again as though a wall of glass lay between the peak and the attacking surf.

Yet there was nothing tangible to be seen, except an almost imperceptible turbulence in the air, like the convection currents of heat which go streaming up from hot iron, or a ledge of blistering rock on a scorching summer day.

To the left lay quieter water. Into this they steered, avoiding the turmoil of crashing breakers ahead. Here, bobbing less furiously, though still fighting eddies and

sucking whirlpools, they could discern that not far
beyond lay an end to the water, a rim over which it
could not pour, a titanic hole in the ocean!

Forging through little choppy waves which, on the
lee side, lapped up against the phantasmal barrier,
they approached it closer. The voyagers soon saw
through it, far below, the shining roofs of stone buildings, glittering metal plate on spire and dome and
pinnacles, gay paint on low stone mansions and high
façaded temples.

Broad white paved streets and avenues geometrically
divided the blocks of buildings, and velvety green
grass in park and plot was set about it all, like a toy
city erected upon a carpet.

And all a hundred feet below the level of the broad
Atlantic, with nothing more substantial than a breath
of quivering air between that land of glamour and the
ocean's fury!

"As Atlantis sank and the glaciers melted, the
waters were released into the oceans. The sea level rose
on all the coasts of the world. It lifted here as well and
at the same time the island settled lower. Through the
ages the power units have lessened in strength. Although
the ocean cannot seep through the force wall, the islanders devised a way to pierce it at its upper edge
where it is attenuated and much weaker," announced
Corenice.

"It is like the magic ring of smoky air within which
Vivienne ensorceled Merlin, in the wood of Broceliande," Gwalchmai said. "No one could enter or leave
until she decided to set him free."

Nunganey only clutched his medicine bag for protection, but his lips moved silently as he stared down,
while they drew closer to that uncanny edge. New
vistas continued to open to their gaze and the men
were bemused with wonder.

A strong wall of masonry, dividing the island into
two segments, separated the city proper from the tilled
fields beyond. Gwalchmai could catch the twinkling
gleam of hoe or shovel as laborers toiled, too far away

for eye to make out their form or dress. The wall was pierced centrally by a single, high-arched gateway, closed and guarded, for he could see the flash of golden armor as a sentry paced his walk. Other glints on the wall proved that it also was patrolled.

Among the fields were set wickams and long houses for the slaves and further yet stretched mile upon mile of forest, interspersed with roofless stone ruins as though there had been other cities now abandoned and overgrown. The tossing green conifers held a scattering of birch and hard woods, thickly covering hills and swales, and out of the dense forest ran a silver streamlet, feeder for a large lake, bisected by the high stone wall. Evaporation from the lake obviously equaled its intake, supplemented by rainfall, so that there was neither dearth of water nor danger of flood.

So lost in these sights had all become that they had no eyes for anything closer at hand, until a loud hail startled them. Looking up, they saw on the peak, less than twenty yards away and about the same distance above them, a crouching white-robed man, peering over the railing set around the platform he stood upon.

He held a mallet poised over the trigger of a stone thrower, which was cranked back and ready. A massive boulder lay in the hopper.

"He says not to move away or he will sink us!" whispered Corenice.

While they still gazed upward, observing now that the mountain was artificial, for the jointings between the black blocks of Cyclopean masonry were clearly to be seen, the sentinel lifted a long trumpet and sent a harsh braying across the city.

Gwalchmai had seen pictures, in his godfather's books, of the pyramids of Khemi, and he had climbed th Mian earth mounds and the myriad steps between the terraces of the teocallis of Tolteca, but this edifice was unlike them all. It much resembled the ziggurats of Babylonia, in the respect that a steep railless ramp wound from base to top in seven decreasing spirals.

However, there was machinery where the sentinel stood in the place of the temple sacred to Nabu.

The ramp now bustled with life and movement. Groups of brown and red-skinned slaves came running up, urged to haste by occasional white, red-haired overseers, busily plying metal tipped scourges as though they loved their work.

The slaves stopped on a broad platform, a little above the water level, seizing windlass cranks, bending to their toil as though their very lives depended upon their efforts. The top of the tower revolved, the sentinel walking around to keep the canoe in view, and the three could see a long beam swinging around like a giant's arm. A large, oval box of metal, shaped like a huge closed clamshell, swung from cables at the beam's end.

The sharp edge of this was forced into the area of disturbed air, which boiled and eddied about it as it squealed and the box, lowered by its cables, slapped into the nearby waves, filling the canoe ankle-deep with water.

The flanges separated then, the upper one raising and swinging back, and the guard above motioned them to enter. Gwalchmai and Nunganey hesitated. That open-jawed black clam looked so much like a trap to crunch them!

"This is what we came for, isn't it?" Corenice said dauntlessly, and she stepped over the rim. The others followed and their little canoe went bobbing away, their last sight as the lid snapped down over their heads and they felt themselves being raised in air.

It was dark as night in the windowless lift and they could not see one another, but they clung together to avoid falling, while it swayed beneath them and the whole fabric rocked and creaked, complaining noisily as ungreased cogs drew the beam and chamber back through the bubble-thin wall of force.

Then the lid of their conveyance swung up and a flood of sunlight dazzled the dilated pupils of the two men. The gaunt-faced guard peered in upon them. His look was strained and wild, and his unkempt, dingy white hair flew free about his head and shoulders.

"Who are ye, strangers?" he creaked in Abenaki. "Why do ye come of choice to Nor-um-Bega?"

Nunganey spoke up proudly: "These be Glooskap and his mate, Bumole, the Night Woman, come to visit Hobbamock the Foul—and I am Nunganey the Abenaki, from Atinien, their friend and guide!"

The hawk-faced ancient laughed—a short, unpleasant sound, with disbelief in it—and they could see that his lips were chewed and ragged. His shoulders and arms bore marks of teeth, white scars and new wounds, some scarcely healed, as though in fits of pain or madness he had gnawed at his own flesh in wolfish passion.

"This has been my home since I was whelped," he growled, "and never before have any come here willingly. Since you are among us, believe now you will surely not go away. Strong men are useful!"

His sharp eyes peered into the shadow of the girl's hood and Gwalchmai feared lest the disguise be pierced, but he only favored her with a sour smile.

"And Caranche, our king, will be well pleased to entertain *you*, Woman of the Night!"

Yet he helped her courteously enough to step over the rim of the lift, as Corenice pretended timidity in crossing to the platform, extending her gloved hand to be swallowed up in his wrinkled yellow-nailed paw. Several metal boats were bottom-up on the platform, ready for launching, and an oar rack was near by. Avoiding these, she stepped aside and her companions, needing no such assistance, jumped down with their hands close to their weapons. No attempt was made to disarm them.

Nunganey narrowly eyed the docile slaves as they filed down the ramp, urged on by the stinging whips. Cosannip was not there, his sad face announced, as the three followed the lead of the old man and joined the tail of that dreary procession.

"Baraldabay am I," the guard remarked. "Keeper of the Tower. Too old for war, too tough to die. I bide here and watch the Killers go and come and long for death myself. But I am forgotten, it seems, so I live on and on in this dull hole and never go a-roving. It is worse when the moon is full and the mood comes upon me to slay. Perhaps I shall ask for one of you. You are the first who ever came here unless they were brought."

"And perhaps we will be the last," supplemented Corenice, very softly, with a somber ring in her voice like a funeral bell.

Baraldabay obviously felt that his position was one without honor and was morosely glad to have someone to talk with, even if only for a few moments. As they passed lower along the circling ramp they went by bays curved into the ziggurat's walls. Here were more close-packed arrays of metal longboats, upside-down on rollers, where the crane jaws could easily grip them and carry them through the thinnest part of the force wall.

Corenice asked, "Will you tell us something of your past?"

"In the beginning, we Nor-um-Begans were a mighty people. It is said that large ships regularly plied the seas between this place and Atlantis, our homeland—"

Corenice and Gwalchmai exchanged quick glances.

"That was when our shores were above the sea. Then danger threatened our beautiful colony. The land sank and the sea rose. Around our island, to preserve us, was set the charmed wall of invisibility, so strong that nothing could penetrate it at its base and only with much difficulty at the top."

Gwalchmai wondered if this horrible old man was really as mad as he seemed. Had time perverted their history until the truth was no longer known? Did he not understand that he was a descendant of generation upon generation of inbred criminals and wanton murderers? A denizen of a penal colony?

"It is said that the original population of the island was divided into two classes—normal people like my-

self and others who were so impossibly good that they
were impossible to live with.

"The latter were the first settlers, old soldiers from
a war who had come bringing their women. They
thought killing was a sin instead of being the proudest
means of gaining honor! My ancestors came later, a
few at a time, and they knew better. They grew
stronger and stronger in numbers, until their descendants far outnumbered the earlier colonists' offspring.

"A high, guarded wall divided the island between
the two classes. *They* held it and also the tower, where
they worshiped Hun-ya, the square-eyed witch, who
is our goddess of battle now. By way of the tower they
lifted in their supplies and their wall kept us away from
it, so we could not leave if we chose. We were their
prisoners, but one night my forefathers carried that
wall and put all upon it and in the city to death!

"That marks the real beginning of our glorious civilization. We stormed out upon the mainland in our
thousands, establishing cities, developing the wilderness, subduing the savages—"

Nunganey grunted.

"We wiped away the budding and rival empire of
the Horicon. Later by many, many years we smashed
the Talagewi—they who began the mound cities the
Mians finished, in the interior valleys, when they came
up from the Hot Lands of the South. Those were good
days, our best days!"

His eyes glistened like a gloating spider. Then his
voice dropped and sadness crept into it:

"But I never saw them. It was all over and done
before my time, those days of glory, long ago! Constant battling sapped our strength. No other enemy was
worthy of us and our cities turned their axes against
one another. One by one, the forest took them back
again. Our women grew less fertile and we were too
proud to mate with the savages, unless for an hour,
with any by-blow from the union slain at birth, lest
the purity of our noble race be impaired.

"Finally Nor-um-Bega, Island of Heroes, took back

all that were left of her mainland colonists and we are
what remains.

"Only once, in all my life, have I known the joy of
fighting in a great army. Twenty years ago, every man
and boy of us allied ourselves with the savages, for the
sport of war, and helped to destroy the Mian Empire
of Tlapallan. We fought to reach that country, fought
in the war and fought to reach home again!

"Hun-ya! That was a great killing!"

Corenice gestured at the encircling wall of jade-dark
water, one hundred feet high, its gentle hundred-mile
curve smooth as polished glass around the sunken
country, and Baraldabay followed her gaze.

Sun rays slanted down through it, in parallel beams,
quivering with the turmoil of waves high above the
level of the street where they now stood. Bathed in
this fluctuating light they walked along. A swimming
school of cod followed their progress, peering in upon
them, marveling, gaping goggle-eyed at the strange
two-legged denizens of this underwater aquarium. As
at some signal they whirled and went as one about
their private business.

"Why do you continue to live here when the mainland would be so much safer?"

Baraldabay was amazed. "Why not? This is our
home!"

"Are you not afraid that someday this may tumble
in upon you and destroy you all and everything you
possess, including your fair city and its wealth?"

The oldster grinned.

"Nay, lady, that can never be. Long ago it was
prophesied by the sorcerers who set the magic wall
here to protect us that never by any will of ours should
it be torn down.

"Never—'until the Thunder Eagle should come to
Nor-um-Bega!' "

"What does that mean?" asked Corenice.

"No one knows exactly. There is a semblance of a
monstrous eagle in the sky, outlined in light, seen when

the Fire Children play along the Road of Ghosts, during the cold winter when the nights are cloudless.

"Some superstitious ones think the prophecy refers to this phenomenon, but often and often it has been a good omen for us. It has predicted great victories for us in the past. It must be Hun-ya's pet. The Killers time their spring raids by its last appearance. It is quite harmless."

Gwalchmai saw Nunganey motioning him urgently to fall back a little out of earshot.

"My people know that Thunder Eagle," he quickly muttered. "The bird lives on Sleeping Giant Cape, on the northern shore of the Inland Sea. If it stays in the sky above the cape, war involves the people of the north countries, but if it moves across the sky, the war takes place in the direction the Eagle travels.

"It never fails to mean sorrow for someone. Sometime it will hang over Akilinek and all the Abenaki will rejoice!"

"Maybe, brother, but I have remembered only now a thing which I had long forgotten."

"And that is?"

"My name! I am called Gwalchmai, not Glooskap, and that word means—Eagle!"

The road they followed diverged from the ocean wall, curving into the suburbs, and as they progressed deeper among the houses they could see that the beauty of the city was viewed best from afar, like that of a woman, once lovely, who retains in age only her dignity of form and carriage.

Beyond a columned portico, a slovenly man was chopping wood upon a tessellated marble floor and the carven pillars were wantonly hacked and defaced as if in some fit of maniac fury.

Between the knife-thin joints of the paved street, grass had found its way and tree roots in thickening had raised and displaced stone slabs weighing many tons. Often they went around or over heaps of rubble, where house walls had collapsed into the streets, so long ago that upon some grew stately oaks, feeding

upon the rotten wood of their fallen ancestors before
them. Many otherwise pleasant homes stood roofless to
the sun and rain, with leaves and mold knee deep over
fine mosaics, fountain bowls and toppled statues of
marble.

Never, apparently, was anything repaired. Nowhere
could be seen anything new.

No dogs, cats or other pets rambled about, and such
children as were visible scowled at the passersby with
such wicked, knowing looks that Gwalchmai wondered
if they ever played and if so what their games could
possibly be.

Some women had built a cooking fire in the center
of a little square, where, judging by the refuse strewn
heedlessly about, most of the surrounding houses
seemed to be occupied, and above it meat was stewing
for the evening meal.

The cauldron was silver and had never been intended for that purpose, but its deeply chased engrav-
ings were blurred with soot and the design could not
be seen.

While waiting, a group of boys and young men were
kicking around a rolling object and Gwalchmai saw
it to be a human skull upon which still hung a few
shreds of flesh and a little black hair. They did not
stop at the approach of the strangers, but went on with
their grim sport in a spirit of dull ferocity. It seemed
to be a duty or a custom, and they appeared to find
little enjoyment in the exercise.

But there was worse to follow before the quartet
could pass beyond this squalid section.

Out of a tumbledown, windowless building a shrieking virago ran, lugging a squalling infant by the heels.
Though it could scarcely be a year old, it scratched at
her flying legs with its tiny nails, biting and yelling
like a changeling imp.

Finally she could stand the uproar no longer and
stopped to pound its head against the stones.

Corenice clutched Baraldabay's robe. "Stop it! Stop
it!" she cried, but he was indifferent.

"What would you? She is the child's mother. Here we do as we please!"

"But why? Why should she do that?" Nunganey asked, in horror at an unnatural parent who would strike a child even lightly, much less beat it to death.

"Who knows?" Baraldabay answered. "Possibly it bit her while it suckled. Woman's temper is always unpredictable, here perhaps more than elsewhere. We are a dying people—let us die in our own way!"

The baby's wails whimpered away into complete silence before they had gone very far. Afterward, they heard a long hysterical cry—half laugh, half scream, as the frenzy passed and the infanticide's shaky reason returned to haunt her. If she was in grief or merely sadistically excited, they had no way of knowing.

They passed on, without speaking, and Gwalchmai's impression was that there had been little sincerity in Corenice's plea. He felt that it had been made only to bring out more plainly the philosophy governing the actions of all the denizens of this grand yet hideously savage city-state.

He wondered anew what her motives were in coming here, a strange missionary from the past. What change did she mean to bring about? What could she hope to accomplish?

In a few more years, at the present rate of declining births and frequent strife, the inhabitants must render themselves extinct. Why not let them eliminate themselves in their own cruel way?

They looked down a lateral street where, at a distance, an old slave was staggering through a gauntlet of young boys, who were striking at him with sticks and light wooden axes. He went down and they fell upon him, but he did not cry out.

Baraldabay saw their glances and their pity. He shrugged.

"He belongs to them. That is how boys learn to become men."

Lost in moody reverie, Gwalchmai took no more notice of the passing scene and was surprised when they debouched into a broad, impressive square. They walked across this, suiting their gait to the old man's halting pace, and climbed a long series of time-rounded steps fronting a high pillared building, once a temple to Poseidon and still in a good state of preservation.

Ancient carvings on the pediment showed men on horseback hunting down a mammoth with bow and lance, but without time for inspection they were hurried through a wide doorway. Choking black smoke rolled out above their heads as they entered, finding egress at its own will. Just inside the portico they stopped where an amorer had set up his forge near the altar, which had been tipped over upon its side to make room for it. He was busily beating out a half-moon head for a ponderous war ax.

He lifted his deep set bloodshot eyes to them, to answer Baraldabay's question.

"Caranche? The king? He went beyond the Wall this morning. There was a disturbance among the field slaves and the foresters gave shelter to the runaways. Some more of them want to be sent into the Hole!"

He chuckled grimly and began to hammer again upon the cooling steel.

They passed down a dark corridor and into an open courtyard.

Here stood the magnificent chariot of Poseidon, drawn by leaping dolphins of bronze, each ridden by laughing Nereids. The chariot, of gold and silver, was decorated with stylized octopi and seahorses swam in dipping procession around the border upon the base. The fountain before it was dry and the statue of the god, still brandishing his trident, was headless.

Corenice gave it one agonized glance and averted her eyes.

"You have the liberty of the building," said Baraldabay, succinctly. "Take any vacant sleep room you choose. Food will be brought you here and you may keep your weapons until Caranche gives orders concerning you. He may be gone two or three days. Until then, all entrances will be guarded. If you try to leave you will be killed!"

When they were alone, Corenice turned to the men.

"What do you think of these people whom Ahuni-i loved—and whose very name has been corrupted by them?"

There was iron in Gwalchmai's voice as he replied, "They cannot be allowed to go on. They are totally evil and a menace to the Abenaki."

Nunganey muttered, "They must be destroyed!"

"I determined that long ago, in my floating prison— looking upon them astrally, abominating their evil plans —knowing what I must do, lest they bring destruction upon the whole world. I know what it may cost me. But we will give them a chance they never gave the Abenaki, brother. I do not remember this king of theirs—he may be of a better breed.

"We will wait his coming. If in that time we find one spark of good in this people, or in him—! Well, let us bide in patience and learn what more we may."

7

The Hole

Caranche, King of Nor-um-Bega, came back to his city before evening of the second day of their incarceration, but when the prisoners were brought before him darkness had fallen, owing to the mountainous wall of water between them and the low sun.

Flaming cressets lit the throne room and one glance told the young Aztlanian that here was a man not likely to be deceived by any naive claims of Nunganey concerning his own and Corenice's divinity. He motioned furtively to the Abenaki, in the almost universal sign language common to all nations of polyglot Alata, that he was to keep silent. Nunganey nodded in answer. But the mischief had already been done.

Caranche was a very ox of a man, bull throated, mightily muscled, his arms and legs furred with red bristles. His mop of carroty hair fell over his fierce restless eyes into his tangled beard.

He sprawled in his seat, peering morosely through his unkempt locks at the strangers, occasionally lifting a hamlike hand to suck a small bleeding wound on his wrist. Gwalchmai saw several in the throne room who wore bandages or moved carefully. He guessed that Caranche's punitive expedition against the foresters had not had everything its own way.

Either the smart or the manner in which the king had received the scratch irked him, making his mood more ugly than usual. The surrounding men-at-arms gave him fearful respect and the three surmised that this man was, like his subjects, of an invariably quick temper and vicious whims.

Baraldabay, their sponsor, went up and whispered something to him which they could not catch. Caranche at once favored Gwalchmai with an intent and interested gaze, centering on the flame-gun at his belt. He motioned Gwalchmai to advance, peremptorily beckoning with a pudgy finger glittering with jewels, and coming to the point without preamble.

"My Tower Man tells me what I can see for myself," he rumbled, in Abenaki. "You have a weapon of the Old Ones who built this city. Where did you get it?"

Gwalchmai stammered, trying to think of an answer which would not disclose the true identity of Corenice.

"Never mind! Let me have it!" the king interrupted, holding out his hand.

Gwalchmai shot a look of indecision at the girl. She nodded imperceptibly and he unwillingly gave up the weapon.

Caranche fingered it inexpertly, turning it over and over, while they hoped fervently that he might manage to blow his head off with it. Scarcely lifting his eyes from it, he grunted to an attendant:

"Bring in those field slaves!"

A group of crippled and bleeding red men were herded in and lined up against the farther wall. None had their wounds attended and some were in a dying condition, being supported by their companions. Obviously these were unfortunates who had been handled with malicious and unnecessary violence, by men who loved the sight of suffering. Nunganey's relieved sigh told the others that his friend was not among them.

The king looked hard at Gwalchmai.

"We have a storeroom filled to the top with these things and not one of them will work. If this one does what our legends say it should, I will make you chief armorer and commander of a hundred!"

He raised it, took aim and pulled the trigger. The echo of the long and continued discharge filled the broad hall with thunder as charred heaps, which had once been men, fell to the floor half buried under cascades of masonry torn from the wall behind them. Heedless of the destruction he was causing, Caranche swung the besom of flame back down the long line. He had not quite finished when the light waned rapidly, running down the spectrum from brilliant blue-white to dark cherry-red, then went completely black like a cooling ember.

Caranche was furious and swung upon the three.

"Did you do that? How can I recharge it?"

"Go to Mictlampa and find out, you blood-soaked murderer!"

Gwalchmai snatched for his sword, while the Abenaki and the girl from Atlantis pressed closer to him in silent approbation. His action was not quick enough. He and Nunganey fell buried beneath a dozen guardsmen and were overpowered at once. They were carried off, weaponless, though Corenice, who oddly enough had not used her miraculous strength, was led peaceably in another direction, smiling secretly at them to be unafraid.

Caranche shouted after them, beside himself with fury:

"Give them a sight of the Hole! Take them down with the relief lot, but bring them back to the pits until morning. They can decide then to tell me or to die!"

The two men were hurried out to the street, where they joined a line of perhaps forty men with only minor wounds, and were linked to them by a long chain. Then, under close guard, they passed out of the city through a gate in the wall and were marched across the open fields beyond. After about a mile of traveling they came to a place where heaps of jagged rock encumbered the ground, in mounds higher than houses.

Far as eye could see in the dusk, these mounds stretched away to left and right, refuse heaps from some industry fit for Titans.

Torches were lit at this point and they pressed forward under the flickering light. They followed a well traveled road and after a half-hour of steady marching among the mounts they came to an unencumbered field. Here stood a high tower of metal with a guiding wheel at its top over which a cable ran, and slaves there were chained to a winch, waiting their coming.

Without delay ten men were separated and led upon a platform which sank into the ground and disappeared out of sight to the creaking accompaniment of the winch and the cracking of whips.

Not long after, it rose again with a load of rock upon it, wet and shining in the torchlight. Slaves came forward and cleared this away and another ten men took place upon the platform and followed the others.

Again this was repeated, and again, and at last Nunganey and Gwalchmai also sank into the depths. The shaft was lined with metal and planks until bedrock was met and from there only the natural living granite met their gaze. Peering over the sides, they saw lights below and soon with a grating bump they came to a stop.

This was not the bottom. The shaft widened out into a chamber, broad and high, with another framework beside them and another contingent of slaves. Here too, another platform waited, and after its load of rock had come down, they stood upon the scarred planks and were carried deeper.

Again they sank from chamber to chamber of this tremendous shaft. There seemed to be no end to lower levels. It became hard to breathe. The least effort was an exertion; the air seemed drenched with fog and the torches would not burn.

They dropped past chambers lit wanly with clustered luminous fungi feeding upon rotten wood left there for that purpose. The floor glowed with foxfire and shining glow worms hung from the roofs of the chambers on long threads, winking like little stars as they swung in the slow movement of the dead air.

They felt their eyes starting from their heads and their eardrums cracking from the pressure. A dead man came up on a rock-loaded platform. They transferred him as well and were lowered once again.

The platforms began fitting the shaft more snugly and were no longer able to hold more than five men. Butterfly valves in the floors opened as the lifts sank and were closed as they rose. Like a piston in a pump, the rising and falling of the platforms helped to change the fetid atmosphere.

Now at this depth the fungi could no longer grow and luminous paint took its place, providing a hazy effulgence in which the newcomers could barely see. The others, though suffering, seemed to experience less distress. They still descended, moving the rock which waited for them and lowered still deeper, from platform to platform by the animalized slaves.

At last they heard picks and hammers below them and came into a partly finished chamber hewn in the basalt, miles below the very lowest of the strata with which men are now familiar. Here, in the very bones of Earth's carcass, the slaves strove and died at the command of Caranche, the king, who carried on the plans of rulers dead long before him.

Here was a man smearing luminous paint, bent over by the weight of his small can and brush, fighting for air with straining lungs. Beside him another had fallen over his hammer and was painting in weakness. His eyes were closed, nor did he open them under the urging lash of an overseer, himself in little better condition.

The picks and hammers rang in the dense air. At each stroke, an echo seemed to rise through the rock below the workmen. At first, Gwalchmai and Nunganey thought it was only an echo, but when the work stopped for the change of workers, the deep sounds continued. It was clearly evident that from some unknown depth of horror a second shaft was being driven *upward* to meet this one which so painfully sank.

The two comrades saw no more than this of the lowest chamber of the Hole. Almost at the same time the dreadful meaning of the years of digging became apparent to Gwalchmai, both of them collapsed upon the splintered floor, bleeding at nostrils and ears. They did not know when they were dragged roughly upon the next heap of rock, hurriedly piled from platform to platform, rising jerkily with it by slow stages once again to the upper levels.

A cool wind revived them. They saw stars shining down upon them through a roughly circular opening. It enlarged as they watched and the stars became flaring torches. They felt hands upon them, cuffing them from their swoon, and then they were stumbling like automatons, stupidly, heavily, back to the city.

Once more at Poseidon's temple, they were led down a steep, dark, poorly ventilated ramp whose walls glistened in the torchlight with stinking slime and luminous molds.

Caranche met and followed them down and saw them locked behind iron bars. The guards left them alone and the king growled:

"So you are the mighty Glooskap, Son of the Mountain? You came here to visit Hobbamock, they tell me!

Well, the slaves here talk of Hobbamock, but we know him not. Could it be possible that you were born to be a slave?

"You shall die a slave's death tomorrow, Glooskap, unless you tell me what I want to know. It may be that you will go back to the Hole, for as long as you chance to live. I promise you, in that case, you shall not come out alive. Possibly we may decide to use some charming little custom of your own country. We must be hospitable to a guest and make him feel at home.

"Shall we wrap you with red-hot chains or warm your feet with coals or throw ashes in your eyes? Eh? Would that help you to remember?"

"The Black Captain take you!" Gwalchmai grunted, and turned his back in disgust. This seemed to amuse Caranche mightily. He went down the corridor, taking the torch with him and laughing in his beard.

When they thought themselves finally alone, but for the scurrying rats, Nunganey turned to Gwalchmai in the dark.

He muttered, "That Sachem! He is no real man at all! Never heard of Hobbamock, said he. I think he *is* Hobbamock the Foul, and none other! The body you chose to dwell in, Glooskap, is too weak to fight these people. They are demons. Do you think the Night Woman can master him?"

Gwalchmai laughed shortly.

"Who? Cor—Bumole? She can take care of herself. Don't worry about her at all. We'll be out of here before you know it. As for that stupid fool—that red bear! If he only knew that he had but to flip up the pan over the butt of the flame-gun and expose the interior to direct sunlight for an hour, in order to completely restore the charge—"

A cackle of mad laughter interrupted him and bare feet pounded in the dark passageway as their unseen listener scurried away to the upper air.

"He may not have known it before," tersely remarked the Abenaki, "but he soon will! All that remains to us now is to pray to Kiehtan and daub on the death-paint."

Gwalchmai groaned. There was only one thought to cheer him in his self-disgust: Merlin's ring lay cold upon his finger. Danger was not very close.

That night, all North Alata lay under a cold, cloudless sky. The very air seemed snapping with electricity and above the Inland Sea the Ghost Dancers roamed, paling the cold majesty of the moon. Perhaps because of the huge copper deposits there, or for other, more terrible, reasons, a broad-winged bird shape took form, high in the heavens.

Beneath it, men looked up and marked it well and wondered whither it would fly to forecast war between the nations. The aged Hayonwatha, called from his lodge in Onondaga, saw the angry crimson of its rippling wings as it hung above the Long House of the Five Nations and his eyes narrowed, thinking that he must call a council to learn what danger threatened.

It moved away, toward the East. He yawned, relieved, and went back to his furs with a peaceful mind.

The phenomenon did not change in formation. It drifted on, a little faster, flickering low, then brightly, pulsating with odd brilliance and changing colors. Riding upon, or driven by, the mysterious magnetic currents of the upper air it hastened easterly along the Ghost Road.

It glowed in pastel shades indicating peace, above the unafraid Abenaki, rosy pearl, shimmering metallic blue, fluctuating yellow, and sped onward in wide curve out to sea.

Its contours had not changed when it poised over Nor-um-Bega, but its color ranged in tinge from blood to flame and now a wrathful aura fringed it like smoke. It hung there, menacing, and hurried on, beyond the world's great round to meet the rising sun.

Caranche heard about it and hastened from his bed to scan the sky, laughing in his strength to see the good omen which meant to him only success in another spring raid. Beneath him in separate cells below ground, where they could see nothing, Corenice nodded secretly to herself and her two imprisoned friends slept uneasily, unknowing of the portent.

8

The Fight for the Tower

The king's throne had been set up in a small courtyard, when the prisoners were brought before him, blinking in the strong light of dawn. Beside him, held lightly, stood Corenice, still disguised. Facing them were two stone posts, their bases blackened with soot, as were also the fire-corroded chains hanging from it. A group of attendants stood close by, near bundles of fagots. Except for these, the enclosure was empty.

Caranche beamed down upon them with a heavy benignancy and indicated their weapons, piled in a small heap at his feet.

"Because you have told me what I wanted to know, however unwittingly, I am minded to spare your lives. Say, therefore, will you be my men? I will make you overseers."

For answer, Gwalchmai spat at him.

Caranche did not fly into a fury, but signed for the two men to be fastened against the posts. While this was being done, he said:

"Since you refuse and, by his silence, so does your companion, most mighty Glooskap who are perhaps no more than an impostor after all, let me mention for your delight that you will soon have ample opportunity to show proof of your divinity.

"An hour, I think you said, in the heat of the sun?

Then the toy yonder will be fully recharged? First we will have wood piled around you." His attendants commenced this work.

"And then, when all is ready, a little practice, eh? If it is fully charged, you should not feel much pain when we burn your legs off—to the hips! If so—well, the burning wood will soon end your troubles.

"Of course, if you are Glooskap it will doubtless not affect you. Surely a god would not permit his friends to feel distress if he could save them—or would he? It is a matter of some interest to me.

"Now, take this thought with you, Glooskap, as you go. In the spring—when the maple leaves are the size of the squirrel's ear—that is the time for war! It is very near.

"Then we will fall upon the Abenaki with ax, knife and fire. We will leave nothing alive, not even the cur at the wickam door! We need no more new slaves. Their work is done once we recharge the weapons of the Old Ones.

"We will blast out the bottom of the Hole during my own lifetime! We will reach the Land of the Dark Sun as they did, learn the powers of that land and become lords among the heathen! Yea, the whole world shall yet bow to the might of Nor-um-Bega! The Island of Heroes shall subdue continents!

"Still we must wait nearly an anxious hour, must we not, in order to find if you have told the truth? Waiting is such a tedious thing that I and thy woman, Glooskap, will while it away in tender dalliance!"

He turned to Corenice, standing patiently, face hidden in her fur-trimmed hood.

"And as for you—you shall come to me for a time . . . then to the commanders of my hundreds . . . and finally to the cauldrons, that the slaves may be fed!"

His men roared with laughter, bending over, slapping their knees, as Corenice with suspicious meekness followed the king into a little chamber. The thick door closed behind them with as final a thud as if a chapter of history closed with it.

A few quiet seconds followed. Then, even as the men were stooping for fagot bundles, they were stopped by a dreadful long screaming from the dark interior of that inner chamber. It was a sound which held the very quintessence of horror—agony—and surprise!

Almost before the startled men could straighten up, Caranche came hurtling out, carrying the door from its hinges. He was no more than a mangled mass of flesh with white ribs protruding from his crushed chest. With all life gone, he flew through the air, to thud with flapping arms and legs upon the stones twenty feet away.

Nunganey gave a wild whoop of exultation as Corenice strode out, but the men-at-arms stared aghast at this stalking figure from their most ancient legends. Her hood was thrown back from off her glittering hair and with her sleeve she had wiped away the masking stain upon the shining metal of her cheeks.

No longer could she be mistaken for anything even remotely human, and the strong men shrank back against the courtyard wall, leaving the stone posts and the prisoners as she approached.

Her face was set in the grim lines of a sad destroying angel intent upon carrying out a just sentence. She swept up the flame-gun and snapped down the butt plate. Her expression did not change or her hand tremble when, with one smooth motion, she waved them out of existence.

The instrument flared briefly and quickly discharged itself again, but it had lasted long enough to bring the wall of the courtyard tumbling down. The street beyond was empty.

She turned to her bound companions and, not bothering to unhook their chains, she twisted the thick links apart as though they had been cast from wax. It was then she spoke in a voice of doom:

"Thus perish the first of the defaming enemies of Ahuni-i!"

Nunganey said glumly, "We got in here easily enough, but we may have trouble getting out."

Corenice laughed.

"Spoken with your usual optimism, my friend. Yonder lies the road and here are your weapons. Let us go, then."

Gwalchmai grunted. "Whither can we go, maiden of Atlantis? There is no spot in all this land that holds a friend to us, except beyond the Slave Wall. There we would be not better off. We are but three!"

She bowed her pretty head. "Nay, man, we are four. Ourselves—and Ahuni-i, for whom I act. As for our destination, I am instructed to take the Tower and wait there for whatever may chance to befall!"

"We go to our deaths," said Nunganey, under his breath. While Corenice was assisting Gwalchmai with the buckles of his sword belt, he surreptitiously rubbed soot off the greasy chains, smearing it upon his cheeks and forehead. Afterward, feeling more suitably dressed for his last battle, he trotted after the others, plotting out a new and magnificent stanza for his death song.

Although the sun was high overhead, it was still early dawn for the late rising city dwellers overshadowed by the dark rim of water. No one was afoot in the mean district that the three passed through to the ziggurat, which was easy to discern, being the highest edifice in the city. Avoiding the ways they had been led before, they passed by heavily shuttered houses, their doors locked and barred against the fear of midnight assassination.

In Nor-um-Bega, no man trusted a neighbor.

Luck was with them also in the next street, a foul lane wandering between heaps of moldering garbage, but it could not long continue. As they turned to the right into a prouder avenue, they saw a man coming toward them not far away. He was fully armed and armored and as he came he was whistling gaily and looking carelessly about him. They shrank back around the corner into the squalor they had just left.

"A change of guard for the Hole," Corenice murmured. "Can you take him Nunganey? Silently?"

A savage gleam of white flashing teeth was her

answer and the Abenaki slipped loose his war hatchet from its sheath and weighed it in his hand, testing its well-tried balance.

On came the unsuspicious guard, obviously in no hurry to take his place in the deep shaft. He strode jingling by the street entrance without seeing them in the deep embrasure of a doorway. As he passed on, Nunganey stepped out to gain the room for a long cast. His hatchet flew, wheeling, spinning, to bury its keen flint edge to the thong wrapped handle, just where basinet did not quite meet gorget and red locks escaped, parted and severed, redder now than ever before.

It was the work of a few moments to strip the dead guard, in the filthy alley nearby. When they were done, out from that alley came an armored man, with brown hair well tucked out of sight. His face was masked with a dropped visor and his sword was out. With it he prodded on before him a red-skinned slave and a hooded girl. The bundles both carried contained Gwalchmai's and Nunganey's own weapons wrapped in the dead guard's inner tunic.

Thus disguised, they came into familiar places which they could no longer avoid and passed down a broad avenue where people were, but without attracting much curious attention. Their next turning took them into the miserable settlement where again the silver cauldron was boiling for the morning meal. Few children were awake, and they pushed on through the square without hindrance or comment. At last they came again to the grass grown pavement which circled along the base of the perpendicular cliff of brine which perpetually menaced this sea-girt land.

Now here, as they walked hurriedly beside the dark unmoving water, they noticed mysterious, ill-defined movements beyond the intangible obstruction between them and the submerged land. They became aware that a blurred and shadowy form was following their progress—outside the invisible wall.

It swerved toward them, avoiding some rise in the sea bottom, and they could see it clearly, nosing against the other side of that transparent dam against the ocean's ponderous weight. A long-bodied prowling shark, looking for food, with others behind it in the murk! Gently fanning the water, it swam beside them, watching them intently with its little piggish eyes.

"The sea-wolves of Ahuni-i!" said Corenice. "They have been sent for and they are gathering!"

Their road veered away from the trailing pack, but they knew that they were still being dogged.

So they came at last to the black stone tower, unchallenged and unharmed, against all of Nunganey's somber expectations. As they set their feet to the first steps of that winding stairway a great shouting and uproar burst out not very far away. They wheeled and saw a confused mass of red-bearded soldiery rushing in pursuit, without discipline or apparent leader.

It was evident that they would soon be overtaken, but the three ran up a dozen steps to a little landing and here, with Corenice and the Abenaki thrust behind him Gwalchmai turned to fight.

Strong as he was and with the elevation of his stand also in his favor, only his fine Roman sword saved him in the first encounter. It was fortunate that his father Ventidius, the former centurion, had trained him well. He had a skill which no Aztec could possess, for the maccahuitl with its teeth of volcanic glass was essentially a striking, smashing weapon without a point. The Roman gladius was a thrusting blade also.

At first, he had no time for science. By sheer weight they pushed him back from the landing, up and up the contested stairs, his blue steel dripping, singing in a circle no man could step inside and live.

Luckily for him, their armor was not the strangely alive orichalcum, but only an alloy similar in color. Like bronze, it turned the edge of a soft iron weapon or hindered an ax of the same alloy, but the good legionary steel shore through it like tin.

Up and back they pushed him along the broad stairway until, when halfway around the first spiral, Gwalchmai heard the thrum-m-m of Nunganey's stout bow. There was a whir above his shoulder and an attacker groaned and fell in midstroke.

A tall, finely armored man ran out from the crowd, tossing his ax from hand to hand. His head was bare and his almost scarlet locks flew free as a flame. There was a rapt look on his face and it was easy to see that he cared little for life.

As he ran, he chanted the Song of the Sun:

> "Earth and Sky are things eternal,
> Man must die!
> Old age is a thing of evil!
> Charge and die!"

He coughed once as Nunganey's arrow took him in the throat, and went down on his knees at the edge of the stair. He cast himself over and down, out of the way of those who came behind him—and even while falling, his joyous expression did not change.

Like venomous angry bees the avenging arrows whizzed and flew, until from very lack of room to fight, the Nor-um-Begans were forced to give way and dodge the rolling dead. Gwalchmai leaned against the wall and panted. Corenice tore loose one of the slabs of stone set here and there to serve as benches and hurled it into the crowd. The three had a short respite.

Then, while a few heavily armored men tried to hook away the bodies and clear the path through the slain, others threw long knives to protect their fellows. This continued until Gwalchmai, in desperation, sprang down and engaged the workers.

Again it was rattle, clang and crash, but the wooden shafted spears, despite their length, were no match for a steel sword wielded by one who had been taught by the finest swordsman in the personal guard of Arthur of Britain. Presently Nunganey, out of arrows, picked up a quantity of the knives and hurled them back with unerring accuracy, a game he well understood.

So they held the stair for a little time. Fresh waves of fighting men washed up against them from the now fully aroused city. Unblooded, new in strength, insanely delighted in the prospect of battle, their numbers forced the valiant three higher and higher toward the next landing. Corenice turned and ran toward it.

Nunganey, struck down by a flying ax, lay stunned but not gashed and Gwalchmai bestrode him, hammering and stabbing at a dozen moving, fighting, golden statues, knowing this to be his last stand and determined to die well.

Corenice's clarion voice cried, "Fall, Aztlanian!" As he instantly did so, the flame-gun's blast turned the very air to fire above them, whiffing away his antagonists in a burst of thunder. With them, twenty feet of the ziggurat's ramp crashed into dust, leaving a gap which could not soon be crossed.

Still, though out of reach, they were not out of danger until, in a shower of spears and knives, with now and then a ponderously wheeling ax clattering down to strike sparks from the worn steps, Corenice lifted the two men by the middles. With one beneath each arm, she ran lightly up the steps and around the next bend, leaving the discharged flame-gun where it lay.

She dropped them upon the platform which ran flatly around the black tower, without proceeding to the stair which led to the peak. Their breathing became less painful. The glazed look passed from Nunganey's eyes. He sprang up with a whoop, tugging at his hatchet, the only weapon now left to him.

A sheepish look came over his face almost at once. It was strange to see the softening of that stern, grim countenance beneath the death-paint. Gwalchmai grinned and a slow, sympathetic smile curved the sweetly formed lips of the metal maiden, for the first time in their long retreat. It quickly passed as cries and the sound of cracking whips came up from below. The three looked over the edge of the platform.

Directly beneath, half a hundred feet away, yawned the gap in the ramp. Toward it a horde of red-skinned Abenaki slaves were being driven, laden with heavy balks of timber, staggering beneath weighty beams and thick planks.

Their respite, it could be seen, would be short.

The work went on swiftly. Planks were stood up on end and allowed to fall and though several rebounded and vanished in the gulf below, finally one lay firm. A slave ran quickly across, holding the end fast, while others carefully slid a beam along it, under the sharp directions of their overseer. With this in place, more beams followed, to be overlaid immediately with planking.

Gwalchmai missed Corenice from her place at his side; looking around, he saw her wedging a pointed bar, torn from one of the windlasses, beneath a ponderous paving stone.

He sprang to help her tip it down upon the bridge, but Nunganey, catching the movement and seeing what they were doing, sprang up, his face working, stoicism forgotten.

"These are my people, Bumole!" he begged. "Not upon them!"

"They *were* your people. They no longer are quite human, Nunganey. These men have been brutalized until their very souls are dead. They will fight you with the vigor of their masters if they can reach you!"

"Perhaps," admitted Nunganey, "but not upon these slaves, Night Woman. Wait for the Chenoo to cross."

Corenice stared at him for a long moment, then flung the bar clanging down and stalked forward to look below.

It was already too late. As though some guiding mind had taken authority and foreseen what she had proposed to do, both slaves and the red-haired ax men were surging across the bridge in an intermingled mass.

She waited until the last slave had crossed, then sent a ton of chiseled stone crashing through the scintillating stream of armored No-um-Begans. The makeshift bridge collapsed with a splintering boom, falling swiftly away from them. It was pursued into the depths by twisting, wailing figures which struck and rebounded from the lower ramps, to tear wide holes in the milling crowd which packed the Square of the Boats.

"Too late," said Corenice, grimly. Already the first of the pursuit had reached the platform and was racing toward them, almost naked Abenaki waving weapons they had picked up from the littered stairs as they came. They seemed as demoniac in temper and visage as the bearded, better armed, grinning Killers, who impelled them on to take the brunt of the battle.

Nunganey shrilly incited them to turn on their captors, but either disregarding his pleas or totally misunderstanding his motives, the frantic slaves flung themselves upon the three. It was well that the two men had been able to rest, for these antagonists, unimpeded by armor, were agile and quick to leap and dodge. Fighting hard, though unwillingly, Gwalchmai and Nunganey were pressed back upon the last stairway leading to the top of the tower from whence there could be no retreat.

Again, in their former order, they contested the way, striking now only to stun when facing an Abenaki, but to kill when opposed by Nor-um-Begans.

Fortunately, this stairway was narrower, steeper and more winding, for the tower narrowed rapidly toward its peak and thus it afforded less opportunity for knife and ax throwing. This was an advantage to Gwalchmai, for the Roman sword was used best in stabbing between armor joints. His antagonists knew the weak spots of armor better than he and presently he bled even more from new shallow spear wounds and could feel his arm weakening, his sword growing heavier.

It was because of this that he could not parry the ax blow which sent his basinet clanking down the steps and which brought him to his knees.

Nunganey sprang in front of him, protecting his friend with his own naked chest, striking out with his flint hatchet, splintering it on the corselet of a burly giant. He roared with contempt and swung up his weightier weapon for the stroke which would finish both at once.

Somewhere in the crowd the Abenaki war-cry shivered up—that yell which chills the blood of the stalking cougar—and a scarred one-eyed warrior ploughed through the press.

"Ho! Ho! Cosannip!" shouted Nunganey, falling forward to grapple the Killer's knees, and as he did so Cosannip came down on the enemy with his own terrible half-moon ax. One horn of it protruded from the nape of the Nor-um-Began's neck, while the other was lodged in the teeth of his lower jaw.

The two halves of his split head lay over upon either shoulder as Cosannip yanked out the blade and the red Killer fell.

Nunganey instantly picked up the dead man's ax, and side by side the reunited blood brothers held the stair, cleared the way and drove back the horde for a precious moment. Gwalchmai dazedly reached for his basinet, but all strength seemed gone from his fumbling hands. Nunganey stooped and clapped it on his head. He wavered to his feet, supporting himself by his sword. The end seemed very near.

A plunging body swooped through the air from above to crash among the yelping pack. Another followed, screaming. Mad Baraldabay, the Tower Man who had lamented the lack of war, hurled now from the tower top. All eyes turned to the pinnacle. Corenice stood there, a living statue of avenging Fury incarnate. Her upper clothing had been torn from her gleaming body and with the wind whipping her skirt, she stared out over the fighting, far across the water.

"Look!" she cried. "Look well, Killers of Nor-um-Bega, for yonder rides your doom, sent by Ahuni-i!"

The fighting stopped. A gasp of horror ran through the assembled throng. The reinforcements charging over the rebuilt bridge slackened their wild pace as they reached the platform and in their turn, from above water level, could look out through the force wall.

Weapons slipped from lax hands and some stout warriors fell to their knees in dread.

For beyond the invisible protection of their little world, only a short distance away, rising and falling lightly to the lift of the waves—the Vimana came hastening over the sea!

9

Vale! Thunder Bird!

Swiftly propelled by its broad webbed feet, the swan-ship of Atlantis breasted the billows. When it drew nearer, Gwalchmai and the two Abenaki could hear, as they hurried up the few remaining steps to stand beside Corenice, the stamp and go of the powerful machinery that drove it. Even over the grumble of the crashing surf upon the impalpable sea-wall, a new sound became audible: a prolonged and dreadful whistling like the angry hiss of a colossal enraged serpent.

Again Gwalchmai sensed that oppressive feeling of merciless hatred which he had so strongly felt aboard the mysterious ship, but not this time directed at himself alone. An alien thought began beating against his consciousness, and it was "Kill! Kill! Kill!" He looked at Corenice. Her face was stern, implacable.

Then the swan-ship drove close, the long undulant neck lay sinuously back upon its shoulders and its beak opened wide. Again the round crystal eyes flared with light and evil life as a forked stream of blazing wild-fire smashed into the force wall. But it was not like the earlier levin bolt which Gwalchmai had himself discharged into the sea of weed or the one which had slain the sea serpent. This was a fiercely livid blue ray, narrow and hard and dazzling to the eye.

As the beam impinged upon the tissue thin barrier a shining iridescent halo took form around the spot which it touched, shot with all the hues seen in a bubble just before it bursts. Seemingly without end the rush of energy poured into that shimmering circle, heating it, breaking down its resistance, destroying the pattern of its composition, rearranging its atomic structure.

The wall bellied in before that wash of fury, deeper, deeper, and in through it tore the strange fulguration to crash halfway across the sunken land. It hung and waved there in their sky like a fiery portent to warn those below of the Day of Judgment. Then the ray died, but all around that evenly punched hole, the edges began to burn!

Slowly at first, then more rapidly as more space opened for their feeding, little smokeless flames licked and ate away the curtain of force. No heat could be felt by those on the tower, closer than any others to the torrent of fire that finally raved by them to the sky, burning high to the attenuated edge of the unseen substance which so long had held the ocean back from Nor-um-Bega. A wide rent opened almost to the water's edge. Away rushed the destroying corrosion to left and right. It became hundred-foot pillars of flame hasting away to complete the circuit of the doomed island and meet once more at its farther end, dashing on with ever increasing acceleration to unite and pass away forever in that union.

Downward also burned the devouring flames. It appeared to be a heatless, cinderless line of light sinking toward the level of the sea. It dropped slowly, as the energy fed by disintegrating atoms in the rock of the sea bottom rose upward, feeding the force-wall, as it had been meant to do by the engineers of ancient Atlantis. Faster than that energy could be renewed, it could be destroyed!

Now the surf beat over the edge, not extinguishing

that steadily lowering mark of destruction. As the waves
came in, gusts of salt rain fell down into the Square
of the Boats, drenching the upturned faces of the aghast
crowd below. A long wail of terror rose up to those on
the tower top.

Already the serrated ramps of the ziggurat were
crowded with climbers. All knew that soon this would
be the only spot projecting above the water and the
last place to offer any refuge. Gwalchmai could see
people setting the inverted boats upright and knew it
to be a hopeless task.

The swan-ship rocked, idly waiting, head craned out
as though it could watch and was amused by the
scrambling below.

Nunganey and Cosannip were staring toward the
Slave Wall. Here there was fighting and already a
dark rush of their enslaved countrymen had crossed
over. No golden Killers could be seen among them as
they streamed through the streets of the ruined city on
the way to the tower. They too had recognized the
doubtful promise of that height.

From the peak, the lamentation of the doomed popu-
lace came up as a moan scarcely to be heard above
the solemn boom of the deluge and the rumble of
tumbling stone houses crumbling like sugar beneath
the force of the cataract.

All the upper curtain of force had vanished away
and in a hundred places along the edge, where energy
units were weaker than others, water poured over in
spurts and splashes.

Little rivulets shone silver as the spray caught the
sunlight or were illumined from beneath by the falling,
unquenched flames. The streams grew to sluices, running together, and cascades came into being as great
combers rolled over the brink without interruption. The
foam and spindrift curved down the thickening glassy
edge in long rivers, tumbling down in an inundation
dwarfing the falls of Ne-ah-ga-ah.

Beyond the immediate flood below, the beleaguered
group could see from their eminence that the water

had surged through the running crowd of slaves, washing them back from their objective. Even further away the rushing streams had coalesced and lipped around the edge of the Hole.

Windlasses, cordage and lumber all vanished into that maw. The structure above, with its pulleys and tackle, collapsed and fell and was carried instantly away. The coping of masonry and the mounds of earth and stone melted away and the Hole yawned wider and wider as though Earth gaped thirstily.

Now, even above the heavy roar of the descending ocean, could be heard the measured thud and boom of *Workers* from the accursed depths who sought to break through the thin shell of rock which separated them from the upper air and domination of the fair green lands above.

Upon that separating layer the cataract thundered down, building up an incalculable tonnage, crushing, splintering away the barrier. A bubble of air rushed up through the zigzag shaft. In it was a mutilated *Shape* whose form remotely approached the human, but which dwarfed man as the mammoth dwarfs the mouse! With it came a battered tree, its trunk and foliage chalk-white from lack of chlorophyll.

The creature waved a gashed and bleeding arm, once only, above the waters, then sank forever.

Momentarily the waters paused at that shrieking blow-hole where spray rose hundreds of feet into the air. The column of froth dwindled, became less high and sank to a widening creamy circle marking where lay the deepest shaft ever sunk by mortal man. This was the only remaining evidence that below lay the ruined labors of a thousand years of toil and slavery. Sealed forever by it was the cavern which to the inhabitants of the Land of the Dark Sun must have been but the merest antechamber.

A tremendous bore of water, carrying with it a scum of debris, rushed down the city's central avenue into the Square of the Boats, overturning the metal craft like chips, washing away the drowning crowd. It thun-

dered high upon the ramps, pounding away the climbers, sucking them under in a welter of spume.

It circled about the ziggurat's base, gnawing into the
green hill the structure had been based upon, under-
cutting its foundation.

The mighty man-made mountain trembled, shook
itself and leaned ponderously toward the sea, bowing
majestically to superior force, shaking from its shoulders the climbing swarm which infested it.

The long boom swung groaning around, hanging far
out over the smooth water where the waves were being
flattened level by the suction of the current plunging
headlong into the maelstrom below. The Vimana, still
obeying the unspoken commands of Corenice, swam
below the end of the boom, fighting the indraught of
the vortex. The four companions, finding it impossible
to use the attached car, clambered recklessly down the
latticework of girders and braces toward the ship.

Gwalchmai cast one hurried glance behind him. A
few islanders and slaves were crawling after. Beyond
them, no edifice cleared the surface of the flood.
Beneath it lay mansion, hovel, palace and fane. Above
it rose a titanic, cold, white column of mist and spray,
bowing, swaying, like the guardian genius of Atlantis
come to mourn over the passing moments of its last,
lone colony, however wicked and forgotten.

The others, already clustered upon the back of the
Vimana, called to him. The boom shuddered and
dipped lower. He leapt upon the wet and slippery
metal. Corenice caught him by the sword belt and drew
him in to safety.

Once more the trap opened and disclosed the stairway and the four hastened below. Already others were
dropping upon the bird's back. The door sealed itself
tightly into its flanges and the machinery drummed
louder as the swan-ship strove to tear itself away from
the suction of the cataract. A terrific blow battered
them under the surface and all could hear the collaps-
ing roar of the ziggurat's destruction. Then the boom
flailed against the Vimana a second time—the power

faltered for an instant and they were drawn into the whirlpool.

Fortunately the depth of water below was now sufficient to cushion their fall, but they were whirled about and up and down, thrown hither and thither by cross eddies. The humans were battered against the unyielding sides of the ship, although Corenice was able to maintain her position at the controls by magnetic attraction, fighting to bring them all safely through.

It was not long before the three men were unconscious. The scene went out in a burst of sparks for Gwalchmai, as his head struck the metal of the ceiling when they were rolled completely over for the last time. Corenice looked on, unable to help, knowing that none other than they still lived who had seen the beauty and terror of Nor-um-Bega, certain that above their heads rolled only a wild and empty waste of tossing waters.

And so it was that the Thunder Bird came to Murderer's Isle—as had been prophesied of old time.

Far to the north, the Vimana lay placidly in a little landlocked bay. A week of tender nursing had brought back strength and health to pounded human bodies, and two Abenaki had been set regretfully ashore to return to their homes. The others were together in the control room poring over a chart, acid etched upon thin metal.

"Observe carefully," she said, looking upon him fondly. "Land has risen and fallen again since this chart was made. Coastlines have trembled and twisted. Mountains no longer exist. Yet the great land masses are much the same and this is the way you must travel to fulfill your vow as I promised I would help you to do.

"North and westerly dwell the Inuete, savages, unfriendly to the people of the forests. Northeasterly, the Beothuks have their home on a fair land, though cold, since the sinking of Atlantis diverted the warm sea currents from their shores. There is no help in either place for you. Northward, still farther, Cimmeria lies, deep down and buried beneath the snows of ten thousand years.

"Beyond these countries lies your road. Here are islands and continental projections leading on and downward into Europe. Here is Estotiland and Miura and the land the Greeks, our ancient enemy, called Thule. So you shall reach, in time, your destination."

"You speak only of me, Corenice," Gwalchmai said, with a somewhat downcast air. "Surely we should not separate?"

She made a little impulsive gesture as though to touch him. Instead she pressed her hand to her side, where a faint glimmer of light shone through her hide garment.

"We must, my dear one, and this is the reason. We have come to an ending, you and I. Both I and the ship which carries us are doomed. Life is departing from us.

"As you have fancied more than once, the Vimana has a life of its own. It may seem impossible, but you must realize that man would not be truly man without the Divine Spark within him which sets him apart from the animal. It was this spark, derived from the Spirit of the Wave, which the Killers allowed to die in themselves, bringing about their own ruin.

"Metal of any kind could never live without the tiny bit of added orichalcum, which like yeast spreads its influence over the whole and transforms the original substance.

"In the beginning, this Vimana was built by human hands, of crass metal, but by the presence of my orichalcum body within it, the particles of its substance have been transmuted. Because it received into those particles energy from the sun, holding, storing it for the thousands of years we drifted over sunken Atlantis, acquiring an affinity with me, the Vimana has taken on a life of its own. A sluggish sentience, it is true, but a real life!

"Because the controls of it were constructed to be

operated mentally and because in my orichalcum body
resides the ego of a human being it derived knowledge
from me. I, Corenice of Colicynos, have an intelligence
superior to that slowly developing metal one and have
been able to control and direct that other ego. I have
a soul—the Vimana has none. Yet, almost without any
help from me, it came to Nor-um-Bega and rescued us.
In its curious way, the Vimana loves me!"

"I can understand that," murmured Gwalchmai.

Corenice hesitated, almost shyly.

"It hates you, because it knew that by your coming,
our long communion would be broken—as it has been.
But, oh, Gwalchmai—it has been so good to be alive!

"It tried to warn you away from the chamber where
I waited, with the only voice it had, the harmonies
built into it, originally placed there for man's amusement. You persisted and came to me. After that, it
sulked—I could feel its thoughts— hating you more and
more, wanting to destroy you, so it and I could be
alone once more. That was impossible because you
and I were always together and my will was stronger.

"Now, soon, I must leave you and you must go on
alone."

Sadness was in her voice. She raised a hand when
he would have spoken.

"You have seen the glimmer which is spreading over
my body, sparkling around me, making the shining
metal turn dull and dead under it. The hard rays emitted
from the burning force wall struck into me when I
crossed above them, setting up a reaction. The Vimana
has caught it from me. Cells in both of us are losing
their vitality, returning to their original state of insensate metal, or decaying away into a fog of glowing
particles inside of which we move.

"When that process is complete, to all purposes we
shall be dead. But before that happens, I will set you
on your path.

"You could not cross the wide ocean from here in a
frail wooden boat. There are dangers. Men of Atlantis
sailed the Worm Sea in wooden ships and were

drowned. Worms ate the bottoms out of their vessels and they sank. Only metal is proof against them.

"The Vimana will not last to carry you straight across to your destination. North we must go, into the cold waters, amid the ice cakes, passing from land to land while I can still force the ship to do my bidding.

"Then we shall part—you to cross whatever land you must, on foot, making friends with its people, securing boats to carry you upon your way, dropping down the continental coasts by easy journeys until you reach your goal and deliver your message. Yet, I have a thought, I know not from where, that it may take longer than you think."

"And you?" queried Gwalchmai. She smiled.

"I? Think not of me. Long ere that, I shall have come to know what end has been reserved for me by destiny and Ahuni-i."

Days of journeying followed. They quitted the coast and sailed northeast, finding and skirting other inhospitable coasts. Folk came out to intercept them in skin boats, but were left behind. In other places shaggy beast-like men came down to the shore, quite unafraid, to shake clubs at them, daring them to come inland and be killed.

They went on, following ancient maps. Corenice spent much of her time in the control room and they were not often together, she fearing that he would be burned in the golden mist which emanated from the walls of that chamber and which was also poised about her own body like a wisp of sunset cloud.

Ominous clankings from the machinery spoke of coming ruin and dissolution, and one day these signs could no longer be ignored.

They had passed the ice pack by this time and were steadily approaching a warmer clime. Finally they made landfall.

The country was rocky and Corenice could not find that it agreed with her maps, but from its position and volcanic smokes on the horizon, she judged it to be a young land upraised since her time.

If there were inhabitants, no sign of them could be seen as the swan-ship limped along the southern coast. Here were no bays and few landing places. The sea beat in upon an inhospitable shore where there was much floating ice from the glaciers which came down from the sea. Dust fell upon them from the frequent eruptions and at night the skies glowed red. They determined it to be an island and the only sign that indicated it to have ever been visited by man came from the sighting of a skin boat floating bottom up. There was no one near it.

A pillar of volcanic ash and smoke stood ten thousand feet in the air over the center of the island as they stood in for a landing. It seemed a dreadful place to set Gwalchmai ashore, yet Corenice knew that there was no alternative. Further traveling was impossible. Helping him with much difficulty, since her refractory body would scarcely any longer obey her will, they carried in supplies to a low shelving beach at the end of a long firth where an ice-river came down to the sea.

Gwalchmai's hair had turned quite white from exposure to the continually discharging rays from the disrupting cells of the ship. He found his faculties were unimpaired and his strength not diminished, when they climbed the gentle slope of land leading to a height overlooking the glacier.

Snow was falling upon the bleak expanse in large soft flakes. They sat and looked down the hill at the waiting swan-ship. It was almost hidden from them by an overhanging cloud of dancing golden motes. Corenice moved within a similar aura, if anything even more lovely because of the deadly mist.

She spoke and moved with difficulty and he felt a throb of heartbreak as he remembered her gay vitality as she had danced and made music for him, so very long ago.

"This, then, must be our place of farewell. Oh, Gwalchmai! Have I brought you so far upon your way only to leave you to your death?

"The Spirit of the Wave cannot have meant to be so cruel to us."

"Your goddess would not have permitted you to become so dear to me if there was to be no other ending. I know now that when I drank my godfather Merlin's magic potion that I prolonged my life. You, my precious one, who have roamed the world in spirit and looked out of the eyes of others in many ages, must find a way to come back to me. Surely it will be allowed to us in time to come that we shall meet again."

She smiled with a great effort.

"Then you feel, as I do, that death of the body cannot be an end of life? This body is dying, but it has brought me little pleasure. To feel myself alive and know that I am metal! To know myself alive, to feel desire and to long for love! To live so long and crave death and now to die and wish to live! Oh, Gwalchmai!

"Yet this life means little to me. You and I would never be nearer in it. If we meet again, let it be in some future existence."

"We must. We shall!" He clasped her tight. She disengaged herself easily and continued:

"There is no time for love-making! No time for anything more. You must flee far inland, for your life, for know that when I am gone the Vimana may return to seek you out and slay you. I am going now, to drive it far to sea and perhaps destroy it if I can, before my faculties fail and the power over it and my body is entirely gone.

"This is my punishment, which I deserve. I completed my vow. I slew murderers and became a Killer myself, the sin I was taught was unforgivable. Because of that sin, I die, but Ahuni-i forgive me, I cannot feel that I am wicked."

"You are not," he groaned. "Oh, Corenice! Murder and the love of killing will not be less in the world because the Nor-um-Begans are gone. Strife is a part of man, born in him, never to be removed."

"Perhaps," she gasped. "But love is better and now that I am dying, I can say it—such an unmaidenly thing, Gwalchmai, and so strange that a girl of metal can love—but it is you who are my heart's darling—I never love another."

Gwalchmai bowed his white head and great sobs shook him. Her little fingers touched his cheek. They were still soft, but burning with the corroding action of the disintegrating metal. There was a rapt look in her eyes. She seemed to be listening. Her voice was very soft.

"I have received the promise. I am forgiven. This is not the end in this place of ice and fire."

He caught her to him again, regardless of the pain the action caused him.

"Let me die with you," he murmured. "Here, together, like this!"

She tore herself violently away and stood up, swaying, with a little of the old imperiousness.

"No!" she cried, but the bell music of her voice was sadly jangled. Then in swift regret she stooped and kissed him with lips that were tender and sweet as any girl of flesh.

"This is not goodbye, my very dear, for now that I know you love me, I will find a way to come again. I will see you complete your vow and somehow I will help you on your long journey. Have faith and we shall be together in some other life. Yea, we shall meet and live and love again—though it be two hundred year!

"Ahuni-i protect you now, my lover, for I cannot any longer!"

She turned away and ran, stumbling down the slope toward the waiting ship, an aura of glowing vapor all about her, a golden ghost in a golden cloud.

"Wait, Corenice, wait!" he cried in anguish, running after. "Let me go with you! When shall we meet? How shall I know you in another life?"

She looked back over her shoulder.

"Know me by gold!" she cried and vanished below

the Vimana's deck. Almost instantly it wheeled, heading out to sea.

He climbed to his former point of eminence, sitting there with his head in his hands, watching the ship until it passed out of sight. The ring on his finger became burning hot.

Disregarding her last warning, he remained motionless upon his rock, eying dully the grim and forbidding horizon. Thick dark clouds let down a heavy sifting of snowflakes upon him and the wind grew bitter, but he did not bestir himself to find shelter, though night was rapidly falling.

Then a brilliant glow became visible upon the far line where sky met sea, as though the sun were rising again. With a start, he realized that it was rapidly growing more huge and distinct. It was an effulgent blur, a cloud of fire tearing across the surface of the water in his direction.

Now it was at the entrance to the firth! The swan-ship on its way back to destroy him—free at last of any restraint!

Without stopping for any of his supplies, he ran inland across the surface of the glacier, far and fast, leaping cracks scarcely visible in the blinding snow which grew momentarily more like falling sparks in the rapidly approaching light behind him.

Frantic, knowing that he could not escape, he turned. The Vimana had reached the strand. Its head lay back for the discharge and the hissing of a thousand serpents filled the air. He stood still to die.

At that instant, an apparition took form on the ice before him. At first, he thought it Corenice mystically returned to be with him, but as she turned and smiled upon him, he saw her to be a stranger.

Her face was oval, but not human! Beautiful it was beyond the telling, but her eyes were square and her skin was faintly edged with jewel-like scales. Sea-green were her robes and dripping with brine. She was armored to the waist and helmeted, but bore no weapon of any kind. Instead, she carried a concave shield, emblazoned with a great serpent, represented as in the act of swallowing its own tail.

The brilliance of her metal hurt his eyes as she waved him behind her. The terrific blast of the Thunder Bird tore over the ice, but quicker even than that the strange being swung up her shield to cover him, deflecting the ray back upon its sender.

Up to the very storm clouds thundered a sheet of fire, a fountain of rocketing heat, as every disrupted atom in the swan-ship gave up its mite to create an unparalleled gush of energy into the heavens.

The bottom of the firth became visible, steaming and black, but the water discharged into the sea soon came rushing back higher than before, thudding against the glacier.

The whole face of it slipped off and splashed down into the turbulent waves, splitting between the two, carrying away his savior into the sea from whence she had come.

Back from the dangerous edge he ran. New cracks had opened from the shock. He avoided these, but a few hundred feet away a snow bridge covered an old crevasse which he did not see.

It collapsed beneath him and he fell with it, deep down within the heart of the glacier, striking, rebounding, striking again, to be buried deeper yet and unconscious in the massed drifts below. More snow, dislodged by his body, fell now upon him, packing itself around him as he lay there, and upon it all, as he lay encoffined, a soft shroud of flakes descended into the crevasse, sealing him away from the world.

A tiny spark of knowledge lit his memory for a brief instant before it went out in the blackness over which he had no control.

"We shall meet and love again—though it be two hundred year!"

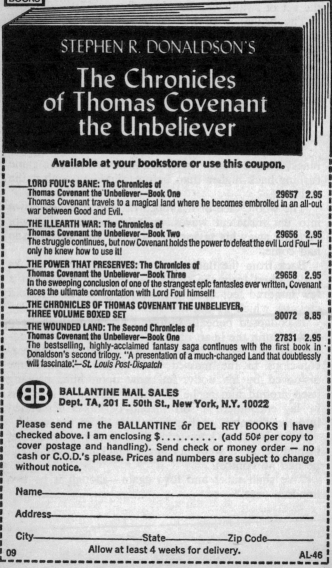